WORTH THE WAIT

As we kissed, his hands swept to the base of my neck and a swirl of sensations, of longing, rushed up from between my legs. I wanted him now, right where we were. But: "Not . . . here."

"What are you doing to me, Red?" he asked, his breathing ragged. "I don't ravage women in the backs of stores. I feel like a horny sixteen-year-old."

"We have chemistry. It's . . . magical." I spoke the truth, if not all of it.

He grasped my hips with both hands, tugging me so that my bottom slid a few more inches along the desk. "Where the hell were you when I was sixteen?"

"I don't know. But when I was sixteen . . . You wouldn't have liked me then."

He kissed the top of my head. "Why not?"

No magic, that's why not. But I couldn't say that. "I was a total cliché: the girl in the shadows reading poetry and daydreaming about the future. Other than a few friends and my sister, I was fairly invisible."

He spoke with absolute assurance: "I would have seen you."

A Breath of Magic

Tracy Madison

LEISURE BOOKS NEW YORK CITY

*To my aunt and godmother, Connie Lynn Tompkins, for
the love you've given and the many, many gifts you've
shared. Thank you for every joy you brought into my life.
I will never stop missing you.*

A LEISURE BOOK®

May 2010

Published by

Dorchester Publishing Co., Inc.
200 Madison Avenue
New York, NY 10016

ISBN 10: 0-505-52836-3
ISBN 13: 978-0-505-52836-0
E-ISBN: 978-1-4285-0851-4

Visit us online at www.dorchesterpub.com.

ACKNOWLEDGMENTS

Some stories are more difficult to write than others, and this was one of those stories. Thank you to the following folks for sticking by me and helping me through the process:

My critique partners, Natalie J. Damschroder: for your support, motivation, and your expert knowledge of hyphens. As difficult as the writing of this book was, it would have been so much more so without you in my corner. Connie Phillips: for your words of encouragement and constant belief in me. You have the ability to see the forest through the trees, something I am always in awe of.

My editor, Chris Keeslar: you totally gave me the confidence I needed when I needed it. Thank you so much for that, as well as for your patience, wit, and belief in me and the stories I want to tell. You rock.

My family, starting with my mom, Krystene Palenske: for truly loving my books and for her excitement to read this one. My kids: for thinking it's cool that your mother is an author and for bragging about me to your friends. My husband, Jim Duncan: for your never-ending support, and also for cooking dinner nearly every night when I was consumed by this story.

And a special thanks to a very special teenager, Katelynn Phillips: for your excitement over this series and for your incredible talent. I love the book trailer you made. Thanks, sweetie!

A Breath of Magic

Chapter One

"Let me get this straight. You want to magically coerce your boyfriend into marrying you? Are you crazy?" My cousin Elizabeth gaped at me as if I'd suddenly sprouted a set of horns. Or maybe a third eye.

"*I* can't magically coerce anyone. And no, that isn't what I want. Not exactly, anyway." We were ensconced in her office at A Taste of Magic, and while I'd known before arriving at the bakery that gaining her approval would be difficult, I'd hoped, at the very least, for her understanding. "It's more that I want to use magic to take away Kyle's reservations about commitment."

Her brown eyes darkened to the same shade as her hair, either in anger or disbelief. Or maybe both. "There isn't much distinction between the two, Chloe. Besides, do you really want to marry a man who wouldn't say yes on his own?"

That same question had been bobbing around in my head for weeks, and my answer changed repeatedly. I inhaled a quick breath, hoping to smother the uneasiness that knotted my stomach. Instead, the thick, buttery, almost too-sweet scent of the bakery assailed my senses, adding queasiness to the mix. "We've been dating for nearly a year. Marriage is the obvious next step."

"But why the hurry? Just let your relationship progress naturally, and you'll end up where you're supposed to."

Her logic, right or wrong, made me want to scream. Of course, I didn't. Doing so would only paint me as an emotional basket case. And I wasn't. Okay, maybe I was *slightly* emotional, but my reasons for going forward were sound. Fidgeting in my seat, I offered, "It's almost like we're already married. He just needs . . . a little shove to make it official."

"And you think I'm that shove?"

"Well, it's not like I can do it myself!" After a few more breaths, I reined in the quick temper that accompanied my red hair. "I'm sorry, but you're the only one who can do this."

Compassion replaced Elizabeth's disapproval. She reached across her desk to grasp my hand. "Is that what this is about? We all believe the magic will find you. Both Alice and I have gifted it to you several times, but maybe you're not in the right place to receive your power yet. Be patient, sweetie. It will come."

Yeah, right. Patient. I'd been best friends with Alice, Elizabeth's sister, long before I discovered we were related, so at first I'd been pleased to learn we were cousins. Now . . . well, the blood relation should have been enough for me to claim the family's Gypsy magic. But so far? Nada. The bluebird of patience had long since flown the coop. Worse, instead of feeling closer to my newfound relatives, I'd never felt more alone.

Except for Kyle.

I pulled my hand away. "I've given up on receiving the magic, Liz. So to answer your question, no, that's not what this is about." I counted to three and then gave my request another go. "What I'm asking for is simple."

She tilted her head, staring into my eyes. "Maybe I misunderstood you. Please ask again."

No way had she misunderstood, but I'd ask again. Heck, I'd ask one hundred more times if it worked. I wanted to become Chloe Ackers instead of Chloe Nichols so badly, it still surprised me. I didn't understand the urgency, but I trusted it. Straightening my shoulders, I said, "I'd like you to bake something special I can serve tonight, because I plan on proposing."

"And 'special' means what, exactly?"

Liz probably figured that by forcing me to say in detail what I wanted, I'd decide the idea was ludicrous. Of course, she had no way of knowing that I'd been contemplating this for the past six weeks and had long since gotten over my qualms. Well, most of them. "Just bake me a cake with the wish that Kyle's fears about commitment vanish. That's it. After he eats the cake, I can propose. If he says no then, I'll know the reason is because he doesn't love me, and I can live with that. But if I ask him without your magic, I'll never know if his rejection is because his feelings for me aren't strong enough, or if it's because he's too afraid of marrying *anyone*."

With a sigh, Elizabeth tucked a stray strand of hair back in place. "It's not a good idea, Chloe. It isn't fair to Kyle, and it isn't fair to you, either. You deserve a man who wants to be with you because of *you*—a man who loves you so much, he'd never need a spell to push him along. Don't you want that?"

I heard her words, and the sentiment behind them, and a sudden longing for exactly that pulled at me. But I knew better. Other than with Kyle, I'd never had a relationship last more than a few months. Besides, Kyle was my high-school sweetheart, my first love, and after years of separation we were a couple again. That had to mean something. Otherwise, why had fate bothered to bring us back together?

"Not everyone is as lucky as you and Alice," I said softly.

She snorted. "We weren't always so lucky in love—or are you forgetting that? What we have now isn't luck. Sometimes, it takes a while. But trust me, the wait is worth it."

Maybe. If I believed that what she'd found with Nate, and what Alice found with Ethan, would happen for me, then maybe the wait would be worthwhile. But I didn't. "I've never asked you to use your magic for me before. I swear, Liz, if you do this . . . I'll never ask again."

"Why is this so important to you now?" She gasped. "Are you pregnant?"

"No!" Not that I hadn't thought of going that route, because I had. For about three seconds flat. Trapping Kyle, no matter what Elizabeth thought, was not my intention. "Besides, if I were, we wouldn't be having this conversation."

"We wouldn't?"

Exasperation curled in my chest. I freed it with a loud sigh. "You know Kyle. If I told him he was going to be a father, what do you think he'd do?"

"Run for the hills?"

"And no amount of magic would get him back." I shook my head. "No, this is the only way."

Liz picked up a stray pen from her desk, fiddled with it for a minute and then plopped it back down. "And yet, you want to marry him."

"Just because he isn't ready for kids doesn't mean he won't ever be. And we have to start somewhere." I stared at Elizabeth, trying to find the right words to get her to agree. "You used your magic for Alice," I pointed out.

"Uh-huh, to help her *find* Ethan. Not to compel him to be with her." Elizabeth stood and paced the small area in front of her office door.

"But we are together, so I'm not trying to force him to be with me. Why are you opposed to this? It's not a big deal. Not really."

She stopped. Turning to face me, she planted both hands on her hips. "Don't ever say that to me again, Chloe. Altering Kyle's perception so he'll agree to something he normally wouldn't is a huge deal. Massive. And the result—good or bad—would rest on *my* shoulders."

My bottom lip twitched. My stomach somersaulted. I opened my mouth to argue, to tell her all the things I'd already said, but I couldn't find my voice. The seconds ticked by with neither of us speaking. She was waiting for me to back down so she wouldn't *have* to say no. But I couldn't. Not for this. "Please," I implored.

Disappointment flashed over her features. "I can't—won't— help you make a mistake of such magnitude."

"No? You're saying no? There isn't anything I can say that will change your mind?"

She approached me and then knelt down so we were eye to eye. "I don't know what's going on inside of you, but I don't believe you really want to marry Kyle Ackers. Not with everything Alice has shared with me, and not with what I've seen for myself. What's really going on here, Chloe?"

Mentally, I searched for an avenue I hadn't yet tried, for something—anything—that would change the direction of this conversation, and therefore her decision. I wanted exactly what I'd said. I didn't have a hidden agenda. And even though I stood behind my belief, that relaxing Kyle's fears was not the same as forcing him into marriage, I understood where Elizabeth was coming from. I just didn't agree with her.

As we stared at each other, I saw the conviction of her answer in her gaze, and my desperation—my want to finally be a part of something I'd never truly experienced: a family—crawled through me. The feeling swirled inside, swelling until I almost gasped in agony. But I held my breath and instead wished with every part of my being that Elizabeth would change her mind, that she'd do this one small favor for me. Seriously, if I could have bent *her* will at that moment, I would have. Even knowing how wrong that was.

Putting my hands on her shoulders, I worked to keep my voice steady so she wouldn't hear my anxiety, my desperation. "I *need* this, Liz. I'm just trying to find my own happy ending."

She blinked. Not once or twice, but three times. The air shifted around us, somehow the weight of the tension easing as it did. Shivers danced and rippled along my skin.

After a long breath, she covered my hands with hers. "Okay, Chloe. If this is truly that important to you, I'll cast your wish."

I ignored the cake as best I could while cleaning up after dinner. It sat there on my counter, in all its chocolaty goodness, taunting me to slice it, to move ahead with my plan. Only, the prospect of feeding the magical dessert to Kyle was wigging me out. Just a little. But not because I'd changed my mind, because I hadn't. Nope, what bothered me was the possibility that he'd still say no, even with the help of Elizabeth's magic. If that happened, we'd have to break up. Again. And honestly, it had taken me years to get over Kyle the first go-around. I wasn't eager to go down that path again. But the idea of waiting for my life—our life—to begin thrilled me even less.

Drying my hands on a dish towel, I pushed the kitchen door open with one shoulder and peeked around the corner into my living room. Kyle was sprawled on the couch, TV remote in hand, clicking through the channels. My nervousness ramped up another notch. He wouldn't say no, would he? We'd been together almost constantly for the past eleven months, and he seemed content. Happy, even. But was that enough? And did that mean he loved me? A voice inside my head countered with Are you sure *you* love *him*?

"Of course I love him," I whispered. Love could mean a zillion different things, and really, what wasn't there to love? He made me laugh, he was easy to be around, and being with him was far better than being alone. That last thought strengthened my resolve. I was ready.

"Kyle? Do you want dessert? We have chocolate cake." A tingle sped down my spine. I was really going to do this.

He groaned and rubbed his hand over his stomach. "I'm stuffed. How about we start the movie and have dessert later?"

"Um, sure. Later is fine." Kyle always stayed over on the

weekends. Eventually, he'd eat a slice. Even if it was for breakfast. I'd waited this long for my happy ending, what did a few more hours matter?

I joined him on the couch and his arms came around me. I settled against him, nestling my head against his chest. Comfort eased in, and I began to relax. Yes, I could definitely see us spending the next many years curled up on the sofa together.

He'd already put the DVD into the player, and with a few clicks the action movie I'd rented began to play. I spent the first fifteen minutes obsessing over the cake in the next room, however, and the next hour or so debating with myself over how to pop the question. You'd think I'd have given more thought to the actual proposal, but most of my concentration had gone into convincing Elizabeth.

Kyle didn't go for grand romantic gestures, so anything too mushy would likely undo any of the good Liz's magic managed to accomplish. Okay then, so reciting a poem or serenading him would fall flat. I'd just say it straight out. Simple and direct. Easy enough. But how long to wait after he'd eaten the cake? Would the magic take effect immediately? Or should I give it an hour or two? God. I wished I'd asked Elizabeth for more details on how her specific brand of magic worked. I'd just have to wing it and hope for the best.

Sliding to the side, out of Kyle's grasp, I took stock of my potential husband-to-be. His denim-covered legs were outstretched and crossed at the ankles, and his slim shoulders were slumped forward. The faint wrinkles in his shirt, along with the tiny hole in the heel of his right sock, brought a grin to my face. They were proof he found the same comfort with me that I found with him. And weird or not, that realization made me feel a heck of a lot better. We were good together.

As if he heard my thoughts, he turned, his amber eyes meeting mine. I waited for him to say something, to offer me a grin or to pull me toward him. He ran his hand through his already mussed brown hair and returned his attention to the screen. Fighting frustration, I leaned back against the couch.

When the credits finally rolled, I grabbed the remote and clicked the television off. I wanted to work in a little romance, maybe a kiss or two, before serving the cake. Silly, maybe, but even with the magic, the night I became engaged should be special, something to be remembered and cherished.

Making my voice bright, I said, "That was a fun movie!"

His lips quirked. "If you call kidnapping and murder fun, then sure."

Kidnapping? Murder? I should have paid closer attention. Going on a hunch, I said, "There was a chase scene! Those are fun!"

"I've seen better." He scooted forward, grabbing his shoes from where he'd kicked them off. "It was a nice evening, though."

I processed his flat tone and slow, purposeful movements. Moisture beaded on my forehead. "Are you going somewhere?" My voice shook, just a little, and that ticked me off.

He stopped and looked at me. Really looked at me. Another blast of uneasiness rose to the surface. All through dinner I'd chatted nonstop, but Kyle hadn't. That was unusual for him, but I'd passed it off as nothing more than hypersensitivity on my part. Now I wondered if there was something bothering him.

As quickly as the thought came, it flitted away. Nah . . . it had to be me—and everything I'd planned for this night. "Kyle? Are you leaving?" I asked again.

He shook his head. "I wasn't thinking, Chloe. Of course I'm not going anywhere."

"Good. I like it when you stay."

"I like staying over too." He wrapped his arm around my waist and dragged me to him. "You're sweet for making dinner tonight. Thank you."

"You're welcome." I smoothed his hair back with one hand and leaned forward, giving him a soft kiss on his lips.

His arm tightened around me as he deepened the kiss. I waited for a spark, still hoping it would reappear, that it would be as strong and hot as when we first met. Prodding my mouth wider with his tongue, he moaned when it slipped inside. Warmth seeped in, and it was nice. Reassuring, even. But it didn't speed my pulse up, and it didn't turn my insides to jelly. Leaning into him, into the kiss, a whisper of doubt crept in, but I set it aside. There was no reason the fire couldn't be there. Pushing my fingers into his hair, I pulled his head closer and kissed him with everything I had.

A noise, more of a gurgle than a groan, erupted from Kyle's throat, and he twisted his body in an attempt to pull away. I squeezed in closer, my only goal to prolong the kiss. No way was I giving up; a little perseverance would bring out the desire. Only Kyle moved his hands to my shoulders and gently pushed.

As we separated, his fingers went to his lips and he grinned. "You're a vixen tonight. You drew blood," he said with a small laugh, wiping at his mouth.

"What? I bit you?" My cheeks burned when he nodded. "I'm so sorry. Are you okay?"

Before he could respond, a series of loud knocks echoed through my apartment. Startled, I looked at the clock. When I saw the time, my heart slammed in my chest so hard that Kyle probably heard. Unexpected company after ten tended to mean trouble. I started to rise, but Kyle put his hand on my leg. "Let me get that," he said.

Sweet, right? Yep, but I couldn't just sit on the couch and wait, so I followed him to the door, hanging back slightly when he swung it open. A gaggle of voices—female voices—sounded, and a petite elderly woman dressed in hot pink and lime green appeared. She pushed her way inside, and her faded blue eyes landed on me, laced with worry. Right behind her came her granddaughter, my best friend Alice, who didn't appear worried so much as murderous.

Crap! Double crap with five million exclamation points. Elizabeth had ratted me out. Awesome. Just what I needed.

I sucked in a breath, my brain rapidly going through possible routes to defuse the situation. "Um. Hi? What are you two doing here?"

Grandma Verda pointed at me. "Where's the cake?"

"Grandma!" Alice said, flipping her head toward Kyle. At least I could count on her for some modicum of privacy. Grandma Verda? Not so much.

"What? I think the boy should know."

Kyle's back stiffened, and he glanced from Verda to Alice, and then to me. "Know what?"

"Know how good Elizabeth's cake is," I blurted. "They know I asked her to bake it special. Because chocolate is your favorite." Ugh. On the plus side, I hadn't lied. I shot a fierce look in the general direction of my surprise visitors. "You two didn't have to come all the way over to share dessert with us. Especially without calling first."

Alice blinked. "That's the best you have? Really?" She separated her legs into an offensive stance—as if she was about to clobber me—and crossed her arms. "We need to talk. Now."

"Uh . . . what's going on here?" Kyle inched a few steps back, away from the craziness. Who could blame him? Sweat trickled down my neck.

"This is a terrible mistake, young lady! Are we too late?" Verda's eyes scanned my living room, probably looking for signs of cake consumption.

"Too late for what?" asked Kyle, his voice an octave higher than normal. Without a clue as to what all the fuss was about, he obviously felt the tension emanating throughout the room. I needed to get him out of there. Fast.

"Dessert. No, we haven't eaten it yet." I smiled sweetly. "And when is chocolate ever a mistake?"

Alice's eyes narrowed. "Chloe? I'd really like to chat with you for a few minutes." She spoke calmly, but steel threaded every word.

Fine. We'd talk. But not with Kyle in the room. I turned my attention to him. "Could you wrap up a few slices for them to take home? Seeing that's the reason they came over in the first place?"

"Um. Sure. No problem." He tossed one last look of confusion at us before making his escape. As soon as the kitchen door swung closed, my chest loosened until I was able to breathe again. Thank God.

"Are you crazy?" Alice asked, unknowingly echoing her sister. "What do you think you're doing? And how in the hell did you get Liz to agree?"

I countered her question with one of my own. "Why did Elizabeth tell you? I thought I could trust her to keep this between us."

"Because she came to her senses. That's why," Verda interjected. "And she hoped we could stop you. Have we?"

"No. All you've done is delay the moment. Kyle isn't going anywhere, and my decision is firm."

Alice huffed out a breath. "Damn it, Chloe! Using magic like this is wrong, and I'd think you'd know that better than most people."

She referred to the fact that I own and operate a New Age store. Well, that, and my general beliefs tend to expand beyond what one can merely see. But she was wrong. The magic she and Elizabeth have is a gift, and gifts are meant to be used. I kept my gaze glued on the kitchen door. "Fate brought me and Kyle back together. All I'm doing is speeding things along a little."

"Fate? You believe that you and Kyle are fated for each other? When did you decide that, and why haven't I heard about it?" Alice situated herself in front of me, and because she's eight inches taller than my five-foot height, doing so broke my eye contact with the door.

Her chestnut-colored hair was up in a ponytail, and if it weren't for the fire in her eyes, I'd have said she looked cute. I lifted my chin. "Why would I tell you? You don't like Kyle. You never have." I mean, yeah, Alice is my closest friend, and normally we share everything. But when it came to Kyle? Well, let's just say she had a sore spot. Possibly leftover protection from the past, as she'd been the person who'd been there when he'd dumped me for another woman.

"That's not true, but that's beside the point. If you'd told me—" She broke off, biting her lip. A whisper of intuition sneaked into my senses, surprising me. Maybe even scaring me a little.

"What?" Even as I asked, I wasn't so sure I wanted to hear.

Her face held an emotion I couldn't identify. My fear increased. "Kyle is not the man you're supposed to end up with. That's what," she said without a trace of doubt.

"You can't know that," I snapped.

"I *do* know that."

"How?" I demanded.

Her jaw opened, and then she jerked it shut. With a shrug, she reached into her purse and retrieved a folded piece of paper. Wordlessly, she held it out.

"What is that?"

"Proof that Kyle isn't your happily-ever-after."

Comprehension twisted in my stomach. I felt the blood drain from my face, and while I'd be lying if I said part of me didn't want to grab the paper and open it, most of me had never been so afraid. Where Elizabeth's power is in her baking, Alice's magic exists in her artwork. She has the ability to see glimpses of the future through her sketches and paintings. She'd drawn herself with her soul mate—now her husband—before they ever dated, and she'd drawn a picture of Elizabeth and Nate's wedding day before he even proposed. So yeah, whatever existed on that page scared the crap out of me.

"Tell me what you drew."

"Take it. See for yourself."

Without thought, I reached for the page, my fingers barely brushing the smooth texture of the paper before Kyle sauntered out of the kitchen. He carried a plate holding a half-eaten slice of Elizabeth's cake in one hand and a fork in the other. Every nerve in my body seemed to pulsate. Static electricity danced in the air, saturating the room—and me—with an uncomfortable buzz.

"You're right. This is damn good cake." He took another bite. "Want some?"

Alice gasped. "Don't do it," she whispered. "Trust me on this."

I looked into her eyes, then down at the page I hadn't fully grasped, and finally, back to Kyle. What should I do? Stick with my plan, or toss it away over the unknown?

Even with her magic, Alice's path to Ethan hadn't been easy. Whatever that paper held, it wasn't anything real. It couldn't hold me at night while I slept, it couldn't bring forth a chuckle after a bad day at work, and it certainly couldn't bring me the family I craved. Kyle could. My decision was really that simple. I dropped my hand away from the paper, away from the unknown. "Kyle, will you marry me?" I asked.

He coughed, and for a second I worried he might choke. Panic clouded his eyes and the muscles in his arms tensed.

He worked his jaw but didn't actually say anything. His body stiff, he set his plate on the dining room table and just stared at me.

Crap. Either the magic hadn't taken hold yet, or it had and he didn't love me, didn't want to be with me. Both scenarios sucked. Everything inside me hollowed out, and the ache of loneliness I'd barely kept at bay returned with a vengeance.

"Chloe, honey," Alice said. "It's okay. Really."

Ignoring her, I focused all of my energy on him. "What do you say, Kyle?" *Say yes. Please.* The hollow ache disappeared, and as if all of my hopes, wants and dreams channeled together, my body flooded with warmth.

"Yes," Kyle said. "I'll marry you."

Chapter Two

Soft snoring came from my right. Kyle's arm rested heavily on my side. The sheets felt scratchy, and my pillow seemed hard as a rock. All of this, combined with the craziness of the evening, had put me solidly in the no-sleep zone.

Part of my inability to relax most certainly had to do with Kyle's abrupt acceptance of my equally abrupt proposal. Would he wake up in the morning with a change of heart? And even if he didn't, would the magic wear off at some point in the future, and he'd walk away? Obviously, as much consideration as I'd given this, it wasn't enough.

Ugh. Turning over on my other side so that my back faced Kyle, I carefully removed his arm from my rib cage. My breathing improved instantly. Closing my eyes, I attempted to push every thought from my mind. Bit by bit, the tightness in my muscles eased and the stress in my shoulders lessened. I began the tumble toward sleep, and I would've made it except for the sudden low buzz of my cell phone sitting on my nightstand.

I groaned and cracked one eye open before pulling myself upright. Grabbing the phone, I flipped it open without glancing at the display. "Hello?" I whispered as I tiptoed out of the bedroom.

"Oh, Chloe! Thank goodness you answered!" said Grandma Verda.

A knot of stress, the same one I'd just gotten rid of, appeared smack-dab in the upper middle of my back. "It's late, Verda. I know you're unhappy with me, but couldn't this have waited until tomorrow?"

A loud sigh reverberated through the phone. "That's not it, dear." She hesitated, and I heard her take another breath. "I'm in a pickle here. I need your help."

Help? My annoyance disappeared and concern took over. The eighty-something-year-old Verda was spry, but she wasn't indestructible. "What is it? Are you hurt?"

"I wouldn't say hurt, exactly," she hedged. "I didn't wake up Kyle, did I?"

Okay, she couldn't be too bad off if she was worried about disturbing Kyle's sleep. "I had the phone on vibrate. He didn't hear a thing."

"Oh, good! Can you help me?"

"Of course!" I wondered why she hadn't phoned Alice or Elizabeth. "If I can," I amended. "What's going on? Where are you?"

"Right outside your apartment. In the parking lot."

"What are you doing in my parking lot at"—I found the glowing numbers of the clock on the cable box—"twelve thirteen in the morning?"

"Well, you see, Chloe . . . I never actually left. I was with Alice when Lizzy phoned her, so I followed her over in my car."

"And?" I waited for the rest of the explanation, far more curious than afraid.

"When you kicked us out—that wasn't very nice, by the way—Alice left before I did. I was putting my seat belt on and I dropped my . . . um . . . keys. Somehow, they ended up beneath the driver's seat," she explained in a rush.

"Can't you find them?" I guessed.

"Hm." She gave a little laugh I chalked up to embarrassment. "I couldn't get to them from the front, so I crawled in the backseat to see if that would work. Anyway . . . I'm stuck."

"With your hand under the seat?" Oh, my God. Poor Verda!

"It's my foot. I can't get it out from under the seat no matter what I try."

"Why didn't you call me right away?" I slipped into the shoes I'd kicked off by the door earlier and then dashed out of the apartment into the cool May night, keeping the phone to my ear. Images of a frail elderly lady with her foot wedged for over an hour made me move as fast as I could in two-inch heels. I hurriedly scanned the parking area in search of Verda's Mini Cooper. "Where? I don't see your car."

"Take a left out of your door and follow the sidewalk. I'm three or four doors down."

I counted the doors as I walked, dismissing one car after another until I finally spotted hers. "There you are. Just hang tight, Verda. We'll get you out of there in no time."

"You're such a sweet girl."

Stopping at her car, I went around to the driver side and closed my phone before sliding it into the pocket of my pajama bottoms. I opened the door and knelt down. "I can't believe you didn't call me sooner. You shouldn't have waited out here for so long!"

"Oh. Well . . . I didn't want to bother you. I really thought I could handle it myself." She smiled, as if pleased with herself. "Thank you for helping out a silly old lady. I think, though, you'll have better luck from the other side. So you can get to the leg that's stuck easier."

Her calm demeanor impressed me. In her position, I'd be freaking out. Taking stock of the situation, I nodded and closed her door. On the passenger side, I slid the front seat up and climbed in the back. "Wow, it's tight in here. No wonder you got stuck."

"I feel so ridiculous." She craned her neck to the side and glanced out the back window. Weird, but I'd have sworn she was looking for someone.

Scooting farther in, twisting on my side, I leaned over as

much as a person can in a space the size of a sardine can. "Is it your ankle or your foot? And does anything hurt?"

"Oh . . . both, I think. And no, I'm not in pain." She shifted in her seat and did that neck-craning thing again. "Your legs are hanging out the door, Chloe. You should pull them in all the way."

Yeah, right. In this tiny car? "Um, this probably won't take but a minute . . . hang on. Let me get my hand under the seat—"

"It makes me nervous, is all," she interrupted, speaking quickly. "With your legs hanging out, someone unsavory could see us."

Humoring her, because even though she had a point, I didn't really think it was necessary, I tried to resituate myself. Rolling from my side to my stomach, I bent my legs backward at the knees and slithered my body forward. "There. Better?"

She clapped, knocking my temple with an elbow. "Yes! Now!"

"Now? Now, what?" Something odd was going on. I knew it, but I couldn't put my finger on what. Crooking my neck so I could see Verda's face, I barely registered her cat-that-swallowed-the-canary grin before the passenger door slammed shut. "Who did that?" I nearly screamed.

"Alice. You can sit up, dear. I'm not really stuck," Verda confided. The driver-side door opened, and the car shifted slightly as someone—Alice?—climbed in. Verda patted my head. "And don't be mad. This is for your own good."

By the time the engine purred to life, I'd managed to get into a half-sitting position. "What the hell is going on here?" I asked, not bothering to keep my voice down.

"We're kidnapping you," Alice said over her shoulder as she backed out of the parking spot. "And Grandma's right, it's for your own good."

* * *

Alice drove us to a small, historic hotel in Chicago's central business district. From what I gathered on the ride over, Verda and my friend had hatched their kidnapping plan within minutes of leaving my place. They'd contacted Elizabeth, who'd jumped on board, taking care of "other details."

Those details were apparently the hotel room I now sat in. Three chairs formed a half circle around a fourth—mine—in the center. A few lit candles were scattered around the room, their vanilla scent filling the air, and soft music played in the background. If I were there with a guy, I'd have thought it was a scene set for seduction. In this case, I figured they were trying to relax me. Which was so not happening.

"She's angry. That's why she won't talk," said Elizabeth. "Maybe this wasn't such a hot idea."

"Of course she's angry. But she didn't give us much choice in the matter," said Grandma Verda. "And she can leave anytime she wants. It's not like we have her tied down."

Leave and go where? Traversing the streets of Chicago in the middle of the night, in my pj's, was not a smart move. I didn't have any cash on me for cab fare, and I distinctly remembered Kyle powering off his cell before going to bed. I had zero options. Which, I'm sure, was the entire point.

"We should have waited a few days." Elizabeth rubbed her eyes. "Or at least until morning."

"No. Grandma's right," said Alice, who for some reason had a baby rattle clutched in her grip. The toy belonged to her daughter, but Rose wasn't with us. "This can't wait. She acted totally out of character tonight. The quicker we resolve this, the better for everyone."

"Hello? Crazy women? I'm right here. Stop talking around me!"

Verda winked, as if delighted by my outburst. "Oh, good! You've decided to talk! We can get started now."

"Started with what?" I crossed my arms, absolutely positive the forthcoming conversation was not one I wanted to have.

"Your intervention, of course. Unless you'd like a snack before we begin? Elizabeth brought goodies," said Verda. "Cookies, I think."

"My what?" I tightened my hands into fists.

"Intervention," Verda said again. "This is a safe place. We're here for you."

While I'm quite sure she meant to reassure me, the result was anything but reassuring. I glared at Alice. "What is she talking about? And it better not be about Kyle, because that horse is dead and buried. Why can't you just be happy for me?"

"Wait!" Verda grabbed the baby rattle from Alice. "We need to go over the rules."

First a kidnapping, then an intervention, and now rules? Awesome. The night I became engaged would definitely live in my memory, just not in the way I'd hoped. Holding my hands up in defeat, I muttered, "Fine. What are the rules?"

Verda shook the toy, the clattering nearly loud enough to overwhelm the music. "Whoever has the rattle is allowed to talk. If you don't have the rattle, you can't say anything unless you're asked a question by the person who's holding it."

Elizabeth and Alice nodded in agreement and looked at me. At that second, it became clear how serious they were. Suddenly, the thought of walking home in my pajamas became a lot more appealing. What were the chances I'd be kidnapped twice on the same night, anyway? They had to be low. Low enough to risk it.

"This is ludicrous. You all realize that, right?" I said evenly. "I don't need an intervention because I'm engaged."

"This won't work unless you're open to the process." Verda sighed, her eyes bright with emotion. "We're family, and we care about you. All we ask is that you give this a shot. Okay?"

"Do I have a choice?"

Elizabeth waved her hands in the air. Grandma Verda

tossed the rattle to her. "Listen," she said. "We've all noticed some changes in you, and we're concerned. I think you're more upset about not receiving the magic than anything else. What do you think?"

I shook my head, not wanting to respond. I was related to these women by blood, which meant I deserved the gift just as much as Elizabeth and Alice. They had their magic, but where was mine? "I already answered that."

"Right. You did, but I don't believe you."

I gritted my teeth so I wouldn't argue.

Verda retrieved the rattle. "Try to be open to this," she reminded me. "We can't help unless you tell us how you really feel!"

Elizabeth snatched the toy back. "It would bother me," she admitted. "I would care very much if the people closest to me had something I should have but didn't. I would feel left out. Alone. And maybe I'd stop believing in the things I used to. Is that what's going on, Chloe?"

The walls closed in. I pushed out a shallow breath, trying to alleviate the suffocating pressure. It didn't work. What she said had hit a nerve. I had a choice here: tell them this part of the truth, like they thought they wanted, and open the wound that had only begun to close, or continue the charade.

"Nothing is going on," I said, choosing the charade.

"Why won't you talk to us?" Liz inhaled a breath, and a tiny grin appeared. "Besides, I think your magic *has* started."

Okay, this was not a development I'd expected. "What do you mean?" I asked, barely daring to hope.

"The cake, Chloe. I was somehow . . . compelled . . . to do what you wanted, to cast that wish. And I'm telling you now, I had no intention of agreeing."

I thought back to that moment in the bakery, to everything that had occurred. Maybe, just maybe, I'd be able to believe Elizabeth if the family ghost, Miranda, the source of the Gypsy magic, had visited me even once. But she hadn't, and from what I knew, that only meant one thing. I shook my head. "No. Nothing happened that was magical. But thanks for trying. Really."

Alice reached over and grasped the rattle. "If it's not the magic, then what? Why do *you* think you've changed?"

"I don't know what you're talking about," I shot back, still going with the charade. "Changed how?"

"You refused to look at the picture." Leaning forward, she centered her brown-eyed gaze on me. "The old Chloe, the one who tackled life instead of being resigned to it, would have leaped at that drawing. But you didn't. And that's when I got scared. That's when I realized something was very wrong."

She was right. The old Chloe would have jumped for joy. But I wasn't that Chloe now, and thinking about that draw-ing, and about whatever future of mine that magic had shown Alice, would ruin everything. I shrugged, as if I couldn't care less. "People change. That's life."

"Bull. Not like this. You're a completely different person."

So are you, I thought. Saying that, though, would just hurt her. "What do you want from me?"

"I want the truth. Whatever it is, Chloe, just lay it on me."

I noticed that Verda and Elizabeth had scooted their chairs back slightly, to give me and Alice an impression of privacy. Nice of them, but totally unnecessary. Because I didn't plan on telling Alice the truth. Not now, not ever. So what if I felt left out? So what if I felt forgotten in the happi-ness of her new life? If she knew, not only would she be hurt, but it might damage our friendship even more.

She continued to stare at me, waiting for my answer. Beg-ging me to answer. Reaching deep, I found the anger from earlier. Anger was better than tears. Anger shielded me from everything else.

I grabbed the rattle from Alice's grasp and shook it. "I'm

done here! This is dumb, and all you really want is for me to break things off with Kyle. But that's not going to happen, so this intervention is over!"

Everyone was silent. Alice shook her head in either disappointment or sadness; I wasn't sure which. Verda began clearing up the room. After a few more minutes, Elizabeth joined her. But Alice stayed in her chair and just looked at me.

I grinned, trying to ease the tension between us. "I'm sorry. I know you all meant well, but come on . . . This was a little much."

"You're right that it was drastic, but we felt—hoped—that drastic would get your attention and you'd open up to us. To me."

"I know you don't believe me, but I'm fine. Really I am. I just wish you could be happy for me." Squeezing my thumb and forefinger together, I said, "Just a little bit? Can you do that for me?"

Indecision colored her features, and I thought she was going to say no. But then a glint appeared in her eyes and she smiled. "I can be, yes, if you'll do one thing for me. Just one."

Immediately suspicious—because, come on, with the night I'd had, why wouldn't I be?—I said, "What's the one thing?"

Before answering, she called out to Verda. "Hey, Grandma? Do you mind if Chloe uses your car tonight? Elizabeth can take us home."

"I can?" asked Elizabeth.

"Yes, you can." Alice's tone was firm.

My curiosity and my suspicion climbed.

"Um, yeah, whatever," Elizabeth said.

"That's fine, dear," Verda agreed. "I trust Chloe with Greta."

Greta? Cute. She'd named her car. I thought only men did that. "What's the one thing, and why do I need Verda's car to do it?"

With a smile very reminiscent of Verda's canary-swallowing version, Alice said, "I want you to stay here, in this room, for an hour after we leave. You'll need the car to get home, but we'll come by for it later."

"That's it? Truly?"

"That's it. Consider it a little 'me time.'"

While I figured there was more to her request, and honestly, I'd had plenty of time alone over the last few months, I couldn't say no. I desperately wanted my best friend at my wedding. And really, what could an hour do? "Okay. You have a deal."

Pleased, Alice stood and gave me a tight hug. "I'm going to help them carry everything out to the car, and then I'll be back."

"I thought it was supposed to be alone time?"

"It is. I'll only be here for a few minutes." Another quick hug. "Be right back."

I washed my face while I waited, using the activity to keep my emotions in check—something I'd gotten pretty good at lately. Then I paced the room, not wanting to sit down, but unable to stand still. For the first time, I wondered why they'd brought me here, to this hotel, for their intervention. There were plenty of hotels closer to my home.

Before I could give it any further thought, Alice barged in. She tossed Verda's car keys on the bed. "You remember where we parked?"

"Yep. Just down the street a little."

"The hour doesn't start until I leave," she pushed.

"Then maybe you should leave?" I stifled a yawn. "I'm sorry, I'm just really tired."

"It's okay." She walked to the other side of the room and took a seat on the wide windowsill. "Come here, there's something I want to show you."

"I'm not looking at that drawing, Alice!"

She showed me her empty hands. "I don't have it with me. Come here. Please."

Hesitantly, I crossed the room and sat next to her on the sill. "What?"

Turning her head, she looked out the window. "It's still dark out, but do you see that building across the street? The one with all the black glass?"

I played along and glanced out the window. "Yeah. It's sort of big, and there are streetlights, and I'm not blind. Kind of hard to miss a building, Alice. So what's this all about?"

"In that building is an architectural firm called Malone & Associates. Have you ever heard of them?"

"No. Why?"

"I lied to you last year," she said, changing the subject. "Remember when you asked me to use my magic to draw a picture of your wedding day, and I told you that nothing happened?"

My throat tightened. "So . . . it did work? You drew my wedding day, and you've had that drawing for this long?" Somehow I'd thought the drawing was a recent thing, something done at the last minute to try to change my decision. The knowledge that she'd had it for nearly a year spun around in my head, clogging everything up. A shiver rolled down my spine, and a hairline crack appeared in the wall I'd built around myself. "Why didn't you tell me before?"

"To protect that day. To protect your future."

Okay. Whatever. It didn't matter. This altered nothing. "So why are you telling me now?"

She nodded toward the building. "Shortly after I drew your wedding day, I was having tea at a café up the road. And the man from your drawing—your groom—strolled in to buy a cup of coffee." Her eyes gripped mine. "I followed him, Chloe. And he walked to that building, to Malone &

Associates, swiped a card to unlock the door and let himself in. Which means he probably works there."

I didn't respond. I couldn't. The hairline crack widened, and the wall began to crumble. "No. I don't want to know this. Not now."

Alice stood and pointed out the window. "Don't you get it, sweetie? Your happily-ever-after is literally across the street. Not lying in your bed, sleeping. Across the freaking street." With that, she turned on her heel and left the room.

I sat there for longer than my promised hour of "me time," long enough to see the early sun of the morning. I didn't once remove my gaze from that building. My body trembled at the very thought, I wanted to grab on to this new future so badly. But actually taking the steps toward that future, the one I couldn't see, petrified me beyond reason. Kyle was safe. Comfortable. And I could visualize my future with him.

Taking a deep breath, I closed my eyes and turned away from the window. Then and only then did I open them. Numb, cold and exhausted, I retrieved the car keys. Then I left and drove home to where Kyle waited.

Chapter Three

In the week that followed, I did everything possible to stay on course. I kept busy at the store, cleaned my apartment, went to the gym every day, read three books and watched four movies. Also, unbeknownst to Alice, I drove by Malone & Associates a total of seven times over four different days. Basically, I was a well-read, physically tired, emotionally drained mess.

I was also still engaged, but now, my prior positive feelings weren't quite so positive. Kyle hadn't mentioned our upcoming nuptials once in the entire week. It bugged me. A lot. I'd fought hard for our future, and I'd have appreciated a sign that he was at least interested. Hell, that he even *remembered*.

So today, when Kyle asked me to go with him to buy luggage for an upcoming business trip, because the airline had permanently lost his last suitcase, I didn't believe him. I thought he wanted to buy a ring.

When we arrived at the mall, we headed directly to the luggage store. He hemmed and hawed over whether to buy a larger suitcase or one that he could carry on. His uncharacteristic indecisiveness struck me as nervousness, which was kind of sweet. But his dithering went on for so long that I started to get antsy, so I convinced him to buy both sizes.

As we left the shop, each of us carrying a bag, I said, "You leave on Monday?"

"Nope. I have to be at the Cincinnati office by eight Monday morning, so I'm flying out tomorrow afternoon." He nodded toward the food court. "Want to get something to eat before we head out?"

That did not sound like ring shopping. Or maybe he was being coy? "With the luggage? Nah, let's go somewhere else, so we don't have to lug them around with us."

We trudged along without trying to hold a conversation. It was a Saturday afternoon, which meant the mall had loads of people crawling everywhere. I saw the jewelry store before we reached it. Would he stop? If nothing else, maybe the sight would bring the subject up.

I stole a sidelong glance at Kyle, but his gaze remained straight ahead. "There's nothing else you need?" I asked.

"Huh? No. I'm set." Then, as if realizing I might want to shop somewhere, he asked, "Do you need anything?"

"No. Nothing at all." And with that, we walked by the jewelry store, with all its glittering diamonds, and didn't stop until we reached his car.

Swallowing heavily, I buckled my seat belt and turned my head away from him. I stared out the window at moving pavement for a while before finally deciding that enough was enough. I hadn't imagined my proposal. And unless Kyle had been afflicted with some type of magical malady, he hadn't forgotten it, either. Clearing my throat, I said, "I've been thinking about when we might want to have the wedding."

He grunted a nonreply.

"I'm partial to spring. Or maybe fall. What do you think?"

"I haven't really thought about it yet," he said, easing on the brake for a red light. "Do we need to decide this second?"

"Nope, we can talk about it later." And probably, I should have dropped the subject altogether, until he was more receptive. But I couldn't get that damn drawing out of my head, so I forged onward. "What about size? Any preference there?"

He reached into his shirt pocket and pulled out his sunglasses. Once they were on, he said, "Size of what?"

"Of the wedding. Small? Large?" I patted his knee. "It'll help me plan if I know what you want."

"Um. Small. I like the idea of small."

"Okay, small it is." Deciding that was enough for now, I went back to staring at the pavement. A small wedding would be good. Perfect, really. My guest list consisted of maybe twelve people. If my sister Sheridan flew in from Seattle, I'd have a baker's dozen.

Ha. Chances of that were slim to none. My baby sister and I hadn't been close for years. A decade or more, really. After our parents died, we'd moved in with my dad's sister. Sheridan and I were a team then, because Aunt Lu was not the motherly type. We took care of each other. Then I left for college and nothing had ever been the same. I sighed, pushing the thought away. The days of sisterly love were long gone.

Kyle pulled the car into a parking space at one of our favorite restaurants. He turned the ignition off and cleared his throat. "Chloe?"

"Yeah?"

"We're not in a rush to get married or anything, are we?"

"I don't know. I guess not. I'd like to set a date, though."

Playing with his sunglasses—one of his trademark signs of anxiety—he frowned. Uh-oh, this reminded me of that long ago day he'd broken things off with me. The day he'd told me about his love for another girl. Is that what this was?

"What's wrong, Kyle?" I asked carefully.

"Nothing, babe. Just thinking. How about I give a date some more consideration when I'm in Cincinnati? And then we can talk about it on Thursday, when I get back?"

Oh. Wow. Not a breakup. "Yeah, that would rock."

"Cool. Let's go eat."

I trailed him into the restaurant, relief suffusing my every step. If Kyle and I weren't meant to have a future, then fate would have to play her hand and tell me so in no uncertain terms.

Since the day I opened the Mystic Corner, Mondays were the slowest of the week—so slow, in fact, I'd recently begun toying with the idea of closing the shop on Mondays and increasing to a full day on Saturdays. It made good business sense, and that should have been reason enough to move forward. I kept dragging my heels, though. I liked the hours as they were, and the staff, as small as it was, was accustomed to having most of their weekend free. As was I. Still, business is business. I'd talk to Paige, my manager—and the only full-time employee—about changing the schedule. Seeing as we currently traded off on working Saturdays, her opinion mattered just as much as mine.

I returned to the crystal order I'd been placing, picking up where I'd left off. As a spiritual gift store, we carried everything from tarot cards to rocks and minerals to books on a variety of spiritual subjects, and more. While we didn't stock many big-ticket items, our inventory tended to turn over fast. The slowdown of the economy hadn't hurt us and, in fact, brought more business our way.

Well, except on Mondays.

Most other days we were busy from open to close. Which made perfect sense. People facing tough times naturally seek out ways to improve their situations, and many of them, the open-minded ones, found us. Crystals, with their mystical properties, remained top sellers.

I double-checked the order on my computer screen, hoping I hadn't forgotten anything, typed in my account information and clicked *send*. There. Done. Barely midmorning, and my to-do list for the day was nearly completed. Another reason I enjoyed Mondays.

My fingers hovered over the keyboard. Without allowing

myself to think about it, I opened the browser and began typing in "Malone & Associates." I got to the first *s* before common sense took over. What was I doing? Something stupid, that's what. I stared at the cursor, fighting the urge to continue, because yeah, part of me figured, "What the hell?" The other part, the engaged part, freaked out. Pushing away from my desk, I went to see if Paige needed any help.

The store was empty, which didn't surprise me. Paige had set up in one of the back corners, resituating shelves to better showcase the spiritual artwork we'd just been shipped. I stopped behind her, pleased with her progress. "It looks great!"

Turning, she grinned. Her jet-black hair was slicked back into a short ponytail, and I saw with great humor that she'd matched her purple eye shadow with a purple stud in her left eyebrow. "Yeah, I like it too. I should be able to finish before I take off."

Paige was slowly working her way through college, which for this semester meant half days on Mondays and Wednesdays. I gave her a lot of credit, because she made up the missed hours on other days. "Do you need any help? I'm almost caught up," I offered.

She considered it, but shook her head. "It's kind of tight back here. We'll just get in each other's way."

"Okay. Let me know if you need anything." She nodded and got back to it. I spent a few minutes walking around the shop, ascertaining that everything was neat and orderly. It didn't take long, as the store itself was only about four hundred square feet and wasn't overly cluttered.

When I was done with that, I hesitated. The joys of payroll waited, but I sort of thought staying away from the computer for now would be smart. Luckily, the bell jangled a customer's arrival, and then a few minutes later, another's. The first customer, a middle-aged woman who was a regular, selected three chakra-energy candles.

"These are gifts," Mrs. Delinsky confided at the register. "I'm giving the abundance candle to a friend who lost her job, the healing one to my aunt, and the happiness candle is a wedding gift."

"How nice of you to think of them! I'm sure they'll appreciate it," I said, ringing up her purchases.

We continued talking for a few minutes, and then, out of nowhere, goose bumps coated my arms. Strange, because the room didn't feel cold. I brushed it off, glancing up to see how the other customer was doing, only to find a third customer I hadn't heard come in. She hovered in the middle of the store, and she appeared young, maybe around sixteen or seventeen. She had long blonde hair, sky blue eyes and a turned-up nose. As if sensing my gaze, she turned and smiled.

I smiled back. Her eyes rounded, and very slowly, she lifted one hand and waved at me. I held up a finger to tell her I'd be with her in a minute and returned to wrapping up the candles for Mrs. Delinsky. Tucking them in a bag, I handed them over. "Here you go," I said, just as the phone rang.

She nodded her thanks and took off. I rubbed my arms to chase the chill away before grabbing the phone. The caller wanted information on the next month's tarot class. Facing the wall, I referred to the calendar of June classes we'd posted, and gave her the details. By then, the second customer—a young man—was waiting to purchase the books he'd selected.

When he was taken care of, I went in search of the girl I'd seen. Except, other than Paige and I, the shop was empty. Apparently, she'd gotten tired of waiting. "Hey, Paige? Did that girl have any questions?"

Paige stopped arranging the artwork. "What girl? I only saw Mrs. Delinsky and that guy."

"Sweatshirt, jeans, long blonde hair?"

"Nope. Didn't see her."

"Weird. Oh well, no biggie." The chill from earlier returned. I shivered and wrapped my arms around myself.

Paige grimaced. "I'm sorry. I'm focused on an exam I have this afternoon. I guess I'm more lost in my thoughts than I realized."

"It's cool. If she needs something, she'll likely come again."

I only had an hour before Paige left, so I confined myself to completing the payroll. With that done, I took my lunch to the front counter and settled in for a long afternoon.

A few customers were in and out over the next few hours, but it was quiet enough that I delved into my latest mystery novel. I was up to my eyeballs in the murder of a politician when the bell on the door jangled. I jumped, my heart in my throat, and my book flew out of my hands, landing on the other side of the counter.

The newly arrived customer stopped just inside the store, probably thinking I was a nutcase. I raced around to pick up the book and smiled in greeting. His return smile lacked warmth, but I found I didn't care. At all.

Because this man . . . ? Wow. Tall, probably around six foot, with short hair the color of burnished gold, and his eyes . . . Well, they were simply the bluest I'd ever seen. A vast, endless ocean. And he had a body that only comes from serious workouts. Merely stating he was fit didn't do the man justice. He was hot-man-of-the-month-in-a-fireman-calendar gorgeous.

Wiping my suddenly damp palms on my slacks, I squealed, "Hi! Welcome!" Guys that look like him live in movies, not real life, and certainly not in my store. I imagined every one of my muscles relaxing and tried speaking in a nonsqueal. "Can I help you find anything?"

"Ah . . . yes." His long legs ate up the floor between us quicker than I'd have liked. I smiled wider, trying to appear calm and collected. "My assistant's birthday is later this week," he said. His jaw was hard. Firm. Chiseled, even. As if cut from granite.

"And you'd like a gift?" I breathed. Like a really bad Marilyn Monroe impersonator. Lovely.

"A pendulum. She's partial to them, and while I think they're nothing more than pretty little gadgets, she disagrees."

His tone, crisp and to the point, stabilized my suddenly out-of-control libido. Obviously, he was a nonbeliever. I shouldn't have been surprised, but I was. And oddly disappointed. "May I ask why you're buying one for her, then?"

Scrunching his eyebrows together, as if my question was ridiculous, he leaned forward. Now I really couldn't breathe. "She's a good assistant. She seems to like pendulums. I'd like to give her one."

"Um . . . that makes sense." Was I trying to drive customers away now? I needed to chill out. Immediately. "Let me show you what we have."

I led him on shaky legs to the display case that held our array of pendulums, wondering if my reaction was based solely on his outrageous amount of sex appeal, or if the tuna I'd eaten for lunch took part of the blame. "Take a look and see if you like any of them."

He laughed, a surprisingly warm, if raspy—as if he didn't laugh often—sound. "My goal is for *her* to like it." Kneeling down, he stared into the case for a while. His shirt stretched tight over his well-muscled back. An image of him naked from the waist up smacked me senseless. My belly quivered, and a heat I hadn't felt for way too long took residence deep in my stomach. I gripped the counter, trying to find my balance.

"Can I see the rose-quartz one in the back? With the gold chain? And the selenite one here in front, with the silver chain?" he asked, pointing.

"You know your stones." Selecting the two pendulums he'd chosen, I laid them on top of the case. "Are you romantically involved?" I blurted, then winced.

"What? With my assistant?" He did his bunched-up eyebrow thing. "Are you hitting on me?"

"No!" Shaking my head vehemently, I sputtered another "No!" for good measure.

He tipped his head to the side, all of his attention on my face, humor clear on his. "Interesting," he murmured.

"What?"

"Your eyes. They just changed from sea green to rich, dark emerald. Like green fire." He winked. "You should hit on men more often, Miss . . . ?"

"Nichols. Chloe Nichols. But I was *not* hitting on you." Where was my equilibrium? Dumb question. I knew where. In Cincinnati with Kyle. "Rose quartz is known as the stone of love." Hitting on him? Who did he think he was? "If she uses pendulums, she'll probably know that. I was actually trying to be of help."

"Uh-huh. If you say so."

I wanted to kick him. Obviously, he was accustomed to women coming on to him—and full of himself.

"I'll take the selenite. Which," he said with a grin, "is known as the stone of mental clarity. A beautiful gift for her, and a huge benefit for me."

"I'm sure she'll love it." The guy probably *was* involved with his assistant. Sexually, not romantically. Men like that? Well, they knew better than to give their conquests any gift with the word *love* attached.

With quick, jagged movements, I replaced the rose-quartz pendulum and picked up the selenite one. "Anything else I can help you with?"

"Do you gift wrap?"

"We can."

"Good. Can I arrange for delivery? I'm much better at

remembering to give gifts if they're not sitting in my desk drawer all week."

"Sure, I'll just need to know when and where you want it delivered." Except we didn't offer delivery, so why did I agree? "And there's a fee." Hey, if I was going to do it, I was going to be paid.

"Not a problem." He chose the gift wrap he wanted and then paid for the pendulum in cash.

I jotted down the name of his assistant on a notepad, asking, "Where is this going to, and on what day?"

"Friday before noon, if you can manage it. Deliver it to my office." He opened his wallet and withdrew a business card, offering it. "My work address, phone number, everything you need is right here."

I was hot. Too hot. Maybe I was getting sick? "Thank you for shopping at the Mystic Corner."

"You're welcome." He hesitated for a beat. "Take the card, Chloe."

"Oh! Yes. Of course." My fingers brushed his and the floor wobbled. Bright sparks of electricity, millions of them, whisked over me, through me, and my body swooned toward him. As if he were a magnet I couldn't resist. The air grew so thick it hurt to breathe.

"Thank you for your help." He tossed me another grin and headed for the exit.

I collapsed on the chair behind the counter and tried to catch my breath, tried to will my body to behave. Wow. Just wow. Now I understood what people meant when they talked about spontaneous combustion. I'd felt sexual attraction before but nothing like this. Nothing so fast. Nothing so hot. Which, I guess, is why they call it spontaneous combustion.

I closed my eyes, huffed the air in and out of my lungs and then realized I still clutched his business card. The card sizzled, begging me to lift it up, to look at it, to put a name to the man who'd just knocked me senseless. One more deep breath and I opened my eyes, hoping his name was something dorky. Something I could laugh at. Something I could focus on instead of those eyes.

Initially, all I saw was a blur of black on white. When my brain was finally able to absorb the fancy raised lettering, everything I thought I knew spun around me at warp speed, stopped on a dime and exploded into a million little pieces. Ben Malone, CFO, Malone & Associates.

Yeah. Fate has a wicked sense of humor.

Chapter Four

I pulled my car to a stop on the street in front of Alice's house, flipped off the car ignition and tried to figure out why the hell I was even there. It wasn't reasonable, and I hadn't made my mind up, but I'd operated on instinct. Quite possibly, the instinct of a crazy woman.

Exhaling a breath, I slumped in my seat, trying to convince myself that Ben Malone appearing at the Mystic Corner three hours ago boiled down to nothing more than a strange coincidence, and that my reaction to him, along with the location of his employment, held zero meaning. What I really wanted to believe was that the drawing wouldn't be of him, and as soon as I proved that, everything would settle.

"Liar," I whispered. After all, I already knew the picture wasn't of Kyle, the man who at this very minute was likely contemplating the perfect date for our wedding. Now, literally out of nowhere, Mr. Ben Malone with his firm jaw and firmer body and ridiculously bluer-than-blue eyes had waltzed into my life, shaking everything up.

I felt as if my body had betrayed me, and seriously? That totally ticked me off. So what if Kyle and I weren't magical together like Ethan and Alice? So what if touching Kyle, kissing him, didn't turn me into a burning pile of mush? These things didn't—shouldn't—matter when contemplating a life with someone. Our relationship was fine. We were fine. Yet here I sat, in front of my best friend's house, emotions churning away, with my heart and soul begging me to reach for the sky. That ticked me off too.

I stared at the house Ethan and Alice had moved into a few months earlier, as if somehow I'd find my answers there. Built in the Craftsman bungalow style, it had stone siding, a porch surrounded by four blocky columns, and a bright red door. A large silver-maple tree graced their front yard, a few of its branches scraping the roof.

A comfortable home. Charming, even. The inside was even more so. With hardwood floors, beamed ceilings and a mishmash of furnishings from Ethan and Alice's former lives, their house was a place meant for gathering, laughing and loving. At that instant, it was the last place I wanted to be.

"You know what? Screw this," I whispered. I didn't have to do it now. No one was forcing me to look at that drawing. Even more to the point, the picture wasn't going anywhere. I could go home, think things through and come back when—*if*—I decided the risk was worthwhile.

My body relaxed. The stress that had balled up in my muscles lessened. Even the aching pain in my temples lightened. Relieved, because these had to be signs I was making the right decision, I started the car's engine. Instantly, the radio blared on, Kelly Clarkson's voice saturating the space. It was loud. Too loud.

My muscles jerked in response. I stared at the radio in confusion, nearly positive I'd left it off during my hurried drive to Alice's. Odd? Yes. Odder yet: when I attempted to lower the volume, nothing happened.

I turned the knob on the radio with more force, and again nothing happened. Desperate to shut the music down, I hit the power button over and over and over with so much force that the tip of my finger turned a splotchy red. But the damn song refused to turn off. What the hell?

"I'll do what it takes to touch the sky."

My hand dropped to my lap.

"Make a wish, take a chance."

The air whispered around me, caressing my skin. It washed into my body, a cool but uncanny breeze, stealing my breath away and igniting a series of shivers that refused to stop.

Slowly, too slowly, the chill faded away, my shivers disappeared and my breathing eased. The moment had seemed to last forever, but Kelly Clarkson still sang, so probably only a few seconds had passed. Dazed and trembling, I reached over and powered the radio off, only half-surprised that it actually worked. The song still pounded through my head, though. Like a skipping record. Over and over and over.

Make a wish, take a chance.

Oh, hell. How many signs was I willing to ignore?

"So this is the way it's going to be, is it?" I demanded. "And why'd you wait for so long? Is this fun, watching me go crazy?" I didn't know whom my questions were directed at— God, fate or Miranda—but whoever's hands were at the wheel of this particular mess, I'd have really liked an answer. Not that I got one.

By the time I reached Alice's front door, the song had, thankfully, stopped playing in my mind. Though I was pretty sure if I retreated to the safety of my car, it would come back. I raised my hand to knock, but Alice opened the door before my fist made contact with wood.

"I was wondering when you'd come inside. Good song on the radio?" she asked, bouncing her seven-month-old daughter on her denim-covered hip.

I narrowed my eyes. "What do you mean?"

"You know. A song on the radio? One you liked enough to maybe camp out in your car to finish before coming in?" She stepped to the side and I eased past her. "I'm not surprised. I do that all the time."

"Right. Of course." I struggled to regain my clarity, my sense of normalcy. "It's been a wild day."

Rose scrunched her face up and yawned long and hard, as if I'd already bored her with the few words I'd managed to say, before burrowing her head into Alice's shoulder. "She's tired," her mother explained.

I followed Alice into her living room and perched myself on her papasan chair, devoutly ignoring the crazy beat of my heart and the perspiration building on the back of my neck. Alice tucked Rose into the baby swing that rested in a corner of the room, covered her with a sunny yellow blanket and put the swing in motion. The baby didn't so much as coo before closing her eyes and dropping off to sleep. After ascertaining she wasn't going to wake back up, Alice crept quietly to the sofa, crossed her long legs and settled in.

I swallowed, trying to find the words I'd decided to say, but couldn't. I was an engaged woman, damn it! I had no business even thinking about that drawing . . . about Ben. The song, which had barely left my consciousness, returned.

I'll do what it takes to touch the sky.

Okay, that had to stop. Like now.

Maybe if I chatted for a while, I'd calm down. And the singing would cease. Smiling weakly in the direction of Rose I said, "Has she shown any signs of magic yet?" Between Miranda's warnings and Alice's own power, we all knew that Rose would someday have more magic than anyone else in the family, save Miranda. We just didn't know when to expect it.

Alice's posture stiffened. "Maybe. But I'm not positive."

"There's been something?"

She glanced at Rose, a mix of worry and love in her expression. "Nothing definite. But the other night, Ethan swears he took her stuffed bear out of her crib, but it was there when I checked on her in the morning. That and a few other similar occurrences have made me wonder." She tried to laugh it off with a shrug. "Of course, we're not sleeping as much as we used to, so it could be a combination of our own forgetfulness and being too watchful. You know . . . when you're looking for something, you tend to find it—or think you do."

Maybe. Maybe not. "It will be fine. Her future is secure. You made sure of that."

Alice rubbed her arms, as if chasing a chill away. "I know, but that doesn't stop me from worrying. Or Ethan."

No, I suppose it wouldn't. "So . . . uh . . . Ethan still hasn't adjusted to the idea of magic?"

"He's fine with me, Elizabeth and Miranda. It's just Rose he's concerned about. Too much too soon, getting things too easily. Stuff like that." Alice's brown eyes bored into me. The thing about having really good friends is that they know you, and that means you can rarely surprise them. Or fool them. Chitchat time was over. "But enough of that. Let's talk about you. What brings you here unannounced?"

"I used to stop by without calling all the time," I pointed out, wincing as Kelly Clarkson's voice grew in strength.

"Uh-huh, before husband and baby. Now I have to resort to kidnapping to get any time with you." She grinned.

"That's not true! You're busy . . . and, well—"

"Give it up, Chloe. Why has today been a 'wild' day?"

Make a wish, take a chance. Why wouldn't my brain let go of that song? "Remember last year, before you and Ethan worked things out, how"—I searched for the correct word—"*unusual* everything seemed?"

"No, I've completely forgotten," she said, deadpan. "Of course I remember. I didn't know which way was up. It was a never-ending cocktail of vertigo and hormones."

"Yeah. Exactly like that!"

My voice was louder than I planned, as if I were talking while wearing headphones, and Alice raised a finger to her lips. "I don't want Rose to wake up." Her gaze hit my stomach. "Oh wow, Chloe! Are you trying to tell me that you're pregnant?"

"No! Why do people keep asking me that?" Oh. The hormones part. I wagged my head to the side, as if I had water in my ear. Works okay for water, not so much for evacuating a song. "I'm talking about the vertigo!" I yelled.

"Chloe, shhh! Have you been drinking or something?"

I lowered my voice. "Sorry. I meant the vertigo part."

"Something's happened?" she asked.

Not trusting myself to speak, I simply nodded.

"Are you going to tell me, or do I have to guess?"

I gestured that guessing was the way to go.

Wrinkles creased her forehead. "Hm, let me think. Has Miranda finally made an appearance?"

I shook my head.

"Has your magic started?"

Another shake.

Alice sat up a little straighter. "Has Kyle broken off the engagement?"

Even with the racket blasting in my head, her hope rang loud and clear. "Don't sound so pleased." I placed my hands on my ears, for some reason thinking that would drown out the noise. No dice, for obvious reasons. "Not that I know of! He's not even in town right now."

"Then, what? Are you having second thoughts?"

"No!" Too loud. I sighed. "Sort of, but I don't want to."

"Now we're getting somewhere." She leaned forward and cupped her chin in her hands. "Have you thought about why you're having second thoughts?"

"Signs. A lot of them. And they keep coming." *Make a wish, take a chance.*

"Like what?"

"Kelly Clarkson," I blurted. "And my traitorous body

becoming all turned on because of a stranger. Singing in my head. The radio refusing to turn off. And a business card!"

Flipping her fingers over her mouth, Alice tried to mask her grin. "As cute as Kelly Clarkson is, she isn't the person in your drawing." She winked. "But hey, I hear fantasies are healthy."

While I appreciated her levity, the joke escaped me. "What are you talking about?"

"Not so quick on the draw today, are you? Think about what you just said," she said with a straight face.

It took another few seconds before I got it, but once I did, all of my pent-up stress, worry and emotion burst out in choked laughter. Leave it to Alice to find a way to make me laugh when I felt as if the very ground had dropped out from beneath me. I smacked my hand over my mouth, trying to muffle the sound, to no avail.

Alice tossed a concerned frown toward Rose, who thankfully still slept, and then rose to her feet. Grabbing my hands, she pulled me up. "Out of this room."

I trailed after her to the kitchen and sheepishly took a seat at the table. "I'm sorry," I wheezed. Then, miracle of all miracles, I was able to pull myself together. "Your fault. You shouldn't have made me laugh."

"Right, completely my fault." She plopped a glass of water on the table before sitting down in the chair next to me. "Drink this. Your face is flushed." I swallowed a large gulp and then, at her prodding, another. When I slid the glass away, she reached over and felt my forehead. "You're a little warm. Are you ill?"

"*Confused* is the more appropriate term."

Alice's oh-no-my-best-friend's-gone-off-the-deep-end look vanished. "Talk to me."

"Maybe I should look at the picture. Just for informational purposes."

Bam, the singing disappeared. It was oddly disorienting,

as everything inside of my head, even my thoughts, seemed to vibrate from the sudden silence.

Alice raised an eyebrow. "Really? Why?"

"I'm curious." Now, my head throbbed. "Can I see it?"

"Why the change of heart?"

"Does it matter?" I shot back.

"Not really, because I don't have the drawing anymore. I ripped it up and threw the pieces in the garbage after your intervention the other night."

Her matter-of-fact tone startled me, and for about half a second I believed her. Then I thought of the signs. "No, you didn't. Just go get it for me, please." No way would Alice destroy that picture. Even so, the mere possibility of the drawing not being in existence any longer brought goose bumps to my skin.

"Yes, I really did. I thought you wanted me to support your decision, to be happy for you. I couldn't do that with that picture here, because every time I looked at it I wanted *that* future for you. So after talking things over with Elizabeth and Ethan, we decided on a course of action."

I weighed her words, which made perfect sense, with everything I knew about her. Again, I shook my head. "I'm serious. It's time for me to see it."

Exasperation floated out of her in a loud sigh. "You can't have it both ways, Chloe! Either you want to marry Kyle or you don't. Either you believe in magic—fate—or you don't. Either you want to see the picture or you don't. You were very specific in your wishes the other night, and as your friend who was trying to do what you asked, I disposed of the drawing." She crossed her arms. "So I could try to be happy for you."

I should have been relieved, because without the drawing I'd never have proof, and that would make it far easier to continue along the path I'd started down. Instead, disappointment gathered in my throat. "You're serious? But now—"

"Now *what*?" she demanded. "Tell me what's happened to make you come here today."

I nearly told her to forget it, but the thought barely entered my consciousness before Kelly began an encore performance. Apparently I was supposed to lay it all out for Alice—for better or for worse—so I did, as quickly and succinctly as possible.

When I finished, she grasped one of my hands. "It's okay to be scared, but sweetie . . . you should also be excited! This is good. You can see that, can't you?"

"I'm not sure. But I don't see as if I have a choice." I let go of her hand. "Everything's getting all messed up."

"Can I ask you something?" At my nod, she continued. "When I drew my picture, the one of me, Ethan and Rose, you didn't have any trouble believing in that future. Why is it that now, when it's *your* future my magic has shown, you can't accept it?"

"I don't know," I admitted. "But right now, that doesn't matter. Now I need to see it, so if you really destroyed the drawing, you're going to have to recreate it." I exhaled a long, slow breath. "Can you? And if not, then I guess you'll have to go with me to deliver the pendulum to Ben, so you can see him for yourself. You'll recognize the man from the picture again, right? Even though it's been a while?"

Bolting from her chair, she raced out of the room. A few minutes later, she returned with a book in hand. Opening it, she pulled out a piece of folded paper, set the book on the counter and approached. "Here."

"Ha! I knew you were lying." The relief poured in that I'd wanted to feel earlier.

"I needed to be sure that you wouldn't destroy the drawing the second I gave it to you." She held the paper in front of me. "So yeah, I lied. Sue me."

Maybe I should have been angry with her, but I wasn't. I understood her motives, and when push came to shove, she'd done what I'd asked. No reason to be upset. But as I stared at the paper, a tremor whisked along my skin. Was I sure about this? No, but my arm remained steady as I reached for the drawing. "I'm as ready as I'll ever be."

She handed it over. My fingers touched the heavy paper and my heart rate sped up. I held the page, trying to draw the strength I needed to open it. Knowing you *should* do something doesn't necessarily make the doing itself any easier. Especially in these circumstances.

One quick breath, and I opened the first fold. Every single hair on my body stood up. The throbbing in my head increased. My stomach dipped. I felt a little like the way I had the one and only time I'd gone skydiving—that millisecond before the jump, when a rush of fear, excitement and adrenaline pushes through every nerve, every muscle of your body, and you have to force yourself to take the leap. To step out into the air and trust that your parachute will open when you need it to. It's mindboggling. And scary as hell.

One fold to go. I sucked in another mouthful of air, let it back out and opened the page fully. My eyes were scratchy, almost irritated, so I couldn't see anything of merit immediately. Just a bunch of lines blurring together. Tears fell, but I couldn't stop them. I didn't even want to. But they blurred my vision, so I wiped them away.

The trembles grew stronger and I shivered. I blinked rapidly, and for a brief, glowing second, the drawing came into perfect focus. My eyes rested on the image of me, and then, out of nowhere, a burst of bright light turned the room upside down and sent it spinning in dizzying circles. As cold as I'd been earlier, my body now surged with heat.

The fire continued to climb upward and then outward. My throat grew parched. I reached out, hoping to find the table, grasping for some type of stability. Nothing met my fingertips. The weight of my legs, arms, my entire body disappeared. Fear pummeled through me fast and furious.

Had I lost my mind, my grip on reality? Or was I in the process of dying from some freak accident? A heart attack, maybe, or a plane crashing into Alice's house. Or hell, maybe an earthquake. All of these seemed like reasonable and perfectly possible, if ridiculously unusual, explanations.

Again I tried to find stability, something to center me, by clutching blindly for the table. The heat suddenly vanished, the swirling ceased, and limb by limb, the weight of my body returned to me. I blinked again, opened my mouth to ask Alice what the heck had just happened, except she wasn't there. Neither was her kitchen. I now stood outside, and an arm rested on my waist while the sun warmed my shoulders. Some type of soft fabric—silk?—cascaded along my skin. Instead of the drawing in my left hand, I held a bouquet of flowers: vanda orchids, a glorious combination of purple and white, surrounded by a sea of lush greenery I couldn't identify.

"Chloe! Smile for goodness sake. This is your wedding day," an unknown male voice called out from in front of me. "Stand a little closer to your handsome groom."

As if on autopilot, my body obeyed the commands. I tightened the gap between me and the unknown masculine form next to me. My lips stretched into a smile. I heard the whir of a camera.

"Good! Perfect!" the same man shouted.

What the stranger initially said finally penetrated through the thick smog that coated my brain. My groom? My wedding day? Had I somehow become a part of the drawing? I'd seen enough strange occurrences in my life to accept that as a reasonable explanation.

But wow. A rush of lightheadedness hit. My legs grew weak. I leaned farther to the right, using the solid, firm form of the man standing beside me to stay upright. His arm tightened around my waist, adding support, shoring me up. The camera made more whirring noises, and while I tried to tilt my head to look at my groom, I couldn't. An unexplainable force held me still, and I could do nothing but stare straight ahead. Not a pleasurable feeling.

"We're set for now. We'll get some more shots at the reception," the photographer said. "I think you'll both be really pleased!"

Whatever vise had seized me suddenly evaporated, so I slowly tipped my head, intent on learning who stood beside me. Excitement, anticipation, fear, worry and a host of other emotions I didn't bother trying to name swarmed my senses. I saw a black tux, a white shirt, a strong physique. Slanting my vision up another degree, a chiseled chin came into view, and then . . . Oh, God.

Ben Malone.

All the blood-pumping desire I'd experienced earlier came back in a flash. No surprise there. But when he angled his body toward me, dipped his chin so our eyes could meet . . . Well, that was when the real bombshell hit. This Chloe, the one in the drawing, loved this man with an intensity I'd never before felt. Bright. Strong. Everlasting. And that same love reflected back to me in the bluest eyes I'd ever seen. This Chloe—the girl who wasn't yet me, but whom, if I played my cards right, I could potentially become—was loved. Truly, to the depths of her soul, loved.

"Kiss me," I whispered.

He smiled, bent over and pulled me against him. I closed my eyes, ready to finally experience the kiss I'd waited my entire life for. Would his lips be hard or soft? Would his mouth ravage mine, or would his kiss be slow and intoxicating? I wanted to know, and I wanted to know right that instant.

"Kiss me," I said again.

"Chloe. Wake up, honey." Alice's voice seeped into my awareness first. Her hand, lightly slapping my cheek, came next. "Snap out of it."

My eyelids were heavy, almost impossible to lift, but I

heard the panic in her voice, so I forced them open. Her face was over mine, concerned. "Thank God! You scared the crap out of me. What happened?"

With her help, I pulled myself into a sitting position but stayed on the floor. The hollow ache I'd lived with for the better part of a year was back, only it was stronger, deeper, and hurt like the devil. "Where's the drawing?" My voice came out in a thick rasp.

"You dropped it when you passed out. How are you feeling? Do you need to go to the doctor?"

"Give me the drawing, Alice. Please. I need to see it."

She didn't argue, just reached to the side to grab the paper. Handing it over, she asked again, "Honey? What happened?"

Please, please let me go back, I prayed, clasping the paper tightly. Just for a few more minutes. Just for the kiss. I stared at the image, not seeing the black and white sketch as it actually was, but in living color, smelling the scent of flowers in the air, enjoying the warmth of the sun and the feel of Ben's arms around me. But nothing else happened. It was just a drawing, nothing more, nothing less.

"If you drew this, does that mean this is definitely my future?" I asked.

Rocking back on her heels, Alice frowned. "I wish I could answer that. I don't know."

"But what do you think?"

She bit her lip before responding. "I think, because my magic showed me this future, that this day is within your grasp. But I also think that the future is fluid, and that every choice we make can alter the outcome."

"But it's possible," I whispered. "It *can* happen. It *can* become true. Like with you and Ethan."

"Oh, sweetie, of course it's possible!" A sigh shuddered out of her. "But I nearly screwed everything up with Ethan by almost making the wrong decision. Every time I think about what I could have lost . . ." She shook her head. "No. As happy as we are now, getting here wasn't all that easy."

My hand gripped the drawing tighter. Did it matter how difficult the process was if it resulted in what I'd just seen? What I'd just experienced? No. It didn't. I wanted this more than I'd ever wanted anything else in my life.

Kyle flitted into my mind then, and while I didn't have a ring on my finger, I felt the burden of it nonetheless, tying me to him. Tying me to *our* future.

"Come on, let's get off the floor," I said. We both crawled to stand and reclaimed our seats from earlier.

"What exactly took place here?" Alice asked for the third time.

I shook my head, trying to deny the words even as I spoke them. "I became a part of that picture, and that Chloe—the one you drew—is head over heels for a man who is not my fiancé." Bringing my hand to my chest, I felt the thud of my heart, the steady beat of it somehow reassuring. "I fell, Alice. I fell hard. So what am I supposed to do now?"

Chapter Five

The following Wednesday I still hadn't settled on an answer. Oh, I knew what I wanted to do, but I wasn't entirely sure if *want* equaled *right*. I'd spent the last few days going about my business as if nothing out of the ordinary had transpired, and other than Alice, no one had a clue that I was completely freaking out.

That "no one" most definitely included Kyle. He remained in Cincinnati on business, and as was his custom, he hadn't called other than to let me know his plane had landed safely late Sunday afternoon. What wasn't normal, and what I hadn't been ready to confront, was that I hadn't contacted him, either.

Arriving home, however, with less than two days before the scheduled delivery to Ben and only one before I saw Kyle, it was time to figure this out. After dropping my mail on the dining-room table, I headed for my bedroom and then quickly changed into a pair of loose pajama bottoms and a T-shirt. Ignoring the nervous energy pumping through my blood, I knelt down in front of the antique mahogany armoire that had belonged to my parents. My fingers rubbed along the rich grain of the wood, my mind flashing back in time, seeing my mother hurriedly selecting clothes to pack. I was twelve and had watched her from across the room, upset that she and my father were going away on a weekend trip without me and Sheridan.

I hadn't been nice to my mother. I'd called her selfish and stomped around in a huff, trying to get her to change her mind. Of course, she hadn't. They'd left with a list of rules and contact numbers for the sitter, hugs and kisses for us and the promise that the three days would speed by. Instead, a rainstorm, flooded roads and a driver who lost control of his car made certain my parents never came home again. Shaking my head, I pushed away the pain.

Opening the bottom drawer, I glanced at its contents: a variety of candles, several types of tarot decks, my pendulums, and a few other odds and ends of a spiritual nature. I grabbed a white candle first, for truth and purity, and next, a blue candle, for wisdom and understanding. My hand hovered over the purple candle, unsure, because the use of it along with the others might be more powerful than I needed. Purple enhanced all other spiritual activities, and should increase magical power—if I had any. Since I didn't, and because I needed all the help I could get, I figured it couldn't hurt, so I added that candle to my pile.

Situating the three candles on the top of my dresser, I carefully lit each before tossing the drawing and my MP3 player on my bed. Scooting into position, I supported my back against the pillows I'd fluffed and puffed along the headboard and closed my eyes.

A dream had haunted my sleep for the past two nights. Pulling the dream to the forefront of my mind, I envisioned myself standing in the middle of a crossroads. One direction led to Kyle, a second toward Ben and the other two paths led to destinations unknown. Even so, I knew without a shadow of a doubt which path beckoned. The strength of the pull didn't so much surprise me as scare me, because I didn't trust it.

It seemed fake. As if I were Eve being tempted by the most succulent fruit in the Garden of Eden. What if, like Eve, I gave in to temptation only to discover I'd made a horrible mistake? Maybe the dream was a warning, cautioning me that all of this could be nothing more than a test of fate, to see how committed I was to Kyle. If I turned away from that now, if I proved to the universe that I'd bolt at the first sign of something possibly better, then maybe I'd end up on one of the other paths, the ones I couldn't see, with years of misery as my future.

I needed to reenter the drawing. To capture the kiss I hadn't, and not just for the emotional punch but for the tactile experience: the taste of Ben's lips, the scrape of his cheek against mine, the weight of his arms around me. Feeling the reality of us together again, when I was prepared for it, seemed crucial, for without that push, I didn't know if I had the courage to proceed in *any* direction.

Praying for clarity, I picked up the drawing and pushed the MP3 player's button with my thumb. The song that had driven me crazy the other day began to play. I set it on repeat, cranked up the volume and centered all of my attention, all of my energy, on my wedding day.

The colors, scents and emotions whirled around me like a kaleidoscope, tugging at the very core of my being. Whatever line separated my current reality from the one that existed on the page blurred, and the tug grew stronger. But it wasn't enough. A wall stood, tall and solid, between me and the world I yearned to enter.

The music played on for a while—I'm not sure for how long—but when the last drop of hope drained out of me, I gave up and turned the MP3 player off. Crinkling the corner of the page in frustration, the sigh I'd been holding back escaped. Why wouldn't this work? What was I missing?

"Help me," I whispered. "I don't know what to do."

The air turned then. I gasped as pinpricks of cold darted down my spine. Next, the awareness of being watched plunged into my consciousness, followed by the scent of freshly picked roses, fragrant and rich. My muscles tensed, my breathing hitched. Could it be—?

"You already know which direction calls to you, Chloe. Is it so hard to heed that call?"

That musical voice, which I'd heard only once before, came from my right side, just beyond my vision. My body went rigid. I didn't move, not even to turn my head to face her. Emotion clogged my throat. The heavy weight of unwanted tears gathered behind my eyes. How long had I waited for this moment? How many nights had I sat in this very spot, calling out to her? I swallowed, tried to find the courage to speak, but couldn't.

A rush of colors slipped into view as she walked— glided—into position in front of the bed. Her tall, lanky, almost willowy form appeared solid, but a shimmer of light surrounded her, an ethereal glow. She had large brown eyes, deep and fathomless, as if they'd captured the secrets of the world; long dark hair that fell in luxurious waves around an elegantly featured face; skin as white as the finest porcelain; and rich bloodred lips. Myriad hues rippled over her like a rainbow's reflection in a pool of water—there, but not concrete, unreal. As if one skipping stone would break the illusion.

Miranda.

Spiderlike shivers cascaded over me, through me, as I fought to stay calm. Again, I tried to voice my thoughts, but they remained locked inside, caught in the storm of emotions I couldn't seem to stop. The minutes ticked by in my head until fear that she would disappear pushed out the words I needed to say, the one question I needed answered before anything else. "What took you so long?"

She emitted a light laugh. "Silly girl. I've been with you all along, in one way or another. You simply haven't been ready until now."

"That's not true! I've been ready for months."

"Ah, if you had been, I wouldn't have had so much difficulty connecting with you, now, would I?" She gestured toward the candles, the movement stirring the flames, making them dip and bob, nearly extinguishing them. "These helped clear the way tonight, even if they didn't serve the purpose you intended."

"I needed you," I said in a halting voice. "But you left me alone. Wondering if everything Alice told me is even real—if I really am a part of something bigger, or if I'm just the girl I've always been. Why would you do that?" The words gushed out.

"Such emotion! Why do you find it so difficult to believe that we share the same blood? You come from me! And yes, Chloe, you are indeed the girl you've always been. But you are also, as you say, a part of something bigger."

I opened my mouth to argue but promptly shut it when she raised her hand.

"There is much to say, and too little time, so listen carefully. That long-ago night when I nearly cursed a man, the night I instead created the gift that has been passed from one daughter to another, I did so out of love, but also because I could see the futures of my girls. I was shown that cursing him would then curse everyone who came from me."

"This man. What was his name?" I already knew the story. Miranda, a powerful Gypsy, had been lied to by the man with whom she'd fallen in love. Seeking revenge for his lies, for his cruelty, she'd almost cursed him, but instead she had changed her direction by gifting magic to the baby—babies, it turned out—she carried, who then gifted it to their daughters. So it went, from daughter to daughter. Supposedly, I was part of this chain.

She hadn't yet answered, so I asked again, "His name? Please tell me. I need to know."

Still she hesitated. A flash of emotions—anger, sadness, fear—plunged in and out of her eyes, but finally, she nodded. "His name was Bartholomew Bennett. Your great-great-great-grandfather."

There it was: the missing puzzle piece, the connection between me and the ghost standing before me, and therefore, my connection to the ever-elusive magic. "He raised my great-great-grandmother? What was *her* name?"

Miranda's eyes narrowed, and a longing entered her voice. "He stole her from me. My Evelyn. I only saw her once, from a distance, and I couldn't bring myself to disrupt her life. As much as I despised Bartholomew by then, he was a decent father, and his wife a good, loving mother. Besides, the world was vastly different then, and no one would have believed the word of a Gypsy over his. I might have lost Amelia in the process."

"I'm sorry," I said softly. I didn't have to be a mother to understand the pain Miranda felt.

"I never told Amelia she had a twin sister. I regret that." Translucent tears appeared in Miranda's eyes. She lifted her chin, forcing them to drip down the sides of her face, past the planes of her cheeks, until they dropped away into nothingness. "This regret is what has allowed me to remain in this world, to reforge the ties that were broken, so all of my daughters will recognize each other."

"And you've done that, but what about—?"

"No, Chloe, I haven't," she said firmly. "Not yet."

Disappointment slammed into me. "So that's what this is about? You want me to search out long-lost relatives? What about me?" I held up the drawing. "What about this? Is this my fate?"

"That depends." Miranda waved her hand, and the drawing shot from my grip to hers. "And it's not really the question you should be asking. You're expending far too much concentration on this picture, Chloe. You need to look inside yourself. You need to trust in yourself and in your power. Find that trust, go with it, and all will become clear."

"What power? I'm as powerless as I've always been!"

Her image flickered, as if my outburst had interrupted her energy and, therefore, her ability to be present. I held my breath, my gaze fixated on her, hoping that she wasn't about to disappear. But then her image solidified, and the tightness that had appeared in my chest relaxed in relief. For better or for worse, I wanted her here. More than that, I *needed* her.

"You are far from powerless. Can't you feel the magic inside of you?" She smiled then, a hauntingly beautiful smile, and the light around her brightened, became more iridescent. She literally sparkled.

"What magic, Miranda? I feel nothing. Shouldn't I feel something? I can't bake wishes into cakes, and I've yet to draw a picture of the future. So, what magic?"

Her nostrils flared, as if she'd exhaled a breath. "Stop comparing yourself to others! You have always been acutely aware of the magic in this world, of the power that exists in objects and people around you. How can you not recognize it within yourself?"

"I don't sense magic anywhere. Not like I used to." My admission startled me. When had I stopped sensing magic? When, exactly, had I begun ignoring most—if not all—I believed in?

"The magic, *your* magic, exists within your will—as natural as breathing. It flows from you to those around you effortlessly, often without your ever being aware of the power you're wielding. Think about it, Chloe, and you'll recognize the truth I speak."

My will? I thought back to what Elizabeth had said at the intervention, that bit about how she'd felt compelled to do what I asked, to bake the magic cake. I remembered how strong my emotions were as I'd pleaded with her. Comprehension slid in, along with the faintest ember of excitement. "All I have to do is make a wish, want something to happen, and it will? It's that simple?"

"Yes . . . and no. What you feel, what you want and desire, feeds this portion of your power. And yes, the more intense your emotions are, the more intense your magic is."

Her eyes clouded with a hint of darkness. Fear? Not of me, but *for* me?

"Listen closely. This gift is yours, and it is meant to be used, but be cautious. Mistakes can be devastating. Not only to you, but to those your power touches. You have a journey, my dear great-great-great-granddaughter, and it is about far more than this picture."

Before I had a chance to ask another question or, hell, even take a breath, the light vanished, and with it, Miranda. My mind whipped through everything she'd said, and while the fear in her eyes and her warning worried me, it was the rest of her message that gleamed bright and true.

The ember of excitement, of anticipation, grew in strength until it hummed through me, pushing everything else out. All this time, I'd been so sure the magic had skipped over me. Now? Well, this changed everything. The drawing lay on the floor where Miranda had stood. Catapulting from the bed, I grabbed it. I looked at it, still reeling from seeing and talking with Miranda—from learning that I was, indeed, more than the girl I'd always seemed. My eyes fell to the sketched image of me, of Ben. My heart cried out, my soul begged me to take a chance. Trust in yourself, she'd said. Trust in your power.

Every part of me wanted this. The fear of choosing the wrong direction skittered away. Confidence soared. I had magic on my side. How could I lose? And with that, I stepped out of the middle of the crossroads, chose a destination and began walking, all the while hoping like mad that what I saw at the end of the path was real and not a trick, not an illusion.

"So. Not. Cool," I mumbled early Thursday evening, punching the button on my cell to replay Kyle's message, hoping and praying that somehow I'd heard wrong.

A series of small beeps sounded, followed by, "Hey, babe.

It's me. Change of plans. I need to stick in Cinci through Friday. Not making it home until Saturday. I'll call when I get in."

Nope, I hadn't heard wrong. Damn! I hit the *end* button and dropped the phone on my desk. This was so not the way I'd envisioned the forthcoming evening. All day long, I'd gone over and over what I would say to Kyle. What words to use to end our relationship. How to explain my change of heart. Even though I'd made my choice, even though I'd taken Miranda's message to heart, that didn't mean all of my doubts were gone. They weren't. My love for Kyle hadn't vanished. My belief that we could have a good life together still existed. But I'd found a truth inside of myself that refused to be ignored, so . . . now what? Everything hinged on meeting Ben again with a clear conscience. How could I do that as an engaged woman?

"Fuck," I murmured. "Why can't any of this be easy?"

I started to give my available options some serious consideration when the telltale clomping of Paige's blast-from-the-past, 1970s-era platform shoes broke into my consciousness. A few seconds later, she pushed into the back room at the Mystic Corner like a woman on a mission, matching my barely-stuck-on artificial grin with one of her own.

"We're all locked up," she announced. Folding her arms across her chest, she leaned against the wall, her posture stiff.

"Awesome. Thanks, Paige."

"No reason to thank me. Locking up is part of my job. Right?" Fiddling with an invisible thread on her sunflower-laden dress, she kept her eyes planted somewhere to the side of mine. Suddenly concerned, I set my own worries on the back burner and gave her all of my attention.

"Is everything okay with you?"

A painful silence drifted between us. Grabbing my cup of cold coffee, I swallowed the last gulp, playing for time, giving her a chance to respond. But when the quiet seemed as if it would never end, I gave it another go. "Is there something you want to talk about?"

"I don't know. Is there something *you* want to talk about?"

"Um . . . no?" Had I upset her somehow? "Help me out here. What's bothering you?"

"Fine." She slapped her ring-adorned hands on her hips. "Is the store in financial trouble? Should I be hunting for a new job?"

"Whoa!" Talk about coming out of left field. "Where are you getting that from?"

"You're either in the middle of some hushed phone call, or you're staring off into space, or you're disappearing back here whenever you can. I wasn't going to bring it up, but your snapping at Jen today made me rethink that." The words tumbled from Paige's mouth in a mess of syllables. "As long as I've worked here, I've never seen you behave so . . ." Breaking off, she twisted the mood ring on her right index finger.

She had a point. "You're right, I have been a little crazy lately. But the store is solidly in the black, and your job is one hundred percent safe. I promise."

"Really?"

"Really," I affirmed, happy to be able to solve at least one problem. Yay for me.

She puffed out a breath. "Okay. Good. But what's up with the weirdness, then? Jen is really upset. She thinks you're about to fire her."

"God, I'm sorry." And I was. Poor Jen. She was one of my two part-timers, and had made a minor error on a return. Rather than calmly explaining the mistake, I'd lost my patience. Not in a bitch-boss-from-hell way, but still. "I apologized already, but I'll talk to her again tomorrow."

"And the weirdness?" Paige prodded. "Are *you* okay?"

I meant to say I was fine, I really did. But what came out

was "No. Not really. I'll figure it out, though, and I'll work harder at keeping my personal garbage away from the store."

"Understood." Crossing the room, she retrieved her backpack from a cupboard. "Can I say something else?"

"Go for it."

"This store is a reflection of you and your beliefs, Chloe. This might sound really stupid, but the last few weeks I've felt this weird energy at the shop. Nothing bad, just . . . unsettling, I guess. Kind of freaky. And I think some of our customers are feeling it too. My guess is that whatever's bothering you is . . . um . . . somehow disrupting the good vibes here."

"That doesn't sound stupid at all." Geez, and here I was thinking I'd done a great job of covering up all my personal stuff. Apparently, not so much. "It should get better soon."

She gave me another long, searching look. "Just let me know if I can help in any way."

"Will do." And really, that should have ended the conversation. For some unknown reason, I found myself asking, "Do you believe in fate?"

She slipped her arms into her backpack straps. "Sort of. I guess I don't believe that our fates are predetermined, but that we have several possible destinies we can claim. That's where free will comes into play, you know? One choice leads to one future, and a different choice to something new."

Similar to Alice's take on the situation, but . . . "That's not really fate then, is it?"

Paige bit her lower lip in thought. "Let me say it like this: even if three choices out of four will eventually lead to some variation of the same endgame, we have the ability to choose door number four. And who the hell knows what lies on the other side? Free will." She shrugged. "I prefer to believe that my decisions matter, and that my life isn't all laid out from the second I'm born. Why such a heavy question?"

I forced another smile. "Just wondering. Have a good night, okay?"

"Um . . . yeah. Sure. You too." She tossed me another curious glance. "Hey, Chloe? Don't worry too much about the future. It's the present that matters, you know? Be happy today. Tomorrow will take care of itself."

The door slammed shut behind her. Her words swirled in my brain as my gaze landed on the cell phone. Kyle was a good man, but could I say I'd truly been happy this past year? Content, maybe, but not really *happy*. The truth of that settled inside, adding weight to the decision I'd already made. I had to move forward. I had to see if I really could reach the sky.

But I wasn't free to begin anything with Ben. So . . . what to do? Have Paige make the delivery to Ben's office and then find a reason to contact him after my conversation with Kyle? Or should I just bite the bullet and call Kyle and do the breakup thing via the phone, with approximately three hundred miles between us?

Yuck. Double yuck. No way would I break up with Kyle during a freaking phone call, and no way was I going to skip out on going to Ben's office. Okay then, my choice fell somewhere in the middle. Wait for the face-to-face to end the most important relationship I'd had the past year, because it mattered—*he* mattered—and both of us deserved nothing less.

But I'd also go ahead and make the delivery to Ben as planned. Business only, though. No hanky-panky. No funny stuff. No kiss. And definitely no magic. Not that I'd purposely tested my powers yet, because I hadn't, but the rule needed to be set for my own sanity.

My resolve strengthened as I completed the day's deposit. I could do this. It was just a delivery, after all. I'd behave, follow my rules and hopefully set the stage for another meeting after Kyle and I worked everything out. I mean, really, how hard could it be?

Chapter Six

"Do-or-die time," I mused late Friday morning. The package for Ben's assistant firmly in hand, I strode into the Malone & Associates lobby with a confident gait. Inside, I was a pile of mush, a messy concoction of anticipation and anxiety with a generous side helping of guilt. Luckily, no one but me knew that.

Do not flirt. Do not say anything stupid.

The not-flirting thing I could handle; it was the "stupid" angle that worried me.

I continued on toward the bank of elevators, my thoughts wholly centered on the image I intended to present. Basically, that of a woman whom Ben would want to get to know better. That seemed simple enough, but based on our last meeting, chances of failing were high.

Alone in the elevator, I pressed the appropriate button and drew in a breath. He was a businessman who focused on the absolute fact of numbers to earn his living, whereas I— at least in his mind—dealt in the weird and unexplained. So yeah, on the outside, we were a totally mismatched pair.

But I knew better. Or rather, I *hoped* I knew better. God help me if I was wrong.

My cell phone buzzed the second the elevator doors swished open. I stepped out before answering, taking a place along the wall. Across from me were two glass doors into the floor's offices.

The phone buzzed again and Alice's number lit up on the display. "What's up, Alice? I thought the plan was for me to call you when I left?"

"I know, I know, but this can't wait. Something strange happened this morning. You haven't seen Ben yet, have you?"

"Not yet." Her uneven tone registered, and a swift bolt of apprehension tightened my hold on the phone. "What is this all about?"

"Well . . . you see . . . Miranda was here, and she—"

"She what?"

"Indicated that I should draw another picture of your future. So I did."

Uh-oh, this didn't bode well. At all. My grip tightened even more. "And?"

"It might be better if you pop over here and take a look yourself. I'm not sure what to make of it." I heard Alice exhale. My foreboding increased tenfold. "Them. I'm not sure what to make of *them*."

It took a minute, but when I understood what she was getting at, I gasped. "Them? As in more than one picture?"

"Chloe," she said softly. "I have three new pictures of you spread out on my kitchen table. None of them depicts the same future! So . . . uh . . . I have no idea what this means."

Her confession hit me about as hard as a dozen semitrucks gunning along at top speed. I pushed myself against the wall for support. "How is that possible?"

"Oh, honey. I just don't know. My magic has never worked this way before. I'm at a loss."

All my confidence bled away. "I can't deal with this right now," I choked out. "I'm here. I'm going to do what I came here to do."

"Don't you want to know what the new drawings are of? *Before* you see Ben?"

"No. I really don't." As much as this new knowledge sat inside, mucking everything up, I'd made a decision. Come hell or high water, I was seeing it through. "Later is fine.

After work. Can you bring them to the Mystic Corner tonight? And can you see if Elizabeth and Verda will come too?"

"Absolutely. Just . . . well, go slowly for now."

"I will." I made the promise and disconnected the call. Nothing had changed, really. Regardless of what Alice had now drawn, her magic had shown her the wedding-scene picture first. And my reaction to Ben had been immediate and strong. Both of these things pushed me forward.

Straightening my spine, I tucked my phone into my purse and marched toward the glass doors. *Ben.* He was in there somewhere. Quivers of anticipation, of longing, licked through me. Being here felt right. Whatever the rest meant . . . Well, I'd deal with that later.

On the other side of the door stood a large, circular desk where two women—one blonde and one brunette—clicked away at their keyboards. Both young, both attractive. Were one of these Ben's assistant? The one he might be involved with?

The brunette glanced up first, smiling widely with perfectly even, if a little large, white teeth. I stopped in front of her. "Do you have an appointment?" she asked in a nasal twang.

"Um . . . sort of. I'm supposed to drop something off for Ben Malone. Personally, that is. I can't just leave it here. With you. In case you were wondering," I blurted.

"And your name?"

"Chloe Nichols. He's expecting me."

She clicked on her keyboard. "Take the hall all the way to the end. You'll see his office."

My knees nearly buckled as I walked past the desk and down the hallway, but I pulled myself together. When my eyes landed on the office that had to be his, I stopped. This was it. Once I walked in there, once I saw him again, I somehow knew there would be no turning back. Taking a deep breath, I stepped to the edge of his doorway and peered in.

Instead of seeing him, as I expected, I saw another desk with another woman—I guessed her to be in her late forties, possibly early fifties—also typing. "Um . . . excuse me? Am I in the wrong office? I'm looking for Ben Malone."

"He's expecting you." Her fingers kept clacking away without missing a beat. Impressive. She tipped her head to the left, toward a door I hadn't noticed. "Go right in."

Even as I crossed the room, relief sluiced into me. Obviously, neither of the women out front was Ben's assistant, and this woman—well, I doubted he had any type of romantic entanglement with her, based on her wedding ring. Not that the possibility was completely out, but it certainly seemed unlikely.

God. What was I doing? I knew what: I was totally getting ahead of myself.

Reminding myself yet again to stay on course, to not act like a loon, I evened my breathing and finally stepped into the lair of the man who, unbeknownst to him, had completely taken over nearly every waking moment of my life. Crazy. Just crazy.

I scoped out the room before announcing my presence. "Spare and Clean" seemed to be Ben's design motto. A long, lean, so-dark-it-gleamed-nearly-black walnut desk took center stage. Behind the desk, a tall credenza, also walnut, housed a plethora of books along with his computer. Not one framed photo could be seen on any of the surfaces, nor were there any other types of personal mementos. Obviously he was a man who kept his business and private lives in separate compartments.

As for the man, his dark-blond head was bent forward, immersed in whatever data existed on the printed-out page in front of him. My heart pounded faster and harder, as if I'd just run uphill several miles. I fought the nearly irresistible urge to throw myself at him, to run my fingers through his hair, to give him that kiss I so badly yearned to experience. I felt as if I already knew him, as if our being together wasn't a question mark but a definite. And that made it so very hard to not give in to temptation. But you know, I couldn't. Mostly because leaping into his lap and draping my arms around him was sure to give the wrong impression.

So I resisted. But it wasn't easy.

"Chloe?" His deep voice broke into my daydream. "Come on in! You have the package?"

Blinking several times, trying to catch up, I shut the door behind me. Damn those urges, anyway. "Oh! Yes. Of course. It's right here." I waved the wrapped gift in the air like a loon. "All ready to go!"

His unbelievably blue eyes met mine, igniting a tingle of warmth that began at my toes and, inch by tantalizing inch, crawled all the way up my body. "It's a pleasure to meet someone who loves her job as much as you do," he said. "I don't see enough of that."

Wide, full lips turned upward at the corners as he spoke. My eyes fastened onto them. All I could think of was kissing him. "Happy to pleasure you," I murmured. "It's my job."

"Really?" he drawled. "And I haven't even tipped you yet."

"No tip necessary. Just—uh—here." I snapped my mouth shut and walked forward, placing the package on his desk. "I hope she likes it."

"She will. But I'm curious. Is that a benefit exclusive to your specific niche in the business world, or have I been missing out with all of my other deliveries?" he teased.

"What benefit?" I felt clueless.

Tapping his long fingers on his desk, he didn't answer. But his mouth softened into a broader grin, and a glint of humor whisked over his expression.

I replayed the conversation thus far, and when I realized exactly what I'd said, heat gathered on my cheeks. "I didn't actually mean . . ." Well, that was a lie. The thought of giving him pleasure and getting some back reddened my cheeks even more. "I'm a little out of my element here."

His smile vanished. Standing, he rounded the space between his desk and where I stood. He stopped in front of me, so close I could smell the shampoo he'd used that morning. And that made me think of him wet, naked and soapy. I cleared my throat, trying to remove the unbidden image from my mind. It didn't work.

"I'm sorry if I made you uncomfortable. Thank you for the delivery." He held his hand out. "It's been nice seeing you again."

I grasped his hand, the feel of it warm and electrifying all at once. I wanted him to pull me to him so badly that I nearly couldn't stand it. "You're welcome, Ben."

Dropping his clasp from mine, he nodded toward the door. "I think that's everything . . . ?"

This was it? It couldn't be. I had to say something. Preferably something intelligent and witty. Something that would drag that smile back to his lips and light his eyes up with interest. But nothing came to me, so I stood there like an idiot while my brain rapidly flip-flopped through possible points of conversation, searching for anything that would lead us to where I wanted to go. I grabbed on to the first semirational possibility that came to me. Okay, the second. Because sadly, asking him to kiss me seemed rather forward.

"No, not everything! I still need to congratulate you!"

His eyebrows bunched together. "For?"

"For . . . winning a free class at the Mystic Corner. We . . . uh . . . conduct a monthly drawing on each month's customers." The lie slipped out easily. "You're our winner this month!"

He rubbed his jaw with one hand. Which brought my attention back to his mouth, and how much I still wanted to kiss him. To taste him. So. Very. Much.

"Is the prize transferable?"

"No. Yes. I . . . gee, no one's ever asked that before." That wasn't a lie. "Why?"

"No time for classes," he said easily. "And no offense intended, but I'm about as far away from your target market as you can get. But if the prize is transferable, I'm happy to pass it along to my assistant. Otherwise, you should offer it to another customer."

"Oh . . . well. Sure. That's fine. You can give it to someone else." Damn! How in the hell was I going to set up another meeting now? And why didn't he appear interested? "I'll mail the gift certificate out at the end of the month," I said, completing my lie. "To your assistant."

He nodded. "Good marketing strategy, giving a monthly prize out to a brand-new customer. Great way to get them to return."

Ha. It *was* a good idea. Maybe I'd actually start using it. Knowing I couldn't extend this visit much longer, I threw caution to the wind and went with my gut. "So . . . um, I was wondering. Any chance we could get together again. Socially?"

I'd startled him. It was obvious by the way his eyes widened. His mouth started to form what I was sure would be a negative reply. I couldn't have that, so rules or not, I decided it was time to let my magic out to play.

Focusing all of my energy, emotion, wants and desires about Ben—about us together—I visualized my power wrapping around him, washing into him, changing the words he planned to say. I latched on as hard as I could, and this time I felt the magic—the power—as it whooshed from me to him. My nervousness trickled away. My breathing quickened. Energy whipped through the air. It buzzed in my ears, tickled my skin and stung my eyes until they watered. My entire body quaked as the magic surged from the very core of my being, from who I was, feeding off of all I felt, all I wished for, all I yearned to be.

Say yes, I thought. Accept me. Want me. Desire me.

His eyes narrowed, and if I hadn't known better, I would have sworn he knew precisely what I was doing. With a slight shake of his head, as if waking up from a trance, he said, "A date? But I don't—" He stepped backward, nearly knocking into one of the chairs in front of his desk.

I stared at him, not speaking, staying as still as possible. *Just. Say. Yes.*

He rubbed his hands over his face and then combed his fingers through his hair. Retreating another few steps, he braced himself against his desk. Then, when I'd about decided his will was stronger than my magic, he nodded. "Why not? What do you have in mind?"

Not exactly the enthusiasm I'd hoped for, but hey, we had to start somewhere.

Several hours later, I found myself in a strangely positive mood. Sure, there were plenty of issues still requiring my attention: Kyle, the three new drawings and the undeniable reality that without my magic, Ben's answer that morning would have been an indisputable "Thanks but no thanks"— which pretty much sucked. Even so, for whatever reason, on this day and at this moment, I felt pretty damn good.

Though I was incredibly, out-of-my-skull, antsy-as-all-get-out bored. The shop had been quiet all day, unusual for a Friday, and I'd sent Paige home early. Jen had called in sick, and my other part-timer had requested the night off. So I was alone with nothing to do but think. And frankly, I was tired of thinking.

I checked the clock for what had to be the one hundredth time in the last fifteen minutes and groaned. There were still hours to go before the Gypsy brigade's planned arrival, and until then, I needed to keep my mind occupied. Racing to the back room, I grabbed Jen's teen magazine, which she'd left at the end of her last shift, and took that with me to the front counter.

Hot pink letters on the cover promised to "uncover your dating style," a splash of turquoise offered "amazing hair, skin, and nails," and along the bottom, a ribbon of red detailed this year's "hottest beach fashions." Geesh.

I'd barely flipped to the first page when I caught a glimpse of someone hovering near the counter, followed quickly by the sound of that same someone clearing her throat. My heart thumped an extra beat in surprise as I glanced up to see a customer. She looked vaguely familiar, so I smiled, trying to place her. And then, all at once, I got it. She was the blonde girl who'd been in the store the previous Monday. The girl Paige hadn't seen.

"Oh! I didn't realize anyone was here," I blurted. "Sorry about that."

Arms hanging loosely at her side, the girl offered a tentative smile. As before, she wore faded blue jeans and a white zip-up hoodie. "I like it here," she said quietly. "It feels like a good place."

"It is a good place," I confirmed, waiting for her to say more. Possibly to ask if love potions were real or if I carried any books on Wicca, which were the two questions I received the most from young women.

Instead, she backed up a few paces, her gaze taking in the shop in one full sweep before returning to me. "I'm supposed to be here."

Her statement didn't shock me. Lots of people visited the store searching for answers. "Then I'm glad you came back. Do you have any questions, or are you looking for something in particular? I'm Chloe, by the way."

The blue in her eyes darkened in confusion . . . and something else. Sadness, maybe? "I'm Mari. I guess . . . well, I guess I'd like to know more about all of this." She gestured with her hands, encompassing the entire shop. "And you. I'd like to know more about you."

My intuition kicked into high gear, and an unexplainable need to help saturated me. "What do you want to know?"

She hunched her shoulders forward. "I don't know. I was here the other day, and then I left, and today I came back." She stiffened, glanced around the shop again and shivered. "I came back."

"Yes, you did," I said softly, reassuringly. "How can I help you?"

"I don't know," she repeated.

Something was off. Way off. I just didn't know what. I couldn't decide if this girl—Mari—was ill, high on something, scared out of her wits, or something else entirely. "Okay. That's okay. What can—?" The phone rang, interrupting me, startling the girl enough that her complexion drained of what little color she had. "Give me a second, Mari." I grabbed the phone but kept my eyes on her. "The Mystic Corner. You got Chloe."

"Hey, it's me," said Alice. "Have a minute?"

"Actually, no. Can I call you back? I have a customer here." Mari turned, as if she was going to leave, so I covered the phone with my hand. "Almost done," I said to her.

"I'll be quick," Alice interjected. "It's just that I won't be able to make it tonight, but Liz will bring the drawings."

The rushed, worried tone of my friend's voice finally penetrated. I held a finger up to Mari to indicate I'd be a few more minutes, and then faced the wall for a little privacy. "What's wrong?"

Alice drew in a breath. "Nothing."

"Alice? It's me you're talking to. Did something else happen?"

"Not everything is about you, Chloe!" she snapped.

"That's not even what I meant," I said.

"I'm sorry. You didn't deserve that." A long, frustrated sigh poured out of her. "I can't talk about this with you until I've talked with Ethan. Please don't ask me any more about it."

"Oh. Okay, then." A blast of hurt surfaced. Sure, I understood that my role as Alice's best friend now belonged to Ethan, though my relationship with her was still important. But even with this comprehension, I missed being the person Alice turned to first. "I'm here if you need me."

"I know that, and thank you."

We hung up. I pasted a smile on and turned back to Mari. Except she wasn't standing in front of the counter any longer, and a perusal of the shop proved she hadn't decided to browse. "Well, shit," I murmured.

She'd surprised me twice now: once on her arrival and once on her departure. And honestly? Being alone in the store on a fairly regular basis meant that I never wanted to be taken unawares by folks strolling in and out. The fact I had been, more than the girl's odd behavior, gave me the heebie-jeebies.

Striding to the front door, I tested the bell-like mechanism that was supposed to announce comings and goings. I swung the door open, and the bell rang just fine. Repeating my actions a half dozen times resulted likewise. It seemed I simply hadn't heard her. Strange? Yes. Impossible? No.

"Better pay more attention, Chloe," I muttered to myself. Once again, I grabbed the teen magazine and settled in for the last few hours of the workday. Thankfully, business picked up, and before too long there was at least one customer in the shop at all times.

Though whenever the bell rang, I'd stop midsentence or midactivity and look up, 100 percent expecting to see Mari. Of course, it was never her, and as the evening continued, my concern for her ebbed away. Instead, my thoughts drifted to Alice and whatever was going on with her, as well as to the three new drawings I'd yet to see. Thus far, I'd done fairly well at not obsessing over them. But now? Well, I wished I'd gone directly to Alice's when she originally phoned.

My apprehension kicked up another notch as the last of the customers filed out of the store and Elizabeth and Verda appeared. I ushered the two women in, locked the front door and was all set to grab the cardboard tube clutched in Elizabeth's hands when my gaze landed on Verda. Laughter burbled inside, so I squeezed my lips together.

"Was this done on purpose?" I asked, referring to her new do.

Verda nodded solemnly, but mischievous glints sparkled in her pale blue eyes. "What do you think? Be honest!"

Her hair, normally a gray-streaked white, now greatly resembled the interesting pale pink color of cotton candy. "It . . ." I searched for a compliment that wouldn't be completely false. ". . . is certainly colorful! And . . . uh . . . bright!"

And really, it matched Verda's fashion style to a tee. Today she wore lemon yellow slacks, a purple shirt, and glitter-speckled high-tops. So yeah, the pink hair was sort of like the cherry on top of a tutti-frutti sundae. "It suits you," I said. "Truly."

"Thank you, dear." Preening, she patted her hair and then winked. "Verda needed a new groove."

"Even better, the dye will wash out." Elizabeth chuckled. "In case she decides pink isn't the right groove for her."

"I might try blue next time," Verda confided. "Or maybe lavender."

The laughter I'd barely held back erupted. "You're awesome, Verda." Interesting fashion choices or not, when I reached eighty-whatever years, I wanted to be just like her: confident, totally at ease with myself, ready to fight any demons necessary to safeguard those I loved. Or even just to make them laugh. "Thank you."

"Whatever for?" Verda asked in an oh-so-innocent tone of voice. "All I did was give you something else to focus on, something you could laugh at. Besides, I'm old. Us old folks can get away with anything." She winked again. "Even pink hair."

Overcome by emotion, I whispered, "I love you."

"Well, that's good, dear. Because I love you too." Stepping forward, she held out her arms. I walked into them and hugged her close. "We're family. Don't you ever forget it," she said when we separated.

Nodding, feeling like an idiot for not recognizing the love around me sooner, I pivoted my head to hide my suddenly moist eyes, only to find Elizabeth wiping at hers. Reaching out, I clasped her hand and squeezed tight. A few minutes of perfectly balanced silence fell upon the room and we simply stood there, united as only family can be. It felt good. So good, I didn't want to ruin it.

"Maybe I don't have to look at those now," I said, my gaze on the cardboard tube that held the three new drawings. "We should go to Alice and make sure she's okay."

"Alice is with Ethan and Rose, and they're fine," Elizabeth said. "If they weren't, do you think Grandma and I would be here now? Do you think *you'd* be here now?"

"No, but—"

"Listen to me, Chloe," Verda said firmly. "Those drawings hold information that Miranda feels you need. Don't let fear stop you from understanding why."

"She's right. What would you have done differently if you'd seen the other picture earlier? Would you still have proposed to Kyle?" Elizabeth asked.

I knew she expected me to say no, but I honestly couldn't. Nor could I say yes. I simply didn't know. So much depended on the day, hour—hell, the very minute—I'd have come into contact with the original drawing.

But her point was clear, and Verda's sensible, so I reluctantly accepted the cardboard cylinder. Without allowing myself a second to reconsider, I marched to the counter and flipped the plastic lid off. "Here goes nothing." I tipped the tube so the paper-clipped and rolled-together pages fell out onto the glass surface.

Verda and Elizabeth approached from behind, each laying a comforting hand on my back, showing their support and love. Sweet of them, and I oh so very much appreciated the sentiment, but I didn't react. Too much was at stake. Too much required my concentration.

Hesitantly, I touched the still rolled-up papers and removed the large paper clip, nearly expecting to be torn from this reality into one of these futures I hadn't yet seen. But the floor remained solid, the walls didn't spin and electrifying heat didn't course through my body. Thank God for that. One skip through time was more than enough.

I unrolled the drawings but didn't separate them. As soon as I lifted my hand, the pages immediately rolled together again. I bit my lip in frustration and repeated my action. This time, though, Elizabeth reached forward to hold the right side down, and Verda did the same with the left. Perspiration broke out on my forehead, and my skin grew clammy.

A little voice inside pleaded with me to close my eyes, turn around and run away. I'm not ashamed to admit that I almost gave in, but the stabilizing presence of Elizabeth and Verda bolstered my courage.

Tilting my head downward, I stared at the top picture, wondering if this was the first of the three Alice's magic had shown her that morning, or if she'd just bundled them up in no particular order. Not that it mattered. What did matter, what I needed to pay attention to, was the future each drawing depicted. And this picture—this future—held only two people: me and Kyle.

My hair hung slightly longer than I presently wore it, and

we were sitting in the middle of a room I didn't recognize. But the furniture in the room I did. Some of the pieces were mine and some of them were his. Wedding bands circled fingers on our left hands. Neither of our smiles reached our eyes, but we appeared at ease with each other and whatever life we were leading. A shudder of relief racked me, because I knew what this future represented: The one I'd already envisioned, the one I'd put into motion with my proposal. The one I'd already decided to turn away from.

I pushed the picture up so I could view the one beneath. My vision blurred with tears as I stared at possible future number two, because in this image I was completely, heartbreakingly alone. I stood somewhere in the dark, with only the faintest edge of light illuminating my face. There were no distinguishing features in the space around me to tell me if I was in a room, outside or hovering in some strange abyss. I didn't like this future. I didn't like the way it made me feel, and I really didn't like the haunting misery I saw on this Chloe's face.

Not able to handle the emotions that this drawing brought forth, I shoved it out of the way, unearthing the last drawing. My breathing eased and the strangling tightness in my chest loosened, because in this image, I was surrounded by others. Again, though, I stood in the center of a room, but all around me were the people I loved: Ethan, Alice and Rose were in one corner, Nate and Elizabeth in another. Verda and Miranda were there too. And while in this picture, I wasn't completely alone, I wasn't specifically *with* anyone, either.

I dragged the other two pictures apart, so I could see all three at once. My eyes flipped from one to the other, trying to understand what each one meant, and then trying to understand what they meant as a whole—if anything at all. The answer sat there, on the edge of my consciousness, forcing me to stare at each picture again, looking for something but not sure what. The crossroads, and me, standing in the center of it with four different paths to choose from, entered my mind in a dizzying rush.

"Elizabeth?" I said, my voice strangely calm, belying the frantic nerves jumping like grasshoppers in my gut. "The wedding picture is in the back room, in the top drawer of my desk. Can you get it, please?"

She didn't bother with a reply, but I heard her footsteps as she raced through the shop and then back again. "Here." She thrust the drawing into my grip.

I added the picture to the counter, so all four were in a neat little square. I soaked them in one at a time, looking for the clue that I knew was there. A crossroads. Four paths. Four futures.

But which path, which choice, led to which future? Finally, after what felt like forever, I saw the sign I'd been searching for. Or rather, I saw *me*.

In the three new drawings, the eyes of the Chloes staring back at me were, in all cases, flat and resigned, as if I'd given up on the world. Sure, the levels of desperation—sadness— differed slightly in each, the worst being the drawing in which I stood completely alone, the best with my family around me. And my future with Kyle? Solidly in the middle. Even so, they were eerily similar.

Or as Paige had so eloquently said the other day, all variations of the same endgame.

But in the wedding scene, standing next to Ben? My eyes were alight with love, happiness and excitement for a future that wasn't shown in any of these drawings, a future that Alice's magic hadn't shown her: my life with Ben and whatever that might bring.

"Door number four," I whispered. "I want door number four."

The path that would lead me to *this* future seemed clear, and I'd already started the journey. Whatever doubts I'd had about spelling Ben—about compelling him to agree to a date—vanished in a blink. A delicious curl of anticipation brought a smile to my face and a fluttering in my stomach.

I couldn't wait to see what would happen next.

Chapter Seven

How, exactly, does one dress for a breakup date, anyway? Common sense dictates the obvious: nothing too sexy or revealing, nothing too flamboyant or bright and certainly nothing that might bring to mind any previous romantic encounters. Because you know, putting those thoughts into the head of the breakupee would only lead to disaster. Or at the very least, an uncomfortable moment or two.

Scowling at my reflection in the mirror, I confronted the truth I'd thus far avoided, and it had zero to do with what clothes covered my body. I hated hurting Kyle so much that I'd battled queasiness all day. Now, with his arrival imminent, I wished I'd listened to Elizabeth in the first place and allowed my relationship with Kyle to progress—or end—naturally. But I hadn't listened, and the responsibility for the fallout rested solidly on my shoulders. Or in this case, swirling in my stomach.

Another glance at my reflection convinced me that the jeans and T-shirt I wore were perfectly acceptable for a variety of situations, including breaking up with someone I still cared a great deal for. But my cheeks were a smidge too pale, and the dark circles under my eyes clearly broadcast my fatigue. Hurriedly I applied a thin sheen of cosmetics, just enough to put me in the living and breathing category, and then I retreated to the living room.

Maybe if I thought about Ben and our date the following day I'd be able to calm down. When I left his office, we'd set the day and time but not the actual activity. I figured by his suggestion of an early meeting that his plan was likely a quick cup of coffee, perhaps breakfast, and that would be that. But I had other ideas. That was why I'd insisted on picking him up, so what we did was in *my* control.

Three sharp knocks sounded, interrupting my thoughts. I sat up straighter, my eyes on the door. My queasiness spiked, reminding me that tonight wasn't about Ben. It was about Kyle. It was about us. The door opened and Kyle stepped inside, smiling as he entered the living room.

I returned the smile and patted the space beside me on the sofa. Dropping down next to me, he rested his head against the cushion and closed his eyes with a sigh. "Hey, babe. Am I glad to be here."

"Hey, yourself." I watched him warily, remembering how comfortable we were with each other. As little as a week ago, I'd have scooted closer and given him a kiss. I might have laid my cheek against his chest and chatted, or I might have rubbed his shoulders to help him unwind. But I couldn't do any of these things. Not anymore.

Sliding to the side slightly, to put a bit more breathing room in between us, I kept my voice on an even keel and started with a general, if boring, topic. "How was your flight?"

"They didn't lose my luggage." He opened his eyes. "And the plane didn't crash, as you can see."

"Well, you're home now." I touched his knee, skimming my hand up and down his leg in comfort—an old habit, and at first I wasn't even aware of what I was doing. But when his hand caught mine, panic welled into a nearly bursting bubble in my chest.

Shifting forward, he kissed me lightly on the nose. I gasped and pulled away, removing my hand from his. He stared at me in question. "Is something wrong, Chloe?"

I didn't—couldn't—reply. An awkward quiet lurched between us, tainting the air with unease.

"Kyle . . ."

He held his hands up, stopping me. Which made me think that maybe, just maybe, he'd had second thoughts all on his own. Maybe *he* was planning on breaking up with *me*? I grabbed the throw pillow from my left side, clenching it in my lap, squeezing the dang thing so hard that my knuckles turned pink.

Reaching over, he tucked a strand of hair behind my ear. "We need to talk, babe."

Oh, my God, I was right. Relief filled me. But also, somewhere deep inside, was an old hurt. "It's okay, Kyle," I began again. "There are things—"

"Let me get this out first. Cool?" At my nod, he continued. "I owe you an apology. When you suggested marriage, I was taken off guard." Red blotchy circles appeared on his cheeks. "But I have to tell you . . . It's important that you know . . . I came here that night seriously thinking about ending our relationship."

Somehow, this didn't come as a surprise. Maybe it should have. Maybe another woman would have cried. But at that moment, I was absolutely calm. "I'm glad we're being honest with each other. We haven't been for a long time, have we?"

"I just thought you should know—"

Before he could continue, I took over, wanting to save him from as much discomfort as possible. "It was awfully quick, and I shouldn't have put you on the spot like that. Especially in front of Verda and Alice. I'm the one who should be apologizing." I gulped a breath before forging onward. "So I totally get that you want to back out now. Really, it's okay."

I was about to give him my rehearsed speech, but he surprised me again. Lacing his fingers into my hair, he cradled my head. "No, babe. You got it wrong. I wasn't sure about ending things. I planned on getting your take on it. But then you proposed, and I can't explain it, but something flicked in my brain like a light switch. I saw that what we have is good."

"But"—I fought for words, for comprehension—"you haven't seemed happy."

He laid another kiss on me, this time on my forehead. "I gave this a lot of thought while I was gone. Like I said I would. And I'm ready to comm—"

"Stop!" I jumped off the couch, feeling cornered, the pillow falling to the floor. "Don't say it. Please. Just . . . stop."

A confused haze flitted over his features. He picked up the pillow and replaced it on the sofa. "What am I missing, here? I thought you wanted me to pick a date for our wedding."

"I did. But Kyle . . ." I forced the image of Ben into my mind. "We can't get married." Instantly, I winced. "God, I'm sorry. Let me explain."

His confusion increased. Bolting from the couch, he paced the room. Suddenly, he stopped and faced me. "Is this about before? About Shelby?"

My jaw dropped open. Shelby was the girl he'd dumped me for during our last year of high school, and then, a year later, she'd dumped him for his best friend Grant. Kyle and Grant remained friends, and we visited him and Shelby on a regular basis. So yeah, the fact that Kyle mentioned her now, so many years later, in conjunction with our relationship, weirded me out. A lot. "What does Shelby have to do with anything?"

"I hurt you then, so you're trying to hurt me now? Or are you afraid I'll change my mind, so you're doing it first?"

"No . . . and no. It's just . . . well, you don't really want to marry me. Can't we just admit that and get it over with?" Ugh. Even though I believed that, it wasn't the whole truth, now was it? "And Kyle? I don't want to marry you, either. Proposing was a mistake."

"Right, you expect me to believe that now? You've wanted to get married since we were seventeen! I'm gone for less than a week and you suddenly change your mind?"

I heaved a shaky breath. "I care about you *so* much. But what we have isn't enough. You deserve more, and I want more. I want everything, Kyle! I want a man who looks at me and wants no one but me. I've never had that with you. Not really."

"Then why propose? You must have thought we could make it work. I believe we can! That's what I've been trying to tell you, Chloe. I believe we can be good together."

Okay, this conversation was spiraling downward fast. Going with the one thing I knew with complete certainty, I asked, "Do you love me the way you loved Shelby?"

He flinched as if I'd struck him. Closing his eyes, he cursed. When he opened them again, there was a pain I'd never seen before. That's when I got it. "You *still* love her, don't you?"

"I'll be good to you, and I know you'll be good to me." He lifted his chin as a shudder whipped through his thin frame. "Shelby was my dream girl. Yes, I still love her, but she's happy. I want her to be happy. And I'm tired of waiting around for whatever happened with her to happen again. So let's do this, Chloe. Let's make a life together."

The room whirled around me, not in a magical take-me-to-some-weird-reality way, but in an I-can't-believe-what-is-happening way. All at once, every last thing that Alice, Elizabeth and even Verda had tried so hard to bang into my head about my relationship with Kyle slid into focus. "You should have your dream girl, and she isn't Shelby. But she's out there . . . somewhere, and you'll never find her if you're with me."

He lifted his shoulders in a faint shrug. "I don't get this. Any other girl would have dropped me months ago, but you didn't. Until now. Why now, Chloe?"

"There's someone else," I admitted. "We haven't even had one date yet, but I know I'm supposed to be with him. I won't explain it. You wouldn't understand anyway. But I'm telling you the truth."

Kyle's face froze as all emotion drained away. "In five days? I don't believe that. That's crazy!"

"What's crazy is staying with someone you don't love. And you don't love me, do you?"

His lips thinned into a straight line as he struggled to find an acceptable answer to my question. I waited, the beat of my heart echoing loudly in my ears, knowing what his answer should be but needing to hear him say it. He stepped toward me, his honey brown eyes beseeching me. "Yes . . . and no. Not like you want. But can't it be enough?"

Even with everything I knew, everything I'd experienced, part of me wanted to say yes. But I couldn't, and not for the reason you might expect. This, for once, had nothing to do with me and everything to do with Kyle. "No, it can't."

"Is that your final answer?" He voiced the question lightly, as if he were joking around, but I was pierced by the sadness lurking beneath.

Nonetheless, I said, "Yes. It's my final answer."

And that, as they say, was that.

You know how some days start off perfect and then somewhere along the way one little thing pushes into your head, and suddenly you wonder why you even bothered to crawl out of bed? I woke the next morning to a sunny, nearly cloudless sky, my shower had plenty of hot water for once, my hair behaved exactly how I wanted and even the traffic lights seemed to be on my side during the drive to Ben's house.

His house, by the way, sat in the middle of a well-to-do suburban neighborhood on an exceptionally large lot. The neighborhood definitely had all the trappings of the traditional. The trappings were just bigger, shinier and far prettier than those found in smaller neighborhoods.

Maybe the visual of Ben's financial success should've

made me even happier, but it didn't. It's not that I'm opposed to wealth, but I lived in a tiny one-bedroom apartment, clipped coupons and had gotten to the point where I rarely bought anything unless it had a sale tag affixed. I am, however, a relentless saver, and I had a decent savings account to show for it.

No, it wasn't so much Ben's apparent wealth that bothered me. Rather, the increase in my stress level had to do with two things: one, it made me feel not in his league, and two, why did he live in such a large house that was so far from where he worked? Did he have a family I didn't know about? Had I used my magic to coerce an already-married man? It was that particular thought that had me wondering if maybe I'd have been better off snuggling beneath my covers all day.

I passed Ben's house for maybe the fourth time and started weaving my way through his neighborhood again, trying to remember if I'd seen a wedding band. Which was ludicrous. Because no way in hell would I have missed that. But not all married men wear wedding rings, do they?

I was probably overreacting. It was just a house, after all. But if even the thinnest sliver of a possibility existed that he was already tied down, I had some serious thinking to do. Was I, even with the proof of the drawing, willing to break up a marriage? How far was I willing to go? There are a million reasons why people cheat, and I'm not such a Goody Two-shoes to proclaim that there is *never* an acceptable reason, because frankly I could think of several. Well, one or two, at least. But would *I* cheat? And would I be happy with a man who cheated on me, or even *with* me?

My grip tightened on the steering wheel. No, no and fuck no. I might be a lot of things, but I am not a home wrecker. So if this was some stupid test to see how I'd react, then fate could take a flying leap and leave me the hell alone.

This time, I slowed the car as I approached Ben's home

and actually made the turn into the driveway. Getting out of the car was easier than I expected. Knocking on Ben's door proved to be a little more difficult, because yeah, I was still obsessed with the freaking huge house. When the door swung open, I sucked in a breath and held it, sure that the person on the other side would be a very pissed off woman demanding to know what I thought I was doing cavorting with her husband.

"So you didn't stand me up," Ben said, leaning his long, sexy body against the doorframe. He wore rough-around-the-edges jeans that looked to have been washed dozens upon dozens of times, a not-tucked-in white T-shirt that very easily could've been one of the three-to-a-bag variety, and boots. Cowboy boots, to be exact.

My breath escaped in a strangely odd combination of a wheeze and a squeal.

"No . . . of course not." Oh, God. He was also fresh from the shower. I knew this by his damp-at-the-edges hair that curled slightly around his perfect face. I swallowed again. "You . . . ah . . . live in a really big house," I murmured.

Sticking his thumbs into the front pockets of his jeans, he lowered his chin in a nod, but an uneasy glint flashed in his eyes. "I do."

He could have said "Yes," or "Sure do," or even "Hell, yeah," but no. The words he chose to say were I do. You know, the I-pledge-my-life-to-you wedding-vow words? Just like that, my wife-wanting-to-beat-the-crap-out-of-me paranoia returned with a vengeance. "Do you have a wife and two-point-five kids?" I blurted. "Or just a wife? Or just the kids?"

His skin paled a shade. Those glorious blue eyes went flat. In a cool, emotionless tenor, he said, "I'm sorry you drove all this way for nothing. It's probably best if you leave." And then, as if realizing how impolite he sounded, he finished off with a "Drive safely on your way home."

He stepped back into the house and started to close the door. I stuck my foot into the rapidly decreasing space and cried, "No!"

Luckily for me and my foot, he paused. "Why would I have given you my address if I were married?"

Um. Magic? But I couldn't say that, so I shrugged, feeling completely, hopelessly idiotic. "Good point."

"And why would you ask me out if you thought I had a wife?" His scowl deepened. "Are you attracted to men who are already taken?"

"No!" I repeated in an even louder screech. Fisting my hands, I strove for calmness. "I didn't think you were married. And then I saw your house and your neighborhood, and . . ." I shrugged. "It made me think of family. So I'm really sorry if I upset you, but before we went out, I had to ask. Because I am *not* the type of woman who dates a man who is taken."

He regarded me silently, trying to decide if I only talked the crazy or if I actually was crazy. Finally, his lips curved into a semblance of a smile. "I apologize if I overreacted. Cheating . . . angers me. Considerably."

My entire body trembled as most of my tension eased away. "And well it should!" I said in an overly bright voice. "I probably should have explained better. Or at all, actually. But I'd still really like to go out. So . . . uh . . . don't close the door on me, please. How about we have fun today?"

Leftover doubt lingered, both in his gaze and expression. But then he said, "Why don't you wait in the car, and I'll grab my wallet?"

"Cool! And Ben?" I said, hoping to wipe away his doubt. "I swear we'll have fun. My goal is to make you laugh lots and lots and lots."

That got a semireal grin. "I wouldn't bet on it. I'm not much of a laugher."

"You'll see," I said, already backing off the front porch. "By the end of the day your cheeks are going to hurt."

And maybe, if things worked out as well as I hoped, I'd snag that kiss.

Chapter Eight

A little over an hour later, I sort of wished I hadn't made that proclamation. Because at the moment, I didn't see even a hint of laughter. Ben hadn't so much as chuckled during the drive from his place. At least we'd managed to hold some type of a conversation, a slow, painstakingly awkward exchange where I worked exceptionally hard to get the ball rolling.

While I hadn't exactly failed, my success was limited. I'd learned that Malone & Associates was a family business, started by Ben's father and uncle when Ben was a child, and that a good many Malones were employed there. With some prodding, Ben shared that his favorite television station was the History Channel, his favorite spectator sport was hockey, his favorite actually-getting-in-the-game sport was soccer and he absolutely despised fast food.

Which, uh, sort of pointed out how very much we didn't have in common. Well, except for the TV thing, because while I didn't watch the History Channel, I loved old movies. *Gone with the Wind* being my top favorite, and that has oodles of history. So yeah, close enough. But I didn't watch or participate in any team sports, and I adored fast food, even if I didn't allow myself to indulge that often. But no way were these differences going to dissuade me.

Except now we were standing in line waiting to buy our amusement-park tickets, and Ben's complexion had turned a faded, sickly gray. Not only that, but his body language was off-the-charts uncomfortable. Add in the unexplainable, miserable feeling of gloom that descended upon us, and I didn't have the slightest clue what was wrong or what to do about it.

I touched his arm lightly to gain his attention. "I bet we can grab some Dramamine inside. And if not, then we can just take in a bunch of shows or something."

"Dramamine isn't necessary," he said quietly, avoiding looking directly at me. "I don't suffer from motion sickness."

Well, there went my best guess. "So . . . you just don't like amusement parks? We can go somewhere else!" I tugged on his arm, my intention to pull him out of line, but he didn't budge. "How about . . . uh . . . putt-putt? Or maybe—"

Gently twisting out of my grasp, he angled his head downward. I nearly choked on the storm of emotions coloring his features. Despair? Maybe. But I definitely saw the fire of anger. When he spoke, his voice was clipped. "I used to love amusement parks. That was a while ago."

I waited for more, but apparently he must have decided he'd said enough. Frustration and a good dose of bewilderment settled in, dampening everything I'd hoped for this day. How in the world were we to get from this to that drawing? Why did it seem as if the last thing Ben wanted was to be here with me?

"Fine," I said softly, somehow already feeling bruised and betrayed, sad and disillusioned. "If you want to forget this, we can leave. I'll take you home."

The shouts and laughter from the group of teens in front of us made Ben pivot. He stared at them for a minute. His back stiffened and then slowly relaxed. When he looked at me again, the anger had lessened. "Actually, I'd like to stay," he said, his tone gruff but subdued, with an underlying thread of pain.

"Are you sure?"

His Adam's apple bobbed as he swallowed. "You promised that my cheeks would hurt by the end of the day. I think I'd like to see if that's possible."

Going with the flow, I winked. "Well, I didn't stipulate which set of cheeks would hurt, now, did I?" A raspy chuckle escaped him. Score one for me!

Folding his arm around my shoulders, he nodded to the line. "It's moved up. We'll be through the gates in no time."

I think I nodded back; I'm not sure. We walked forward together, inching closer to the ticket booth, the feel of his arm bolstering my sagging confidence. But it wasn't enough. I wanted to see the love in Ben's eyes that I had seen in the drawing. The intensity had blown me away, made me believe in a happily-ever-after I'd given up on.

"Where to first?" he asked as we headed into the actual park. "Rides, food or some type of show?"

"Rides." So that for a little while we wouldn't have to talk. I simply didn't know what to say, how to shrink whatever gap existed between us. A few hours of one ride after another seemed like a great way to break the ice. As an added bonus, nearly every ride would have us sitting thigh to thigh. "You like roller coasters?"

"Used to," he said tersely. "Let's see if I still do."

The first coaster we came to was of the corkscrew variety, and as luck would have it, the line was blessedly short. Once we were in the car and all buckled in, I said, "You have to hold your arms above your head for the entire ride."

He raised an eyebrow. "Oh, I do, do I? Says who?"

"Chicken?" I teased. "Trust me; it's more fun this way."

"Then you have to keep your eyes open . . . for the entire ride," he countered.

I chewed on my lip, a happy little bubble growing inside. "How'd you know I normally close my eyes?"

"Good guess." The car jerked as we started to move. He turned his head, gaze on me. "Open eyes, arms up. Deal?"

I pretended to ponder the challenge. I mean, it wasn't that it was impossible to keep my eyes open when going a zillion miles per hour. I just didn't like it. Which was the main reason I never skydived again: you sort of have to keep your eyes open for that. But for Ben? "Deal," I said, as we started up the first hill.

His arms went up, and mine followed suit. Our eyes locked, the anticipation in his matching my own. My stomach somersaulted, both from said anticipation and the oh-so-close proximity of Ben. He grabbed my hand in the air just as the car hovered at the edge of the peak.

My stomach plunged and twirled, and then we were off. Wind hit my face, blew my hair back. The screams from the other passengers were all around. Ben's hand tightened around mine as we came out of the dip and immediately went into a spin. Laughter burst from my chest, but the wind whooshed it away. I tried to scream through the second upside-down maneuver, but the look on Ben's face plugged the sound before it left my throat. Happy. Smiling. Exhilarated. *This* was the man in my drawing. This Ben. My Ben. Even if he didn't know it yet.

My fears about his odd behavior rippled away. Maybe he'd had a bad experience at an amusement park once. Perhaps he'd forgotten what it was like to live, to have fun, so the concept of spending an entire day focused on nothing but had weirded him out. Or hell, any one of a hundred other reasons.

The coaster slid to a jumpy stop, and it was with great regret that I let go of Ben's hand. My legs shook as I stepped out of the car, both from the ride and the man, and I nearly tripped. But he was right behind.

"Careful," he said as he caught me, his breath tickling my ear, tantalizing me. "Don't want you to get hurt." He flashed me a smile that made my legs go even weaker. "What's next?"

Without thinking, without even the slightest hesitation, I stood on my tiptoes and stroked his cheek. "Whatever you want."

"Anything I want, eh? No backing out, whatever it is?"

"I was just thrown upside down multiple times. It's a pretty safe guess I'm up for anything."

"Good, the Ferris wheel it is! They have a huge one here, and I could never get—" Abruptly, he stopped speaking. His jaw locked. Tension crept into his body, literally tightening every muscle. His demeanor changed so fast that it sent a shudder through my body.

It seemed that, like it or not, today was going to be a series of one-step-forward-and-two-steps-backs. I forced a breath, calmed my jitters and tried to find a way to calm his.

"Is there something about being here that upsets you?" I voiced the question carefully, not wanting to upset him further but dying to help. "Should we go find a place to sit and talk?"

He blinked, and in the space of that blink, whatever emotions he'd been feeling disappeared beneath a facade of cheer. "Come on," he said. "I think the wheel is this way."

"I'll take that as a no." Patience is a virtue, I reminded myself as I hurried to catch up.

We stopped in front of the Ferris wheel. My eyes rounded when I saw its size. My mouth went dry. "How about we ride another coaster first," I suggested, attempting to sound nonchalant. "And come back to this later." Like when it was dark. So when I was at the top of the freaking thing, I wouldn't be able to see the ground and the distance between me and it, and how fast I'd hit bottom if I somehow managed to fall.

"You ride coasters, but this scares you?" Ben's lips twitched, but he had the grace not to laugh. "Is that a girl thing?"

I stood as tall as my barely five-foot height allowed. "There is a massive difference between this thing and roller coasters. And I'm not afraid. Just . . ." I narrowed my eyes at the grin spreading across his face. "I'm not! These things make me nervous. And what do you mean, 'Is that a girl thing?'"

His grin disappeared again. "If this really scares you, we'll skip it."

"No. Let's just do it later." I'd absolutely be able to ride the monstrosity when it was dark. But . . . if it would make him happier, I'd do it now. Anything to get his smile back. "Let's just get in line," I huffed.

His fingers grazed my chin. Applying the lightest bit of pressure, he pushed so I could do nothing but look up at him. "My . . ." He inhaled a breath. "Someone I used to know once told me that Ferris wheels are the 'scariest ride ever' because of the slow backward climb to the top in a seat that 'wiggles and jiggles.'"

"Exactly!" I said. "But I'm happy to go. I don't throw up or anything. In case you're wondering. Not that you are or anything, but . . ." Oh, God. Babbling about puking was sure to win him over. I crooked my neck toward the Ferris wheel. "Let's just get in line."

"Nah," he said easily. "We'll catch it later, if you're up to it. How do you feel about bumper cars?"

"I don't know," I said honestly. "I usually stick to the fast rides. But I'm game to try."

He pulled me toward him by the shoulders. "Chloe Nichols, are you seriously telling me that you've never experienced bumper cars?"

I shook my head in mock sadness. "I have never, in my life, driven a bumper car, ridden in a bumper car, bumped or been bumped by another bumper car."

"Well, Red, I'd say it's time you got bumped." Lacing his fingers with mine, he tugged. "You're going to love every second of it."

My cheeks flooded with warmth. The image he evoked made me gasp, and I got hot all over as we started off.

He stole a sidelong glance at me and then immediately changed direction, pulling me toward one of the many gift stores dotting the main strip. "Your face is already getting sunburned," he said. "Let's get you some sunscreen or you'll be miserable later."

"Yeah," I choked out. "Miserable. Good idea."

After we made the purchase, he squirted a glob of lotion onto his palm. "Pull your hair back so I don't get any in it."

I did as asked, and then his fingers gently touched my skin, rubbing the lotion into my cheeks, my chin, my nose and my forehead in small, even circles. My eyes closed at the thought of him touching my breasts, my stomach—hell, my entire body—in exactly the same way. A sigh escaped. I wanted him, every part of him, so much that my muscles literally ached with it.

"Wow, you're really sensitive to the sun, aren't you?" Ben's voice shook me from my fantasy. "Your skin is turning redder by the second. I'm surprised you don't carry sunscreen around with you."

"I probably should start," I mumbled, opening my eyes. His hands moved to my neck, softly massaging, his fingers dipping ever so slightly inside the collar of my shirt, eliciting a yearning that tingled through me. Warm hands. Strong hands. Hands I simply wanted everywhere.

Struggling to regain my sense of equilibrium, I stepped back. "That should do it. I can do my arms." The words were short, quaky little bursts.

Concern lit his expression, which was sweet. But what I wanted to see was attraction, desire, passion. Reminding myself once again that there was plenty of time for that, I finished applying the sunscreen and tucked it away in my purse.

"Ready?" he asked.

"Ready." For the moment, I very purposely pushed everything else away, intending to focus 100 percent on just having a good time, on enjoying Ben's company and using everything in my arsenal to make this day the first of many, many more.

We rode the bumper cars twice, but that was mostly for Ben. Why smacking into other cars as fast as possible made him appear as happy as a little boy on Christmas morning, I didn't know. But I honestly didn't care. It was just nice to see.

As for me, well, I could barely maneuver the stupid little cars. In between watching him and recovering from being pushed all over the place, I was totally out of my element. I even managed to get stuck in a corner. Repeatedly. Which, I soon discovered, made me target number one for all the other drivers.

And yes, that included Ben, though I sort of thought he was helping me out, because after he smacked into me a few times I got unstuck, while the other smackers always buried me deeper in the corner. Of course, I'd barely get myself turned around before I'd end up back where I started. Let's just say that bumper cars are not my strong suit.

Next we hit a few more roller coasters, the big merry-go-round, which was far more thrilling than it sounds, and then the worst ride I've *ever* been on. Literally. I groaned to Ben, clutching his arm. "Whoever thought that a huge pirate ship suspended in midair and rocking back and forth at top speed was a good idea is an idiot."

"I kind of liked it." He stared at me for a second before running his finger down my cheek. "But you're looking a little green." Pointing to a bench a few feet from where we stood, he said, "Why don't you go sit, and I'll get you something to drink."

"That would be heavenly. Thanks." The ground swayed beneath me as I walked; my stomach sloshed and grumbled. Somehow, I was queasy and hungry all at once. Sitting down on the bench, I rested my elbows on my knees and my chin in my hands and sighed.

While I waited, in addition to staying as still as humanly possible, I couldn't help but think of the day so far in plusses and minuses. Plus: he'd laughed several times, though not nearly enough to make his cheeks hurt. Minus: every now and then, the darkness from earlier returned. Plus: he shook that off fairly fast, or at least appeared to shake it off fairly fast. Minus: he seemed more interested in proving an unknown something to himself than he did in spending time with me. Plus: we'd held hands on the coasters and the godawful boat thing. Minus: we hadn't kissed yet. And oh, how I needed to feel his lips on mine.

My stomach sloshed again, so I dug a peppermint Certs out of my purse, and popped it into my mouth. Ben joined me with two icy cold bottles of water. Collapsing on the bench next to me, he stretched his long legs out and unscrewed the top from one. Handing it over, he ordered, "Drink up."

I swallowed a large gulp and then held the bottle to my cheek, my eyes on Ben. His own were focused straight ahead, taking in the strolling and chatting crowd: families, tourists, teens, adults. Anywhere but on me.

I ached to touch him but didn't feel as if I should. Well, that's a lie. I certainly felt as if I should, as if I had the right, but I knew *he* didn't.

Touch *me*, I thought instead. Please. Look at me. Focus on me. See me. Touch me.

The queasiness gave way to the faintest tingling of warmth. A hot ball of energy in my stomach slowly expanded, licking through every nerve, every muscle, rippling into my skin, until every part of me vibrated with power. The magic took hold, frightening me with its quickness, with its potency. I tried to rein the energy in, but it continued; my emotions were too strong to turn back. I breathed in through my nose, out through my mouth, focusing on banishing the power. I hadn't meant to cast a spell—cross my heart and hope to die, I hadn't!

I gulped more water, not to quench thirst but in the hopes that it would drown out the magic. The fire burned on, so I tipped the bottle higher, dumping the rest of the water into my mouth. That's when I saw it, out of the corner of my eye: a sparkle. Lots of sparkles. Holy crap! My hand was *glowing*. Not like one of those glow-in-the-dark green-tinted sticks for kids, but more like I'd dipped my hand into iridescent glitter. Not bright or showy, but very, very real.

The bottle fell from my grasp. Curious, I held my hand in front of my face. On closer appraisal, it wasn't so much the skin that glittered and sparkled, but the veins beneath and, when I turned my hand over, the little lines in my palm.

"Chloe?" Ben asked.

I whipped my hand behind him, placing it in the space just below his neck. So he wouldn't see the magic literally running through my veins. "I'm not a litterer. I swear! That bottle . . . uh . . . slipped."

He blinked. His eyes deepened in color to a nearly black indigo. The heat in my hand increased, but it wasn't uncomfortable or alarming. Rather, it was a lot like the rush of warm water from a faucet. Another blink, and he bent his head toward me.

Three of my fingers rested on his neck, the other two on his shirt. Warmth was everywhere: my fingers and wherever I touched him. Before I knew what was happening, before I could even begin to process the change in me, in Ben, his face came closer to mine. We were eye to eye, nose to nose and very nearly lip to lip.

"Chloe," he said again. "Do you know how beautiful you look right now? Your skin is radiant, almost luminous. Is that—?"

"Cosmetics! The sun! It's . . . uh . . . girl stuff," I whispered in a rush. I moved my hand up, wove my fingers into his wind-blown hair and tugged his head forward. "Kiss me. I want you to kiss me."

Gripping my arms, he dragged me even closer. Everything slowed down. The sounds around me disappeared. This—oh, God—was the moment I'd been waiting for.

He brushed my lips with his, just the slightest of touches, and a physical jolt fired through me, sending everything into a whirling, dizzying, breathless spin. He deepened the kiss, whirling me even further into the maelstrom of emotions, of sensations, into a level of intimacy so deep, so baring, that it seemed impossible.

I moaned as my tongue slipped inside his mouth, tasting him, savoring him, enjoying him as I'd never enjoyed a kiss—a man—thus far in my life. His hands slid from my arms, wrapped around me, enfolding, capturing me. And I knew in a way that the drawing hadn't shown me that I belonged to this man. He belonged to me. We belonged to each other. And I would fight to the death to win him over.

He pulled back, desire in his eyes.

"Why . . . ? Don't stop," I whispered. "Don't ever stop."

This elicited a grin and a chuckle. "Sweetie, we're in the middle of an amusement park. If I don't stop now, I won't be able to." He winked. "And then we'd get kicked out."

I stroked his cheek as I had earlier, barely noticing the glitter had disappeared from my hand. "I don't think I care. But you're probably right."

He cocked an eyebrow. "Probably? You're . . . you're like no woman I've ever met. But, Chloe—" With a quick shake of his head, he retreated. "Never mind. This isn't the time."

"No *never-minds*. What?" I pressed. "You can say anything to me."

His face became serious. So serious that my stomach hurt. "I started to tell you the other day, but I don't date anymore. I'm not interested in settling down or finding a wife or becoming involved in a relationship."

"Oh." His words were a bucket of cold water in the face.

"And you're the type of woman who's looking for serious."

"How do you know what I'm looking for?" I raised my chin, straightened my backbone. "So you're just out for some fun and games, is that it?"

He had the courtesy to look ashamed. "I wasn't. I'm not. You're the first woman I've gone out with in a long time. Hell, Chloe, I still can't figure out why I said yes."

Ha! Well, I knew the answer to that one. "Maybe you're drawn to me. Maybe I'm the girl of your dreams, but you don't recognize it yet."

"No, Chloe, you're not. I met the girl of my dreams a long time ago, and it didn't work out. I'm not in the market for another."

He looked so darn serious, and he believed every freaking word of his spiel, but that drawing told me different and our kiss told me different, so even though his declaration hurt, I swallowed the pain. "I just got out of a year-long relationship, myself, so I'm not looking for serious," I lied through my home-bleached teeth. "I'm looking to have fun. And games. And honestly, Ben, I can't think of anyone I'd rather do that with."

Relief washed over him. In any other circumstance, my heart would have crumpled into a thousand and one slivered pieces. As it was, it merely split in two.

"You're up for that? Because I'm not going to change my mind," he said softly, his gaze searching.

Giving him my best possible come-hither, slutty-girl-from-the-wrong-side-of-the-neighborhood smile, I winked. "Oh, baby. I'm up, down and all over that."

"Well, then, Miss Chloe Nichols, I'm game. It will be my pleasure to be your rebound." He tipped my chin with one finger and kissed me gently. "I'm starving. Do you think you can handle some food?"

"I'm famished," I said, still smiling brightly through my lies. "Food sounds terrific."

He stood and pulled me up too. "Let's do it. Then, if you're ready, we can give the Ferris wheel another try. What do you think?"

"Sure, why not?" The sky hadn't even begun to darken,

but I sort of figured I wouldn't notice the size of the wheel or how far the ground loomed beneath us. Not with my mind, heart and soul rehashing every last word of the crummy conversation we'd just had. Besides, I'd had my share of roller coasters for the time being, literally and figuratively. Not his dream girl, he said? Didn't want a relationship? My rebound guy?

Yeah, well, we'd just see about that.

Chapter Nine

Tuesday evening, I was curled up on my couch trying to pay attention to one of my favorite old movies, *Arsenic and Old Lace*. Unfortunately, that was a no-go. Not only was I bummed that I hadn't heard from Ben since our date, I'd spent half of every night fantasizing about him touching me and the other half nearly sick to my stomach worrying about the darkness inside him. I was flat-out exhausted.

I kept coming back to that one moment, the one on the roller coaster when he'd looked at me with that too-sexy-for-real-life smile. *That* man, the one I'd so briefly glimpsed, was the real Ben. I needed to find him, to draw him out, because that was the man who would fall in love with me. I was sure of it.

Learning the origin of his darkness seemed the ideal place to begin, but the idea of investigating filled me with more than a little fear. Delving into his past could potentially have the opposite effect I intended, pushing him further away. And even with magic on my side, there were no guarantees, which Sunday's date had proved well enough.

Sighing, I switched the television off. Cary Grant and his on-screen, homicidal spinster aunts would have to wait. So would Ben, for my thoughts turned to Kyle. I'd left him a few messages, just wanting to know how he was doing, but he hadn't returned my calls. I hoped he was okay.

Standing from the couch, I went in search of something to munch on, but stopped midstride when the doorbell rang. I wasn't expecting visitors, so I peered through the peephole before unlocking the chain. Grandma Verda was on the other side.

"Hey, Verda," I said, opening up. Glancing over her shoulder, I gestured for her to come in. "Are you alone?"

"Yes, dear. It's just me." She whisked inside, a blur of orange and white—and pink, naturally, as her hair remained reminiscent of cotton candy. She held her handbag tightly in front of her while she glanced around my apartment. "Do you have company?"

Memories of the last time made me pause. "Why? I'm not in the mood for an intervention tonight."

She chuckled. "That's not why I'm here. What with your magic arriving and Miranda's help, I think you'll be okay. There isn't any reason to steal you away."

"Well . . . good. And no, I don't have company." We'd already discussed both Miranda and the arrival of my magic that night at the Mystic Corner, so I figured Verda's visit was somehow related to my friend and cousin. "Is Alice okay? I tried calling, but no one answered."

Verda headed directly for the living room. Normally, she moved as if she were twenty years younger than her actual age. Not tonight. Her slow, shuffling gait and the slumped form of her shoulders reflected every one of her years.

When we were seated, I said, "You look a little tired. Are you feeling all right?"

Her hands shook as she deposited her purse on the floor. "No need to worry yourself over me. I'm just dandy. As for Alice, she's also well enough."

"I'm . . . uh . . . glad to hear that."

"I probably should have called first," she admitted. A quiver rippled through her, making her hands tremble more. Clutching them together in her lap, she fidgeted and then spoke so softly, I had to lean close. "I have a favor to ask."

That put me instantly on alert. "What kind of favor?"

She sat up straighter. "You have to promise that you won't share this with anyone."

"Of course I won't." I mimed zipping my lips shut. "Completely confidential."

"That means Alice and Elizabeth too. Are you willing to keep something from them?"

I'd somehow assumed Alice and Elizabeth already knew. "Can you give me a hint as to what this is about?"

Her watery blue eyes were full of defiance. "No. You have to trust me, and then you have to promise. I'm sorry to do this to you, Chloe, but I need your absolute assurance that you'll keep this quiet."

I hesitated, not liking the idea. "I don't know if I can. It depends on what this is about."

She wrinkled her nose, searching for a loophole she could use to get me to agree. "How about this?" she said with a tiny grin. "You make your promise on the contingency that I'll promise to let them in on the secret when the time is right."

"Who decides when the time is right?"

"Well, I do, of course. Who else?"

I pressed my lips together so I wouldn't laugh. "So the time could be a week, a month or never?"

She snorted. "You're too smart for your own good. Fine, you win. I promise I'll spill the beans—if there's anything worth spilling—within . . . oh, say no more than two months' time. Does that work for you?"

"One month," I countered.

"Six weeks."

While I still had my reservations, I also didn't see how I could say no. "Six weeks and not one day longer?"

Crossing her fingers over her heart, she grinned. "I promise."

"Then I promise too. Now, what's this all about?"

As soon as I made the vow, her entire body visibly relaxed. "Well, see, now that you have the magic . . ." Stopping, she rubbed her arms, as if to chase away a chill. "You know the history of the magic, and how Elizabeth was the first in our family since Miranda to keep the gift and also to pass it on, and how that will continue for you, for Alice, for Rose and whoever comes after. Right?"

"Yeah. No one else will lose the magic by passing it on, but what does that have to do with—?" I clapped my jaw shut. "You want me to try to gift the magic back to you, don't you?"

"Yes." Her frail shoulders lifted slightly. "I know it sounds crazy, and it might not work, but I have to know for sure. The magic was a part of me for most of my adult life. I feel as if I've lost a leg or an arm. I look around at my beautiful family, and I rejoice that you girls have our family's gift . . . but oh, do I miss it."

I understood her feelings well enough, but I didn't get the secrecy. "Why don't you want Elizabeth and Alice to know? They'd support you in this. I'm sure of it."

"I'm not as sure. Besides, I have my reasons." Hope shimmered over her, as bright as a starry sky. "Will you try, Chloe?"

I heard the yearning in her voice, and my heart broke a little. "Why did you pass the gift on, if you weren't ready to give it away?"

"I'm old, kiddo. Too old to have kept something that might have gone to the grave with me. I had to give the magic to Elizabeth. It was the only way. But now . . ."

"Everything has changed."

"Exactly. I've tried to deal with the loss. I've told myself I'm a silly old woman who has no need for magic any longer. That I'm happy with my life and to let this go."

"But you can't."

"Not without knowing for sure. So, Chloe, will you humor me and give this a chance?"

I reached over to grasp Verda's hands in mine and squeezed.

She was the core of our family, the sun we all revolved around. I could do this for her. No. I *would* do this for her. Focusing inward, I envisioned my power as a clear, brilliant stream of light. It whirled and bobbed inside of me, mixing with my energy, with my emotions, gaining strength from both until the light swirled and jumped outside of and around me . . . around us.

My breath caught in my throat. Energy sizzled along my skin, making the hair stand up. Warmth flooded my body, beginning as a tingle at my toes and then quickly rising through me, until it seeped from my hands into Verda's. I totally expected to see the sparkling, glittering array beneath my skin, like what had happened with Ben, and I realized belatedly that I should've warned Verda about it. But as the power grew, as it pulsated inside of me, my skin remained its normal pale shade.

I finally formed the words that seemed necessary: "I wish for Miranda's gift to touch you again, for you to reclaim our family's magic. This is my wish for you, because you deserve it. Because I love you."

I repeated the wish several more times while the energy continued to work its way from me, through me, bleeding into Verda. I felt the power. I *knew* the wish was working.

Suddenly, the power stilled in the room, hanging in the air like the heaviest of weights, as if time had been halted by some unknown force. Fear that something had gone wrong overcame me, but I refused to let it take hold. Digging as deep as I could, I funneled every last drop of my energy into repeating the wish.

I heard a snap. Electricity crackled bright, fast and hot, almost as if bolts of lightning had zapped through the room, through me, through Verda. Another second passed, and then another. Oh so slowly the power trickled out of me, evaporating into the air, and in barely a heartbeat, everything reverted to normal. I collapsed against the back of my chair, even more wiped out than earlier. Verda still sat in the same position, but her eyes were wide, shiny with unshed tears.

"What do you think? Did it work?" I mentally crossed my fingers and toes.

Her cheeks became a full shade darker than her hair. "I think so! Of course, a few practice sessions will be necessary to be sure. But thank you, Chloe!"

"You're welcome. Just remember our deal: six weeks from today, and absolutely no later." Because Alice and Elizabeth would definitely want to know.

"I won't forget." Standing, she came to me for a quick hug and added, "Is there anything you want to chat about?"

Happy to see her normal verve had returned, I grinned. "Nope. I know you're dying to test your power out. But . . . uh . . . try not to do anything too crazy."

"That, my dear, is not a promise I recall making!" Retrieving her purse, she just about floated to the door. "Besides, I'm a little old lady. Nothing is too crazy for little old ladies. It's the best part of aging!"

She let herself out, and I was once again alone. Dear God, what had I done? Hopefully, whatever craziness Verda planned would, at a minimum, fall into the legal category. Otherwise, there would be hell to pay, and I'd be the one paying.

I locked the front door and then nearly crawled back to the couch. The extra few feet to my bedroom seemed far too vast a distance. Yes, I really was that tired. Covering myself with a blanket, I closed my eyes and emptied my brain. Exhausted or not, too many thoughts would keep me up.

My breathing slowed and my body relaxed, but mere seconds before I completely dropped off, the faint scent of roses tickled my nose. Instantly awake, I sat upright, my heart already zipping along at top speed, expecting to see Miranda perched on one of my chairs. Or maybe watching me from the dining room. No . . . and no. I sniffed again, wondering if I'd imagined the scent, but the fragrance still lingered, reaffirming my belief that Miranda was in my apartment. Somewhere. But a quick search of each room, including the bathroom, came up empty. The ghost wasn't in residence.

Shivering, as if I'd caught Verda's chill from earlier, I wrapped my arms around myself. Every single instinct insisted that Miranda had been here, watching me. So why had she left without saying a word? What could she possibly have wanted?

Chloe!" Paige hollered from the front of the store the next morning. "You have a delivery!"

I tossed my pen on my desk and rubbed my temples, a headache already brewing, the result of not enough sleep combined with the sheer agony of balancing accounts. That, along with all of the other strange events highlighting the past several days, had made me solidly cranky.

I stomped out of the back room in a huff, ready to raise hell. "Why is anything except for the mail being delivered through the front door? That's why we have a back door: for deliveries! And why are you screa—?" My eyes fell on the huge, blossoming bouquet of flowers that Paige held. I stopped in my tracks. "Oh. Wow."

"Yeah." Paige's lips curved into a quirky grin. "Wow!"

In the snap of a finger, a rush of giddy, schoolgirl elation replaced my crankiness. I crossed the rest of the room so fast that my legs probably blurred. "Are those for me?"

"Unless you know of some other woman named Chloe Nichols at this address." Paige shoved the bouquet into my hands. I dipped my nose down, smelling the intoxicating fragrances, already forgetting every last worry that had kept me awake.

"Oh, wow," I repeated. "These are gorgeous." And they were. White daisies, purple lilacs, some plum-colored bloom

I didn't recognize and sunny yellow daffodils. *Ben*. They had to be from him. Who else?

On the other side of the counter, I shifted items on the shelf that lined the wall, freeing a spot for the large green glass vase. Carefully I set the flowers down, and then stepped back and stared at them.

"There's a card," Paige prodded. "Don't you want to know who they're from?"

"I know who," I said, my eyes still on the flowers. "Aren't they beautiful? And so romantic!"

"I think you should read the card, Chloe," Paige pressed. "If you don't, I'm going to."

"Of course I'm going to read it!" I slid the florist's white envelope out of the plastic holder. Pulling the flap free, I carefully pried the card out, shivers of anticipation rolling over my skin.

Aw . . . a splash of red and pink hearts covered the front. I teased the card open with my thumb, but read the printed words slowly, wanting to savor the moment.

> *Chloe, I can't get you out of my mind.*
> *Maybe I was wrong and you are my dream girl?*
> *I'm willing to find out.*

I did a happy little strut, my eyes still on the message. Ben wanted to move forward in a relationship. With me. After just one date! Somehow, something had shifted inside him, leading him toward me—toward the future we were going to have. Hardly able to contain my excitement, I reread the card, this time noticing the last line.

"'Love, Kyle,'" I whispered.

I brushed my finger over the writing, trying to ignore the stabbing sensation in my chest, hoping that somehow I'd read wrong. Of course, I hadn't. Why oh why couldn't Ben have sent this? These were the words I wanted *him* to say, not Kyle. My grip tightened on the card, and that annoying little voice inside my head piped up, reminding me that not that long ago, I *had* wanted this—and so much more—from Kyle.

"Geez, I'm a bitch," I said. "A fickle bitch at that."

A burst of laugher erupted from Paige. "What are you talking about? You can be a little bitchy sometimes, but can't we all? It's like a woman's prerogative," she teased. "You just received beautiful flowers from a very good-looking man! Aren't you all melty inside?"

"I'm serious, Paige! Look at this." I held the card out so she could read the message herself. "I broke up with him on Saturday. Sunday, I spent the day with another man. I thought—hoped—the flowers were from him." I sighed. "I really want them to be from B—"

Paige grabbed my wrist and shook her head wildly back and forth. With her other, she held a finger over her lips.

My assumption, based on her odd body language, was that a customer lurked in the recesses of the store and that I should keep my voice down. Nodding, I lowered my tone. "It's just that I proposed to Kyle, ended the engagement, fell for someone else . . . and now Kyle's sending me flowers. He has never given me flowers! So why now . . . when it's—?"

In an abrupt movement, Paige angled herself over the counter and slapped her hand over my mouth. It kinda stung. "Be quiet," she whispered. I tried to talk, tried to ask what the hell she was doing, but she pushed her hand tighter. "Seriously, Chloe. Shut. Up."

I'm not normally so dense. I swear. I blame my lack of understanding on the craziness my life had become. Even so, I finally began putting two and two together, but before I reached four, Kyle stepped out from behind one of the counters in the middle of the shop.

Paige shook her head again and dropped her hand. "He wanted to surprise you," she said in a soft tone. "I didn't know . . ." She took one last look at me, and then moved toward the back of the store. "I'll . . . uh . . . find something to do so you two can talk."

Unfortunately, my foot was now wedged firmly in my mouth, leaving me utterly speechless. Not to mention embarrassed and ashamed. I gripped the counter, my gaze on Kyle, who'd yet to speak. He stared right back, in shock and sadness and confusion.

Feeling like a heel and willing to bet the word itself was stamped on my forehead, I mumbled, "I'm sorry. I didn't know you were here. You didn't need to hear . . ."

"Hey, no big deal." His was an easy, nonchalant tone. As if he couldn't care less. "I took a shot and it backfired. Not your problem."

I closed my eyes for a millisecond and inhaled. "It *is* my problem, because I care about you. That hasn't changed." And yes, I could still see myself with him. Even knowing it—we—were wrong. "I'm sorry you heard my disappointment. You don't deserve that. The flowers are beautiful and I appreciate them so much."

"Stop, Chloe. This was my call. I should've known better than to hang around." He shrugged, again playing it cool and carefree. I wasn't fooled, though. The Kyle I knew, the one I'd dated for these last many months, had never, not once, attempted to romance me. This action alone spoke volumes.

"Listen. Let's go grab a cup of coffee and talk. Maybe find a way to resolve whatever you're feeling . . . what I'm feeling . . . so we can find our way to friendship. How does that sound?" I put the offer out, hoping he'd agree. Wanting to do something to settle the weirdness between us. "What do you say?"

Pulling his sunglasses out of his shirt pocket, he slipped them on, hiding his eyes. And therefore, his emotions. "I should go. Sorry for interrupting your day."

"Please don't leave! Not yet. If we could just talk, I'm sure—"

"Talk about what, Chloe? I put myself out on a limb. I wanted to show you that I'm serious." He shoved his hands into his pants pockets, the movement quick and jittery. Covered eyes or not, I'd have sworn he was glaring at me. Who could blame him? "I thought showing you that might make a difference. It's cool, though."

My throat tightened, so I swallowed. "I know you don't believe me right now, but our being together is a mistake. This is better for both of us. I swear. You'll see that, eventually." Or at least I hoped he would.

He came forward in five large steps, stopping abruptly in front of the counter. He tilted his sunglasses up with his knuckles, his amber eyes transfixing me. "This is better for you. Not me. Got it? Don't confuse the two." His voice wasn't so much angry as annoyed.

"I don't understand. This isn't like you," I murmured, confused.

Letting go of the sunglasses he said, "Maybe you don't know me as well as you think."

Well, gee. That was kind of apparent. "I understand what you're going through. I felt this way before. You know that."

He chuckled without humor. "No, Chloe. You do not understand. For some reason, I can't give you up. It's like I have no choice but to try to win you back. Can you explain that? Do you understand that? Because I sure as hell don't."

My mouth opened and then closed. Oh, dear God. I understood. Completely. It was the magic cake coming back to bite me in the ass. Just as Elizabeth predicted. It had to be that. What else? "Um . . . no. I don't know what that means," I lied. Something, it seemed, I'd been doing a lot of lately.

"That's what I thought." He twisted around and strode toward the exit. Right before pushing open the door, he paused but didn't turn his head. "I don't get what's going on, but don't call yourself a bitch. You've always been good to me. Better than I probably deserved. I'm . . . sorry it's taken me so long to recognize that."

He left before I could reply. I nearly ran after him, but was quite sure that he'd agree I was a bitch if he knew I'd bespelled him with a magical cake. As it was, I needed to find a way to fix this. Like yesterday. Because somehow I didn't think his sudden fervor to make our relationship work was going to go away on its own.

Chapter Ten

"Are you and Kyle really through?" Paige asked minutes after his abrupt departure. Idly she picked up one of the spritzer bottles from the counter display and sort of juggled it from one hand to the other. "What happened? And who's the new guy?"

"Yes, we're really through. As to what happened . . . well, that's a long story." I shrugged. "Easier to say that we're not right for each other."

"It's better to decide that now. Besides, if some other guy has already changed your feelings for Kyle, then he can do better than you." If she hadn't said the words gently, without even a hint of censure, I might have gotten upset.

"I know." Having that knowledge didn't mean jack when someone I cared about was going through pain caused by me, by magic. "Anyway, I'm going to get back to work. Finish the . . . oh, hell, whatever I was doing when you called me."

"You didn't answer my other question." She replaced the bottle. "Who's the new guy?"

"Oh!" My tension eased slightly. "His name is Ben Malone. I took one look at him and felt as if my life had been jumpstarted. And now . . . well, there's no going back."

"I get that. I totally do. It's a defining moment, an instant where you know that your life will never be the same. Even if things don't work out—"

"Exactly. But things with Ben *are* going to work out." I pushed the statement out with total confidence, needing to hear myself say the words, even if the situation was more along the lines of blind hope.

"Cool. I'm happy for you." She busied herself with putting new stock out. "Remember, I leave even earlier today than normal. For that class project I told you about."

"Yep. Got it."

Retreating to my office, I laid my head down on my desk. How in the hell was I going to get out of this mess with Kyle? Magic was supposed to make life simpler, not more convoluted. "Fuck," I whispered. Maybe Elizabeth would have some ideas on how to fix things. And if not her, then Alice or Verda. Thank God they had more experience with magical mishaps than I did. If I was really lucky, they might even have some advice on what was going on with Ben. What to do, how to make him love me, stuff like that.

Or not. The truth was that a tiny, miniscule part of me wished I'd never met Ben, had never seen that damn drawing or the three others. Because as much as I wanted to be with him *now*, the whole kit and caboodle surrounding that want was just too damn hard. I barely knew him, yet felt as if I'd known him forever. Which was crazy. And yes, without the knowledge I currently held, staying with Kyle would for the most part have been enough for me.

But I *had* met Ben. I *had* seen those drawings.

"Fuck," I murmured again, as a light knock sounded on the door to the back room, followed by the door creaking open.

"What's up, Paige?" My voice came out muffled, because my forehead remained pressed against the desk. "Need help with something?"

A rumble of deep laughter met my ears. "If that's an example of your psychic powers, I'm not impressed."

Ben! Just that quickly, the wish to have never met him vanished. Lifting my head, I tried not to smile too hard as he approached. Today he wore a dark gray suit, white shirt and a black tie. He appeared formidable, larger than life and totally hot.

"I've never claimed to be psychic." While I far preferred the jeans and cowboy boots look, this wasn't so bad. "Calling you Paige was more of an assumption."

"I met her out front. When I gave her my name, she said I could come on back." He leaned one delicious hip against the side of my desk. "Hope you don't mind."

"No! Of course not! I'm . . . uh . . . happy to see you. Surprised, though."

"I was in the area for a meeting. Thought I'd stop in and thank you again for Sunday." His gaze zeroed in on me, and the corners of his mouth twitched. "Do you realize you have a paperclip stuck to your forehead? It's quite fetching. Almost sexy."

My hand shot to my forehead. "Great. Just great." I sighed and peeled it off.

Bright sparks of humor glittered in his eyes. "Now you have the imprint of a paperclip on your forehead. Catching a nap while Paige works the front?"

"Not napping. Thinking about you. About our date." The admission slipped out before I could squelch it. "Wondering again if you had fun or not. I didn't know the park held bad memories for you," I said softly. "I'm . . . uh . . . sorry. I should have checked it out with you before going there."

"The park doesn't hold bad memories for me. Good ones, actually. It was just . . . difficult to be there." He cleared his throat. "But I had fun, and I'm glad you chose that particular destination." Drumming his fingers against the desk, mere inches from the folded up drawing of us together, he said, "Glad I was there with you."

"Yeah? Really? Even with whatever was bothering you?"

"Of course. You're fun to be around, Chloe," he said, neatly avoiding my reference to his moody behavior. "I have a question for you. I hope you'll say yes."

"Yes," I said immediately, not caring at all what the question was. I was quite content just staring at his face.

He gave me his sexy-as-sin smile and I melted. It was, at once, that simple and that complex, that thrilling and that scary. "You don't even know what I'm going to ask. Maybe I want to take you skydiving this weekend. Feel like jumping out of a plane?"

Ha! I resisted sticking my tongue out. "You made your point. What's the real question?"

"There's a charity event happening next Friday night. My firm is hosting it, and I was wondering if you'd like to go with me. As my date."

I tilted my head to the side, pretending to give his offer serious consideration. "Hm. A week from this Friday? I'll have to check to see if I have plans." A date—a real, honest-to-goodness, go-out-and-have-fun date with my someday groom that was totally his idea! Okay, *maybe* totally his idea! But still . . . a date! I sent a silent prayer of thanks to Miranda. "Let me see." I grabbed my datebook and flipped to the appropriate page.

He leaned forward. "Seems you're free."

"So it does. So, yeah, I should be able to make it work. What kind of event is this?"

"Like I said, it's a charity thing. It might be boring through dinner," he warned. "But afterward, it should be fun. Casino theme, including roulette, craps, poker and blackjack. You like to gamble?"

Remember that happy little bubble from the other day? It was back. In force. "Love it. What time? And where is the event being held?"

"Oh no, Red. I let you drive on our first date. I'll do the driving for this one, so you'll have to cough up your address."

Grabbing the Post-it pad near my computer, I scrawled my address and phone number down. I slapped the note on his suit jacket. "There, all coughed up. But I still need to know a time, and is the dress formal?"

A wicked gleam gathered in his baby blues. "I can't hear you, Chloe. You'll have to speak up . . . or come closer."

Delicious shivers of anticipation danced over me. "Oh, I will?"

He cupped his ear with one hand. "What?" Patting the desktop, the gleam brightened. "Can't hear you."

Stifling a laugh, more than happy to oblige, I pushed a sheaf of papers to the side, including the oh-so-incriminating drawing, and slid onto the desk, mere inches from where he leaned. "Okay, so . . . what time, and is the dress formal?" I asked again in a lower and, hopefully, sultrier voice.

"Dinner is at eight." He touched my lips, the feel of his finger surprisingly gentle and erotic at the same time. In a slow, sure, sensual glide, he began tracing my mouth's outline.

"So . . ." I gulped. "You'll pick me up around seven-thirty?"

"Let's say seven." Oh so slowly, he swept his thumb over my bottom lip. My mouth trembled, opening slightly. He continued brushing the lower line of my lip, his thumb dipping down and then up around the contours of my mouth, until it reached the opposite corner. "And yes, the dress is formal."

"Sounds . . . wonderful," I breathed.

"I've been thinking about you," he admitted.

Just kiss me already, I thought. "Good stuff, I hope."

"Good . . . ? Yes, you could say that."

Kiss me, Ben. Lean over, pull me to you and kiss me.

His entire body surged forward. He wove all ten fingers into my hair, dragging my head toward him. Fathomless, bluer-than-blue eyes met mine, searing in their intensity as he came closer . . . closer . . . closer, until his lips found mine in a hard, ravaging kiss. My mouth parted easily when his tongue thrust inside, eliciting one shudder after another of heavy want from me.

I moaned and moved my hands to his chest, wishing we were somewhere else, somewhere exquisitely private, so I could rip his shirt off. So I could run my fingers over his skin, feel his muscles as they tensed against me, rub my hands over his bare back. Need and desire were making me wet, making me ready for him. I pushed my tongue into his mouth, tasting coffee and something else, something sweet.

His hands swept to the base of my neck, his thumbs pressing lightly at the nape, his fingers curving around and brushing lightly over my collarbone. A swirl of sensations, of longing, rushed up from between my legs, spreading through my limbs and turning my skin to fire. I wanted him now, right where we were.

"We . . . Paige," I murmured against his mouth as a dose of cold reality, of common sense, clicked in. "Not . . . here." With great difficulty I pressed on Ben's chest, pushing myself back, my lips swollen, my body vibrating with need. I buried my head in his shoulder, focused on breathing slowly and tried to cool the inferno of my senses.

"What are you doing to me, Red?" he asked, his breathing ragged. "I don't ravage women in the backs of stores. Or at an amusement park, for that matter. I feel like a horny sixteen-year-old."

"We have chemistry. It's . . . magical." I spoke the truth, if not all of it. "And we're both consenting adults. Relax and go with the flow." And while you're at it, I thought, fall head over heels in love with me. Please.

He grasped my hips with both hands, tugging me so that my bottom slid a few more inches along the desk. "Where the hell were you when I was sixteen?"

"I don't know. But when I was sixteen, I was stealing cigarettes from my aunt and barely passing algebra. You wouldn't have liked me then."

He kissed the top of my head. "Why not?"

No magic, that's why not. But I couldn't say that, so I

went with the other truth. "I was a total cliché: the girl in the shadows reading poetry and daydreaming about the future. Other than a few friends and my sister, I was fairly invisible."

Speaking with absolute assurance, he said, "I would have seen you."

Tears pricked my eyes, because that one little statement softened the calloused heart of the sixteen-year-old girl who still lived inside of me. She'd been sad, that girl. But then, several months later, Kyle had come along and made me happy. The happiest I'd been in years. Shoving the memories out of my mind, I shrugged. "Maybe. Maybe not. But you see me now. That's what counts."

We stayed that way for a few minutes. "I should go," he murmured, his lips on my hair. "I have to get to the office for another meeting."

Regret simmered in his voice, and I smiled. "I want you to come to dinner before next Friday. So we can have some privacy." Looking up, I lightly touched his lips. "So we can be alone."

Hunger and desire roared to life in his eyes. "How about this Friday?"

"Sounds perfect." I stood from the desk and tugged the Post-it that was still amazingly stuck to his suit jacket. "Don't lose this." I folded the paper into a little square and tucked it in his hand.

"I won't. Mind if I wait a few minutes before leaving? I'm . . . ah"—he lowered his chin—"not fit to be seen in public."

My eyes drifted downward. "Wh—? Oh! Yes, of course."

"You're all red again, Red. And today you can't blame it on the sun," Ben teased. "I think I'm going to like being your rebound guy."

My heart fell in two all over again, but before I could come up with a response appropriately flirtatious yet noncommittal, a loud knock pulled my attention. "Come on in, Paige," I called, knowing she probably needed to leave.

She stepped into the room with a saucy-ass grin. "Sorry to interrupt, but I gotta get out of here or I'll be late for class. And I'm parked a couple of blocks away."

"I can give you a ride to your car if you want," Ben offered. "I'm right out front."

"Cool! That would rock." Dashing to the cupboard, she grabbed her backpack. "I'll just wait . . . um . . . out there for you." She slipped out of the room as quickly as she'd appeared.

"That's really nice of you, offering her a ride. Thank you."

"It's my fault she's running late. But . . . do you have a book or something I can use for . . . er . . . camouflage?" It was his turn to blush. My smile returned.

"Just take your jacket off and carry it in front of you. It's probably pretty warm out."

"Smart as well as beautiful." Doffing his jacket, he folded it over one arm. "Come here."

I stepped forward, and he leaned in, giving me one more kiss, albeit a short and fast one. "I'll see you on Friday," I said when we separated. "Say, around seven?"

He agreed and took off. As for me, I collapsed in my chair and closed my eyes, listening for the bell on the door. Paige would've told me if any customers were in the shop, so I felt safe giving myself a few minutes to calm down, to find my balance. I touched my lips, reveling in the sensual hum Ben's kisses had brought to life inside of me. Why my physical reaction to him still stunned me, I didn't know. I wondered if I'd ever get used to such a strong, visceral response.

I hoped not. How awesome would it be to marry a man who could do that to you for the rest of your lives together? A man who could make you hotter than hot with just a kiss? That little thought piqued my desire again, so I inhaled a breath deep into my lungs and then pushed it out. "This is not the way to calm down," I whispered.

"Chloe? I waited out front—"

I jumped from the chair so fast that I banged my knee on the desk. It hurt like hell. Very likely, I'd have a bruise there within the hour. Turning toward my unexpected guest, I worked hard to keep my voice even. "I really wish you'd have knocked on the door, Mari. You scared the crap out of me."

"I—I'm sorry. I waited out front but you weren't there. I . . ." She hovered near the door, dressed in the same clothes she'd worn the last time. I felt like a heel. Again.

"Hey, it's okay. You just surprised me! Was Paige helping you with anything before she left?"

"Paige? The girl with the dark hair? No . . . I don't think so. She d-didn't see me."

Annoyance blistered over me. It wasn't like Paige not to pay attention to customers. But then I realized that Mari had likely walked in as Ben and Paige were leaving. Which was why I'd only heard the bell once. "Okay, that's fine. What . . . um . . . what can I do for you?"

Eyes filled with pain and confusion settled on me. "I don't know. I . . . I think I need your help."

I told myself to proceed carefully. "I'll be happy to help if I can. How old are you, Mari?"

Her chin trembled. She shook her head slightly, as if in a daze. Again, I wondered if drugs were involved, but her eyes looked clear and she appeared healthy. Physically, anyway. "Sixteen?" she murmured. "I think I'm sixteen."

"You don't know how old you are?" Maybe the girl suffered from some type of mental illness. That thought brought a tremor of apprehension, because I was, after all, completely alone in the shop.

"I'm sixteen. I'm sure of it," she said with more decisiveness.

Then she should be in school. But I didn't mention that,

because if she were in trouble, the last thing I wanted to do was send her scurrying away. "Is there anyone I can call for you? Someone you trust?" She didn't respond, so I pushed forward. "A teacher? Your mom or dad? Another relative? A neighbor, perhaps?"

Fear loomed in her sky blue eyes, in the hunched way she held her body. "There is no one I can talk to except for you. It has to be you."

Okay, I was completely out of my league here. But the desire to help flooded in, drowning out all of the perfectly sound reasons why I should excuse myself and make a quick phone call to the authorities, to someone who might be able to get to the bottom of this, to someone who might be able to offer Mari real assistance. Instead, I said, "If I can help you, I will. What do you need?"

"I don't know." She said the words with despair, with a ring of finality that made zero sense. "I just know . . . I feel that you're the only one who can help."

"Is someone hurting you?"

She blinked, and a solo tear dripped down her cheek. "Please help me."

Oh, God. "If someone is hurting you, we can get you help. But you have to tell me what's happening. Is it your parents? A boyfriend?"

The barest shimmer of light grew, as if the sun shone through a window behind Mari, illuminating her. But there wasn't a window, just a wall and the door. "My mother . . . She was sad and crying. I was mad and . . ." Mari broke off, overcome by emotion. By memories, by something I didn't understand.

Perhaps she was a runaway. The desire to help her, to understand, curled in my belly in a pulsating wave of pure energy. Comprehension that my magic, my ability, might give me the answers I needed, the power to actually offer assistance to this girl, slammed into me. I grabbed onto it with everything I had, letting the magic rip through me, allowing the power to take control, feeding off of my emotions and off the emotions I felt emanating from Mari.

Without thought, without dissecting what I was doing, I reached for her, my magic strong and forceful, once again burning through my blood, glittering and glistening and glowing on my skin. She gasped and took a step backward. The light around her brightened to a clean, pristine white that nearly took my breath away. I focused in on the light, the barest of images beginning to appear within it, startling me.

Pushing myself mentally, I fought to clear the haze that covered the image, fought to see what my magic was trying to show me. I imagined peeling back layers, like on an onion, one at a time, to reveal what the light hid. Only the harder I worked, the more my eyes watered. A rush of dizziness swooped in, making my vision swim, turning the room topsy-turvy.

I held on, intent on using my magic for good, intent on helping Mari. The faintest outline of the image began to come into focus, so I pushed myself harder. I saw darkness. I saw two streams of beaming light. I heard a scream, then another.

"Are you okay?" Mari's concerned voice came through the fog.

I nodded but didn't speak. Hurt, pain, loss and betrayal twisted in my mind. Anger. Lots of anger. Again, I tried to focus in, tried to see the rest of the image, tried to understand, but the sound of a bell broke my concentration. In an instant, the magic bled from my body, the light and the image around Mari dissipated, disappearing as if neither had ever existed.

My entire body shook. My skin was ice cold and covered in a light coat of perspiration. I attempted to breathe evenly, waiting for the effects to subside, not daring to talk. I heard a voice call out, "Excuse me? Is anyone here?" And then, all at once, I realized where I stood, what the sound of the bell signified.

"Someone's in the shop, Mari. I—I have to get out there. Wait. Wait right here and I'll be back as soon as I can." I looked at her. "Do you understand? I'll be right back."

She tilted her head, and her sky-blue eyes searched my face before she nodded. "I understand."

"Okay. Good. Just wait." I stepped around her and tried to walk straight, but felt as if I'd just downed several glasses of wine in quick succession on an empty stomach.

The customer in the shop wanted advice on cleansing her pendulum, as well as information about how to use charts in conjunction with it. I answered her questions and showed her the charts we carried, pointed out a few books that dealt with dowsing, and finally rang her up. By then, two other customers were in the shop. I blew out a sigh of frustration. The pair had arrived together, were apparently friends, and their slow, methodical appraisal of one item after another showed they weren't in a hurry.

After ascertaining there was nothing they needed immediate assistance with, I opened the door to the back, wanting to tell Mari I'd be a little longer. But she wasn't there, and when I dashed to check the restroom, she wasn't there either. My eyes landed on the back door and I cursed. I should put a bell on *that* door. Probably, I'd scared the poor girl out of her wits, and she'd run the second I left her alone.

While I didn't blame her, my worry and fear for her ate at me the rest of the day. God help me if she was now too terrified to come back. I was fairly certain that my earlier assessment of her being a runaway was right on. And while I didn't have a clue as to what that barely seen image meant, I didn't believe she'd go anywhere else for help. Why she'd come to me, I wasn't sure. But she had, and the weight of that responsibility hung heavy.

Miranda's message about my having a journey, one that

had nothing to do with the drawing, came to mind. Maybe, just maybe, Mari was part of that journey? Maybe my powers were meant to be used to help someone that no one else, for whatever reason, could? If that were the case, had I already screwed up?

"I want some answers," I said to the now empty store. "I want to know what the hell I'm supposed to be doing."

Chapter Eleven

Verda stared at me with unblinking blue eyes. "You cursed that boy, Chloe."

We, along with Elizabeth and Alice, were gathered around Alice's kitchen table early Thursday evening. Ethan and Rose were in another room, and I'd already caught everyone up to speed on Ben, but had just finished explaining the Kyle debacle.

I glared at Verda, not liking the sound of that. "What do you mean?"

"You bespelled him twice: once with your magic and once with Elizabeth's." Verda smacked her hand on the table for emphasis. "Double-whammy magic! Poor Kyle never stood a chance."

Oh, shit. Why hadn't I thought of that? I mentally revisited the night of my proposal, and my emotions—the strength of my want to cement a future with Kyle—returned in a flash. I looked to Elizabeth. "Can you bake something else to fix this?"

Elizabeth chose a home-baked—presumably magic-free—chocolate chip cookie from a box emblazoned with the A Taste of Magic logo and dunked it into her cup of coffee. "I can certainly try. But it might not work."

"It's worth a shot." Alice slumped in her chair. "I'll stop by A Taste of Magic tomorrow and pick up whatever you bake, Liz, and then deliver it to Kyle myself."

"Don't be silly. I'll take care of it." Though how I was going to explain bringing Kyle anything was beyond me.

Knowing my luck, he'd dump the contents of the bakery box over my head.

Alice shook her head. "You shouldn't see him right now, Chloe. Let's give Elizabeth's magic a chance first. Without your interference."

My *interference*? And that meant what, exactly? Somehow, Alice, Verda and Elizabeth seemed all in on some little secret that they weren't sharing.

Trying not to sound as defensive as I felt, I said, "I think I can handle delivering baked goods to Kyle. But if you want to take care of it, I won't argue."

"Good." She shot me an uneasy look. "Don't misunderstand me. I'm just worried that you'll accidentally respell him."

Verda tightened the shawl around her shoulders. "You have too much going on, Alice. I'll make the delivery." She spoke in her don't-argue-with-me voice, but I totally expected Alice to argue. She didn't.

The fact that she didn't, along with Verda's statement and the weird energy in the room, bothered me. What did Alice have going on, and why hadn't she told me? Once again, as I had been for so many months, I became the odd girl out. And petty or not, I didn't like it. "Fine. Verda will make the delivery. But what if that doesn't do the trick?"

"Then you'll need to find a way to fix this. Just be sure you're not holding on to any doubts about your relationship with him," Verda said. "Because otherwise, whether you meant to or not, you *have* cursed Kyle. You'll leave that boy miserable for the rest of his life, wanting you and not being able to have you."

An uneasy chill overtook me. "I won't let that happen."

Elizabeth sat up straighter in her chair. "I warned you of this." She broke off a chunk of cookie. "Magic isn't a game, Chloe."

Riled up but not sure why, I forced myself to remain calm. "I know that."

"Do you?"

Now why did that feel like a trick question? "I just said I did, didn't I?"

A gush of words erupted. "You begged—coerced—me into using magic on Kyle to marry you, and now you're using your magic on Ben."

"The situations are completely different," I argued. "I have a picture that shows me marrying Ben! If I have to use my power . . . my gift . . . to get to that day, then I don't see how that's a huge issue."

"You also have a picture showing you already married to Kyle, one of you alone, and one of you with us. So why is this the one you're so focused on?" Elizabeth asked.

"Because it's the *right* future. Those other three? They're showing me what could happen if I don't go down this path. The right path. I'm sure of it." Or I thought I was. I'd given those four pictures and my dream about a crossroads a lot of thought. This was the only scenario that made sense. "Besides, kissing Ben is like magic."

"That's because it *is* magic. Your magic." Elizabeth frowned. "I asked this before, but it bears repeating. Don't you want a man who will want you for you?"

"He will! Eventually."

"And how do you know that?"

"Calm down. Both of you." Alice's voice of reason slipped in. "We're all on the same side here."

"Too late," I huffed. But she was right, so I looked at Elizabeth, lowered my tone and tried to cool my anger. "You were right about Kyle. I get that, and I'm sorry I didn't listen to you. But this, with Ben, is different. Everything I feel for him is so strong, and it started before I ever saw that drawing. I'll do anything I have to do for that future to come true."

In a softer tone, Elizabeth said, "All I want is for you to understand that there are ramifications whenever you use magic. Sometimes, they can be good. But sometimes, like with Kyle, you can . . . well, you can screw things up. Just be careful."

"I just need to get us on the right path. That's all I'm doing." And even though I believed that to the core of my being, Elizabeth's words and the situation with Kyle struck deep. "But, yes, I will be careful."

"Good. That's all I need to hear."

Silence descended on the room, but unlike the comforting quiet at the Mystic Corner the other evening, this one was filled with unsaid words, conflicting emotions and who the hell knows what else. I squirmed in my chair. I'd planned on asking Elizabeth to ask her cop husband, Nate, for advice in dealing with Mari. In case the girl returned. But with what had just occurred, I decided to keep Mari to myself.

"So . . . has Miranda been around lately?" I asked Alice. "Since the morning she told you to draw my future again?"

"Nope. And I'd really like to talk to her." Alice frowned. "Have you seen her?"

"I thought I felt her a few nights ago, but if she was there, she kept to herself."

A few more minutes of conversation surrounding our ghost relative ensued, but then, once we'd exhausted that topic, no one appeared to have anything else to say. Elizabeth and Verda kept darting glances at me, and I sort of thought that they wanted to me to leave so they could talk to Alice in private. But nope. I wanted some privacy with my best friend, so I settled in, prepared to wait.

It took a lot less time than I figured, and before I knew it Elizabeth and Verda were saying their good-byes. When I hugged Verda, she whispered in my ear, "Remember our deal! I'm counting on you."

"I remember," I whispered back. "But that deal goes two ways."

We separated, and she grinned conspiratorially. "Don't worry. I know what I'm doing."

I couldn't help but smile back. "You have five weeks and five days."

She wrinkled her nose but didn't respond. Then she and Elizabeth went home, leaving me alone with Alice.

Fiddling with her now-empty coffee cup, my friend asked, "How are you. Really?" But while the words were appropriate, she seemed preoccupied.

"I'm fine. I want to know what's going on with you."

Her shoulders stiffened. "You should focus on *your* life right now."

"I can do that and care about you. Why are you keeping me out of the loop?" I bit my lip, staring at her, waiting for her to grin and spill whatever secret she was keeping from me. She didn't.

"Because right now all I want is for you to work out what's happening in your life." She heaved a breath. "I'm not going to weigh you down with my own burdens."

I shook my head. "You're seriously not going to talk to me about this?"

"Not this time, Chloe. Not now. This is . . . Well, Ethan and I are dealing with it."

"So you haven't told Elizabeth and Verda? This is a husband and wife thing?" That, at least, I could understand.

She shifted in her seat. "They know, but please don't push this. It's nothing about you. I promise."

"You *have* told them?" All of my feelings from the past year returned. Where had my best friend gone? Why was I suddenly the only person being kept in the dark? I stared at Alice without speaking, wanting her to open up, wanting her to turn to me the way she used to. Even if her intentions were good, I hated being shoved to the side. As if my opinions didn't matter. As if *I* didn't matter.

Giving it one more go, I said, "Please, Alice?"

She shook her head, not looking me in the eyes.

"Fine. If that's how you want it."

I was going to stand up and leave, take my hurt feelings home with me and pout . . . but then I realized I *could* get her to open up. Without giving myself the chance to think twice, I breathed deeply and focused on the power inside of me, going for a gentle push, and not an outright takeover of her will. Tell me what's going on, Alice, I thought.

Trust in me. Trust in our friendship.

Warmth flooded my body and tingles leaped across my skin. "Alice? I want to know what you're keeping from me."

She blinked. Then, in a soft voice, she started speaking. "It's about Rose. Are you sure you want to hear this?"

"Yes. What's going on with your baby?" I pushed the magic forward again, from me to her, energy saturating the air. "Tell me."

Tiredness and worry seeped over Alice, darkening the brown in her eyes. "It's the damn magic! I just want Rose to grow up normal and happy, and . . ."

"And?" I gave another mental push.

"She's doing things. Not just little stuff, like with the bear in her crib, but big stuff."

Oh, this had to do with the magic. *Rose's* magic. "Like what?"

"She . . . she can heal, Chloe." Alice sucked in a breath and blanched. "She healed me. I cut myself while preparing dinner, and I was running my hand under the water. Rose woke up from her nap and was crying, so I wrapped a paper towel around my hand and went to get her. I took her into the bathroom with me and sat her on the counter while I got out the bandages. Rose leaned over and touched the cut . . . and I felt this almost-burning sensation and watched the cut heal." Alice snapped her fingers. "Just like that. There one minute, gone the next."

As soon as she finished speaking, the magic whooshed

away. "Oh . . . oh, wow. That's huge! Imagine what she'll be able to do—how she might help people!"

"And imagine the circus her life will become." Tears dotted Alice's eyes. "It scares me. I'm not even going to be able to send her to school with normal kids."

"Whoa! You don't know that yet." But she had a point. A very good one. "Between you, Ethan, Verda, Elizabeth, Miranda and me, you'll figure this out."

Alice wiped her eyes. "I wasn't going to tell you, but . . ." She stared at me, confusion and questions rippling over her. Uh-oh. She'd already caught on.

"I'm glad you did. But now I should probably get going," I said. Before she clobbered me.

"No. No you don't. You just spelled me, didn't you?" Her voice trembled with anger and disbelief. "How could you do that? To me? Your best friend?"

"I'm sorry. But why wouldn't you tell me about this if I *am* your best friend?"

"I was trying to be conscious of what's going on with you! And you're so wrapped up in the magic right now, I didn't think you'd understand why I'm upset. I figured it was better to not even go there." She narrowed her eyes. "I understand why you did it, but Chloe . . . I don't like being forced to do anything. Don't ever do that again."

"I'm sorry," I repeated, hoping she'd let me off the hook. And I was sorry. Hugely. "But it doesn't matter what's going on in my life. You can always come to me. Just like I can always come to you. Magic, husbands, children—none of that changes that you're my best friend. I love you, Alice."

"I know that. And I feel the same." She sighed in exasperation. "But if you ever use your magic on me again, then I'm going to have Elizabeth bake you one hell of a cake."

I gulped. "Understood. Completely."

"Okay, then." The tension eased out of her, but it still weighed in the air. Her eyes drifted to the clock. "It's getting late, and while this might not be the best time to get into this, there's something else I need to say. And it can't wait."

"I'm all ears," I replied.

"It's about Grandma. Has she come to you with any type of requests lately?"

"Um, er . . . you mean Verda?"

"Is there another grandmother that I don't know about?" Alice asked, deadpan. "Yes, I mean Verda. She's been hinting about getting her magic back, but she hasn't actually asked me or Elizabeth straight out yet. Neither of us are prepared to say yes, even if she does. But . . . well, we thought she might go to you."

"Why wouldn't you say yes?" I asked.

"She keeps rambling about a dream." Alice twisted her wedding rings. "Sh-she thinks she needs her magic to accomplish something—whatever the dream is warning her of—and, well, that she has to do this soon. Before she dies."

Oh, no. Verda dying? That's what her request was all about? Not only did I hate that, not only did the thought bring tears to my eyes, but I should've known that Verda wouldn't have come to me without knowing Elizabeth and Alice would refuse. Manipulation 101 at its finest.

"Did she actually say that?" My voice quavered. "That she dreamed she was going to die?"

"Not exactly, but close enough. So I can't—won't—gift her magic to her. Not if that means she's going to give up on life once she's done whatever it is she thinks she needs to!"

"Verda loves life, Alice! You're worrying too much. She's not the type to just give up because some dumb dream showed her something."

"Maybe I'm using the wrong words." Alice's eyes clouded with fear. "But if she believes things are going to happen in a certain progression, and receiving the magic happens first, then that's enough reason to keep the magic away from her."

"So, you want me to . . . what?"

"If she asks you, tell her no. Please."

"I see." My voice was barely a whisper. "But what if she's right? What if she needs her magic returned so she can . . . oh, I don't know, set something straight? Or make sure that something that's supposed to happen will?"

"How can you say that? I know how Grandma's mind works, and she'll focus in so hard on this that she'll believe in everything that dream is telling her. And if that dream says . . ." Alice stood and strode to the sink, filling a glass with water. "I can't lose her. Not yet!" She drank a gulp and turned back to me. "Just promise me that if she comes to you, if she asks you to try this, that you'll say no. Please?"

I looked into the pain-filled eyes of my best friend and I did something I never wanted to do. I outright lied. By omission, but still. "If from this moment on, Verda comes to me and asks for her magic, I'll tell her I can't give it to her. That's my promise."

Alice's entire body slumped in relief. "Thank you. And you'll tell me if she does ask, right?"

Hating myself, I continued. "Of course. If she makes this request in the coming days, I'll tell you at once."

Under normal circumstances, Alice would've caught on to my odd wording, but with so much on her mind, she heard only what she wanted, what she expected to hear. She thanked me again, and shortly afterward, I took off for home.

I should've been angry with Verda, but I wasn't. Sure, she'd manipulated me by not giving me the entire scoop, but I didn't really blame her. Especially now that I understood Alice's and Elizabeth's issues. Verda in her wisdom probably figured I'd react similarly, because she knew how much I loved her, or that I, at the very least, would insist on talking with Alice and Elizabeth first. But honestly? She needn't have worried, because even knowing what I now knew, I wouldn't have done anything different. I trusted Verda, and if she said she needed her power back, then I believed her, no questions asked. My only real fear resided in Alice, in what her reaction would be when the truth came out.

Suddenly, five weeks and five days seemed way too short a time. I should've given Verda a couple of years to come clean. Maybe a decade.

"Why haven't you phoned your sister, Chloe?" Miranda asked in her oddly lilting way.

I'd just arrived home from Alice's to find the ghost of my great-great-great-grandmother reposing like a queen on my bed. It was slightly disconcerting. Mostly because she looked like she belonged there.

"Were you here the other night?" I asked, rather than responding. "I felt but didn't see you."

She shrugged, a light grin playing across her lips. "I check on you every now and then."

I scowled. "So, what? You're like a Peeping Tom? Hovering around to see what I do and how I do it? Not cool, Miranda."

"Oh, hush. I leave when you're involved in"—she cleared her throat—"intimate matters."

Yeah, that made me feel better. Not. "So were you here for a reason? Or just to spy."

"I wanted to be sure you'd help Verda. You did, so there was no reason to make myself known." She spoke with such conviction that my lingering stress over Verda lightened. "But tonight, I want to know why you haven't contacted your sister."

"Sheridan has my phone number. She can call whenever she wants." I made my voice as cool as possible. "If you're here to push me into mending fences with her, you're wasting your time. 'Cause that is so not going to happen."

The colors around Miranda bounced and shimmied. "She needs you, but she's too proud to tell you that herself. And you're too stubborn to make the first move."

"I've made the first move, and the second, and the third. She isn't interested." I kicked off my shoes and heaved myself up on the dresser, taking a seat there, pretending unconcern. "But what do you mean, she needs me?"

"I mean exactly that. You might be surprised at how interested she is." Miranda lifted her hand and an image appeared between us, like a movie screen suspended in thin air. It showed my sister sitting in what I assumed was her living room. Of course, I didn't know this for sure, as I'd never visited her in Seattle. She had a photo album in front of her, and she was crying as she slowly turned the pages. "Those pictures she's looking at are of you and her, of your life before your parents died. She misses you, Chloe."

My sister. How had I not realized how fully I missed her? I reached out toward the image as if I could touch her, soaking in every detail: her chin-length strawberry blonde hair, her wide blue-green eyes so much like our father's, her long, narrow face with a spattering of freckles. Oh, how she hated those freckles. Whenever I thought of Sheridan, I thought of her laughing and smiling, of her sunny, optimistic outlook on life. But this image of my sister was anything but happy.

"What's wrong with her?"

"Maybe you should call her and ask her yourself?"

I cannot even begin to express how much I wanted to. But you can only get burned so many times before you quit reaching into the fire. "She knows how to get a hold of me," I said again. "If she wanted me in her life, she'd let me know."

"Why do you try so hard to dismiss the connection between you? You need Sheridan just as much as she needs you."

I continued to stare at my baby sister as she wept. The anger and hurt from years of avoidance softened, bringing tears to my eyes. "I thought she was happy," I murmured. "I thought she was so happy, she didn't want me around, because I just remind her of everything she's lost."

The image disappeared, and I had to force myself not to cry out, not to beg Miranda to bring it back. I turned my focus to her, tried to empty my mind and heart of my sister's tears.

"What you've *both* lost," Miranda pointed out. "But you still have each other, and I'm growing tired of waiting for one of you to get off your ass and do something about it." Yes, the ghost actually cursed. If I weren't so upset, I might have found it amusing.

"Is this what you were talking about before? About all of your daughters recognizing each other? Because I'm not going to tell Sheridan about the magic, or you, or about our connection to Verda, Elizabeth and Alice." I pushed myself off the dresser, annoyed and angry and sad and scared.

"And why is that?" Miranda tipped her head, looking as if she could see my soul.

"She's like Isobel!" I shouted, referring to Verda's daughter, and Alice and Elizabeth's mother, who knew about the magic and Miranda but wanted nothing to do with either. "Sheridan is ridiculously practical. She organizes her cupboards in alphabetical order, she buys clothes that never go out of fashion and she follows the rules and does every last thing by the book! She thinks my business and my beliefs are ludicrous, and I'm telling you now that she won't believe in any of this. If I try to convince her, it will just make things worse between us."

"From what you say, things can't really get any worse, can they? So, what do you have to lose? Perhaps opening up to her will draw you closer." Miranda beckoned. "Come here, child. Sit next to me."

With jellylike legs, I stumbled across the room and perched on the edge of the bed. Instantly, and weirdly, my swirling emotions calmed. "I know Sheridan better than you do. She will not accept this. Besides, you told Isobel it was her choice to take the magic or not, to accept it or not. Why is this any different?"

"Because Isobel knows the truth, accepts the magic as being true even if it scares her but chooses to turn away from the gift. That is her right. However, Sheridan does *not* know, so you are making the choice for her. And that, my dear, cannot be."

"Then you tell her. You go and give her the news."

"I've tried," Miranda admitted. "But she doesn't see me. She isn't ready to see me. And my time is growing short."

That startled me. "I thought you were here to stay. Elizabeth said that you planned on being here to help Rose grow up."

"I'm still hopeful that will be the case, but I'm feeling a pull, a very strong pull, and I don't know how much longer I'll be able to resist it. So I need you to go to Sheridan. Even if you aren't ready to tell her everything, you need to begin to find a way to cross the chasm between you. Then someday, when the time is right, you can tell her the rest."

My jaw twitched. "I don't know. I'm tired of her rebuffing me."

"She's ready to hear from you. Trust me in this," Miranda pushed.

Feeling as if I had no choice but to agree, I made the promise. "Okay. Fine. I'll call her."

Miranda smiled, and a luminous glow shone over her. "Thank you. I think you'll find her far more receptive than you imagine."

I nodded, still unsure about following through but knowing I would. Eventually. However, at the moment my entire attention was drawn by the light surrounding Miranda. While different, it somehow reminded me of Mari. "Last time, you said I had a journey. Does that journey have anything to do with helping others?"

Miranda's smile broadened, and a glint of satisfaction gleamed in her dark eyes. "Yes. You have the ability to heal, Chloe."

I frowned. "Like Rose?"

"Rose will have many abilities. Your healing power isn't for physical wounds, but those of the heart . . . those of the soul." Again, Miranda looked at me so deeply that I felt as if my entire being was opened up to her. "Your magic is already growing and changing, yes?"

"Yes," I confirmed, thinking first of my sparkly veins, and then of the strangeness of Mari's last visit. "And there's this girl, she—"

"Everything has a connection," Miranda interrupted. "Your abilities, the people who come into your life . . . even the drawings that Alice has created. All of these are connected to each other. It's up to you to figure out how. It's up to you to decide how to use your power properly, which future you will claim and which futures are there because of, shall we say, certain choices and decisions."

I let out a sigh. "Can you possibly be any more evasive?"

She laughed like a tinkling bell. "If you'd like me to, then yes, I'm sure I can pull it off."

"Stop, Miranda. Everything is a mess. Between Kyle and Ben and those drawings and this girl . . . I don't know which way is up. I don't know what I'm supposed to be doing."

"Trust in yourself. Trust in your instincts. And Chloe? Your gift is very powerful. As I said before, you've always had the ability to sense magic in objects and people around you. Because of this, your magic can do so much more than either Elizabeth's or Alice's."

She rose from the bed, hovering above it as if residing on an invisible throne, sparkling with colors and light. Really, not all that different than what I saw running through my veins when my magic was strong. "But I'm confused by the drawings, by—"

"I have to leave now, granddaughter. If you look inside of yourself with complete and utter honesty, you will find the answers you seek."

Annoyance zipped into me, but before I could speak, her form glimmered and then faded away. I was left sitting with an open mouth and a rapidly beating heart. "Come again soon," I muttered.

Laughter echoed through the room. "Oh, I will return. When you're ready."

"Lovely," I whispered. "Just freaking lovely."

Chapter Twelve

"Is this sexy enough for you, Ben?" I asked my reflection in the mirror, my hands skimming over my sheerer-than-sheer black lace negligee. This little number came from a shop across the street from the Mystic Corner. I'd popped in earlier on my lunch break, and one look had sealed the deal. I'd even paid full price. Not only was the lingerie the sexiest garment I'd ever owned, but my plan was to greet Ben that evening while wearing it.

I know. Crazy.

And if this evening worked out as well as I thought, Ben would be staying over. For the whole night. Seeing how Paige had asked for more hours and was now taking over Saturdays for a while, that left me free and clear to spend the entire next day with Ben. Assuming he stayed the night, of course.

I sort of thought he would. Because rather than continuing to be upset about his rebound comments, I'd decided to use our fun-and-games agreement to full advantage. And that meant no rules. Not one. I was going to do whatever I wanted. Even if that scared me senseless.

Meeting Ben and then dropping into the drawing of our wedding scene had changed the course of my life. And while I knew we were just getting started—had barely met, even!—I wanted to move forward as quickly as possible. I figured a night of passion would help hugely in that regard, and that after we had mindboggling sex, he'd start to come around to my way of thinking. And yes, if our kisses were anything to go by, then I was fairly certain that sex with Ben would definitely be mindboggling.

Narrowing my eyes, I tried to see myself as Ben would. The negligee was open in front, held closed by a tiny black ribbon under my breasts, and the hem skimmed high on my thighs, leaving very little to the imagination. Skimpy black silk panties made sure I didn't show everything. Because yeah, I'd like him to have to work at least a little. I tipped my head, giving myself a once-over, wishing for ampler curves and longer legs, for a body that called out to the other sex. But my muscles were firm, and while my breasts barely weighed in at a B cup, they filled out the negligee well enough.

I tightened the spaghetti straps a bit more, helping to push those barely B-cup breasts up, to give the illusion of greater cleavage. I'd already brushed my hair until it gleamed and had applied my cosmetics expertly enough that my eyes had a smoky, sultry look. No lipstick, though. I didn't want anything between my lips and Ben's.

"You'll do," I murmured. I mean, hey, if the guy found me sexy in full clothing, then this should blow him away. And if not, I was definitely doing something wrong.

I slipped on the matching black lace, barely-longer-than-the-negligee robe and tied the ribbon at my waist. My eyes darted to the clock, which ignited the nervousness I'd thus far ignored. Twenty-five minutes until Ben arrived. If I stopped dawdling, I had just enough time to finish setting the stage.

In the kitchen, I placed onto a tray the various bowls and dishes I'd prepared earlier, along with the bottle of wine I'd already opened, and carried everything into my bedroom. I returned to the kitchen to get the wine glasses, some napkins and a few other items that hadn't fit on the tray. Once those were also in my bedroom, I pushed out a breath. Fifteen more minutes.

I lit some candles, closed the drapes, folded the bedcovers back and plumped the pillows. I didn't bother with music, because the only sounds I wanted to hear were the ones that Ben and I were bound to make. As he ravaged me. As I ravaged him. As we kissed, talked and touched each other. I brought my fingers to my lips, already feeling the effects of his kisses, already feeling the heat. With great effort, I shook myself out of my daydreams and got back to work. I didn't want to leave one thing to chance.

When all was ready, I stood in the doorway, taking it all in. I had never, ever, not once in my life gone to such extremes. Up until now, I'd totally been the type of girl who let the guy make the first move. Another shimmer of excitement whipped through me. This was fun! Scary, yes. Nerve-racking, yes. But also a hell of a lot of fun. And I couldn't wait to see his expression when I opened the door.

I didn't have to wait long. The knock came five minutes early, fueling my excitement and nerves to a degree just short of boiling over. Before letting him in, I closed my eyes and silently wished that this night would bring everything I hoped and yearned for, everything I wanted. Then I formed my lips into the best sultry smile I could and answered the door.

Ben opened his mouth to say something, probably just a greeting, but then he closed it. Fast. In barely a breath, his eyes darkened with desire and longing. Oh so slowly, his gaze dropped from my face to my chest, to my stomach, to my hips, to my legs and then back up. A sigh whispered out of me as my skin warmed beneath his intimate appraisal. I felt completely naked, as if he truly saw me. The real me, the entire me.

"You are luscious." His baritone held the slightest of tremors. He stepped inside and closed the door, locking it. The click echoed in my ears. "Exquisitely luscious. And totally unexpected."

Butterflies swam in my stomach. I tipped my chin up, so I could see into those remarkable eyes of his. "I told you I wanted us to be alone."

"So you did. I—"

I didn't wait for whatever he was going to say. Standing on tiptoe, I grazed my lips over his jaw. "I hope you don't mind a slightly unorthodox dinner."

"I'm"—he coughed, as if to clear his throat—"fine with whatever you've planned."

"I'll remember you said that." Hooking my finger into his waistband, I batted my lashes. "Dinner and entertainment is this way."

A rough-and-tumble laugh poured out. "What type of entertainment?"

"You'll see." I tugged him toward me and led him to my bedroom. We stopped just over the threshold. Nervousness made my hands shake as I started to unbutton his shirt.

His hand came down over mine, stilling my movement. "Look at me, Chloe." I did, and he brushed my mouth with his thumb, as he had at the Mystic Corner. "This is pretty much every man's fantasy," he admitted with a wicked gleam in his eyes. "But Red, don't you think we're going a little fast here? We've only known each other a short time."

"Trust me. I'm not going to rip off all of your clothes and leap on you. But . . . well, I thought we could have a little fun getting to know each other better." A shiver coursed through me. "And then we'll see where that takes us. Maybe you'll be ready to leave, or maybe we'll decide to watch a movie, or maybe"—I whisked my knuckles lightly over his still-clothed chest—"*you'll* leap on *me*. I'm happy no matter how it goes."

"Sounds . . . more than fair." His voice had deepened. "I'm in your hands tonight."

Liking the sound of that, I finished unbuttoning his shirt and with his help slid it off. "Oh!" I said in a very mouselike squeak. "You're . . . Wow, Ben. How many days a week do you work out?"

"Almost every one," he said, sounding embarrassed. As if he were caught doing something naughty. "As a stress reliever."

I nodded and swallowed. My gaze drifted slowly down his torso and then, just as slowly, back up. His muscles, rather than being huge and bulging, were tight: hard and smooth, both well proportioned and extraordinarily well-defined. He looked like a Roman gladiator. And he was mine, all mine. At least for tonight.

I swallowed again. My tongue darted out, licking my lips. Yum. Just *Yum.* And yes, I totally mean with a capital Y. He was without a doubt, absolutely mouthwatering, the hottest guy I'd ever dated, let alone had shirtless in my bedroom.

I slid my palm up from his washboard abs, feeling the soft dusting of curly, dark blond hair on his chest, muscles rippling beneath my touch. "I—I'm breathless."

"I take it you approve?" When I nodded, he breathed in deeply through his nose. His eyes drifted over my head, taking in the scene. "Are we eating in bed?"

Again, I nodded. My hand went to his belt. "What do you have on under your pants?"

He pushed out a short, ragged breath. "Boxers. Why?"

I began working at his belt, undoing the buckle and sliding the belt from the loops. "If you were going commando, that might"—heat touched my cheeks—"make what I have in mind a little difficult." Because as much as I wanted to see him naked in my bed, that wasn't how I wanted to start. Mostly naked would do just fine.

"And what devious plan is in that mind of yours, Chloe?"

"I'll tell you. But first I need you to take your pants off." I rolled my bottom lip between my teeth. "If you do that, I'll take off this robe. Then"—I flipped my head toward the bed—"we can get started."

He worked his jaw as he looked at me with questioning desire. For a split second I worried what he might be thinking, but then a dark and dangerous smile split his face, and he bent over and unlaced his shoes. When those were off, he unbuttoned and unzipped his pants. He removed and folded them into a neat square and placed them on my dresser. Then he grabbed his discarded shirt and draped that over the pants.

I held back a smile, which was hard. He stood before me in nothing but a pair of navy boxer briefs and black socks. The boxers fit him like a second skin, hugging his hips, his butt and the tops of his muscular thighs in such a way that I rolled my lip between my teeth again. My God! How could any man look this good and not be taken?

His hand shot out and tugged the bow that held my robe together. It slithered apart, and I pushed my shoulders back, letting the lacy piece of fabric fall to the ground. A groan choked out of his throat. His fingers brushed the negligee's gap, softly and languorously stroking my belly. "I might very well die tonight," he said in a very serious tone. "You are bewitching."

I arched a freshly plucked eyebrow. "Like 'Witchy Woman' bewitching?"

"Maybe." His fingers wrapped my waist, his touch searing, branding me. "But you're definitely bewitching. And bewildering. And breathtaking."

"Damn straight," I teased, as if I were used to hearing such compliments. In truth, his declaration zipped through me, filling me with pleasure, heating my cheeks another degree. Most of my life I'd heard how cute and perky and girl-next-door-like I was. Not bewitching. Not bewildering. And most definitely not breathtaking. I found I liked his assessment quite a bit.

"Can I kiss you, Chloe?"

"Not yet." I walked to the bed and climbed on. Crossing

my legs, I patted the space next to me. "Will you join me? Please?"

He did and, mimicking my position, crossed his legs. I carefully lifted the tray I'd prepared earlier and put it in front of us, within both of our reaches. I picked up a bowl off of the tray and set it down between us.

He gulped. "Are we playing a game?"

"We are. In this bowl"—I nodded to it—"are questions. I'll ask you a question, and if you answer it, then you get to choose something off of the tray to eat . . . and you can choose anywhere on my body you want to eat it from. Then it's your turn to ask me a question."

"What happens if I don't answer?"

"Then I get to ask another question. Until you answer one, you don't get to eat."

"But if I do . . ." His eyes swept my body. "Anywhere I want?"

"Within reason," I said, my voice way breathier than normal. "You can't remove any of my clothing. That's the only rule. Do you want to play?"

"I do." He gulped again. "Yes, Chloe. I want to play."

A surge of power—not of the magical variety—rushed into me. It was the type of power that being a woman, a desired and sexy woman, brings. I found I liked the feeling quite a bit. It was new, exciting and more than a little heady. "Do you want to go first, or shall I?"

The blue in his eyes became dark indigo. "Your home, your game, your rules and your bed. You should go first."

Heat and hope brought a tremor to my body as I dipped my hand into the bowl, selecting a folded slip of paper. I'd written down every question I could think of, from the silly to the mundane to the serious, that just might help us get to know each other better. I'd also thrown several away, deciding they were either too serious or too silly.

"Okay. My question is 'How old were you when you had your first crush, and what was this person's name?' "

"That's an easy one. Her name was Wendy LeBlanc, and she was my nanny when I was ten." He whistled. "Dark brown, almost black hair, brilliant blue eyes, and she had a mole"—he pointed to the spot just above the left side of his mouth—"right here. I asked her to run away with me when I was eleven."

I grinned. "What did she say?"

He pouted. "She said her heart belonged to another, but that someday I'd make some girl a very lucky woman."

"And did you?" The question came out before I could stop it.

"Play by the rules, Red. Unless that question is in that bowl and you happen to choose it, I don't have to answer." His eyes locked with mine. "Besides, I'm suddenly starving."

I dropped the slip of paper on the bed. Stretching my arms behind me, using my hands to brace myself, I arched my back into a curve. My negligee fell open, draping backward at the sides, baring everything from the line of my panties up to the ribbon beneath my breasts. "What are you hungry for?" I asked, another tremor tickling along my skin.

"Most men would go for your breasts." He reached over and plucked a strawberry out of a dish. "Maybe they'd put this in your cleavage and bury their heads in your"—he waggled his eyebrows—"heaving bosoms."

The image sent a wave of heat through me. "What about you?"

"I am not most men." He very purposefully and slowly dipped the strawberry into a bowl of chocolate syrup and then held it over his tongue, letting chocolate drip into his mouth. My body quivered.

"So . . . um." I swallowed again. "What's your choice?"

Sliding the question-filled bowl to the side, he leaned over and drizzled chocolate from the strawberry onto my navel. The muscles in my stomach clenched, then the ones in my thighs. Another quiver stole over me. His hand dropped down and he skimmed the berry along my skin, the syrup spreading into a thin, warm layer. My muscles bunched again and then released in a jerk. I tried to breathe, but my lungs refused to cooperate.

He shot me a look of pure anticipation before letting go of the strawberry. It landed perfectly on my belly button, and then he bent his head. His tongue caressed my skin in a sensual rhythm, swirling into the chocolate, eliciting a rush of goose bumps. I tipped my head back, closed my eyes and tried to relax, tried to keep my muscles still.

They refused. Again, they tensed. Again, they released. His mouth found the strawberry and he nibbled it until his teeth scraped oh-so-gently across my belly button. I moaned. My hips moved, pushing my belly up tight against his mouth. Another languorous slide of his tongue across my skin brought forth a fresh crop of goose bumps. And then, far too soon, he lifted his head.

"My turn," he said, as he returned to his prior position. "But I'm happy to answer another question first, if you'd like."

I pulled myself upright and dragged air into my lungs. Before I even dared attempting to speak, I poured us each a glass of wine. After giving him his, I drank mine down in two gulps. "You're scary good at this," I managed to say. "Seeing how this was my idea and all."

He winked. A light grin teased at his lips. "I should've warned you how competitive I am. Had to come out of the gate at a full sprint."

I choked out a laugh, though my body was still trembling. "Remind me never to play Monopoly with you." Inhaling another breath, I indicated the bowl with the questions. "Go ahead. I'm getting hungry."

Unfolding the paper he'd selected, he scanned it. Then he cocked his head to the side, a devilish smirk on his face.

"What did you think the first time you saw me? Be honest, Red."

Damn it! I wanted to ask *him* that question. "I thought you were too handsome and too sexy to be real," I admitted. "I also thought you were having an affair with your assistant."

"We are. Or, we were." His tone was even and his face straight, so I totally believed him. "But she hated the pendulum so much she went back to her husband. I'm hoping when she gets your gift certificate she'll have a change of heart. The workday is so much longer without our midday sex romp." He sighed piteously.

I still would have believed him, but his lips twitched from his effort not to laugh. My lungs squeezed out the air I'd held in. "Geez, you're evil! You almost had me!"

"I know. You have a horrible poker face." His hand touched my knee in a gentle glide, sending another bolt of hot, heady awareness over me. "I believe you said you were hungry?"

"Oh, yes. Very, very hungry." I focused on the tray of food, considering what I might want to taste and where I might want to taste it from. Deciding how bold I could be. I had one thought, one utterly delicious, specific image in mind, which would require a fair amount of boldness. Not sure I was quite ready to pull it off, I went with my second choice, and selected the canister of whipped cream. "Lie down, Ben."

"On my back or on my stomach?"

"Your back."

He complied, and I scooted closer. My eyes soaked up the pure masculine beauty of his body. A ball of warmth ignited deep in my stomach, teasing out until every inch of me radiated heat. Straddling his waist, I closed my eyes for one beat . . . two beats . . . and then opened them. "Most women,"

I said, barely noticing the catch in my voice, "would probably squirt the whipped cream into your mouth. And then devour it slowly."

"But you are definitely not most women."

"No." I shook the canister hard. "I am not."

I pushed the nozzle down and sprayed the whipped cream in a circle around his left nipple. A breath shuddered out of him as I created a peak and filled the circle in. I searched the tray until I found the bowl of maraschino cherries. My fingers slid around a slick, wet cherry and I oh so slowly placed it on top. The whipped cream canister slipped out of my other hand, landing softly on the bed.

"Nice," I whispered. "Very, very nice."

His muscles clenched so tightly that I saw them tremble beneath his skin. I swished my bottom on his waist, teasing him. Tantalizing him. He shuddered again. His lips formed an O.

Dark, sensual, heavy-lidded eyes watched me, begging me to get on with it. Happy to comply, I leaned forward, keeping my eyes on his, until my lips touched the cherry. Using my tongue, I scooped the cherry into my mouth. I bit down, the juices exploding in my mouth, sweetness dripping down my throat. Licking my lips in my best porn-star move, I smiled. He groaned, so I must have been successful.

Scooting backward from his waist, I tightened my thighs around him. I felt the hardness of his cock pushing against his boxers, pressing against my panties, making me wet. So very wet. I moaned at the feel, at the reality of the position we were currently in, at the realization that nothing but a few pieces of fabric lay between us.

His hand came to the small of my back, teasing the lacy sheath up so he could touch my skin. "I think you should clean up your mess, Red," he said, his voice rough.

I blinked, not sure at first what he meant. But then, with

his other hand on the back of my head, he applied a small amount of downward pressure and I saw exactly what he meant. My whipped cream peak was melting—from the heat of him, from what I was doing to him—and dripping down the hard planes of his chest onto my sheets.

"I always clean up my messes," I said, and with my tongue I lapped up one mouthful at a time, catching the drips, tasting his skin again and again until he was, quite simply, licked clean. His erection throbbed beneath me when I sat fully up.

"You're a devil woman," he rasped. "How . . . how long is this game?"

I slid off of him, my muscles like jelly, my belly quivering, the power of the desire I'd engendered warming through me. Once I was back on my side of the bed, I batted my eyelashes. "We've hardly started. Don't tell me this is too much for you? I thought you were competitive."

"Oh, Red . . . you've seen nothing yet." And over the next hour and a half, he proved that. One question, one mouthful of food and one seductive taste at a time, we kissed, touched and savored each other in ways I couldn't have imagined.

Through the questions, I learned that Ben had one sibling, a brother, but that he didn't like talking about him. So much so, he wouldn't even tell me his brother's name. I also discovered that Ben was an Ivy League graduate, that he preferred summer to winter and that his favorite sex position was on top with a woman's legs wrapped around him. He learned that I believed in ghosts, hated slasher flicks, indulged in one glass of wine almost every night and fantasized about having sex outside beneath a star-filled sky.

At last, with only two questions remaining, I grabbed one from the bowl, just wanting to get this game over with so we could move on. Frankly, I didn't know how much more foreplay my body could handle. But I cleared my throat when I saw the question: "'Do you want children someday? If yes, how many? If no, why not?'"

He swallowed heavily. His body tensed and his shoulders stiffened. "No, I do not want kids."

His brusque tone startled me. "Why not?"

A veil came down, effectively hiding the emotion in his eyes. His tension increased, and the vein in his neck pulsated. Knowing I was cheating but unable to stop myself, I sent a mental push toward him, wanting to hear his answer.

He shook himself, drew in a breath and then said, "Kids require more than I'm able to give."

I sent another push. "What do you mean?"

"They take too much time. Too much love. I don't have enough of either."

I stared at him, trying to see inside of his head, wishing I could read his thoughts. No way did I buy his explanation as the full story, and seeing how I hoped to have children someday, his response shocked me. Saddened me, even. But rather than focusing on that, rather than using my magic to get more out of him, I set it aside. Whether children were in my future or not, I didn't know. What I did know, thanks to Alice, was that Ben *did* exist in my future, as long as I played my cards right.

I simply nodded and smiled. "You're right. Kids do require a lot of energy and resources. So"—I dragged my eyes from him and planted them on the tray—"what are you hungry for now?"

His tone became sexy, teasing . . . relieved. "I don't know, Red. What haven't I tried yet?"

I shrugged. "I think you've tried nearly everything. Haven't you?"

"Turn over and lie down," he ordered. "There's one thing left."

Without saying a word, I flipped myself over and pressed

my cheek into the pillow. I felt him shift on the bed. Then, something warm and sticky drizzled into the shallow depression at the back of my knee. I groaned.

"Chocolate?" I asked.

"Honey," he responded. Pleasure whipped through me as his tongue once again burned into my skin. My leg flinched and clenched as the pleasure turned to spasms of delight. I gritted my teeth and clasped the pillow. And then, I groaned again.

He stroked his tongue along the depression, and I had to work to keep my leg flat. With his mouth against my skin, he asked, "Do you know what this area is called?"

"The back of my knee?" I said in a breathy voice.

"Actually, this space here"—another languid glide of his tongue—"is called the popliteal fossa."

I gasped as tendrils of pleasure rippled out from my leg, through my body, tearing through my muscles. "How in the world do you know something like that?"

"I did a stint in premed before becoming a numbers man. And—you might find this interesting, Red—for some women, the popliteal fossa is a highly erogenous zone." Then, as if to prove his point, he suckled.

Good God, who knew that such an obscure area of your body could be so extraordinarily sensual? Not me, that's for sure! "It . . . um . . . feels pretty cleaned off back there now," I whispered. "Not that I'm not enjoying this."

"Ready to finish this game of yours?" Anticipation and longing hung in his voice, churning my own into a near frenzy.

"Yes. Are you?" I turned over and sat up, pulling my knees to my chest. My legs still trembled, my stomach dipped.

He pushed himself away, retaking his place at the head of the bed. "One question remaining. And it's *my* turn."

I knew what the question was, obviously, and again, it was one I'd hoped to ask him. "Go ahead," I said.

"Name something you'd change if you could."

"My relationship with my sister. We aren't . . . haven't been close for a while. I miss her, but"—I tightened my arms around my legs—"it's too late. Or maybe it's too soon. Regardless, now isn't the right time."

He reached over and ran a finger down the side of my cheek, looked into my eyes. I let my face drop into the touch. "Do you want to talk about it? We can hit the pause button. I'm a good listener," he offered.

Rebound guy, my ass. He'd turned me on repeatedly that night, but this one little gesture gave me more hope, and sooner than I'd expected. But no, I didn't want to talk about Sheridan. Not tonight. "I'd rather continue on. I've . . . ah . . . been waiting for this last question all evening."

He raised an eyebrow. "Oh you have, have you? Feel like telling me why?"

"Nope. I'd much rather *show* you. So, what I want you to do"—I placed the tray on the floor, but not before I grabbed my chosen food—"is to lean back on your pillows, but don't lie down all the way."

Curiosity and desire battled in his expression, in the deep blue of his eyes, but he obeyed instantly. Once he was in place, I straightened his legs and straddled myself low on his hips. He was hard. So very hard. I wiggled my bottom, feeling him throb beneath me, and I grinned. He choked out a laugh, but his gaze remained firmly planted on the fruit I cupped in my hands.

"What are you going to do with that?"

I cocked my head and winked. "Let me show you." And then, at a leisurely pace, as if I weren't dying to feel him inside me, I unpeeled the miniature banana. "These," I said with a heavy drawl, "are called Lady Fingers. Sort of appropriate, don't you think?"

He cleared his throat, a mix of danger and humor in his eyes. "What I think, Red, is that you've underestimated me."

In a purely male gesture, he drove his hips upward so that I could feel him pressing against my panties.

A shiver of anticipation rolled over me. "Such ego," I teased in a breathy whisper. "I chose this particular type of banana for one very important reason, and it has nothing to do with *that*."

"Then what would it be?"

"Ease of use," I replied. "Let me show you."

Leaning to the side, I dropped the peel into a wastebasket. Heat trickled into my cheeks, seeped into my body and made my hands tremble ever so slightly as I lifted the waistband of his boxers. Very carefully, in a slow and measured movement, I slid the minibanana into his waistband, leaving it at an oh-so-cute, if somewhat awkward, angle.

My lips quirked when the muscles in his abdomen shuddered. I loved seeing this: the proof that I affected him as much as he did me. Resting my palms on the bed for support, I slid myself down the length of his body just a little, and then I tilted my head and broke off the tip of the banana with my mouth.

He laced his fingers in my hair as he groaned. I lifted my chin enough so he could see into my eyes as I chewed. As I swallowed. As I licked my lips. And then I went for more. He muttered a curse. "You really are going to kill me tonight."

"That would be a pity." My lips wrapped around the banana again, and I took in another mouthful. I scooted myself backward a bit more. Nearly lying flat, my breasts tight against his thighs, my chin pressed into his groin, I used my tongue to retrieve the remaining fruit. Then, very slowly and very efficiently, I licked all leftover residue from his belly. His muscles tightened and released over and over and over again. My nipples hardened and fire pulsated in my blood.

"Enough," he said, his voice thick. "I can't stand any more of this."

Twisting my neck so my cheek rested on the hard angle of his hip, I looked into his eyes and licked my lips again. "The game is over. Want to go watch a movie? Or leave?" I inhaled a long, deep, deliberate breath. "Or would you, perhaps, like to leap on me?"

He growled and grasped me, pulling my body up, up, up until my lips hovered above his. "I want you." His eyes searched my face for confirmation. I nodded, and in one swift move he rolled us over so that he was on top. The kiss, when it came, was hungry and hard. His tongue invaded my mouth almost desperately, as if what he found there was the one and only thing he desired. I moaned as his hands slipped inside my panties, squeezing my butt and then traveling up to my hips, up to my waist, where he grabbed on, holding me close.

I ground against him as we kissed, enjoying the feel of him, savoring the sensations our touching bodies elicited. A sigh whispered out of me as he moved his lips to my ear and then to my neck, seizing my throat in an explosion of suckling and kissing, of tasting and exploring. One hand left my waist, skating up my body, until he found the ribbon that bound my negligee.

"I've wanted this off of you from the second you opened your door," he said.

"Then by all means, take it off," I whispered.

One quick tug and the loosely tied bow came undone. His mouth found my right breast, and he teased my nipple with his tongue before shifting to my left breast. I gasped in pleasure as a series of shivers coursed through me. His tongue moved between my breasts, igniting new fires along my skin until he reached my belly button. His hands found my bottom again, and he pushed me up tight against him. He groaned when I shoved my hips harder, when I pressed myself as close to him as I could, when I gyrated against him.

"Take. Them. Off," I whispered, ready to feel him, all of him, against me, on me, inside of me.

With one hand, he dipped a finger into my panties and yanked them down. For a few seconds, trying to remove this damn scrap of fabric that kept me away from him, I felt as if I were all leg, like a newborn colt. But finally they were off and instantly forgotten.

He dragged his eyes from my face to my breasts and down, then back up, locking his gaze with mine. "You're stunning, Chloe. I'm—"

"Shh. Just kiss me," I whispered. "Kiss me, Ben."

His lips came back, but this time the kiss was slow and intoxicating, as if he were putting his mark on me, as if he were making me his. Every muscle, every nerve, every bit that made me who I was tensed and released, relaxed and stiffened, yearned for and desired this man. My man.

I jerked at his boxers. "Now, you. Please."

Again we did the shimmy, the always-somewhat-awkward dance of pulling and tugging and removing. His erection pushed and throbbed against my stomach, his eyes were the darkest I'd ever seen them, far more black than blue, and his hands . . . well, they were simply everywhere.

"Condom? Tell me you have some, Red, because I—"

"Top drawer, left side."

He nodded, shifting his body even as I spoke, reached into the drawer and came back with a foil-wrapped condom. Using his teeth, he ripped the packaging off and rolled the condom on. "Are you ready?"

"Yes."

He spread my thighs open with his hands and then slid his finger inside, feeling my wetness, feeling my desire. My muscles tightened, heat and pleasure and want thrumming through me. "Are you ready?" he asked again.

"Y-yes."

His pushed another finger inside and rubbed both in slow, heavy circles. I thrust forward, pushing them deeper in, perspiration slick on my face, on my body. I rolled my bottom lip between my teeth as he took me closer, closer, closer to the edge.

"Are you ready?" he asked for the third time.

"Yes! P-please." The words shuddered out of me.

Pulling free his fingers, he pushed my legs up and toward me with his hands. My stomach clenched from need, my legs trembled from want. His eyes focused on mine, staring into me, seeing me as no man ever had. His hips pushed forward, the feel of him right there, right where I wanted him, and then, with one deep thrust, he entered me.

He groaned in that guttural way that speaks of absolute pleasure, absolute satisfaction. With both hands on his butt, I pushed him in deeper and harder, and I moaned as my body accepted him. Reveled in him, even. Letting go of my legs, he touched my breasts, rubbing his thumbs over my nipples, making me moan even more. I gasped as pleasure swirled in fast and heady. I wrapped my legs around him tight and ground my hips against his, over and over and over.

He picked up my tempo and thrust harder, his eyes never leaving mine. This, without a doubt, was the most intimate moment of my life. I pushed a breath out, pulled one back in, and then, when I thought I couldn't handle it any longer, when I was sure I was just going to flat-out die from the overload of emotions and sensations wrestling through me, I came, in a tingling, mind-numbing, all-consuming blast of pure energy.

"That's my girl," Ben whispered. Another thrust and his body tightened, stilling inside of me, above me, as he groaned. His eyes closed and the muscles in his cheeks flinched, the line of his jaw hardened as he held himself for one second . . . two seconds . . . three seconds, and then a long, slow tremble overtook him. I tightened my legs around him, watching as he reached the place he'd already brought me to. The beauty of him—of this moment—stole the last breath I had from my chest.

He crumpled against me, wrapped me up in his arms and, with his lips on my ear, said, "Good God, Chloe. This . . . you . . . Never in my life." His voice was rough, ragged and more than a little shocked. Capturing me in a tighter hold, he murmured again, "Never in my life."

"Me neither," I whispered, snuggling into his embrace. "Me neither."

I whipped the sheets off of the bed late the next morning while Ben showered. I'd already had my shower, as Ben insisted I go first. His original plan had been for us to shower together, which would have been lovely on all counts except for the fact that two people in my tiny shower would be far more awkward than erotic.

My entire body hummed with the aftereffects of his touches. I liked this. I could definitely get used to it. Grinning, I picked up the condom wrappers from the floor—four, to be exact—and tossed them into the trash. Three from last night, and one from this morning. Sex with Ben, by the way, beat the pants off of "mindboggling."

I'd just finished remaking the bed when a towel-wrapped Ben entered the room. Everything inside of me softened and heated up simultaneously. "You're so freaking sexy. How'd I get so lucky to meet up with you?" I asked.

"I was just thinking the same thing." He came to me and kissed me lightly on the lips. "We need to talk. There's something I've decided to tell you."

Oh, God, was this going to be another I'm-not-a-relationship-type-of-guy speech? Rather than saying that, though, I nodded. But everything inside of me hollowed out, terrified and sick at the thought. "Okay, sure. What . . . um . . . do you want to talk about?"

He grabbed his clothes from the dresser, sat on the edge of my bed and looked up at me. "This is difficult, and not something I'd planned on talking to you about." His face drained of color. "But I want you to know." He swallowed heavily. "I want to tell you about my family. You asked me the other day if I was married."

My heart stopped. "You said you weren't!" But then I realized he hadn't exactly said that. No, what he had done was skirt the issue by asking me if I'd go out with a married man.

"Tell me you're not married," I whispered, dropping onto the bed next to him. "I don't think I'll be able to forgive you if you are. Not after last night. Not after this morning."

"Look at me, Chloe." I did, and he stroked my hair. "I'm not married now, but I was, to a woman named Sara. We had a child together. A daughter."

"Oh! That's okay, that's fine. I love kids!" A huge amount of relief slid in, extinguishing the panic that had begun to build. A kid? I could handle a kid. No problem.

His Adam's apple moved with another swallow. The darkness from the day at the amusement park returned. Without knowing why, I put my hand on his bare knee, trying to offer him comfort. Pulling his wallet out of his pants pocket, he flipped it open and removed a picture. "This is Sara and Rissa, taken almost three years ago."

I accepted the photo and looked, curiosity about the woman he'd married forcing my eyes to her picture first. She was a long, lithe and very pretty blonde. My gaze then moved to the figure next to her, to Ben's daughter.

Goose bumps came in a rush of awareness. I brought the photo closer, squinting my eyes, thinking I must have lost my mind, thinking I was wrong. I had to be wrong. Because this was no child staring back at me, but a teenager. A girl with long blonde hair, a turned-up nose and strangely light sky blue eyes. *Mari.*

My Mari. Or rather, *Ben's* Mari.

"Did Sara get full custody or something?" I asked, every part of me totally fixated on the girl in the photo, on the help she claimed to need. On the help that only I could give her.

"No." Distress and agony weighted his voice. "Marissa and Sara died in a car accident a little over two years ago."

The walls closed in. I couldn't breathe. I tried to put my head between my knees to stave off the dizziness. But all I heard were Ben's words echoing in my head. *Marissa. Car accident. Over two years ago.* My mind latched on to his statement, to all that it meant, to the look on Mari's face when she'd pleaded with me for help. To the image, the two beams of light, the screams. To the light behind her, glowing upon her in an iridescent way. Like Miranda.

Mari was dead? A . . . *ghost?*

The room spun faster, and the dizziness took over, swallowing me away.

Chapter Thirteen

Fifteen minutes later, a fully-clothed Ben sat next to me on the sofa. I stared at him, not sure what to say, still in complete and utter shock. The universe was playing some sort of huge cosmic joke on me.

"You're sure you're not sick?" Ben asked. He reached over and felt my forehead. "No fever. That's good."

"Nope, not sick. I'm sorry for scaring you. I think . . . um . . . my blood sugar dropped or something." I sipped the orange juice Ben had brought. Rather than helping, the citric acid made my stomach churn all that much more. "H-how did they die?"

"As I said, a car accident. Rissa was driving, practicing for her driver's exam later that week." Grief and anger thinned his face, accentuating the planes of his cheeks and jaw. "I was supposed to take her out but got held up at work, so Sara did it."

"A c-car accident?" I'd almost forgotten that part of the revelation, what with all of my energy focused on Mari being Ben's daughter and, apparently, a ghost. Another round of lightheadedness forced me to gulp more juice. "My parents died in a car accident when I was twelve."

His eyes softened. "I'm sorry to hear that, Red. That must have been horrifying for you."

"It was. Still is, sometimes. But I had my sister, and we had an aunt who took us in. Not the same as losing a child, though. That's"—I closed my eyes and inhaled a breath—"incomprehensible. That sort of loss . . . Well, I . . . I'm just so very sorry."

"But you understand how this feels—waking up one morning to a completely normal day and then having everything drop out from beneath you."

"Yes. I do understand that." Too well, actually. "Do you know what happened? What caused the accident?"

His shoulders lifted in a heavy shrug. "From what they could tell, Marissa took a turn too fast and lost control. They think she overcompensated, veered into oncoming traffic." He grimaced and my heart ached for his pain, for his loss. "She slammed into a truck. Sara . . . wasn't wearing her seat belt. She died instantly. Rissa hung on for a few days."

"Oh, Ben. I'm so sorry. So very sorry." I flinched at the pain in his voice, but also at a bit of comprehension: the scarcely seen image of two beams of light must have been the oncoming headlights of that truck. I squirmed again.

"It just doesn't make sense. Marissa was a careful driver. We spent a lot of time on the road, and she took to driving easily. And Sara always wore her seat belt."

Okay, so something had altered their normal behavior. But what? I remembered the desperate whirl of emotions I'd experienced the last time his daughter visited. "What . . . um . . . type of girl was Mari? Was she happy?"

He gave me an odd look. "I've never heard anyone but her girlfriends call her Mari. She was always Marissa or Rissa to Sara and me. But yes, she was as happy as any other teenage girl. Some days more than others."

I downed the rest of my orange juice and set the glass on the end table. Mari hadn't been happy at the time of her accident, and she wasn't happy now. But I didn't know how to say that, how to explain to Ben that his daughter was somehow still around, looking for some type of help. "I'm sorry," I repeated. "I can't begin to imagine how difficult this has been for you."

"Listen. I didn't tell you about my family to make you feel bad. I wanted to be honest. I wanted you to know why I acted the way I did at the amusement park." Shifting slightly, he laid his hand on my shoulder. Weirdly, it seemed as if *he* was comforting *me*. "I was there the summer before Rissa's accident. We were there together. It was a yearly thing for us. She's the person who told me why Ferris wheels are 'the scariest ride ever.' You would have liked her, Red."

"I'm sure I would've." I breathed deeply, hoping to calm the swirl of nausea in my stomach. "I didn't know . . . I wouldn't have taken you there if—"

"Of course you didn't know. How could you? But I meant what I said the other day. I'm glad I went back, and I'm glad you were with me." He smiled sadly. "Being there helped me remember so many things about Marissa, things I hadn't thought about in a long time. So, thank you. You actually gave me a gift."

I opened my mouth, all set to just get the truth out there, knowing he deserved it said and hoping he'd listen, believe and understand. But before I could form my confession, a strange sensation overtook me. Goose bumps rose, an icy cold tingle sped down my backbone, and every hair on the back of my neck stood up. And then I saw her. *Mari.*

She stood on the other side of her father, looking every bit as solid as he did, and a deep, heartbreaking sadness emanated from her. Tears sparkled in her eyes as she shook her head. She held a finger to her lips and then, quick as a blink, she faded away in a ripple of colors. Again, I was reminded of Miranda. I wondered why I hadn't recognized the similarity before.

I swallowed as a new round of shock whipped through me. Mari wanted help but didn't want me to tell her father about her?

"Are you sure you're feeling better?" Ben's concerned voice cut in. "You look like you've seen a ghost."

A hyenalike laugh erupted from me. "I'm . . . um . . . just feeling a little overwhelmed."

He mumbled a curse. "I'm sorry for dumping all of this on you. You want some fun and games, not all of this baggage." In a jerky movement, he combed his fingers through his hair. "Not what you expected from a rebound guy, huh?"

I held back a sigh and returned my focus to him. "No, that's not it. I'm just so very sad for you. And I *want* you to be able to tell me things." Deciding to go for some modicum of the truth, I stroked his cheek. "Can we put this 'rebound' stuff away somewhere? Whatever we are, we are. I like you and I enjoy being with you. And when you say that stuff . . . it sort of eats in and makes me a little crazy."

A shroud of stress filtered over him. Grasping my hand, he squeezed. "I like you too, Red. Last night was wonderful and I loved every minute of it. We just don't know each other all that well and I can't—won't—make you any promises. I need you to understand that." His expression became even grimmer. "I don't know what any of this means. But after last night, keeping my family from you seemed wrong. I hope you can understand where I'm coming from."

"I totally do. And I'm glad you trusted me enough to tell me." Maybe he hadn't said exactly what I wanted to hear, but I'd accept it. For now. One day at a time and all that. "And I'm not asking for any promises. Just be you."

He sighed in relief. "I can do that."

I cleared my throat and pushed forward, intent on gathering more information. "You . . . um . . . must have been fairly young when Mar . . . Marissa was born."

If my change of subject surprised him, he didn't show any sign. Instead, he simply nodded. "We were. Sara was eighteen, just finishing up her first year of nursing school, and I was nineteen, in my second year of premed. When we found out she was pregnant, we married immediately." He blinked, lost in his memories. "That's when I switched majors, knowing that with a family I couldn't devote the years it would take to become a doctor."

"Were you happy? You and Sara?" I asked the question with the full realization that I didn't truly have a right. But I had to understand. And Mari's comments about her mother's sadness and her own anger refused to leave my brain. "I just mean . . . well, if you married that young . . ."

Ben stiffened and a glint shone in his eyes—a reflection of anger? Maybe. Or maybe something else. I just didn't know.

"We were focused on Marissa, and she made us happy. But if you're asking if Sara and I were happy as a couple, then no. Not for a long time, anyway."

"H-how come?"

"Sara . . . didn't love me. It's damn hard to make a marriage work when one partner wishes they were with someone else." He shook his head, a new battle raging in his eyes, in his expression. "We kept all of that from Rissa, though. For all of Sara's faults, she agreed that our daughter came first."

"You know . . ." I spoke carefully, knowing I was wading into murky waters. "Kids sense a lot of things that parents don't realize. Maybe Marissa knew more than you thought."

"Marissa didn't know," he said firmly. "We took every caution to keep her life steady and secure."

I pressed my lips together. Mari *had* known. I was sure of it, but it would get me nowhere arguing with Ben about a daughter whom, as far as he knew, I'd never met. Likely it would push us apart. "How are you?" I asked instead. "Dealing with a loss like this . . ."

"It's been over two years. The worst of the pain . . . I'm usually okay. As long as I focus on work and staying busy, I do fine. I can't allow myself to think about Marissa that often," he admitted shakily. "When I do, I can almost smell her. Sometimes I'm sure she's there, but I turn around and she isn't." He closed his mouth abruptly, as if he'd said far more than he planned.

Probably, in those moments, he *had* sensed her. Thinking I could broach the topic indirectly, I said, "Well . . . you know, I believe in ghosts."

Whisking a strand of hair off of my cheek, he tossed me a smile I pegged as completely false. "Let's move on to happier topics. You wore me out last night and I'm starving. Why don't you finish getting ready and we'll go get something to eat?"

I wanted to argue. I wanted to push him for more information, because there was more to this story, more that he wasn't saying. The temptation to use my magic was strong, and I gave the idea some serious consideration, but in the end I resisted the pull. I'd wait until I talked with Mari, until I learned more, before going down that road.

Or . . . maybe I was just chicken. Because the thought of ruining what had so recently begun filled me with terror. So right or wrong, I latched on to the promise of a day spent with Ben, of possibly reclaiming our momentum from earlier, before his revelation.

"That sounds terrific." I leaned over and gave him a long, slow kiss. His arms came around me, and for a few fleeting minutes everything felt exactly right.

Now, if I could only find a way to turn fleeting minutes into forever, to help Mari, to convince Ben I wasn't a loon, to mend fences with my sister and figure out the mess with Kyle . . . well, I'd be all set, wouldn't I?

By the time Paige arrived at the Mystic Corner on Monday morning, I'd decided on a course of action. Ben and I had spent the rest of the weekend together, and for the most part, every minute of that weekend had been luscious, wonderful and illuminating. Not only hadn't he referred to himself as my rebound guy again, but he seemed relaxed and at ease. Which, taking everything into consideration, I took as a good sign.

He hadn't brought up the subject of his daughter or wife again, though, and I—following his lead—hadn't done so either. That didn't mean they weren't on my mind, because they were. Especially Mari. So when Paige waltzed in through the back door thirty minutes before we opened, I was ready and waiting.

"I have a surprise for you!" I said as enthusiastically as possible.

She yawned and slipped off her backpack. "What type of a surprise?"

"Five days off with full pay. Starting now!" After all, Mari had only spoken to me when we were alone, so I wanted to give her every chance in the world to pop in. Even if that meant I flew solo for a few days.

Paige stowed her backpack and turned, eyeing me with confusion and a fair amount of suspicion. "You're going to pay me for the week? I've already used up most of my vacation time this year."

"Consider this a bonus. For your exemplary work ethic. You've earned it!"

Rather than the excitement I expected, Paige planted her hands on her waist and frowned. "What's really going on? Why do you want me out of here so badly?"

"Geesh, Paige. Most people wouldn't care why. They'd just be thrilled to have some extra paid time off." I gave her a bright smile. "Just go and enjoy your week. I'll still need you on Saturday, though. And before you ask, the store is still solidly in the black."

"Ohh-kay. Whatever you say." She went to retrieve her backpack but stopped midreach. "Actually, how about if I work this morning and then take off tomorrow through Friday? I mean, I'm already here, and I leave early, anyway. And that way you can get the payroll done, so I can get my check before I leave?"

Ugh. I'd forgotten about payroll. "Yeah, that will work. But I'll get moving on it right away, so you can get out of here extra early."

She gave me another curious glance but didn't argue. Once she headed to the front, I heaved a sigh of relief. Hopefully, Mari would show sooner rather than later, and hopefully, she'd be ready to tell me whatever it was she needed from me.

I turned my computer on and went to start a pot of coffee. Everything I did brought a twitch to my muscles, a reminder of every last thing Ben and I had done to each other over the past two days. Glorious, really, feeling like this. I waited for the coffee to brew, poured myself a cup and dealt with the payroll. While the checks were printing, I opened my browser and typed in "Sara and Marissa Malone, car accident, Chicago, Illinois," and then clicked *enter*.

After the results appeared, I clicked on a link to an article with the headline, CHICAGO AREA MOTHER AND DAUGHTER KILLED IN CAR ACCIDENT. I read the text quickly, looking for any bit of information I didn't already know but finding none. The story was short and to the point, stating that the accident was Marissa's fault, that Sara had been ejected through the window of the vehicle, the name of the driver of the other vehicle and that he had escaped free of injury. The article itself was probably no more than two hundred words, and even that bothered me. Two lives lost were boiled down to the barest minimum.

I closed the browser, not able to stomach looking at the article for another minute. "What really happened that night, Mari? What had you so angry, and why was your mother sad? Were you two arguing about something? The man she loved, perhaps?" I whispered the questions, somehow hoping the answers or the girl herself would appear before me. No such luck.

Pulling the checks off of the printer, I ripped off Paige's and started toward the door, ready to send her on her way. But before I walked even two feet, the door swished open and a very flustered Paige stepped in. "Kyle's here again," she said. "He wants to talk to you. Should I send him back?"

I swore. After not hearing so much as a peep from him the entire weekend, I'd begun to believe that Elizabeth's wish had fixed everything. Apparently not. I gave Paige her check and worked to keep my voice steady. "He didn't bring flowers again, did he?"

"No, but . . . he seems kind of angry. We were talking and . . ." She slicked her hands down the front of her skirt. "Should I send him back?"

"Yeah. Go ahead." I knew, after my intimate weekend with Ben, that even if everything with him exploded in my face, I would never be happy with a man who didn't make me feel as alive as Ben did. So at least my lingering doubts regarding Kyle were gone. Now I just had to remove his own so that *he* could be happy.

I stood in the open doorway, watching him approach. I gestured for him to come in and closed the door tightly behind us. "I'm glad to see you," I said softly. "I was hoping we'd have a chance to talk."

"I have one question," he said. "Did you use magic on me to make me say yes to your proposal?"

"Wh-what? Where did that come from?" Stupid question. This had Grandma Verda's name written all over it. I just wished she'd given me a heads-up. So I could've had some semblance of an appropriate response ready.

"Just answer the question, Chloe." He narrowed his eyes. "Is. It. True?"

Fisting my hands, I nodded. "Yes, it's true. But you've never believed in anything supernatural or metaphysical, so what . . . what did Verda say to make you believe?"

"She brought me cookies. 'Magic cookies,' she said. I told

her I didn't want them, and she started talking crazy—said you'd cursed me, and that I needed to eat the cookies to undo part of the curse."

"And that was enough?" I pushed out a squeaky laugh. "Verda has some . . . odd ideas."

"Yeah, that's what I thought, but I ate a cookie anyway. Then, over the weekend, I gave it a lot of thought and realized something." He shot me a look that dared me to argue. When it became apparent that I wasn't going to, he continued. "I've thought more about you since the night you proposed than I have for the entire time we dated. Like an addiction I can't get rid of. Is that just a coincidence?"

"It's not as if I gave you a love potion or anything. It was just a little spell that was supposed to relax your fears about commitment. But"—I swallowed—"it seems I spelled you twice, and that's why you're so . . . um . . . dead set on us being together." Oh, did Verda have a thing or two to hear from me. I'd done her a favor. A freaking huge favor. One her granddaughters wouldn't even do, and how did she repay me? By ratting me out!

"Say I believe this, and I'm not saying for sure that I do, but pretend I believe. Can you fix it?"

"Yes. Or . . . I think I can, anyway. You say you ate the cookies?"

He glowered at me but didn't speak. Then he nodded.

"Have they helped at all? Do you feel any different? Maybe everything is already fixed, but you're thinking too much about it so you haven't realized. Is that possible, Kyle?"

Crossing his arms, he stared me down. "I'm standing here and all I can think about is how I can get you to agree to marry me. But I know I'm not in love with you. Does that sound like whatever the hell was in those cookies worked?"

"N-no. Not at all." I sucked in a lungful of air. "Let's do this . . . So, um, close your eyes. I don't want you to see this. It might, uh, freak you out a little."

"You're serious? You want me to close my eyes?"

"I'm not going to beat you over the head or anything. I just . . . well, I'll have an easier time doing it if you're not staring at me. Okay?"

"Whatever." He grumbled and frowned and his entire body tightened, but he did as I asked. "Just hurry up. I'm late for work."

Nervousness whisked through me, but I centered my thoughts and focused on my breathing. I thought about Kyle, about how much I cared about him, about how important he was to me, but that I knew we weren't right for each other and that I wanted to set him free so that he could find the person—whoever, wherever she was—who was right for him. I envisioned him locked in a cage, one that I'd built with magic through my misguided emotions and wants, and then I imagined the bars melting to the ground and disappearing. When I saw this clearly, I reached deep inside and grabbed my magic. It switched on, fast and furious, alive and potent, whipping through me, feeding off of my thoughts, off of the image, off of everything I felt and wanted for Kyle.

I grabbed Kyle's hands and thought, I abolish whatever spells have been cast on you by my hand so that you'll regain full control of your will, and your choices, feelings, wants and desires are yours and yours alone.

I opened myself fully to the energy, allowing the magic to zip from my hands into Kyle's, knowing the physical touch wasn't necessary but not wanting to leave anything to chance. Several seconds, maybe a minute, passed in a blur of pulsating power that electrified the air. My lungs hurt from the effort to breathe, and my body trembled from the outpouring of magic, but I held on with everything I had, refusing to give up, refusing to turn away. Finally, I felt the subtle shift of power that told me the spell had been cast.

Squeezing his hands tighter, I breathed in through my nose and out through my mouth, trying to find my balance.

Another long lash of energy trickled through me, the air returned to normal, my shivers vanished and the power evaporated.

I dropped his hands and backed up a step, and then another, until I bumped up against my desk. "Done," I whispered. "That should . . . well, that should do it. You should be back to normal fairly fast."

Kyle opened his eyes and the tension in his shoulders eased. "How will I know if it worked? Not that I'm saying I believe in this or anything, but if I were to believe, how would I know?"

Good question, but I had a better one. "Do you still want to marry me?"

He didn't answer immediately. Angling his head to the side, he grew pensive, as if searching himself to find the answer. This, believe it or not, told me that the magic *had* worked, that I had cleansed him of the other spell. If he had to think about whether or not he still wanted to marry me, the chances were high he didn't.

Slowly, he shook his head. "No, I don't. I remember wanting to marry you, feeling as if I had no choice but to keep trying, but it's barely there now, and even that is fading away the longer I think about it." Clearing his throat, he stepped backward toward the shop door. "Magic," he scoffed. "What was I thinking? Maybe I just had to see you one more time to get those thoughts out of my head. Because we'd been together for so long."

Trying hard not to smile, I nodded. "You're right. That's probably it."

"The simplest explanation is usually the correct explanation," he continued. "So, thanks for humoring me."

My smile emerged. "Okay. If that's how you want to play it, then you're welcome."

His gaze darted around the room. "So this is it, huh?"

"It doesn't have to be. Can't we remain friends?"

A quirky, happy-go-lucky grin lit his face. In that second, my heart squeezed. Our relationship had meant so much to me for a long time. "You still want to be friends?" he asked.

"Of course I do! I owe you a lot, you know. No one else really stuck by me this past year, not the way you did. And back in high school"—I closed my eyes briefly as the memories swept in—"you . . . well, you made me very happy. You entered my life when I needed . . . when I felt lost and afraid, and even though I had Alice and Sheridan, you did something for me that no one else could. You"—I gulped as I made the admission—"took care of me. You made me feel special."

"You are special, and you helped me too, Chloe. It wasn't all one-sided." He cleared his throat again. "Come here."

I did, and he pulled me in for a hug. I held on tight, pressed my forehead against his chest and mourned one final time the fact that we hadn't been more than we were. I'd held on to the belief that what we had in high school was real and lasting, and that he'd made a mistake in leaving me. Letting all of this go was easier now. We separated, and my heart squeezed again. Not so much in pain as in loss, because we were finally, really and truly through.

"Hey, why are you looking so sad?" Tweaking my chin with his thumb and forefinger, he grinned again. "I'm not going anywhere, Chloe. Friends it is."

I gulped, and the tears I'd barely held back dripped from my eyes. Not a gush, not a flood of emotion, but appropriate nonetheless. "I want you to be happy. I want you to find the love you felt—feel—for Shelby with someone who can return it."

He kissed me on my forehead for old time's sake, and then gave me one more quick hug. "I wish the same for you. But I should take off, so I still have a job. Friends, though, right? You're not going to change your mind on that too?" he teased.

"Absolutely not." I watched him leave and then gave myself

a few minutes to feel whatever I was going to feel. The four drawings, the futures that Alice's magic had created, came to mind. Miranda had said that one of those futures would be the one I'd claim, and that the others were there because of certain choices and decisions.

I envisioned the drawing that had shown my future with Kyle, and then I visualized ripping the picture up and throwing the pieces away, because this choice had removed any potential for that specific future. Relief that I seemed to be making headway fluttered in, easing the bittersweet moment. Then, with my romantic relationship with Kyle put where it belonged—firmly in the past—I went to set Paige free so that I could wait for Mari.

Chapter Fourteen

"Sheridan, it's Chloe again. Your sister. You know, the girl you grew up with? I really want to talk to you, so could you please call me back?" I rattled off all of my numbers again then hung up the phone with a frustrated sigh.

Damn Miranda and her assurances. Sheridan obviously did not want to talk to me, did not miss me and had no desire to reconnect. The fact that she hadn't responded to any one of my three messages over as many days broadcast that statement loud and clear. I couldn't decide what bugged me more: that she hadn't gotten in touch, or that I'd allowed myself to believe we had a chance. So stupid of me.

I cursed Miranda again for giving me hope where none existed, and finished closing up the shop. After my luck with Kyle, I'd naively thought that everything else was finally sliding into focus. If someone had asked me Monday morning, I would've sworn that by today—Wednesday evening— I'd already have begun mending fences with my sister, and that I'd have a firm handle on the Mari situation. No and no. Because Sheridan wasn't the only person refusing to reach out. I hadn't seen even a glimpse of Mari since Saturday morning, when she'd phased in for all of five seconds.

Why she'd come to me before I knew who she was, and why she wasn't coming now that I did added yet another layer of confusion atop the already jumbled mishmash of strangeness. So that was why right before leaving the store, I grabbed a book from our stock of spiritual subjects. This one dealt in the afterlife, and within its many chapters existed a message that I wanted Ben to read. Maybe if I could get him to open himself up to the possibility of ghosts, we might have a chance of reaching Mari together.

Besides, I missed him. We'd talked on the phone each day, but hadn't set up plans to see each other until that Friday, for his charity function. I figured, if nothing else, the book gave me an excuse to spend a little more time with him. Nothing wrong with that.

The drive to his place took longer than I expected, partially because every single freaking traffic light seemed to have it in for me, but also because weekday evening traffic proved far busier than Sunday morning's. When I finally turned in at his driveway, a fresh crop of doubts swarmed in. I purposely hadn't called to warn him of my visit, because I worried he might make an excuse, or worse, just outright say no.

"Too late for second guesses," I mumbled after ringing his doorbell. Either he'd be pleased to see me or he wouldn't.

A few minutes passed with no response. I peered in through one of the narrow windows that framed his front door but couldn't see anything. Great. Just great. The guy probably wasn't even home. I pressed the bell again, trying to decide if it would be too stalkerish to wait in my car for him to return or if I should leave and go grab some dinner and then come back. Cupping my hands around my eyes, I peered into the window again just as a glare of lights flooded the interior. Startled, I jumped back and tried to calm my racing nerves, hoping for the best but bracing for the worst.

He opened the door, a quizzical gleam in his gaze. I swallowed and smiled. "Hey, Ben. Hope you don't mind an unexpected visit!"

He gestured for me to come inside. "Not at all. I almost didn't hear you, though."

I entered and took in my surroundings. We stood in a large foyer that had lustrous hardwood floors, expensive-looking paintings and a sweeping staircase. The hallway opened up to several rooms on the left, a dining room on the right and what I assumed was the kitchen straight ahead.

"So, what brings you over?"

Thankfully, he didn't sound displeased or unhappy to see me. Just curious. Taking that as a positive sign, I grinned again. "I missed you," I admitted. "Plus, I have something for you. You really don't mind I popped in?"

"Nope. In fact, I was going to give you a call after my workout."

And that's when I finally processed his appearance. He wore black shorts and a black tank, and his hair curled damply around his face. Beads of perspiration dotted his forehead, his face was slightly red and the muscles in his arms were tensed, almost bulging.

My lips felt dry, so I licked them. "I interrupted you. I'm . . . well . . . God, you look good."

He winked one of his incredibly blue eyes. "You look good too. Have you eaten yet?"

I shook my head, already feeling the heat Ben always ignited in me. "No."

"Want to stay for dinner? We can order out, and I'll go jump in the shower. There's something I want to get off my chest."

"Besides your shirt? I can help you with that." I grabbed the garment and tugged. "I'm quite good at getting your clothes off."

Desire roared to life in his eyes as his lips twitched with amusement. "Did you come over for a booty call, Red?"

I hadn't. Not really, anyway, but now that the subject was broached, every muscle in my body clenched, released and then melted. "Depends," I breathed. "Are you up for one?"

"Hold that thought," he growled. "Let me shower, we'll get some food, and then . . . we'll see where we're at. Sound good?"

Hm. Not exactly the response I was after. I'd have far preferred for him to sweep me up in his arms and then haul me off to the shower. That He-Man-like image brought another flush of longing. "Um . . . sure. Where should I wait?"

He led me to a large, slightly sunken living room off of the kitchen. The room itself was rectangular and boasted a stone fireplace at the far end, a wide, flat-screen television on one of the long walls, an oversized caramel-colored sofa, a couple of chairs and a square coffee table in front of the couch. This room felt like Ben, smelled like him, and just being there elicited all sorts of comfy, homey feelings inside of me.

Handing me the remote, he gestured to the TV. "Find something to watch and I'll be right back."

I nodded and settled into the lush, deep cushions of the sofa, automatically sliding my shoes off and curling up. Curiosity had me looking around for signs of his prior life, for photos of him with his wife and daughter, but other than one framed picture of Mari on the fireplace mantel, there were none. I thought about snooping while Ben showered, all in the name of learning more about Mari, of course, but common sense rode in. Skulking around his home and looking through his things wasn't only rude, but the idea of doing so made my stomach cramp—which was weird, I suppose. Using magic on him didn't make me feel ill, but secretly checking out his home did.

Not wanting to delve into the inane logic of that, I flipped the television on and tried to find something to watch. After clicking through a few dozen channels, I settled on a rerun of *Charmed*, thinking that maybe somehow I'd learn something about real-life magic. No such luck. But the program did manage to hold my attention well enough that I startled when Ben cleared his throat from the entryway of the room.

"Wow," I said. "That was quick."

He strode in, his long legs carrying him to me in barely a

blink. He still wore shorts, but this pair was of the khaki, pocketed variety, and his red short-sleeved shirt didn't stretch tightly across his chest like the black tank. That didn't change his sex appeal, however, or the fact that the very sight of him made my mouth water.

Sitting down next to me, he tossed me a smile that forced me to gulp. He asked, "Are you hungry? We can order a pizza, or if you trust my abilities in the kitchen, I can cook for us."

"I definitely trust your abilities in the kitchen, but how about pizza? That way we can talk." And maybe get to the bedroom that much sooner. But then I remembered he wasn't a fan of fast food. "Or you can cook, if you want."

"Pizza works." He waggled his eyebrows and a teasing glint appeared in his eyes. "But let's use plates this time."

Picturing eating pizza off each other, I laughed. "Absolutely."

We decided on a veggie pie with extra cheese, and he placed the order. While we waited for the delivery, I pulled the book out of my purse. Apprehension crackled in, because I wasn't sure how he'd react. But I had to move forward. "I told you I brought you something." I held the book toward him, and he accepted it.

He worked his jaw as he read the title. "*Understanding the Afterlife: Have Your Loved Ones Moved On?* What is this, Red? I don't think—"

"Just listen," I interrupted. "And then, if you don't want the book, I'll take it back. I . . . I know you don't believe in a lot of the things I believe in, and I'm okay with that. But this is about your daughter . . . so, can you give me a few minutes to explain?"

His complexion paled. Eyes filled with uncertainty met mine, but lurking there, beneath the darkness, existed a tiny speck of hope. "Go on. I'll listen."

"Okay, good." I inhaled a breath, trying to calm my racing

heart and pulsating nerves, knowing that the words I used would either relax his defenses or create a thicker, possibly impenetrable shield. "You told me that there are instances where you feel Mari—um, Marissa—and that you can almost smell her, she feels so close."

He nodded but didn't speak. Gripping the book tighter, his knuckles whitened.

"There is a chance that she's still here, Ben. That something is holding her to this world and she can't move on. Maybe there's something she feels is unresolved, or maybe"—I gulped—"she's trying to get your attention but doesn't know how to reach you."

He shook his head. "That's impossible. I know you believe in ghosts, and while I respect your beliefs, I need you to respect mine. Because, Red, I hate to tell you: when we're gone, we're gone. And Marissa is gone." That last bit tore out of him, right from his heart, and he flinched as he said it.

"There are unexplained happenings in this world every day," I pushed, not ready to give up. "I truly believe that Marissa is still here, and that she's trying to connect with you. What I don't know is why." I bit my lip, watching him carefully for his reaction. When he didn't respond, I continued. "You are her father. You were always there when she needed you in life. What if she needs you now? If there is the slightest possibility that I'm right, and that she is here, wouldn't you want to help her?"

Myriad emotions flashed through his eyes. "I can't deny I've felt something. But this . . . this goes against everything I believe. You"—his voice splintered—"really think this is real? That my daughter needs something from me?"

Believe? I *knew*. "Yes. I do. Don't you want to help her if you can?"

"If what you say is true . . ." The words ground out of him and his complexion paled another shade. "I have a really difficult time with that thought, but yes. If somehow Rissa is still here and needs something from me, then of course I would help."

"Then just read the book. See if anything in there resonates with you. Then, when you're ready, we can talk about this again."

He breathed in and out, the sound ragged. His grip on the book tightened even more, and a tremor whisked through his body. When he looked at me again, the disbelief hadn't vanished, but that speck of hope gleamed just a little brighter. "I can't believe I'm agreeing to this, but okay. On the off chance you're right, I'll read the book. But you need to understand that this is a hard pill for me to swallow."

Shivers of relief spilled through me. "Thank you, Ben. I know this is difficult, and I'm just grateful you're willing to do this much."

He opened his mouth to say something, but the doorbell rang, announcing the arrival of our pizza. Another shudder rippled through him. "Let's enjoy the rest of the evening, and after I've read through the book, I'll let you know my thoughts."

"Fair enough."

Opening the end table next to him, he slid the book in the drawer and went to get our dinner. My anxiety grew to a whole new level while I waited. What if I'd just made a mistake? What if, by pushing him to accept something so foreign to him, I ended up pushing him away from me? That thought settled in, screwing with my appetite and my equilibrium, but then Mari's pain came back. No matter what happened with her father and me, she was more important. Helping her came first. My tension relaxed, and by the time Ben returned, I had a smile on my face.

Over dinner, we chatted about work, politics, our favorite books and a variety of other subjects. When the last mouthful of pizza was eaten, the energy between us had stabilized and we were, thankfully, back on track. "You said there was something you wanted to get off your chest?" I asked Ben. "When I first got here. Remember?"

"Yes. There is." He put his empty plate on the coffee table and faced me. "I've been thinking about what we said to each other at the amusement park, about this being a fun and games thing for us. You said you were just out of a year-long relationship, and I called myself your rebound guy, which you plainly don't like."

Fuck. Oh, fuck. He was about to break things off. "Um . . . actually, it's more that I don't want to define this. I just want to take it one day at a time without rules. But if you want rules, then, well . . . I'll listen and—" I squeezed my eyes shut. Don't end this, Ben, I thought. We have a future to-gether, so hang tight. Stay with me. See where this goes.

The air stilled around us. My ears buzzed and my pulse sped up. Perspiration dripped down the back of my neck while I waited for his response. But I kept my eyes closed, not daring to see what emotions lurked in his.

"Red . . . look at me." His thumb brushed the area just beneath my right eye. "Come on, open up."

Not able to resist his voice or his touch, I did as he asked. He rubbed his thumb down to my cheekbone and then laced his fingers into my hair. I leaned into his hand, my entire body, every nerve and every muscle on alert.

"You said exactly what I wanted to say. I don't want to define this." His husky tone slid over me, easing in, calming my nerves. "But"—he cleared his throat—"I also don't want to think of you dating anyone else while we're figuring out what this is. So I wanted to know if there are any other men in your life right now."

Thank God he hadn't asked that a week ago. "No, there aren't. But what exactly are you saying? You don't want to define us as a couple—which is fine, I guess—but you don't want me to go out with anyone else?"

"Sounds rather selfish, doesn't it? I don't have sex with more than one woman at a time. I never have, and I don't intend to start that habit ever. So yes, Red, if we're going to continue to see each other, to sleep with each other, then I want to know there's no other man in your bed when I'm not there."

"Can I take that as meaning there will also be no other women in your bed when I'm not there?"

"Isn't that what I said? I'm not in the frame of mind to share you, and I hope you're not in the frame of mind to share me."

"I agree! No sharing!" I nearly yelled. Damn, this was good news. On every freaking level. I mean, no, he hadn't exactly declared his love for me, but we were one step closer. I was sure of it. "I'm glad I stopped in tonight," I murmured. "Really, really glad."

"Me too, though if you hadn't, we would've had this conversation over the phone."

"This is much better."

"Yes, it is." The blue of his eyes darkened. He swept his gaze over my face and his fingers tightened their hold on my head. "I don't understand my reaction to you."

"Geez, thanks. That's something every girl wants to hear," I mumbled.

He leaned over and kissed my forehead. "What I mean"—he kissed my nose—"is that you're"—he moved his lips to my ear, bringing his teeth down oh so lightly on the lobe—"affecting me in a way that I've never experienced."

"Not even with Sara?" I whispered, my entire body awash in trembles and shivers. His mouth continued to tickle and tantalize my skin. "And not since Sara?"

"Never with anyone. This is a completely new experience for me. It's . . . you're . . . intoxicating." His tongue found my neck in a hot rush of fire.

"Well, that's okay, then. I like being intoxicating." While

my body responded to his touches, to his caresses, a twisty, almost uncomfortable, sensation pressed in. Why was I intoxicating to Ben? Because of magic, because of my wishes and wants or because of me?

He kissed and suckled down my neck, and I moaned in response. I tried to set the squirmy feelings aside, tried to focus wholly on the wonderful sensation of Ben's mouth on me, but I couldn't stop thinking about what Elizabeth had said to me weeks ago about wanting to be with a man who wanted to be with me for me and not because of magic, not because of a spell.

The truth of those words sank in as they hadn't before. Because yes, I desperately yearned for Ben to want me all on his own, and while I'd accepted that without the magic, we wouldn't be sitting here now, that didn't mean I liked it. Panic started to build in my chest, nearly overtaking the intimacy of Ben's lips on me, but then I remembered that where we ended up was what mattered. Not how we started. I let my anxiety go and turned myself completely over to Ben.

His hand eased under my shirt, traveling up my back. With what could only be a practiced move, he unclasped my bra and pulled it loose so he could cup my breast. I moaned again, every part of me turned on and ready, just like that. Following his example, I pushed my hand under his shirt and stroked his back, delighting in the feel of his muscles as they tensed beneath my touch.

"Want to take this upstairs, or do you want to stay here?" His voice dripped with longing, with need. For me.

"I don't care. Anywhere. I just want you. I . . ." I arched my back as his tongue drove into my mouth, hungry and forceful.

"How about here and then, later, there?" His hands were at my shirt, pulling and tugging.

"Yeah, and then maybe even later somewhere else," I

teased, proceeding to help him remove each article of pesky clothing from both of our bodies.

We spent the next hour on the couch and then made our way to his bedroom, where we spent another delicious hour exploring each other's bodies. Each touch, each sensation drove my need for him deeper, and by the time we curled up together, completely and utterly sated, I couldn't imagine ever being with another man again for the rest of my life. The weight of his arm around me, the feel of his body pressed against mine and the whisper of his breath upon my ear lulled me, relaxed me, and with one last contented yawn, I drifted off, sure that everything was going to work out perfectly.

I woke with a start. My heart beat too fast in my chest and my breath erupted in tiny, wheezy bursts. Unsure of what had awakened me, because Ben still slept, I held myself motionless and just listened. Nothing, not one sound met my ears, but my heart continued to pound, and something—call it a sixth sense—told me to pay very close attention.

I took a few more minutes to come fully awake, and all the while I continued to listen, continued to trust my body that there was something going on that I needed to know. My sleepy, fog-filled brain finally cleared, and I knew without a shadow of a doubt what my instincts were trying to tell me. Mari. She'd been here, and maybe, just maybe, she still was.

Sitting up carefully, to not disturb Ben's sleep, I swung my feet around and stood from the bed. The air felt cold—frigid, really—and I reached around in the dark, looking for the pile of clothes we'd carried upstairs with us. Finding them, I slipped Ben's shirt over my head, the hem of it falling midthigh, and with a quick look toward Ben, I made my way to the door and eased it open as silently as possible.

Darkness loomed in the hallway, but I resisted switching

the light on. Instead, I shuffled slowly, stopping before one door and then the next, waiting for a tremble, a shiver, some physical sign that would announce when I found the right door.

It was the third from the master bedroom. One quick breath and I pushed the door open and stepped inside. I closed the door behind me before turning on the light. My chest tightened as I took in the room that had been Mari's, fully expecting to see her, and surprised and disappointed when I didn't. But yes, this had definitely been Mari's bedroom. I felt her here. Beyond that . . . well, the room had been decorated with a teenage girl in mind.

Deep, dusty pink colored the top of her walls above the chair railing, while the bottom was painted a warm, chocolate brown. A tall, full-sized bed with a comforter dotted in light pink, mauve and brown circles, and large plush pillows in the same colors sat in between two windows that overlooked the backyard. Posters and pictures of varying sizes were hung on the walls, along with shelves that housed books, DVDs, CDs and a few leftover dolls from her childhood. A desk with a computer, a dresser with her jewelry box, and a television rounded out her furnishings.

This room in all likelihood looked exactly the same as it had when Mari lived. The fact that Ben hadn't changed anything here in this space spoke volumes. Maybe Mari was hanging around because he couldn't let her go? Or perhaps he simply hadn't felt the need to change anything yet. It wasn't as though he needed the space.

My eyes searched the room again, and unlike earlier, when I'd pushed away the temptation to snoop, this time I followed through. I went to the desk first and opened a drawer, not even sure what I was looking for, but searching just the same. Guilt crept in as I flipped through pictures of Mari and her friends, as I sifted through papers, memorabilia and other odds and ends, but I kept searching. Closing the top drawer, I moved on to the second, repeated my actions there and then went to the third.

My fingers barely touched the handle when I heard the unmistakable sound of someone clearing their throat. I jumped. With my heart in my mouth, I pivoted on one heel, completely expecting to see Ben frowning, ready to lay into me. My excuses, all of which were lame, rolled to the tip of my tongue, ready to beg Ben for his forgiveness.

Mari sat on the edge of her bed, her arms angled across her chest and her feet dangling toward the floor. Her eyes bored into me, as if she knew how nervous and guilty I felt. "Hi, Chloe," she said, her voice so quiet I could barely hear. "What are you looking for?"

I cleared my throat. "Something to help me help you, I guess. I know there's a reason you're still here, but I don't know what that reason is. I'm sorry. I shouldn't have been looking through your things."

A light smile played across her lips. "Why not? I don't need them. But I don't think you'll find what you're looking for here."

I approached her slowly, trembling, wanting to do whatever I could to help her, to help her father, but still needing to understand how. "Then tell me. Why are you still here? What help do you need?"

Her teasing smile vanished, and just as before, a single tear trickled down her cheek. Again, her sadness and desperation churned inside me as if they were my own feelings. "But I don't know anything," she whispered. "I don't remember anything. I know I'm stuck here, and I think it's because of my dad and how upset he is, but he can't hear me. He can't see me. So how can I make him feel better?"

"What do you remember? Let's start there."

Her chin trembled, and her sky blue eyes rounded. "I only have memories of feelings. I remember my mom being sad and I was mad. So mad. But I don't know why." Another tear slipped out, and her voice clouded with pain. "No one but you can see me, Chloe. You are the only person who can help me."

I swallowed past the lump that had appeared in my throat. "I need more to go on, sweetie. Every part of me wants to fix this for you, but I don't know how. You have to give me something I can work with."

"But there's nothi—" Her gaze shifted to the door. "He's looking for you now. Please help me. Help him. So I can go be with my mother. I hear her calling for me and she sounds so sad."

"I—I'll figure this out. I promise," I whispered, my heart nearly breaking into two, hating how useless and inadequate I felt. "Is—" The door to Mari's bedroom swung open so fast, so forceful that the air blew against my hair.

"What are you doing in here?" Ben's voice was sharp, angry. "You don't belong in here."

I gulped and then bit my lip, knowing I couldn't tell him the truth but not sure what else to say. "You're right and I'm sorry. I . . . ah . . . was looking for the bathroom and stumbled in here."

The line of his shoulders relaxed but his frown remained. He searched my face carefully, as if trying to work things out. "Okay," he said. "I shouldn't have yelled."

"It's okay. I . . . surprised you. I understand that. But can I ask you something?" He nodded, so I forced the question out of my mouth, knowing I was probably going to tick him off all over again. "Marissa's been gone for over two years. Why does her room look as if she lived here yesterday?"

"Because I can't bear to get rid of her belongings. It's the same reason I still live in this house. This was her home." Annoyance flashed bright and hot in his eyes. "Why are you so curious about my daughter?"

I gulped again, not liking this side of Ben even if I understood it. "Because you're important to me and she is important to you. I care about what you care about, and if that scares you then I'm sorry. But that's the way it is." I lifted my chin, defiant.

His face softened minutely, but his emotions were still in conflict. Finally, he huffed out a breath. "God, I completely overreacted. I'm . . . I'm not used to sharing any of this with anyone. Can you forgive me?"

"Yes, if you can forgive me for trampling over your personal life."

"I can. I do." He walked toward me and pulled me into his arms. With his lips in my hair, he murmured, "Come on. I'll show you where the bathroom is, and then we can go back to bed."

As we left the room, I turned back for one more peek before closing the door. Mari still sat on her bed, tears rolling down her cheeks, her thin body shaking. I blew her a kiss—the best I could do under the circumstances—and then, when Ben pulled on my hand, followed him down the hallway.

For the remaining few hours of the night, sleep refused to come. All I saw were Mari's tears. All I felt was her heartache. And all I heard were her words, "Please help me. Help him."

I just wished I had the slightest inkling of how.

Chapter Fifteen

The following evening I gaped at Verda, not fully trusting myself to speak. Why oh why had I told her about Mari? I'd called her that morning to clear the air about Kyle, and somehow I'd spilled the entire story. Dumb, just dumb.

She'd taken action and arrived at the Mystic Corner along with her granddaughters thirty minutes before closing. I'd sent all of them into the back room to wait, because there were several customers in the store, but now the shop was closed.

I flipped my gaze to Alice, and then to Elizabeth. "How did Verda talk you two into something so extreme?"

Verda's faded blue eyes twinkled. "I promised I'd quit asking them to return my magic if they'd do this for you. They were quite happy to agree!"

Nice. Just . . . nice. "You did what? But—"

"Promises are important, Chloe!" Verda's high-pitched voice cut me off pointedly. "They shouldn't be taken lightly."

I narrowed my eyes. "Yes. I realize that. But Verda, don't you think you're crossing a line? Promising something that—"

"No! Use what you got, that's what I say." She gave me her cat-that-swallowed-the-canary grin. "And you're in a pickle and need help. So we're here for you."

"B-but a *séance*?" I gulped the word out, still not able to wrap my mind around the concept. "Mari talks to me without the help of a séance, so what do you think we'll accomplish?"

"She told you that she hears her mother calling out to

her. I bet we can connect with Sara and get the answers you need." Verda shrugged and then looked at me. "Do you have a better idea?"

Rather than answering, I returned my focus to Alice and Elizabeth, who'd yet to utter even a syllable. "You guys are really willing to do this? Séances aren't games. They should only be performed under the direst of circumstances!"

A shudder rippled through Elizabeth. "Hey, I don't even like Ouija boards, so I'm sure I'm not going to like this. But"—she tipped her head toward Verda—"she's going to do this with or without our help. I'd rather be here to make sure things don't get out of control."

"What do you mean she'll do this without our help? You can't really conduct a séance without the combined energy of a group. So if we all say no, then that's that."

Alice squirmed in her chair. "I *want* to do this. Besides, if we don't, she threatened to conduct the séance with her bingo friends. Apparently, they're all very excited at the possibility."

Okay, I have to admit that nearly made me chuckle. I repressed the urge, because a group of old ladies conducting a séance was not a good plan. But neither was this. "Verda, I'm putting my foot down. My foot is down!" I stamped it for good measure. "I absolutely don't think this is the way to go."

"Come on, Chloe—remember what we talked about the other day?" Alice pleaded. "This will make me feel better."

I knew she meant about Verda and the magic, but seeing as her crafty grandmother already *had* it, the worry in Alice's voice didn't sway me. Even so, I hadn't the slightest clue how to argue or convince her that this wouldn't change anything. I exhaled a breath, totally at a loss.

Verda, sensing my weakness, moved in for the kill. "This girl needs your help! You were almost in tears on the phone this morning, and that's when I knew we had to do this,

Chloe." She winked. "I owe you. Let me help you, that girl and her father."

Curiosity glimmered in Alice's eyes. "What do you owe Chloe for, Grandma?"

I pressed my lips together and looked to Verda for her response. Part of me wanted her to just come clean; the other part readied my legs to run in case she did.

"For her dedication to this family," Verda replied without missing a beat. "For all the support she's given you."

Alice nodded, accepting the answer without the slightest hesitation. "Okay, then I'm with Grandma on this one. Let's do this and get it over with."

I sighed in exasperation. "I just don't—"

"If you don't help Mari, then who will?" Verda's entire body vibrated with purpose. "I think about this poor girl and everything you told me, and I want to help her as much as you do. What if she were one of us? Would you hesitate then?"

No, and how fair was that? Everything in me wanted to fix things for Mari, not to mention for Ben. But there had to be a better—and less scary—way. "Do you even know how to conduct a séance? I've only ever sat in on one, and that was a long time ago."

"I did my research. On the World Wide Web!" Verda reached into her handbag and pulled out several folded papers. "It's all right here. And it seems really easy. With our history of magic, I'm sure we'll be able to pull it off."

Biting my lip, I thought about all the reasons I should say no. There were plenty. I opened my mouth, all set to quash this plan once and for all, when Mari's voice and tears and desperation flooded back. I sighed again, giving up. "Fine. I'll give this a chance, but we have to be careful." I glanced at Verda and nodded. "Go ahead and explain what we have to do."

Excitement filled her expression, and she unfolded her

séance papers. "We all have to agree on the purpose of our gathering. That would be to connect with Sara and to find out what's holding Mari to this world." Verda searched each of our faces. "It says this is really important, and that if even one of us has another purpose in mind, it can divide the . . . uh . . . psychic energy and ruin our chances."

"What else?" My stomach cramped. "I don't want to pull in some other spirit."

"That's why we have one solitary goal. And there can be no fear or cynicism inside any of us. And . . . oh! Hm, that's not good." Verda tightened her hold on the papers and she squinted, as if making sure she'd read correctly. "Is there any way we can get inside Ben's house and do this there? It says that we'll have better luck if we gather somewhere symbolic to the person we're trying to reach."

"Uh-uh. No way. Not happening." I shook my head, already imagining that conversation. "I barely got him to agree to read a book about the afterlife, so convincing him to conduct a séance in his house is a big no."

Verda sighed. "Well, we'll have to make do with this space then. Hopefully, the fact that Mari's appeared here before will be enough."

"It will have to be. Ben isn't ready to host a gathering meant to contact his deceased wife." I shuddered at the thought. "Let's move on. Is there anything else we need to know?"

"Nope, that's it. We just need to light some candles, play some meditative music, sit in a circle and hold hands and concentrate on connecting with Sara. This will be easy." Verda tucked the papers away. "You should have everything we need right here in the shop, Chloe. Let's get set up."

Uneasiness swept through me, but I nodded again. "I'll grab the candles and the music. You guys pull that"—I gestured to the small round table in the back of the room— "out more, so we can get chairs all the way around it. And . . . um . . . then we'll get started."

Ten minutes later, everything was ready to go. The four of us sat in an evenly spaced circle around the table. Soft music played, and I'd lit several candles. Weirdly, each of us had started speaking in whispers. "Now what?" I asked.

"I did the research, so I'll act as the medium." Verda sat up straighter. "We need to hold hands and focus on the purpose. You remember what that is, right?"

We all whispered a collective "Yes."

I reached one hand out to Verda and the other to Alice, and Elizabeth did the same. Once we were all holding hands, Grandma Verda closed her eyes. "We're gathered in this circle to reach out with love and positive energy for Sara . . ." She half-opened her eyes and frowned at me. "What's her last name?"

"Malone."

"We're trying to contact Sara Malone, who died in a car accident with her daughter, Marissa Malone. Sara . . . your daughter needs help and we don't know how to help her. We beseech your assistance, your knowledge and your love for Mari so we can clear her way to join you," Verda said softly, her tone mesmerizing. I was impressed. She certainly seemed to know what she was doing.

"Okay, girls. Close your eyes and concentrate on Sara. Make sure you only feel love and positive energy, and try to pull her to this circle."

I brought Sara's face to mind, focusing on how she looked in the photo that Ben had shared with me. Then I thought about Mari and allowed myself to feel every emotion I'd experienced whenever I was with her. Finally, I pulled in that scarcely seen image that must have been the accident itself.

I shivered as the air cooled upon my skin, raising goose bumps along with each and every one of my hairs. I pushed myself harder, trying to use *my* energy—*my* magic—to reach out, to somehow find Sara and bring her to us. This time, the power came slowly, much more like a sluggish drip from a broken faucet than turning on like with the flipping of a switch, but as it grew in strength, my body warmed and tiny tingles rushed through me.

Inhaling deeply, I visualized my energy combining with those of Alice, Elizabeth and Verda, enhancing what I could do alone, hopefully working as a magnet and drawing Sara in. Alice's hand trembled in mine, and Verda clamped down tighter. A wave of pulsating, electrifying energy whipped through me, through Alice and I assumed through Elizabeth, and finally, back to me through Verda. Then, as if I were teleported to some unknown place, everything and everybody disappeared.

A faint tugging sensation pulled at the center of my being, as if something or someone was trying to gain entrance. Fear skittered over me, through me, but I allowed myself to open up, to accept the possibility that Sara was here and that she was trying to reach me. A flickering series of images began to play in my mind, reeling by so fast that I couldn't tell what was happening or what I was supposed to be seeing. Not sure if Sara controlled the images or if they were a result of my magic, I first willed them to slow down and then pushed out a thought.

Slow down, Sara. I can't make anything out.

Almost instantaneously, the flickering paused before continuing onward at a much more watchable pace. I focused in and gasped, my muscles tightening with the realization of what I saw. Playing before me were various images of Sara and Ben. Sometimes they were embracing, sometimes they looked to be arguing, sometimes I saw pure love and adoration in Sara's eyes, and in other instances, I saw . . . well, not much of anything. In some I saw anger and unhappiness.

This continued on for a while, I don't know how long, and I tried to understand why this message was important, tried to comprehend what information I was supposed to grasp. I watched Sara and Ben pass college age and become adults, and still the emotions changed between them in nearly every flash, in nearly every image. They *had* loved each other; I could see that. What I didn't know, what I couldn't figure out, is why Sara's love seemed to switch on and off through the years.

Well, Ben's too. Though through all of the images, I never saw the love in his eyes that I'd seen in my vision of our wedding day. But there were moments, scattered here and there, that I witnessed something very close. As if he wanted to be head over heels but wasn't quite there, or maybe she kept pushing him back. Damn it! I couldn't tell. The desire to learn fueled my power another degree, and then suddenly, the flickering pictures of Ben and Sara vanished.

The energy in the room and in me swirled on. In another minute, something new appeared behind my closed eyelids. Sara stood in her kitchen—Ben's kitchen—with a phone to her ear. Tears were in her eyes, her cheeks were flushed bright red and her arms trembled. Then, as if a camera were on her, as if it panned back, I saw the entirety of the room and the nearby hallway. Standing there was Mari. Her body was pressed against the wall, as if she didn't want her mother to see.

I heard a crackle, a buzz, and then a woman's voice erupted in my head. *Sara's* voice. But like a weak radio station, her words faded in and out, sometimes scratchy and sometimes clear. "I love you! I've always . . . loved . . . should have waited . . . married then," she said. "You know she could be yours! Don't you care? Ben knows now. I told him . . . Rissa. Tired . . . waiting."

Mari barreled into the kitchen. I thought she was going to confront her mother, but she didn't. Instead, she grabbed the car keys from the table and ran out. Sara hung up the phone and followed. The scene blacked out, but then another image appeared, this one showing them in the car. Except now I couldn't hear anything.

My heart rate picked up and I wanted to shout, to tell them to stop the car and get out. But of course I couldn't. It wouldn't have made a difference, anyway. Sara still cried, but now Marissa did too. It was obvious she wasn't paying any attention to the road, but rather to the emotional discussion with her mother. Again, I wanted to scream at them. Why couldn't I stop this? What good did it do for me to see?

Mari turned the wheel with way too much force, and then she tried to correct her mistake. Headlights blared into the car. She opened her mouth in a silent scream. Everything went black. Before I could react, before I could even blink, Sara's voice whispered in my mind.

Tell Ben I'm sorry. Tell him she's always been his.

And then: *Tell Rissa I'm waiting for her, whenever she's ready.*

"Oh, my God," I whispered, still caught in everything I'd seen, everything I'd heard. My body shook and my throat ached. The phone call whipped into my mind, the barely heard words, and they seemed to back up what Ben had told me. That Sara had loved another. My brain zeroed in to that part of Sara's statement, and shock coursed through me. Was there a chance that Marissa wasn't Ben's biological daughter? Is that what Mari had heard?

My heart went out to her, to that moment of stark realization when every truth she'd known was tossed back in her face. If I was right, then her anger at her mother made perfect sense. But then I thought of the first set of images, with Sara and Ben, and the love that was sometimes there and sometimes not. What did that mean?

Opening my eyes, I couldn't talk immediately. I continued to try to make sense of what Sara had shown me, but there was far too much that I didn't—couldn't—comprehend.

"Well, that was a bust," Grandma Verda said. "I'm sorry

this didn't work, Chloe. I thought it was going to at first, what with the blowing wind and all, but then nothing."

I stared at her, incredulous. "You didn't hear or see anything? Really?"

"Nothing at all. What about you girls?" Verda asked Elizabeth and Alice.

They shook their heads.

Okay, so Sara's spirit had contacted me and me alone. I opened my mouth, all set to share everything I'd seen and the little bit I'd heard, when Verda's eyes widened and her chin trembled. "Girls!" She squeezed my hand hard. "Close your eyes again and think of Harry. He's here!"

"Who's Harry?" I asked. But then I realized. Harry was Verda's late husband. He was here?

"Grandpa," Elizabeth answered. "Are you sure, Grandma?"

She snorted. "Of course I'm sure. We were married enough years for me to recognize his presence. Think about him, girls. Remember what he looked like and how he sounded and help bring him in closer." Her voice shook with indignation. "I have a few things I've been waiting to say to him!"

Wrung dry myself, I doubted I'd be of much help but closed my eyes and thought about Harry. Not that I'd ever known him well. He'd passed away just a few months after Alice and I became friends. But I had a vague recollection of his face and a slightly stronger remembrance of his voice. I focused in on those and tried to recreate the push of power I'd experienced with Sara.

The energy fluttered in, even lighter than before but still there. I grasped hold and switched my focus to Verda and how this was important to her, even if I didn't know why. A slight tremble whisked along my skin, and the power throbbed from inside of me, catapulting out through my hands to Alice, then on to Elizabeth, and returning to me through Verda.

"You want me to apologize to you? Why, you old coot! I'm

not the one who took a mistress!" Verda's voice reached my ears, but I didn't open my eyes. Obviously, Verda heard her late husband just as I'd heard Sara. I clasped her hand tighter.

"Grandma? Are you okay?" Elizabeth whispered. Verda didn't respond. At least not to her.

Verda huffed out a breath. "Oh. Well, I suppose that's okay then. I'm sorry I used magic on you, but that spell was supposed to lead you to me. Not to Shirley. How was I supposed to know that you'd choose that ridiculous woman over your own wife?"

I opened my eyes to find Verda had opened hers. Her face was all scrunched up, and if lightning bolts could actually shoot from one's eyes, well . . . let's just say she had that look.

"What's that? I can't hear you. Haven't you learned to speak up yet?" Verda sighed, as if totally exasperated. "That has nothing to do with you! I know what I'm doing, and it has to be done. You don't understand any of this, and I don't have to listen to you anymore!" She huffed. "Oh, just go back to wherever you came from."

As soon as she uttered those words, the energy whipped away in a blinding flash. Verda tilted her head, as if trying to sense if Harry had truly left. Apparently, he had.

"Well . . . that man hasn't changed one iota in the twenty-plus years he's been dead! Telling me I owed him an apology, and then telling me how I should conduct my life. As if he has any right!"

Alice eyed Elizabeth, and Elizabeth shrugged. Turning to her grandmother, she said, "Are you sure Grandpa was really here?"

"I might be old, but I'm not senile. That was him. Sneaky old man, finding a way to reach me." Verda's voice quavered and her eyes were misty. "I shouldn't have told him to leave. But he got me so mad, I spoke without thinking."

Elizabeth scooted her chair closer and gave Verda a hug. "What did he say that made you angry? Is he worried about something?"

Verda's cheeks became a rosy pink. "None of that matters. Not now, anyway." Looking at me, she asked, "Did Sara contact you?"

"Yes. But are you positive you're okay? It's not every day you have the chance to talk to your late husband." Or argue with him.

"I'm fine. I do not wish to discuss Harry any longer. What I want"—she swung a defiant look to each of us—"is for you to share your experience with us. That's what matters."

Elizabeth and Alice narrowed their eyes but didn't argue. Taking my cue from them, I nodded. "Okay. Let me tell you what happened."

When I finished, all three of them gaped at me. "You have to tell Ben now," Verda said. "He needs to hear Sara's message and what you saw. You can't keep this from him, Chloe."

"I don't intend on keeping anything from him, but I'm not going to tell him just yet, either. I'm going to try to talk to Mari first and see if I'm right. I . . . can't tell him that Mari might not be his biological child unless I know that's actually what Mari heard her mother say. I could be misinterpreting, and if I'm wrong . . ." I blinked away tears. "No way will I hurt Ben like that without knowing."

What I didn't say, what I wasn't ready to admit out loud, is that I *was* sure. Between what Sara had shown me and things that she, Mari and Ben had said, well . . . I couldn't see how my perception was off. But there were still things I needed to know, so I held on to the belief that waiting just a bit longer was the smart way to go.

I wanted to protect him. I wanted to hide this from him for as long as I could. Besides which, being the messenger for this totally sucked, and I wished I could forget about everything I'd seen and heard. But I couldn't. Not when this information might be the answer to setting Mari free.

I pulled my car to a stop in front of the house Verda shared with her live-in boyfriend, Vinny, and turned the ignition off. Elizabeth had brought Verda to the Mystic Corner, but I'd insisted on taking her home. She'd been uncharacteristically quiet for the entire drive. Normally, she had a million and one topics of conversation right at hand.

I pivoted in my seat to see her. "Thank you for insisting on doing the séance tonight. I wasn't sure about it, but at least I have a few more answers now."

"You're welcome. I'm sorry you're having such a struggle with all of this, but you know I'm here if I can help. Don't forget that, Chloe."

"I won't. But right now I want to talk about you and this promise we made to each other. Alice"—I swallowed heavily—"told me that you've been having a dream, and that's why you wanted the magic back. Is that true?"

She arched an eyebrow. "So you know, eh? I shouldn't be surprised. You girls share everything. I shouldn't have tricked you into returning the gift, but after Alice and Elizabeth reacted so strongly, I was afraid you'd respond the same."

"That's okay. I'm not worried about that, and I would've helped you even if I had known. But I'm worried about you. And I'm curious if whatever Harry had to say to you tonight has something to do with all of this." I broached the question carefully, not wanting to upset her again, but also with the full desire to figure out exactly what was going on.

She unbuckled her seat belt and took a long, deep breath. "I'm not ready to explain. There are certain steps I'm taking right now that I don't want anyone to interfere with." A small laugh tittered out of her. "None of this is important in the scheme of things, sweetie. But yes, Harry thinks I meddle too much, and he told me so. But he doesn't have all of the information. Or if he does, he doesn't understand it. He's still the same stubborn man I married all those years ago."

I wanted to push her for more but didn't. She had the right to a few secrets at her age, and I had to believe that she'd come to me, to her granddaughters, when she was ready. "Okay. I trust you and trust that you know what you're doing, whatever that is, but remember that I'm here for you too. That road goes both ways."

With a quick, tight squeeze of my hand, she smiled. "I know that, dear."

"Good. I'm glad." I paused. "What was it like, talking to Harry after so many years?"

"Wonderful! I do wish I hadn't sent him away, though. As much as I care about Vinny, Harry was my first real and true love. We built a life together, and for most of those years it was a good life. I've missed him just as much as I've missed butting heads with him." Her smile brightened even as her eyes grew misty again. "That probably sounds silly to you, doesn't it?"

"Not at all. Maybe when this is all over with and things are settled with Ben and Mari, we can have another séance. For the express purpose of contacting Harry, so you can finish your conversation with him. When you're prepared to talk with him."

"Oh, yes. I would like that." She closed her eyes, sighed and opened them again. "There should be plenty of time for that. Thank you for offering, Chloe, but now I need to get inside and check on Vinny."

I watched her until she was inside the house before driving off, wondering what she had going on inside of that head of hers. No matter what she said, hearing her dead husband's voice couldn't have been easy. And that, of course, brought my thinking back to Ben, and to how in the world I was going to explain the fact that I saw and spoke with his daughter on a somewhat regular basis, and that his wife had given me a message to pass on. Why the responsibility had fallen on my shoulders, I didn't know. What I did know, to the bottom of my soul, was that the conversation would be the hardest of my life.

Chapter Sixteen

From the second Ben arrived at my door on Friday night, I felt like a princess being taken to the ball. He looked princely in his black tux, and while my classically styled black evening dress wasn't exactly Cinderella's luxurious gown, that didn't stop Ben's eyes from nearly popping out of his head. Everything seemed perfect. As if we'd truly stepped out of real life and into a fairy tale, where nothing could go wrong and good always triumphed over evil. I knew that this night was going to be fantastic. Well, I thought I knew that. I changed my mind shortly after we actually arrived at the charity event.

Nearly two hours later, I sipped my wine in an attempt to calm my jittery nerves, no longer basking in the fairy-tale glow. Glancing around the room, I tried not to stare too hard at Chicago society's crème de la crème. They were all here: politicians, local and a few nationally known celebrities, and anyone else who might be found on a list of who's who in Chicago. Not to mention gazillions of Ben's relatives. Yes, I mean gazillions. They were everywhere. So to say I was slightly overwhelmed would be a huge and complete understatement.

His family members, upon introduction, always looked at me oddly, as if they were startled to see that Ben had brought a date. After that moment of shock, they began sizing me up. In all likelihood they were comparing me to Sara, and I had no way of knowing how I measured up. Mostly I tried to keep a smile on my face, my posture straight and—throughout dinner—to use the correct piece of silverware.

At the moment, it was dessert: a luscious-looking chocolate mousse of which I'd barely eaten three bites. I gulped another sip of wine before inhaling a breath. Ben's hand skimmed along my knee as if he sensed my discomfort, while he chatted with the man on the other side of him. It didn't help, but I appreciated his awareness.

As people finished eating, they began strolling out of the room, moving into various other areas that had been set up to reflect a casinolike atmosphere. Instead of winning cash, there were donated prizes up for grabs. I'd learned that tonight's event was to benefit a local charity for the homeless. Apparently, Malone & Associates hosted the event annually, choosing a different charity each year out of hundreds of applicants.

Ben leaned over and whispered in my ear, breaking into my thoughts, his breath warm and tingly upon my skin. "There are a few more people I have to say hi to before I'm all yours. Do you want to come along, or are you still finishing dessert?"

"I think I'll wait here. If that's okay?" With the room emptying at a breakneck pace, I might be able to reclaim my balance by the time he returned. Unlikely, but it was worth a shot.

He kissed my cheek. "Enjoy your chocolate and I'll be back."

I picked up my spoon and mashed the mousse around, not really interested in eating, just wanting to get through the evening so I could go home and be with Ben. Alone. Preferably in bed.

"Is there a problem with your dessert?" An older man, also dressed in a black tux—as were most of the men in attendance—eased himself into the chair Ben had vacated. He tossed me a mischievous grin. "Or are you as nervous as you look?"

"I'm nervous." I dropped the spoon on my plate. "There

are so many people here, and way too many of them are staring at me. I'm the white elephant that no Malone can keep his or her eyes off." It was an amazing moment of blurted idiocy.

"You're Chloe, right? I don't think we've had the pleasure of meeting. I'm Jason Malone." His grin grew. "Ben's father."

My jaw opened. I snapped it shut. "Well, of course you are. Who else would you be?"

A delighted laugh boomed out of him. "Now, now, no reason to become flustered. I just wanted to say hello." He angled his mostly gray-haired head ever so slightly toward the next table. "Don't look, but my wife's sitting over there. She's also staring at you."

I grabbed my wine. "It's nice to meet you," I said as primly as possible, hoping to come off as a little more with-it than I felt. "I'm . . . uh . . . having a very nice time tonight."

"No, you're not. But you will. Soon enough the focus will change to something or someone else and you'll be able to relax. We really don't bite. I promise."

I let out the sigh I'd been holding. "It's just . . . a little overwhelming. Ben didn't mention how many of you—um, of his family—would be here. I feel like I'm in the middle of some initiation ritual." Immediately embarrassed, I set my glass down and placed my hands on my lap.

Jason Malone shook his head, chuckling. "Nah, that doesn't start until the third family gathering. Seriously, we're all happy to see you. I hope you'll forgive us for being interested in the girl who's found a way to make that boy of mine laugh again." The man's blue eyes—the same blue as Ben's, by the way—twinkled with good humor, but beneath that twinkle, a layer of concern loomed. "He's had a tough time of it. We all have, but him more than the rest of us."

I angled my head to see if Ben was anywhere close, so I could wave him over, because I thought it strange that his father was totally at ease discussing any of this with me, let alone with Ben in the same room. Unfortunately, Ben was nowhere to be seen. My nervousness ramped up another level.

"I'm . . . um . . . very sorry for all that he's lost," I murmured, not sure of the proper or expected way to respond.

The good humor disappeared as the man's concern deepened. He lowered his voice. "Benjamin has built a shield around himself that none of us has been able to breach. It makes sense and it's understandable, but that's not the life I want for him." Ben's father's gaze shifted away from mine for a second. "Has he mentioned his brother?"

"Well, I know he has a brother, if that's what you mean. Is he here?" Curiosity made me search the room, which was silly, because it wasn't as if I'd recognize him. Well, not unless he had the same bluer-than-blue eyes his father and Ben shared.

Jason Malone's mouth straightened into a rigid line. "No, but he might show up later. I wanted to let Ben know. You might want to mention it if you see him before I do." He cleared his throat as if suddenly uncomfortable, as if realizing that he'd said more than he should. "I'm pleased you're here, Chloe. And I'm pleased to hear my son's laugh again. I genuinely hope both continue."

Emotion welled up in me, both at his candor and his geniality. "I hope so too. I'm . . . well, I care a lot about your son."

"I can tell. And he cares about you. I saw the way he looks at you, and that's something else I haven't seen in a long time." He brushed his clean-shaven jaw with his fingers. "Too long. Might I ask how you two met?"

Happy to be navigating a somewhat safer topic, I smiled. "He came into my store to purchase a gift for his assistant."

Gray eyebrows bunched together, just the way Ben's would. "You must have made some impression for him to ask you out. I don't think he's asked a woman out in"—he shook his head—"a very long time."

Heat gathered in my cheeks. "I . . . uh . . . sort of did the asking."

Ben's father laughed. "Good for you! That's how I met my wife, Clara." He gestured again to the woman at the next table. "She decided I was the man for her and let nothing stand in her way. We've been together for going on forty years."

Wow. Just wow. "You're both very lucky."

"We are." His blue eyes latched on to mine, and I had the sense that he was staring right into my head, deciding my worth. "Ben's going to do well with you. I can feel it."

Before I could think of a reply, let alone voice one, Jason Malone stood and reached out a hand. "I have to schmooze with the guests now, but you have a good time. And don't let any of the family worry you. We're curious, but we're harmless."

I gave him my hand. He gripped it in a tight, firm hold. If a man can truly be measured by the strength of his handshake, then Jason Malone measured somewhere near the top. "It was very nice meeting you, Mr. Malone."

"Jason," he ordered. "Clara will probably bend your ear at some point tonight, but she's harmless too."

I stole a look at Ben's mother. She smiled and nodded her head. I returned her smile, but the butterflies in my stomach fluttered harder. "I'll try to remember that. I . . . ah . . . should probably find Ben and see what he's up to." Ben's father nodded and gave me another searching look, but I was pretty certain I'd passed muster. At least for now.

After he walked off, I sucked in a breath. And then another. I drank down the last swallow of wine and forced myself to chill out. All of this was normal. Of course Ben's family would be interested in the first woman he'd brought into their circle since his wife's death. It made perfect sense. But wow, talk about unsettling.

Ben showed up, stopping beside my chair. "Have I told you how sexy you look tonight?"

"Yes, but that's okay. I don't mind hearing it again." Relieved beyond belief to see him, I stood up. "You're looking pretty sexy yourself, Mr. Malone."

He chuckled, but an uneasy glint flashed over him, surprising me. The look vanished so quickly, I wondered if I'd imagined it. "Be careful, Red. There are close to a dozen men here who go by 'Mr. Malone.' I don't want any of them to think you're referring to them."

Pleasure flushed through me, warming my limbs to a jellylike state. "I'm here with you. I'm not interested in any other Mr. Malone."

"You have no idea how glad I am to hear that."

"Though I did just meet your father. If I hadn't met you first, he might be able to steal my heart," I teased. "He's quite charming."

"How long did it take him to get over here after I left you alone?"

"About three seconds." I was all set to give Ben the message about his brother when his mouth spread into a wide, teasing grin. I narrowed my eyes. "You knew your father would come over if you left? You should've warned me!"

"I wanted you to impress them, and if I'd warned you, then you might have worried too much about what to say." His arm swept around my waist. "So, how'd the meeting go? Did Mom come over too?"

"The meeting went fine, and no, your mother just watched from her table. But she smiled and waved."

Ben tipped my chin up and then bent over to kiss me softly on my lips. "My family will adore you. But even if they didn't, they wouldn't say that. They want me to be happy, Red. And right now, you make me very happy."

"Oh, I feel . . . I'm happy too." A cozy warmth curled out from somewhere deep inside, pushing all other thoughts away. At that moment, I decided to enjoy this evening and whatever it brought. I, for the moment, had the seal of approval from Ben's dad, and Ben was happy with me. Tomorrow or the next day, or whenever I saw Mari again, would be time enough to burst this bubble. And that day, regardless of how necessary it was, would come far too soon.

"So . . . what should we do now? I'm assuming you can't leave yet?"

"Nope, not yet. We can get another drink, or we can try a bit of gambling, or we can meander around and I can introduce you to more of my family." He waggled his eyebrows. "Whatever you want."

"Gambling. Let's do that!" I said brightly. "I'm sure we'll bump into your family as we go, so no need to search them out."

He laughed again. "Gambling it is, but first we have to register. There are prizes to be won, and one of them is a romantic weekend getaway."

An entire weekend away with Ben? My skin warmed even more, and some of my tension eased. "We should go register, then. Before someone else wins our prize! Maybe Lady Luck will be on our side tonight."

His hand flattened on my hip, and a thread of heat seared me. Just a simple touch, but Ben had that effect. "I'd say Lady Luck is already with us. Let's go see if I'm right."

Once we registered, we hit the blackjack tables. Ben sat on one side of me, and a woman he introduced as his cousin sat on the other. I expected a round of questions from her, but other than a friendly smile she focused on the game. Thank God for that.

The table started off hot, with the dealer losing the first five hands. Ben won three of those, his cousin one, and a guy at the far end of the table another. We stayed for four more rounds and then moved to the roulette wheel. Neither of us won anything there, but that was okay by me. Because while we weren't on the fast track to winning any prizes, Ben remained by my side the entire time. That, as far as I was concerned, was a win all on its own.

"Go grab a table and I'll get the drinks. Do you want a chardonnay?" Ben asked as we stepped into the bar after deciding to take a break from the gambling. The room had been recreated to look like a casino nightclub, with flashing lights, scattered tables and a makeshift dance floor.

"Yes, please." While he disappeared into the crowd, I found a table, purposely choosing one near the dance floor. I wanted to dance with Ben. So very much. I wanted to feel his arms tight around me as we moved together to soft music.

I sat there for a few minutes, pleasantly distracted by those thoughts, when a new one reared its ugly head: did Ben know how to dance? Did he even like dancing? Ugh. How could I not know something so simple about the man I was certain I'd be spending my life with? New anxiety lashed through me, chasing away my momentary calm. I fidgeted in my seat, trying to work out why this bothered me so much. It shouldn't have. After all, it took time to get to know someone, to learn about the different aspects of their personality, about what they liked and didn't like.

"You have a frown on your face, Chloe," Ben said as he arrived with the drinks. He handed me my wine and took the chair next to me. "Penny for your thoughts?"

I pushed my lips into the semblance of a smile and attempted to sound lighthearted. "They're worth far more than a penny. You'll have to cough up a whole dollar, at least."

"A dollar, eh? How do I know the info's worth it?" His voice was teasing, but he nervously strummed his fingers on the table. "Really, Chloe, what's worrying you?"

"I'm just . . ." I told the truth because there were already so many secrets I was keeping from him, I didn't want to add even one more to the pile. "Well, I was sitting here waiting for you, and I realized how much we don't know about each other yet. I feel so close to you that I guess that bothered me. Like I should know everything already."

"We have tons of time for that. But ask me anything you want." He tipped his glass, the ice in his drink clinking against the side, swirling around in the amber liquid.

"Okay." I nodded toward his glass. "You knew I'd want a chardonnay, but I have no idea what your drink of choice is. What are you drinking?"

"Scotch on the rocks. Single malt." He swallowed a mouthful, then grinned. "But I don't have a drink of choice."

Still, I filed this information away for future reference. "How about dancing? Do you like to dance?"

"If I'm with the right woman, I do. Maybe we can hit the dance floor after we're done with our drinks and I'll show you that I don't have two left feet. How does that sound?"

"I'd love that," I agreed.

We continued talking while we sipped our beverages, but neither of us seemed to be in the frame of mind for more than general chat, partially because the music was so loud, and partially because of all the people surrounding us. Still, it was nice, and for the first time all evening I truly began to relax. So much so that when Ben pulled me to my feet and led me to the dance floor, every part of me vibrated with a heady warmth.

I stepped into his embrace, and he tugged me close. My arms wove around his neck, and I stared up, lost in the blue depths of his eyes. He bent his head, and his lips began at my ear in a soft nibble and then trailed across my skin with one small kiss after another. The heat in my belly branched out, slowly suffusing me, until my entire body blushed. My mind emptied out, and I allowed myself to experience the moment, this dance, with every one of my senses: the clean, pure, wholly freaking male scent of Ben, the feel of his hands on my back, the stroke of his lips along my skin, his body pressed tightly against mine.

Delicious curls of longing trickled over me, through me, turning the fire up even more. It didn't seem to matter where we were or how often we were together. My body—my soul—recognized this man, and every nerve, every muscle, every tiny molecule of my being came to life under his touch. When I'd dropped into the drawing of our wedding scene, I'd experienced a love I'd never felt before. It had stunned me, changed everything I wanted, and now, as I danced in Ben's arms, I recognized that love as becoming a reality inside of me.

I sighed as the music ended, and the next song blasted out in a fast, upbeat tempo, breaking the soft, romantic mood like a sledgehammer. We separated, but Ben kept his arm on my back as we left the dance floor.

I stood on tiptoe so I could whisper in his ear. "That was lovely."

He tightened his hold on my waist. "You're lovely, Chloe. Every man here is green with envy because you're on my arm."

"I'm sure that's not true, but thank you for seeing me that way." I was about to say more, about to tell him how very much I enjoyed being with him, when I felt that odd sensation of someone watching me. It burned into my back, and I shivered. I scanned the room, but there were so many people that there was no way of ascertaining if I was right.

Probably just another of Ben's relatives sizing me up. I shrugged it off and gave Ben a quick kiss on his cheek. "Let's get out of here. The music is starting to give me a headache."

We walked out of the faux nightclub into the overly bright hallway. My eyes watered from the sudden brilliance, and I stumbled as we rounded a corner.

"Are you okay?" Ben asked, holding me upright. "Too much to drink, not enough food or a little of both?"

"None of the above. The change in lighting threw off my balance. I'm fine now. Really."

He searched my face, nodded, and we continued on until we reached the end of the hallway, merging into an area that resembled a lounge. A few people were milling about, chatting with others, obviously taking a break from the festivities. Ben led me to a sofa and we both sat down. He stroked a finger along the line of my jaw.

"This isn't the place, but later, I want to talk to you about that book. I've read it, and I'm interested in hearing your thoughts."

"Oh . . . okay. That's good." Everything inside paused and went on alert at his words, which was ridiculous. He'd done as I'd asked, even quicker than I'd assumed he would, and was now willing to delve into an area he found uncomfortable. I should've been pleased. This was a discussion we definitely needed to have, both for his sake and for Mari's. Possibly, even for Sara's. But an icy band of fear appeared, making me tremble.

Concern etched Ben's features. "You're not feeling well, are you?" He cursed under his breath. "I'm sorry, Red. I should've been paying more attention. Wait here and I'll let the powers that be know we're taking off."

I felt just fine. Physically, anyway. But I was beyond ready to leave, so I didn't argue. "Who are the powers that be?"

"My father and my uncle." He leaned over and kissed my forehead. "Take it easy and we'll be out of here in no time."

The mention of his father reminded me that I'd never relayed the message about his brother. I grabbed his arm before he could stand. "Oh! Wait a second. I was supposed to tell you that your brother might stop in. I'm sorry, but I completely forgot until just this minute."

Ben stiffened. His jaw tightened, and the vein in his neck throbbed. In a tone far more frigid than an arctic freeze, he said, "And there's another good reason we should leave."

"You . . . uh . . . don't want to see your brother?"

"Not tonight, I don't."

"I take it you two aren't close?" I pushed, knowing I shouldn't.

"No, we're not. But my relationship with Gabe has nothing to do with my relationship with you. And I prefer not to discuss him or our"—his Adam's apple bobbed as he swallowed—"falling-out right now. Especially not here." He looked at me intently. "Okay?"

"Yeah. Sure. That's fine, Ben. I didn't mean to pry." I spoke with the full knowledge that this was a story I needed to hear. But he was right that we weren't in an ideal location. And at least I knew his brother's name now. That was a start. "We can talk about this later. When you're ready."

He gave me a terse nod. "Give me a few minutes, and we'll make our escape."

"I'll just sit here and wait." He took off and I worked through everything I knew, trying to fill in the blank areas, and the answer I came up with was chilling. Was it possible that Ben's brother was the man whom Sara had loved, the man who might be Mari's biological father? Oh, God. If I was right, how much did Ben know? Did Ben know his paternity was in question? What message, exactly, was I supposed to share with Ben, and which one would help Mari?

My confusion increased tenfold when I considered the flickering images of Sara and Ben. Sara hadn't shown me another man in those images. So maybe I'd misunderstood the phone call, and therefore Sara's message?

I leaned back, resting my head on the cushion of the sofa, and closed my eyes. I replayed the images in my mind, trying to remember everything I'd seen and heard. The problem was, they didn't match up. When I thought about the scenes of Ben and Sara, I believed that she *had* loved him, had wanted their relationship to work, but something kept getting in their way. And then, when I considered the phone call and Mari's emotional response, along with Sara's whispered words, I believed Ben's take: that she was in love with someone else. So where did the truth lie?

I groaned, my head beginning to throb from all the questions, from the mystery that refused to be solved. It was as if someone had hidden the most important clues, and with the information I currently held there was no way to find the answer. The pressure of someone sitting down next to me forced my eyes open. Ben smiled and looked at me inquisitively.

"Hey, sexy," he said. Leaning close, he nuzzled my cheek with his lips. "I've been looking everywhere for you."

My heart picked up an extra beat in surprise, but also with something else. Something I couldn't identify. "I've been waiting right here. Just as you asked."

"Oh. Right. I thought you might have decided to come look for me." He winked and then pushed his hand behind my head, drawing me to him. His mouth took mine in a fast, hard kiss while his other hand landed on my knee. I waited for the thrumming pleasure that being near Ben always brought forth, but instead a cold ball of apprehension flared out from inside of my stomach. Panic grew in my chest, stealing my breath away. Trembles of fear slid over my skin. This was wrong. So wrong.

But why? I tried to relax, tried to melt into the kiss, but it didn't work. Instead, my panic built to a suffocating pressure and I pressed my hands against his chest, hard, shoving him back. I shifted farther away and stared at him, looked into his eyes and then dropped my gaze to his jaw, to his tux, to his hands. Feeling as if I'd lost my mind, I shook my head and gave him another once-over. This man looked like Ben, and sounded like Ben. But my body told me he *wasn't* Ben.

I narrowed my eyes, now noticing his hair. Did it look a tiny bit longer? I shook my head again, feeling dazed and unsure, but the panic in my chest increased.

"You . . . Who are you?" I whispered in a halting voice, knowing I sounded like a crazy person but trusting my instincts. "You're not—"

"Wasn't Sara enough for you, Gabriel? This game got old a long time ago." Ben—the real Ben—interrupted, his voice furious. He approached in fast, ground-eating steps, every part of his body on edge and a blaze of anger in his eyes. I catapulted upright, feeling cold and numb and even a little dirty. I looked from him to Gabriel, and my mind solved the question my body had raised so vehemently. They were brothers. Identical twins.

I opened my mouth to tell Ben that I'd known from the moment his brother touched me that something was wrong, but before the words came out he grabbed Gabriel's arm and yanked him up.

"You've gone too far. Get the hell out of my life and leave my women alone!" Rearing back, he punched his brother in the jaw. Gabe crashed backward, once again landing on the sofa.

"Heya, Benji. I figured that was the quickest way to get you to talk to me." Rubbing his chin, Gabe shrugged, as if he'd expected the punch, as if he knew he'd asked for it. "I need you to understand the truth. It's time we resolved this, don't you think?"

Ben reached out to haul his brother up again, but I stepped in between them, totally aware of the growing crowd of onlookers. "Ben, let's leave." I grasped his arm and tugged. "Come on. Please? Let's just get out of here."

He focused on me, anger and betrayal and hurt darkening his features. Without saying a word, he reached into his pocket and pulled the valet ticket out and handed it to me. "Go wait in the car, Chloe. I'm not finished with my brother yet. We"—he spoke the words slowly—"have unfinished business."

I looked from one brother to the other, but neither appeared ready to budge. This, whatever this was, didn't really involve me. And while I wanted to stay, wanted to protect Ben, I also knew he needed me to leave.

"Fine. If that's what you want." I turned on my heel and faced Gabe. "If you ever try to pretend you're your brother with me again, I'll punch you somewhere it will really hurt. Got it?"

His lips twisted into a grin as he nodded. Weird, but I thought I saw a glint of satisfaction in his eyes. Pivoting back to Ben, I stood up on my tiptoes and kissed him on his cheek and whispered, "I knew he wasn't you. But thank you for rescuing me."

Ben's eyes softened. "Please go wait in the car. I won't be long."

Knowing I couldn't dissuade him, I left the room with shaky legs and a rapidly beating heart. I kept my gaze straight ahead as I made my way out into the night air, and while I waited for the valet to bring around Ben's car. It wasn't until I was safely inside and had pulled the car up so that it was out of the way that I realized something I should have latched on to immediately. Gabriel was Ben's *identical* twin brother. They looked exactly alike. Which meant, they both looked like the man in my drawing. *Either* could be the man in my drawing.

Everything inside of me bottomed out, and a whole new slew of shivers overtook me. Fear crawled up my throat. I tried to swallow it away. I tried to calm myself. I tried to think about this new dilemma as rationally as I could. Of course, that was impossible. Because now I had to seriously consider if I'd been focusing on the wrong man this entire time. Was there any chance at all that Gabriel was the man in my picture, the man from whom I'd felt such strong love emanate when I'd fallen into our wedding scene?

Bile replaced the fear in my throat. Nausea twisted and churned in my stomach. No. Just . . . no. He couldn't be.

Not with the way my body reacted to him as opposed to Ben. Not with the heat that had coursed through me the very first time I'd laid eyes on Ben, not to mention the complete and utter intimacy we'd found with each other. So, no. It couldn't be Gabriel in that picture. That would be the worst joke ever. Worse than anything else I could imagine. Because I'd lied to myself earlier that evening, during my dance with Ben. I wasn't *falling* in love with him. I was already there, whether the timing made sense or not, whether other people would say it was too fast or not. I was in love with Ben Malone. Not with Gabriel. Nothing would change that.

But . . . had I fallen for the wrong man? Or was Gabriel yet another test of fate, to see how I'd react? Honestly, if so, I was getting pretty damn tired of fate screwing with me.

It was that moment I decided I'd had enough of fate. It was time—past time—for me to take control, for me to put into motion the future I wanted. I wanted it with Ben. Even if, for some reason, he wasn't the man in my drawing, I didn't even care. He was the man for me. I was as sure of it as I was of the creepy-crawly sensation I'd experienced with Gabriel. That had been pure instinct; it had been my heart and soul not recognizing him as the man I loved.

Feeling better, I closed my eyes and thought about how much I believed in me and Ben. About how I'd been able to see us together almost since the minute we met. Another surge of calmness erupted from deep within, and I smiled.

"Hey, fate?" I whispered. "Go to hell. I'm in charge now."

Chapter Seventeen

Ben drove us to his house in total silence. I figured he needed the time to come to grips with whatever had developed with his brother, and I had my own thinking to do, so the quiet came as a relief. It was also a relief to be going to his house. I'd been half-afraid that he would insist on taking me home.

He carried my overnight bag into his place, and I excused myself to change into more comfortable pajama bottoms and a short-sleeved shirt. When I found him in the kitchen, I had a momentary spasm of panic. This was the setting from my vision at the séance, except Ben hadn't been there. I could almost see Mari huddled in the hallway and Sara in tears on the phone.

With great effort, I shoved the disturbing image away and turned my attention to Ben. He had on a pair of gray sweatpants and a white T-shirt, and a pot of coffee was brewing. He nodded toward the table. "We should probably talk."

"Yes, we should." I sat down. "There are things I need to say to you as well, but I'd like you to go first." Tonight, one or way another, he was going to learn about Mari, the séance and Sara. Even though I'd hoped to see Mari again first, I couldn't put this off any longer. But hearing his side would, I hoped, give me the complete picture before I shared the bits and pieces I knew. Regardless, right now my concern was for him. "Are you okay?"

He shrugged. "I don't know if I am. I've known you for what? Two weeks . . . almost three? You've made me want things I haven't wanted in longer than I can remember. I don't understand that, but when I saw Gabriel with you"—he ran his hand over his jaw—"it brought me back to a place I never wanted to visit again."

"I knew he wasn't you. It didn't make sense that I knew, but when he touched me . . . well, everything inside tightened up." I shivered at the memory. "For a second, I thought I'd lost my mind."

The coffeemaker beeped. Ben brought the pot, two mugs and the carton of half-and-half to the table. Sitting down, he poured two cups. "That's my fault. I should've told you I had an identical twin."

I wrapped my hands around my mug, the warmth soaking into my skin. "Why didn't you?"

"I'm not sure. Eventually, I would have. But I try not to think about Gabe, and he wasn't supposed to be there tonight. That's the only reason I went. We tend to take turns at company and family gatherings now. Ever since . . ." He clamped his jaw shut. "That's not an excuse. I'm sorry, Red. I'm so sorry I put you in that position."

"You couldn't have known he'd be there." I remembered the burning sensation of being watched after our dance. Gabe. Otherwise, how would he have recognized me? "And even if you had, how could you have known he'd pretend to be you?"

Ben drew in a ragged breath. "I might have guessed."

That startled me. A lot. "How so?"

"It's a game we used to play. It started way back in high school. If he was dating a girl he really liked, I'd pretend to be him to see if she could tell us apart. He'd do the same for me." Ben shifted in his chair, obviously uncomfortable with his admission. "We used to say that the girl who could tell us apart was the girl we'd settle down with. Only none of them ever did." He planted his gaze on me. "Until you."

A warm glow of satisfaction unfurled in my chest. I *had* known. Suddenly, the look in Gabe's eyes made sense. "Your brother was happy I knew, Ben! I mean, I don't like what he did, but maybe he had good intentions?"

"No. He wanted my attention and got it. I've painstakingly avoided him, and he decided it was time to get something off his chest. So he used you to get to me." There was more pain in Ben's voice than anger.

Suddenly, sickeningly, what Sara had shown me earlier slid into place. "Sara loved Gabe, didn't she?" That's what those images had meant. They weren't all of her and Ben. Some were of her and Gabe. That's what she'd been trying to show me: how she'd loved one brother and not the other. "Oh, God, Ben. I'm so sorry."

"How did you know that?" He gulped a swallow of coffee and then shook his head, as if how I knew didn't matter. "Yes, and it all started with this stupid game we thought was so clever."

"Tell me," I whispered. "Tell me what happened."

By the way his jaw clenched, I didn't think he would. A few minutes passed, and he nodded. "When I met Sara, I fell for her fast. We slept together after our third date, and by our sixth, I'd already decided she was the girl I was going to marry." He chuckled humorlessly. "I used to be a romantic."

A quick spurt of jealousy tightened my throat. Which was completely ridiculous. "Where does Gabe come into the picture?"

"My brother joined the army instead of going to college. He came home for a two-week leave before deployment. I was under a lot of stress with school, so when he suggested that we play our old game and that he take Sara out so I could study, I foolishly agreed."

"And she couldn't tell you apart?"

"Not at first. They went out, had too much to drink, and apparently she had more of a connection with him than with me. He felt the same connection, so he confessed who he was. They ended up in bed. I didn't know this for years."

Ben gulped down another swallow of coffee "But after their date, Sara ended our relationship, saying that we'd gotten too serious. That she wanted to focus on school. I believed her. And Gabe said very little about their night out. But a month or so later, Sara discovered she was pregnant. So we married."

"But you had no idea she'd slept with your brother? Why didn't she contact him? Why didn't he tell you?"

"He was deployed and wasn't easily reachable, and I don't think Sara knew how to get hold of him. Anyway, he didn't know she was pregnant or that we married until he came home. By then, Rissa was a little over a year old, and he says now that he didn't want to disrupt our family." Ben's eyes clouded with disbelief. "He actually told me that he thought he'd be able to stay away from Sara and let us be happy."

"But . . ."

Ravaged eyes met mine. "Sara and I had an active sex life up until she met Gabe. She had no idea whose baby she carried. With Gabe gone for two years, she . . . she decided to cut her losses with me, rather than being a single mother."

"Wh-when did you find this out? How . . . how could she do that to you? To Gabe? How could *he* do this to you?"

"You think I haven't asked myself that question? I don't know! Sara was excellent at keeping secrets. Gabe didn't live in Chicago until the year before the accident, when he was discharged from the army, so I rarely saw them together." Ben closed his eyes. "I feel like an idiot that I didn't catch on. Our marriage was never easy, but we had Marissa, and there were good moments that I'd hold on to, believing we had a chance. Once a year or so, Gabe would come home for a visit and Sara would change, grow colder and become more difficult for months after. I never made the connection."

At that second, I wanted to strangle both Sara and Gabe. I also wanted to pull Ben into my arms and comfort him. I did neither. "Until?"

"Until a few months before the accident. I came home unexpectedly. They were arguing, and I heard everything. I remember standing there, listening to her wail about how miserable she was, and him telling her repeatedly that they were in an untenable situation. That he wouldn't hurt me by taking my wife away." Ben growled. "What a joke. As if sleeping with my wife throughout my entire marriage wouldn't hurt me."

Anger and pain became a hard, tight ball in my chest. "What did you do?"

"What could I do? I confronted them. Gabe apologized, but it was kind of late. Sara was strangely calm, as if she knew I'd been listening. She . . . seemed relieved that she didn't have to pretend anymore. She asked for a divorce so she could be with Gabe. I told her that Rissa would stay with me, but that she could have the divorce. And then I went back to work because I couldn't handle being around them."

"But you . . . you didn't divorce."

"No. When I came home that night, Sara had a sudden change of heart. Told me she was sorry, that she wanted to make things work and that she'd stay away from Gabe. I didn't believe her, and I didn't want to 'make things work,' but I thought that if we could hang on until Marissa turned eighteen and left for college, things would be easier on her. Rissa was all I cared about." Ben stood and paced the kitchen, lost in his memories.

My heart shattered as I watched and listened to him. No wonder he'd closed himself off from life. He'd thought he had everything and then found out that the two people he should have been able to trust most in the world had betrayed him beyond reason.

He cleared his throat and continued. "What I didn't know until tonight, what my brother has been so dead set on telling me—as if I would suddenly see him as an upstanding man—was that she'd wanted Gabe to fight me in court for paternity of Marissa. He refused. He told her that I was Rissa's father by the very fact I'd raised her, that no court would see it different, and that he wouldn't do that to me or to Rissa even if there was a chance. After hearing that, Sara got cold feet. As much as she claimed to love my brother, she still loved her daughter more."

Okay, that information helped ease the seething anger I was feeling toward Ben's brother and late wife. Not much, but a little. "You *are* her father. You know that, right?"

Ben stopped pacing and faced me. "In my heart I am—was—her father, but I hate that I'll never know for sure. And with her gone, it's like I can't let go of this one thing. Most of my adult life has been consumed by a lie, and I—I just want to know the truth, but I have no way of finding out. Not now. Not ever."

"You could have done DNA testing, couldn't you? We still could! I saw Mari's hairbrush in her room the other night. We could—"

"Identical twins, Red. Our DNA is the same, at least as far as a paternity test goes. So no, I'll never know. It shouldn't matter. I raised her. I loved—love—her. But this is tearing me up. Because if I'm not Rissa's father, then what did all those years mean?"

And there was the answer I'd been searching for. Ben's emotions regarding his daughter were tying her to him, tying her to this world. But how in the hell was I supposed to fix that?

"Mari is still here," I blurted before I lost my confidence. "She's confused by a lot of things, but she wants to move on. I think she can't because of what you just shared."

Icy blue eyes met mine, and a shiver rolled down my spine. "What do you mean, she's still here?" His gruff, doubtful tone sent another shiver through me. "You're saying this as if it's a fact. As if you know it to be true."

"I do know. I've seen her. I've talked with her. Before I even knew who she was, Ben." I grabbed my coffee and swallowed a gulp, burning my throat in the process. I coughed but forced myself to continue. "She . . . she came to me at the Mystic Corner the same day I met you. But she didn't talk to me then. It was . . . um . . . the day I asked you out. And then again the day you came to see me there. Oh, and I also saw her in her bedroom. That night you found me in there. She was there, Ben."

I stopped speaking and watched him, holding myself as still as possible, waiting for the moment he'd either kick me out for being a raving lunatic or accuse me of being cruel and heartless. Asking him to believe in this, in everything I'd just said, was a lot, and for a few devastating minutes I was afraid it was too much to ask.

"Say something." I clasped my hands together in an attempt to stop them from shaking. "Tell me to go to hell or ask me to explain more or . . . or . . ."

"You can see ghosts?" He spoke softly and slowly, as if I were a nutcase and he was afraid I was going to leap up and do something crazy. Like grab a knife and attack him. He backed up a few paces. "How is that possible?"

"It's . . . an ability. She needs help. I'm the only one who can see her, who can talk to her. She was drawn to me somehow, I don't know how. And that's why I gave you that book! That's why I've been so curious about her." I gulped, not liking the expression on his face. "And that's why I agreed to have a séance last night."

He narrowed his eyes and his jaw tensed. "Assuming I believe in the possibility, how do I know you're telling the truth, and that you're not . . . lying in some misguided attempt to make me feel better?"

"I wouldn't lie about something like this! But . . . um . . ." I racked my brain, trying to think of something to prove my honesty. "Mari is always dressed in the same clothes. A pair of faded blue jeans and a white zip-up hoodie. Does that mean anything?"

His face blanched. "That's . . . She . . ." His eyes seared into me, and a tremor rumbled through him. "Rissa was a tomboy. She hated dresses and anything girly, so I refused to bury her in clothes she hated. Those jeans and that sweatshirt were her favorite clothes, so I . . ."

He blinked, and a tear rolled down his cheek, and my heart broke into pieces all over again, for his loss, for his pain, for everything that he'd dealt with.

". . . buried her in those. There's no way you could have known."

"She, um, also introduced herself to me as Mari. You said only her friends called her that. She's very sad, Ben. I wanted to tell you as soon as you showed me the picture and I realized who she was. Until that moment, I didn't even know she was a ghost! I thought she was a runaway or in trouble somehow. But"—I cleared my throat—"she appeared at my place, after I fainted, and she shook her head no and held a finger to her lips. I don't think she wanted me to tell you until I understood why she was here. So I waited."

He dropped back into his seat and stared at me, questions and confusion and hope and want combining into a dangerous mix, darkening his eyes and coloring his expression. "What does she need?"

"I—I think to talk to you. Her memories are broken. She knows she was angry at Sara, and that Sara was sad, but she doesn't remember why. I think she feels your pain and your confusion, and until you can let that go, let her go, she's somehow stuck here." That was the best explanation I had. "But now that I know everything, I—I might be able to help."

"What do you mean, she was angry at her mom? Do you know how the accident happened, Chloe?"

"The séance. I told you we had a séance," I whispered in a

rush. I didn't want to share this with him. I hated bringing him more pain, but he deserved the information. "Me and my cousins, and I . . . Sara came through. She showed me what happened." I told him the rest, trying to keep my voice steady, reciting every single detail.

When I finished, he appeared as if I'd struck him. Empty, shell-shocked eyes held mine, the angles of his face seemed sharper, and his breaths were short, raspy huffs. "That's why the accident happened? She was upset, and she needed me, and I wasn't here. I was supposed to be here! If I had been, she wouldn't have heard that phone call." Ben covered his face with his hands, and his shoulders shook in silent agony.

"Let me help you. Let me help her. I . . . I think if I can speak with her again, I can relay information from you to her, and from her to you. I know it's not the same as talking to her yourself, but . . . but Ben, *I* can see her and *I* can talk to her." But would that be enough? God help me, I just didn't know.

He raised his face and searched the room. "Is she here now?"

"No," I whispered. "Not now."

He jumped from the chair and grabbed my hand. Yanking me up, he tugged me down the hall. "You said she was in her room the other night. Maybe she's there now?"

"Maybe." But I didn't think so. If Mari was ready to see me, she'd show up wherever I was; I'd learned that much. Still, I couldn't refuse Ben this tiny bit of hope, so I let him pull me up the stairs and into Mari's bedroom. Naturally, it was empty.

I fought back tears and shook my head. "But she will come to me, Ben. When she's ready. I'm sure of that. She hears her mother calling, and she really wants to join her. But she doesn't know how to go when you're feeling everything you're feeling."

He placed his hands on my shoulders and swung me

around. "If you're lying to me, Chloe, I will never forgive you."

"I swear to you, I am not lying! I promise you with every part of me, with how much I love you, with how important you are to me, that I am not lying."

His eyes widened. "What did you just say?"

"That I'm not lying . . . that I love—"

Every muscle in his body tensed. "I can't say those words to you. It's too soon, and right now I'm . . ." He thrust his fingers into his hair. "I'm trying to understand what's happening with my daughter. I'm stunned you would use my moment of weakness to—"

I scowled at him, at his statement and body language. "You think that's why I said I love you—to get you to say it back? This isn't about me, Ben!"

I recoiled, startled by my own vehemence, but also by my verbal admission of the feelings I'd only so recently acknowledged. So much of this *was* about me, had been for so long, that it came as a shock to know that this moment, this second in time, had nothing to do with me. And that he thought I would try to manipulate him both saddened and confused me. It ticked me off too.

"I'm not asking you to confess your feelings. I'm telling you why I wouldn't lie to you. Why I *am* being honest." I cringed, knowing how much he still didn't know about me. About my family. About my magic.

He gave me a hard stare. "For now I'm going to take your word on this, because you have a belief system that I don't understand. So I'm relying on you. If my daughter needs me, if she is stuck here, then I need to help her. And if what you say is true, I need you in order to make that happen." He pushed a breath out. "When . . . when we've taken care of my daughter, we'll go from there." Scanning the room again, he walked over to her bed and sat down. "So, what do we do? Just sit here and wait?"

"If you want," I said carefully. "Or we can go back to the kitchen, or we can keep talking, or we can watch TV, or we can go to sleep. She'll find me—us—when she's ready."

"Is this the place you last saw my daughter?"

"Yes."

"Then I'd like to wait here."

"Okay, then that's what we'll do." I joined him on the bed, wanting to touch him, wanting to kiss him, wanting to comfort him, but unsure if I should. Instead, I just crossed my legs and stared straight ahead. I hadn't lied. Tonight, my focus was on Mari, on Ben and on helping them figure this all out. But I would be lying if I said my heart wasn't breaking just a little at his response to my declaration of love. I wanted him to love me.

My power came alive then, unbidden, swirling inside, mixing with my emotions, pouring out in a rush of energy. I tried to stop it. I centered all of my thoughts on Mari, on Ben's loss, on his pain, hoping to rein the magic in.

Ben stroked my cheek and then repositioned himself on Mari's bed. He was half-sitting up, his legs open and bent at the knees. "Come here, Chloe. I'd like to hold you while we wait. I'd like to talk to you about Marissa."

Relief and tenderness and love spilled into me as I scooted into his waiting arms. "I'd love to hear more about Mari. Anything you want to share."

His arms came around me, and his chin settled atop my head. My power ebbed and flowed, wrapping around him, around me. Weirdly, the energy seemed comforting, as if it were easing the ragged emotions we'd both just gone through.

"Rissa loved practical jokes. It started when she was . . . hm . . . probably around six. She'd learned about April Fool's Day at school, and came home with a dozen or so pranks." He laughed, and in this laugh I heard a joy Ben hadn't shown before. "Every year afterward, she'd try to get me with one prank or another. By the time she was a teenager, April Fool's Day had turned into a major holiday."

I loved this: learning about his daughter, about their life together. I settled more deeply into his arms, content and at ease. "What's the best joke she ever played on you?"

Another warm laugh rolled out of him. "It wasn't funny then, but the year before her accident, she called me at work in the middle of the day. Smart, because she knew I had several meetings lined up. She told me she was running away with a boy from her English class, but if I'd allow her to marry him, and if they could live together here, she'd stay."

I chuckled, imagining. "How long did it take you to catch on?"

"Only a few minutes, but those nearly killed me." I heard the smile in his voice. "It was the first year she completely had me, and she loved it. She told me that she had something even better planned"—his tone dropped, heavy with emotion—"for the next year."

I reached up and squeezed his hand. "Memories are a bitch, aren't they? Sometimes they fill us with so much happiness, and in the next they . . . they're heartbreaking."

"That they are." He gave a little cough. "Hey, Red? How *could* you tell that Gabe wasn't me without even knowing I had a twin?"

"I don't know. My body told me. My instincts told me. I just knew."

"Whatever the reason, I'm pleased you did. Thank you for knowing."

I couldn't speak. I just nodded. As his arms tightened around me and he lightly kissed the top of my head, a stream of happiness brought a smile to my lips, easing my worries about us and our future. I reveled in this feeling for all of thirty seconds. Then his earlier comment floated into my head, the one about most of his adult life being consumed by lies. In that second, everything inside me turned cold. His prior life *had* been built on a lie—on a series of a lies, really. Look how well that had worked out. And here I was, using my magic to get us where I thought we should be.

The coldness swept me, filling every muscle and nerve, swallowing me up. Oh, God. How often had I used my magic on Ben? I tried to think of the whens, wheres, whys and hows. I closed my eyes as pain shot through me. Had I learned nothing from my experience with Kyle? How was I any better than Sara? She'd coerced Ben into marriage because she was pregnant. And I . . . well, I'd been coercing him all along in one way or another.

Elizabeth's question from what felt like forever ago came at me again, and this time I had an answer I couldn't ignore: yes, I wanted Ben to want me for me. Not because of a spell. Not because of magic. I had thought—stupidly—that where we ended up was what was most important. I'd been fooling myself. Lying to myself. Pretending that because of that drawing, anything I did, whatever measures I used, were okay. Now? I wanted the journey itself to be real, to be meaningful, and to pave the way to a future that had nothing to do with Gypsy magic.

My earlier proclamation that I was in charge now seemed absurd. I loved Ben, and I yearned for his love to be true and unencumbered. If I continued in this direction, I would lose him. I was sure of that. I would also lose everyone else I cared about. After all, I hadn't hesitated in using my powers on Alice to get what I wanted. This magic was turning into an addiction, and while there were a few times I'd resisted the pull, the temptation was becoming stronger each day I possessed it.

My instincts had been right in the beginning. Alice's drawings had indeed been a test of fate. And wow, had I failed. The only question that remained was whether it was too late to alter my path. I blinked away the tears behind my eyes, and for the first time since starting this particular journey

I truly felt lost, scared and—even with Ben holding me—entirely alone.

I unlocked my apartment door late the following Monday, exhausted and grumpy from the long day and the even longer weekend I'd spent at Ben's. We'd barely slept, with our ongoing lookout for Mari, but she hadn't shown. I'd thought I sensed her once, but in my sleep-deprived delirium and the residue from my emotional meltdown I might have been mistaken.

So now, before heading to Ben's for another long—and, I was fairly certain, fruitless—night, I had one very specific purpose I wanted to accomplish at home: talking to Miranda. I needed her help, and if this particular ghost also refused to show, then I was going to make Verda, Alice and Elizabeth sit in on another séance. I had some questions for my great-great-great-grandmother. Namely about the magic, the drawings and what I might and might not be able to do to rectify all the mistakes I'd made.

Working quickly, I brought out the blue, white and purple candles I'd used before, the first time Miranda visited me, and once again I placed them atop my dresser. After they were lit, I sat on my bed and crossed my legs. She'd said that they'd helped her connect with me before, so maybe they'd do the trick tonight. And hey, it would come in awfully handy if I figured out how to bring her to me instead of waiting around and being surprised when she did pop in. Even better, if this worked, I could try them on Marissa. Helping her move on had become a primary objective.

Closing my eyes, I breathed in deeply and brought the image of Miranda to mind. I imagined her voice in my thoughts, the tinkling way she spoke. Once I had the whole picture, I pulled in another breath and relaxed every muscle in my body.

"Miranda," I whispered. "I don't know what I'm supposed to do or how I'm supposed to help Ben and Mari. I need your help. Please don't leave me alone on this."

Nothing happened, so I repeated my words and waited. When Miranda still didn't appear, frustration and anger rose up inside of me so fast that my voice shook. "I call you to me, Miranda! I call you to me now. I need your assistance, I need your wisdom, and you are to heed this call!"

A blast of wind hit the room, blowing hair into my face, extinguishing the candles and leaving me quite unable to breathe. I focused harder, grabbed hold of my magic and shouted for Miranda with everything I had, "Come to me, Miranda! You cannot ignore this call!"

Colors so bright they hurt my eyes darted through the air. A solid, almost suffocating pressure wrapped me, pressing inward, stealing the rest of my breath away. I held on, refusing to give up, refusing to let Miranda off the hook. And then, in another flash of brilliant, eye-watering color, she hazed into being directly in front of me. And oh, was she mad.

"How dare you pull me to you!" Her body pulsated with power, and for the first time ever I saw with my own eyes how frightening a woman Miranda must have been. "I come to you when I'm ready, not the other way around!"

My own anger grew. "Then where have you been? I've tried to figure all of this out on my own, but I don't know what to do, and there's a girl who needs my help and I can't seem to help her!"

"This is *your* journey! I've given you all the information you need to solve this, Chloe," Miranda snapped. "You are extraordinarily powerful. You brought me to you—no one has ever been able to do that. You brought Sara to you! So why haven't you used your magic, your will, to pull Mari to you?"

Oh. "I didn't know I could."

"Well, you know now." She glared at me. "If you don't find

the way to solving Mari's dilemma, she'll remain just as she is, locked to this world with no hope of moving on. This should be your focus! Not dragging me around."

"Right. I get that," I snapped back. "I just don't know how to help Mari or Ben."

"Get them in the same room. Your power will lead the way. You'll be able to heal both of them. That's what your true gift is." She narrowed her eyes. "As to the other question in your mind: yes. Because of your ability to alter people's wills, you, in effect, can shape their fates. It's a dangerous game you're playing. I warned you to be careful."

And where was that bit of intel when I'd needed it? I shook my head. "I want to stop! This gift scares me and I don't want it anymore. Is that possible? This magic is too forceful, too overpowering, and . . . Can't I give it away so I'm just a normal girl?"

For once, Miranda didn't seem to know how to respond. Tilting her head, she looked into my eyes as if she could read my thoughts and emotions. "This gift has always been that, Chloe. A gift. It is your choice to accept it or not." Then, in an obvious reminder of our last conversation, she heaved a sigh. "Just like with Isobel. But child, your feelings have to be true and sure. If any part of you wants to retain the magic, then you will not be able to lose it."

"But it's possible? If it's truly what I want, then I'll be able to become plain old Chloe again?" Hope blossomed inside, quelling some of my despair.

She smiled in her glistening, glittering way. "You've never been plain old Chloe, and I can't assure you that you'll lose every drop of magic. But yes, the chance certainly exists."

Okay. Good. A relief. "And the drawings—they're what I think they are, right?" I'd given this a lot of thought, and I was almost positive I was right, but I wanted Miranda's assurance. "You wanted me to see what might happen if I altered other people's wills—their fates—and how I'd then alter my own. Is that true?"

"See? You don't require my help. Why can't you trust in yourself? But yes, you have such great power that you can help people beyond measure, or you can deal them—and yourself—incredibly debilitating blows. Everything stems from you. Everything is connected. But as with Alice, there was only so much I could tell you. In your case, I needed you to grab onto your magic with both hands, to experience what you were capable of, so you'd be able to find your true destination. You're far too stubborn to have just listened to me and nodded."

I nearly stuck my tongue out at her, but didn't. Because loath to admit it as I was, she was correct. Again. "Okay. And what about Gabriel? My heart and my body and my soul tell me he isn't the man in that drawing. But is that just wishful thinking?" I bit my lip, waiting for her to respond.

"You already know the answer to that question! You have some serious self-trust issues, don't you?" She shook her head as if greatly disappointed. "Besides, my dear—if a little deluded—great-great-great-granddaughter, who is the man who walked into your shop off the street? Was that Ben or was that Gabriel?"

Oh, God. Thank God. I mean, I was sure of how I felt, of what I believed, but Miranda's declaration helped. I swallowed and tried to breathe, tried to work out if what I wanted to do would be possible, and if maybe, just maybe, I'd end up where I wanted. A new glimmer of excitement appeared. "I'm sure I don't want this gift anymore, because if I keep it, I'm going to turn into a person I don't want to be. But I need to help Mari and Ben first."

"Then do what you must. Trust in yourself. Trust your instincts." She winked, and the colors around her sparkled and jumped, bounced and shimmied. "But listen to this,

Chloe: if you ever call me like this again, then I will have a long talk with Elizabeth."

I chuckled. "I don't think you'll have to worry about that, Grandmother."

Her energy expanded across the room and cascaded around me. In that second, I felt the purity of Miranda's love, of her belief in me. And I gotta say, it felt really, really good. I smiled through my tears. "I love you too."

She nodded, raised her arms and, in a final blast of colors, disappeared.

Chapter Eighteen

Tuesday evening, right after locking the door at the Mystic Corner, I dialed my sister's phone number and waited for her automated, robotic-sounding voice mail to pick up, hoping that maybe she'd actually answer. She didn't.

"Sheridan, I've purchased a plane ticket to Seattle. I'm not telling you when I'll be there, because I'm sure you'll find a reason not to be home then, but I'll see you soon and I hope you'll let me in." I heaved a breath. "I miss and I love you."

My flight was on Friday, a mere three days away. We were going to settle the weirdness between us once and for all, and strangely that decision had come about because of Ben and Gabe. They would likely never cross the chasm between them. With what had occurred, I didn't blame Ben for that at all, but my relationship with my sister was different. We *could* become close again. At least, I hoped we could.

There was something else in my mind too, something that I hadn't yet decided but wouldn't unless I was sitting across from Sheridan. So yes, this visit had to happen now.

I dragged my eyes to the clock, noting that Ben should be arriving soon. I'd called him the prior evening after talking with Miranda. Instead of going to his house as originally planned, I'd stayed at home. Mostly because I didn't trust the strength of my emotions combined with the potency of my magic. I was afraid of myself.

My heart ached as I considered my plans for the evening, what had to happen after I brought Mari to us and, if things went well, she moved on to be with her mother. But I had to trust myself and my instincts. That's what I was doing. Either the result would be huge and glorious, or it would be nothing short of horrendous. I drew in a long, deliberately slow breath and then exhaled just as slowly.

I'd told Ben to come in the rear entrance, so I switched the lights off in the front part of the store and hurried into the back room. There, I continued my methodical breathing and retrieved the candles I'd brought from home. Silly, maybe, but even though I had candles of every size, shape and color here at the store, I wanted the ones I'd used with Miranda. I placed them on the table unlit and collapsed in my desk chair. Ben knocked on the door two minutes later.

"Punctual as always," I said, gesturing him inside. He entered, and I faced him, soaking in his appearance. Just in case I never saw him again. Tonight he wore the same jeans he had during our first date, and he looked just as handsome, just as rugged and just as sexy. My eyes traveled up his body. His cobalt blue shirt fit him well, not too loose and not too tight. Somehow, his eyes looked even bluer than normal. Impossible.

"You look sad," Ben said, advancing into the room. "Are you worried about me? About how I'll react to . . . whatever is going to happen here tonight?"

I nodded. Not only because his assumption was correct, but also because it extended beyond connecting with Mari. "Just a little. But you're here now, and I'm really glad to see you."

"Are you—? You really think you know how to bring her to us? Is there a chance she's already moved on, and that's why you haven't seen her?" Tendrils of doubt clung to his every word, probably because I hadn't "seen" his daughter since my confession.

Well, I'd fix that tonight, if nothing else—assuming Miranda was right. "I've . . . ah . . . done a little research, so

I'm as close to positive as I can be until we try. And no, I don't believe she's moved on."

"But I won't be able to see or hear her?"

I swallowed, trying to dispel the lump in my throat. "If you haven't seen or heard her on your own, then I don't believe you'll be able to tonight. But think of something I can ask her that I wouldn't know. You need to be one hundred percent sure that I'm being honest with you."

This was a must.

He closed his eyes and his shoulders tensed. Without thought, I approached him and lightly touched his cheek and then his hair. "I'd say that we don't have to do this if you're having second thoughts, but we need to. For Mari." For him too, but I knew his concern for his daughter would outweigh his fears and skepticism.

He opened his eyes. "I'm trusting you, Red. I don't know what else to say."

I heard his sentiment loud and clear: I'm trusting you, so don't let me down. "You can have faith in this. I promise." I rubbed my thumb along his jaw. "Do you want to talk about what I think will happen first, or do you just want to get on with it?"

He grabbed my hand in his, shaking his head. "I don't want to have any expectations or assumptions. So yeah, I guess we—you—should do whatever it is you need to. And tell me what I should be doing."

I squeezed his hand and then leaned in and gave him a gentle, lingering kiss. He returned it, his fingers weaving into my hair, drawing me closer. The emotions between us were soft, tender and far more about offering each other comfort than anything else.

When the kiss ended, I forced my legs to take me to the table, where I lit the candles. More nervous than I expected, I skimmed my hands along my pants. "I'm ready. You can stand or sit down, whichever you prefer, and I need you to think about Marissa—her face, her voice, the sound of her laugh. Your memories of her. If you do that, I'll be able to do my part."

He gave a quick nod. "I'll stand."

Then I would too. "There might be wind. Or . . . um . . . colors. Or something else. Just so you're not surprised." He nodded again, and I moved into position next to him, clasping his hand. "I don't know if this is necessary, but it can't hurt."

Faint humor touched his face. "It might even help."

I grinned. "Yes."

With nothing else to say, I closed my eyes and brought every memory I had of Mari to the surface. Again, like with Miranda, once I had the girl's image I grasped on tight and delved deep inside of myself. The power there had almost become second nature. One long breath in, another out, and I envisioned my energy as a vine, climbing higher and higher, reaching from me, beyond me, toward Mari.

Electricity—hot, fast and sharp—sizzled in the air, blazed along my skin and funneled through my hand into Ben's. I heard him gasp, so I gripped his hand tighter but kept my eyes closed. My power swelled, and the vine I'd envisioned climbed even higher, searching for a lost, scared teenage girl who needed her father.

"Mari, honey," I whispered, not wanting to yell as I had with Miranda. "Your dad is here with me. It's time for you to come talk with him, so that together we can help ease your pain. So you can help ease his. Oh, sweetie, he misses you so, and if you can give him the gift of one more conversation, both of you will be able to move on."

I opened my eyes and turned my head, locking my gaze with Ben's. His jaw was clenched tight, but he nodded, as if giving me permission to carry on. I continued to stare at him while my power vibrated within.

"I plead with you to heed this call, Mari! Come to us now!"

A gust of wind, not much more than a forceful breeze, touched my face. Ben swallowed and blinked several times. Next, a strong white light washed into the room, the brightest portion of the glow directly in front of where Ben and I stood. I centered my energy, my power, on that light and repeated my call to Mari.

I blinked, and in the space of that blink, there she was. She stepped out of the middle of the light and stopped before me, before her father. Her eyes went to him first, and I saw her heartache when it became obvious that he couldn't see her.

She turned to me. "I've tried to stay away because, now that I remember, I don't want to hurt him anymore," she whispered. "But you called me, and here I am, and look at him. Look how sad he is. What good is this if my father can't see me? Can't hear me?" Her voice caught and her sky blue eyes welled with tears. "I don't understand how this will help him or me, Chloe."

The distress in her eyes, in her very energy, swirled around us. "Oh, honey. *I* can see you, and *I* can tell him whatever you want."

As I spoke, Ben flinched. "Sh-she's here?" His words held a mix of doubt and hope. "Are you seriously saying that Rissa's here right now? And that you can see her?"

"Yes, Ben, your daughter is with us." God, I *so* needed him to believe this. "What do you want me to ask her? The question that will prove to you that your daughter is standing with us?"

"If . . . if she's here, ask her about the April Fool's joke I told you about. Ask her the name of the boy she said she was going to run away with."

Mari's lips quirked, and the sadness in her eyes lightened. "Marvin Maypole! I made the name up." She splayed her fingers over her mouth and giggled, remembering the prank she'd played on her father. "T-tell him, Chloe!"

"Marvin Maypole," I said. "She says she made the name up, and she's giggling." I watched Ben carefully, worried that as much as he wanted this opportunity, the truth of it might be too much for him to handle.

He gulped. A series of emotions—shock, hope, happiness and another round of shock—flashed in his eyes, over his features, and he reached his other hand out blindly, as if he could grasp his daughter. "Yes," he said in a raspy, thick voice. "Marvin Maypole. That's right. I can't believe . . . Rissa? You can hear me, right? Even though I can't hear you?"

"She can hear you, Ben." I watched him struggle, trying to find the words he wanted to say to his daughter, and when I looked at Mari, I saw the same struggle. At least she could see and hear him, but Ben? Talking into the air, believing with your heart and soul that someone you loved was listening, had to be incredibly difficult.

"I . . . Now that this is happening, I don't know what to say. This is—" He swallowed again and shook his head. "How can you see her and I can't? This isn't fair!" He searched the area in front of him, and another round of tremors licked through him.

Mari started crying again, and I knew in that instant that this wasn't going to work. All of the hope that I could fix this bled away. Why couldn't I do something—anything—so father and daughter could really connect? What in the hell was my role here? It had to be more than as an interpreter. Otherwise, how was I supposed to heal anything, let alone their hearts and souls?

"Take a deep breath, Ben. I'll help you through this." Confidence I didn't feel edged into my promise, and I winced, unsure if I'd be able to follow through. I glanced at Mari. Her tears fell harder, almost desperately, and my heart reacted. And then, so did my power.

It expanded in a dizzying rush. The energy inside me flowed in a burning frenzy through my veins, the power so strong, so forceful, that heat flushed through me, rocking my equilibrium, making my head swim. Ben gasped again, and that's when I saw that my magic was glowing and glittering beneath my skin. Just like with him at the amusement park, and then again with Mari, right here, right where we now stood. Oh my God! This . . . this sparkling, glistening display had only happened those two times. Never with anyone else. I latched on to that, knowing it meant something vital. But what?

"S-something's happening," I whispered. "Give me a second. Let me think."

Almost immediately, I had the answer. But was it possible? Could I really use my gift, this portion of my magic that sped through my blood with such intensity, to bridge the physical world Ben stood in and the spiritual world where Mari existed? As soon as that thought hit, my power rippled in a new, even more potent push, the heat and the trembles and the energy making my body quake.

"C-Chloe?" Ben's voice broke in, awe filled. "You . . . you look like you're lit from the inside. You're . . . What's happening now? Is my daughter still here?" he demanded. "Is this like that movie *Ghost*? Are you like Whoopi's character? Is Marissa going to . . . is she inside—"

"No, but . . . maybe?" Going on a hunch, trusting nothing more than my instincts, I squeezed Ben's hand hard and then lunged forward and grabbed Mari's with my free hand. I was only half-surprised to find that I could touch her, that I could feel her. But somehow, she was as solid for me as Ben.

The energy whipped from me into both Mari and Ben, and they too began to glow. This display—the tiny embers of light that washed over them in a sparkling, dazzling array— made me believe, made me sure that I'd tapped in to a portion of my power I hadn't even known about or understood until that very second. I clutched both of their hands tighter and focused all of my magic on them.

The lights grew brighter, and the air sizzled and zapped, buzzing in my ears, tingling along my skin. "Can you see your daughter now, Ben? She's right here." Another blast of energy weakened my limbs, and I almost toppled over. "Oh, please tell me you can see her."

He shook his head in confusion, but then his eyes rounded and tears poured out. A heart-wrenching sob erupted from his throat. "Rissa? I . . . I . . . You're . . . Oh, God, you're so beautiful. I have missed you so much, baby."

"Daddy?" A look of pure happiness filtered into Mari's face. Stepping closer to her father, she raised her other hand and brushed it along his arm. "Can you feel me? Can I touch you like Chloe's touching me?"

"Yes. Yes, I can feel you. I can't believe you're here, that I'm with you." He yanked his arm, as if he were going to drop my hand so he could pull his daughter into a hug, but I tightened my grip.

"Don't, Ben," I warned. "If you let go of me, you won't be able to see her." Somehow, my magic had become a conduit, a bridge, for father and daughter. I didn't understand how, but I knew it to be true. "If we break this connection, I'm not sure I'll be able to get it back. And I—I know this is private and personal, but I have to be here. I'm sorry."

He squeezed harder and nodded but didn't remove his gaze from Marissa. "C-Chloe says that you're stuck here, sweetheart. Is that true?"

Mari lowered her chin slowly in a nod. "I hear Mom calling for me. And I know you're angry with her, and I was too, but Daddy, I want to go to her. I want to be where she is, but I can't leave. Every time I try to follow her voice, nothing happens." Another tear fell. "You're so sad, and you're . . . I don't want you to be mad at me if I go to Mom. I—I feel bad for wanting to be with her, because it means I have to leave you, but . . ."

Ben's face crumpled. "Baby, you don't have to be afraid of that. I could never be mad at you for . . . for moving on. And I have been angry at your mother, but that's not your fault. She"—he swallowed heavily—"lied to me. And that lie has made it difficult for me to forgive her. But if that's what you need, then I'll work harder. I'll do whatever I can for you."

Mari tipped her tear-streaked face up toward Ben's. "You've wondered if I'm your daughter. I am! It doesn't matter about DNA or Uncle Gabe or whatever they did, Daddy. You were—are—the best father a girl could have. Don't think I'm not yours. Please don't think that. Please don't let this . . . this thing with Mom change us. She can't do that. Only *you* can do that."

Ben's entire body shook with sobs. "Of course you're my daughter! I hate not knowing for sure, though, because I love you so much that I don't want to have any doubt. It's eaten at me, the not knowing, not—"

"But there *isn't* any doubt! You raised me, and you loved me and I love you. You read to me at night and taught me to ride my bike and took me to concerts with my girlfriends and . . . and . . . and you did everything that a father does. So why is there doubt?" She spoke with such passion that her body vibrated. "Do you really think anything else matters?"

"I didn't know. I—" He broke off, overcome. Reaching out with his free hand, he grasped Mari's and pulled her close. "But what matters the most to me is that you're okay. Chloe told me about the accident, how you heard your mom on the phone with your uncle. I'm so sorry you found out that way, baby. I should have told you."

She swung a defiant look toward him, 100 percent teenage girl. "You *and* Mom should have told me! I could have handled it if you had. But hearing the news accidentally made it so much worse. Because of your pain, I thought that maybe you wished you weren't my dad. That if Mom had married Uncle Gabe instead, you'd have been happier because you could've become a doctor. You gave that up for me."

"I would give up the world for you, Rissa. Being your father was the most important role of my life. That will *never* change."

"Promise?" she asked.

Letting go of her hand, he tilted her chin up more and then cradled her cheek. "I promise. Being a doctor would've been nice, but I've lived just fine without it." He tugged her head toward him and then kissed her sweetly on her forehead. "I don't know how I'm managing without you."

"M-maybe it *would* have been better if Mom had ended up with Uncle Gabe, because then you wouldn't be so sad now. I'd just be your niece."

"No! That's not true. As difficult and impossible as it has been to lose you, Rissa, the joy of being your father far outweighs anything else. I would never, in a million years, give that up." He stared into her eyes again. "Do you understand me, sweetheart? I love you and will always love you, and you will always be with me in my heart. Moving on, being with your mother, will not alter that. You're mine."

"And you're mine. My dad. Please don't forget that. Okay, Daddy?"

"Never. I'll never doubt that again."

Suddenly, Mari's face was awash with warmth and serenity. "Daddy? I can leave now if it's okay with you. I'll . . . I'll stay if you want, though."

The realization that this was it, the last moment of time, of space, he'd share with his daughter until the day *he* moved on, coursed through Ben's features. A tremor racked him, and his eyes— Oh, my heart broke as I looked into those sad, sad eyes! But I watched him shore himself up, become strong for Mari. "You go, baby. Be with your mother and be happy, and know that . . . know that I love you and am very, very proud of you."

"I love you too, Daddy." She turned to me with beseeching eyes. "Take care of him, Chloe."

Choked with emotion, I nodded. "I'll try. I've loved getting to know you, Mari. Thank you for choosing me to help you."

She smiled, luminous. "Oh, Chloe. I don't think I chose you. I think maybe you chose me. But thank you. Thank you for fighting for me. For him." Stepping as close to her father as she could, she laid her cheek on his chest. "Good-bye for now, Daddy. Try to talk to Uncle Gabe sometime, okay? He's . . . he's hurting too."

Ben pulled his daughter close, tears dripped from his eyes and he oh so slowly rubbed his chin on the top of her head. "We'll see," he whispered. "I'll try. For you." Then he grazed his cheek along her hair in a final farewell. "I love you, baby girl. You go now. Go to your mother."

Mari's form shimmered. She pressed her cheek tighter to her father's chest before pulling back. "I'm ready," she said into the air. A golden glow appeared to her side. She gave her father one last look, then dropped my hand and walked— literally—into the light.

Just that fast, she was gone.

Chapter Nineteen

Two hours later, Ben and I remained in the back room at the Mystic Corner. After Mari's departure, Ben had pulled me into his arms and held me as he cried. I'd kissed his cheeks, wiped away his tears and given him all of my attention. His strength, the depth of his emotions, his ability to love—these things blew me away.

We now sat across from each other at the table. "How are you feeling?" I asked.

A light of tranquility gleamed in his eyes. "Better. Seeing Rissa and talking with her helped more than I can say. It's as if I've spent the last two years grieving but couldn't complete the process because of my anger. Now don't get me wrong, Red, I'm still sad. I still miss Rissa. I always will. But I finally feel as if I'll really be able to take the best parts of my life with my daughter and carry on." He shook his head. "Does that make any sense?"

"It does," I said softly. "When my parents died, I felt cheated. As if they had somehow chosen to leave me and my sister behind. While different than what you've gone through, I was angry too. So angry that it took a while before I could let them go. After I reached that place, things—life—became easier."

"Did you . . . uh . . . talk to them the way you did with Rissa?" Curiosity and interest colored his tone.

"No. I didn't grow up this way, Ben. What I did for you and Mari was a brand new experience for me."

He reached over and ran a finger down my arm. "Really?

How does that work, exactly? You woke up one day and could see ghosts?"

I swallowed, recognizing this as the beginning of what might be the end. For us, anyway. "It's a gift. You haven't met any of my family, but I'm not the only person who has a"—I pushed out a breath—"magical ability. For my cousins, Alice and Elizabeth, their gifts are closely tied to their talents. Alice is an artist, and Elizabeth owns a bakery. Oh, and their grandmother, Verda, has a gift too."

He bunched his eyebrows together. "Magic runs in your family tree?"

"Kind of," I hedged. "But not exactly. Let me try to explain." Haltingly, I told him about Miranda, and about Elizabeth's brand of magic. When he took that fairly well, I told him about Grandma Verda, and how she recently was able to have her magic returned. Then finally, I told him about Alice's ability to create pictures of the future for the people she cared about. "And that brings us to me."

"So, your gift is to see ghosts and help them move on?" Ben chuckled, but his eyes were serious. "I'm grateful. More than I'll ever be able to say. But wouldn't it be more fun to have your wishes come true? I hope you don't think you got the short end of the stick, because you and this . . . uh, gift, have made a tremendous difference for me. And for my daughter. Thank you for that, Chloe. I'll never be able to thank you enough."

"Helping you and Mari was my pleasure." And an honor. A huge, glorious honor that I would never forget. "But . . . Ben. There's more I need to tell you. My magic extends beyond what you saw tonight." I straightened my shoulders and tried to ignore the sickening swirl of nerves in my stomach. "You're going to be angry. You might never want to see me again." This last comment rushed out, and a tremble of fear whisked through me.

"No. That won't happen." His voice was firm and calm, filled with assurance that nothing I could say would change anything. "I'd like to hear more about what you can do. But Red, I have pretty serious feelings for you. I have from the beginning." He focused those blue, blue eyes on me. "I saw my daughter tonight because of you. That alone gives you a hell of a lot of breathing room as far as I'm concerned."

Oh, how I wanted to believe. The tiniest amount of hope crawled over me. Maybe he'd understand. Maybe he'd listen to my heart more than my words. But even with that hope, I wanted to ignore what I needed to do. Not only because I flat-out hated the thought of hurting Ben, especially after everything he'd just gone through, but because my heart broke at the very thought of letting him down.

Beyond that, it felt wrong—so very wrong—to get into this now. But waiting even a minute longer seemed a greater sin. I loved him too much for that, so I steadied myself and stood. The few steps to my desk seemed to take a dozen lifetimes. I pulled the original drawing out of my drawer and, before I could dissuade myself, returned to the table.

My breath quivered in and out of my chest, and my heart pounded. "I have something to show you." Perspiration beaded on my forehead, on the back of my neck. My hand shook as I slid the paper across the table. "Here. Let's start with this."

He picked it up and held it in front of him. A minute, maybe more, passed where he didn't say anything, where I barely heard him take a breath. Anxiety, apprehension and fear of the future weakened my legs, so I sat down. Still I waited. Finally, after what felt like forever, he let go of the drawing and it swirled down onto the table.

"What is this, Red? It appears to be a sketch—a very well-drawn sketch—of you and me at . . . our wedding? Or is it just a fancy party?" Confusion filled his voice and eyes.

"I told you about Alice, and how she can see the future in

her artwork. She drew that picture a year ago, Ben. Before I knew you. Before you knew me." I pulled air into my lungs, and then wheezed it back out. "She . . . uh . . . didn't show it to me for a long time. Not until I decided to propose to Kyle—the man I was involved with this past year. Even then, I didn't want to look at it. The thought of that drawing scared me, so I refused."

"But you have it now." He spoke calmly, but his voice held a flat, almost emotionless quality, as if he sensed we were heading down a path that would—no matter what he'd just said—change everything. "When did you see this for the first time?"

"The day you bought the pendulum for your assistant. I—I had such a strong reaction to you, I knew I needed to see the picture then." I lifted my eyes to his. "To see if it was you."

"If you hadn't looked at this"—he nodded toward the drawing—"why would you think, after meeting me, that I might be the man your cousin drew?" He combed his fingers through his hair, obviously perplexed. "And did you end your relationship with this other man over this drawing, or because you met me?"

"There's a lot more to it. Let me . . . I should start from the beginning."

"Please do. A week ago I would've laughed at the idea of a woman who draws scenes from the future, but after tonight, after Rissa, I know anything is possible. So tell me. Tell me everything." He narrowed his eyes. "I care enough about you to listen, and then to talk about whatever you tell me, but do not leave anything out, and do not lie to me. Okay?"

"I'm being honest with you now because I love you. And I don't want to lie. That's the one thing you don't have to worry about."

Something in my expression softened his. Again he reached across the table, this time to grasp my hand. "I'm listening."

I closed my eyes for a second, found the strength I needed and began. "Ever since losing my parents, I've felt lost and alone. All I've wanted, almost as long as I can remember, is to be a part of a family. A real family. With people who love me because I belong to them, and they belong to me." In a choking voice, I shared the journey that had started with Kyle way back in high school, and how destroyed I'd been when he left me. I talked about my sister and how much I missed her, about Alice and how she'd discovered that I was a part of her family via her gift and the family ghost.

It was here that Ben interrupted me. "That had to have been some revelation. Not only that your best friend was also your cousin, but that ghosts were real, and that magic existed. How did you handle it?"

"I loved it, Ben. I've always believed in ghosts and magic. When Alice told me the truth, everything seemed to settle inside, and the world—for a little while—made a lot more sense."

"What changed that?"

"Alice falling in love, I think." Now I related the past year. How I'd felt left out, how Alice's priorities—rightly so—had changed and how I'd reacted. The no-show magic, and the feelings of being forgotten, and how all of that had pushed me into proposing to a man that I knew, even then, wasn't right for me. "So I begged Elizabeth to use her magic to bake a cake, to soften Kyle's commitment issues, so I could propose to him and have a better shot at getting a yes. And with that, the family I thought I was lacking."

He removed his hand from mine. "So you tricked him?"

I nodded, hating the censure in his voice, but hating myself more. "I did. And he said yes." The story of the intervention came out next, and how Alice had pointed to the building where Ben worked, insisting that my happily-ever-after was there, and not with Kyle. "But I still refused to see the picture. But then you walked into my shop. I . . . I'd never felt anything like the response just seeing you, talking to you, brought forth. And when you handed me your business card and I saw your name, and the name of your firm—"

Comprehension washed over him. "So, you . . . ?" he prodded.

This was it. There was no going back. I nodded again, and forced out the rest of the tale. Every last thing. How I could change people's wills with my magic, by the strength of my emotions, by my wants and desires. I moved on to the three new drawings, and everything I'd learned about them, about fate and destiny, and how—for me—I could control not only my future but those I used my magic on. The longer I talked, the colder the gleam in his eyes grew, and by the time I finished, he looked at me as if I were a stranger.

"You've been manipulating me this entire time?"

"No. Yes. A little here and a little there, I guess?" I gnawed on my bottom lip, mentally recounting each of the instances I'd bespelled him. There were four, at least, that came to mind. But with the way my magic worked, who knew how often my emotions had pushed from me to him? How often had I affected him that I couldn't recall? My stomach cramped. "Often enough, Ben. I'm so sorry. I believed that getting to that day"—I pointed to the drawing—"was more important than how we got there. It's not an excuse, but I had the best intentions. And I really do love you. So much that I had to come clean. I had to give us a real chance. I had—*have*—to know if whatever you're feeling for me is real or just a by-product of my magic."

"You don't even know if the man in that drawing is of me. It could be Gabe! Have you thought of that?" The words escaped between gritted teeth.

"Of course I have. But, it isn't. I love you. I want you. He—other than how he affects you—means *nothing* to me. You, on the other hand, mean everything." He meant *more* than everything.

A dark and dangerous quiet fell, weighting the air like the calm before a storm. I couldn't speak. Every part of me yearned for him to stand up and pull me into his arms, to tell me that he didn't give a damn about any of this. But of course that couldn't happen. Because not only would I forever wonder if his feelings for me were true, but he would also forever wonder. And that was something that wouldn't bring happiness to either of us.

Finally, I whispered, "What are you thinking?"

He tightened his jaw, but his voice was even. "I can believe that your feelings are for me and not for Gabe. You recognized he wasn't me. But while I'll always be thankful to you for what you've done for me and for my daughter, I've spent enough years of my life being manipulated by other people." He shook his head and continued in a slightly louder, stonier tone. "I will not go down that road again. With anyone. How am I supposed to know if anything I feel for you is really my own? What if you've planted them so deeply that these feelings *seem* real?"

"I can fix that!" My promise erupted in a sob, barely coherent. "I can remove every spell I've ever cast on you. It's what I planned on doing tonight, after we had this conversation. Because I want to know the truth too! I need to know the truth."

"You still lied to me! And with this gift of yours, you'll be able to continue to lie to me. I would never know what decisions, emotions, actions"—a hot blaze of anger ripped into his eyes, darkening them—"were mine, and which were yours. I won't live like that."

I almost told him about my plans to rid myself of the magic, thinking that might just be enough to bring us to a better place, a new beginning, but I didn't. Not because I didn't yet know if it would even work, and not because I'd changed my mind; I hadn't. Whether it was right or wrong,

I wanted him to want me for who I was, even if that meant I retained my powers. So, hoping beyond hope that if I set him free he'd find his way back to me—just like that old quote about love—I gathered together every strand of courage I had left and pushed back my tears. There'd be plenty of time to cry later.

"Okay, then." I was surprised when my voice came out cool and collected. How could that be, when I was dying inside? "I understand and I won't argue or try to change your mind. But removing the spells I cast on you is important. Otherwise, you might try to fix things with me, feeling as if you have no choice." In a slow, halting manner, I relayed how Kyle had reacted, and how Verda had been sure I'd cursed him. "Will you let me use my magic to remove what I've already done?"

Ben's eyes narrowed again and his jaw hardened another degree. "How do I know you're not going to cast a new spell on me? Maybe this is another one of your tricks."

The venom in his voice brought a wave of bile to my throat. I choked it down. He had every right to be angry. I'd expected this, even. But that didn't alter how very much I hated it. "I'll speak out loud, so you know what I'm saying. So you know what I'm wishing. That's the best I can do, Ben."

"Well, I guess I don't have a choice, do I? Being cursed doesn't sound like a hell of a lot of fun." Another round of temper cascaded over him. I wished I had the ability to go back in time, to change my mistakes before I ever made them. Now *that* would be a power worth having.

"I need to hold your hands," I whispered, just wanting to get this over with. I shook my head, flustered and uncomfortable. "Okay, I might not *need* to hold them. But that's how I did this with Kyle, and . . . um . . . I don't want to leave anything to chance."

Ben thrust his arms across the table and gave me a terse nod. "Yes. Let's be sure to leave absolutely nothing to chance."

I exhaled, put my hands in his and closed my eyes. Looking at him, seeing the pain and betrayal so apparent on his face, was simply more than I could handle. My chest tightened, the pressure so heavy and strong I was sure I'd cease to breathe or exist. But this had to be done, so I thought about Ben and how much I loved him. I thought about how sorry I was to have altered his will, to have changed even one aspect of who he was. And then, focusing inward, I found my power. It turned on instantly, burning through me, pulling from my emotions, from my deep and utter sadness, but also from the clarity of necessity.

Using the exact same words I had with Kyle, because they'd worked with him, I whispered, "I abolish whatever spells have been cast on you by my hand so that you'll regain full control of your will, and that your choices, feelings, wants and desires are yours and yours alone." The energy pushed and throbbed, emerging from deep within, and I opened myself to the sensation, to the magic, fully and completely. I repeated my wish three more times, and each uttering fueled the power with increasing amounts of electricity, which zapped and crackled all around us.

There was nothing new about these sensations, nothing that surprised me or halted the flow of power. But then the fire inside flashed hotter and brighter than ever before, tearing through me at a breakneck pace, suffusing me with a type of energy I *hadn't* previously experienced. In that instant, every agony—every bit of sadness, despair and loneliness—I'd felt over the last year saturated me.

Having these feelings all at once was crippling. Devastating. Excruciating. But I held on, repeated my wish again, and suddenly the heat disappeared. A cool, cleansing energy took over, rushing through me like a blast of cold wind, filling me with awe and something new. Something different. Shivers trickled along my skin. My body quaked as the cool tide continued, bathing me in a healing glow, casting out the shadows and the darkness I'd lived with for so long.

Another rush, another brilliant flash of pure, clean power rippled through me. The energy then bled away, leaving me shaking and cold, trembling and exhausted. I opened my eyes, removed my hands from Ben's and focused on catching my breath. This wasn't the loss of my magic, for when I reached within, it was still there, ready and waiting.

"Is that it?" Ben's voice pierced my thoughts. "Am I now spell free?"

I nodded, still unable to talk.

He didn't wait around. Standing, he crossed to the back door. This, it seemed, was really the end. For now, at least. I wanted to say something, but anything I conceived seemed lame and worthless.

Still, I had to try. "Wait. Please, Ben. Give me a minute here," I said softly.

Rotating on his heel, he faced me. "You have one minute."

"I know right now you're probably thinking that I'm not any better than Sara. Maybe you even think I'm worse. And maybe you're right. But I love you. I never meant to cause you pain. If you believe nothing else, please believe that."

A mask slipped into place as he stared at me, shielding his emotions and his thoughts. "I don't know what I think right now." He grappled with himself, trying to find the right words. "You gave me an incredible gift tonight, Chloe. No matter what else, please know that I recognize that and that I appreciate it beyond measure. As for the rest . . . I just think it's more than I can come to grips with."

I nodded, fighting back tears, refusing to cry in front of him. "You know where to find me if you change your mind."

"That I do." He stared at me for a few more seconds. Opening the back door, he stepped out and walked away. I don't know if he looked back. I don't know if he paused. All I know is that the door slammed shut and he was gone.

My tears came. No way in hell could I stop them. They streamed down my face in a never-ending rush. My throat clogged and I had a difficult time drawing air into my lungs. Whatever had happened at the tail end of my spell with Ben had seemed to heal every pain I'd lived with for the past year. For longer, really. Except for the pain that mattered the most: losing the man I loved.

I pulled myself upright and grabbed the drawing from the table. Gathering the other three, in a defiant move I ripped all four of them into shreds and tossed them into the trash. Whatever my future was going to hold, whatever fate waited around the bend, it didn't exist in these pictures. Because even without Ben I wasn't going to throw in the towel. My life was worth more than that.

I hoped and prayed and pleaded that Ben would find his way back to me. That he would somehow see into my heart and begin to believe in me again. But if he didn't, I'd forge a new future, and I didn't need a freaking drawing to show me what that would be. Not anymore.

Chapter Twenty

Three days later, after nearly delaying my trip to Seattle because the thought of leaving without hearing from Ben seemed incomprehensible, I pulled my rented car into Sheridan's driveway directly behind a silver Mazda and let out a sigh. I'd made it.

Turning the car off, I took stock of Sheridan's home. She lived on the outskirts of the city, in a newer neighborhood with about seven different styles of houses dotting the streets, several in the process of being built and plenty of empty lots still for sale. Her house had muted blue siding, shuttered windows, and looked neat, tidy and damn near perfect. Pretty much like Sheridan herself.

My stomach dipped as I forced myself from the car. The butterflies increased with every step. When I reached her miniscule front porch I heard music playing, and that spun my nervousness to even greater heights. How long had it been since I stood in the same space as Sheridan? Years. Way too many.

I banged on the door, lightly at first and then with more force when she didn't answer. That didn't do the trick, either, so I rang her doorbell and waited.

Another couple of minutes passed, and a flurry of fear skittered over me. What if she'd looked out her window, seen me and decided not to let me in? As ridiculous as the thought was, it settled in, increasing my anxiety even more. So I twisted the doorknob and pushed, expecting the door to be locked. It wasn't.

I stuck my head in, noting that her living room was the same as I'd seen in my vision with Miranda. Swallowing, I perused the space, my gaze flickering past her plum-colored sofa, the television, her bookshelf and the two oversized chairs that rested in front of the window. But no sister.

Hesitantly, I stepped completely inside and closed her door behind me, feeling like an intruder. "Sheridan?" I called out, trying to raise my voice above the music. Since she didn't appear, I must not have been successful.

I deposited my purse on one of the chairs and went to find my sister. A narrow hallway jutted off the side of the room, so I followed that. Before I reached the end, I saw her in the kitchen. She stood at the counter with her back to me, preparing dinner. Her hips swayed back and forth to the beat of the music, and her strawberry blonde hair was tied into a loose ponytail.

Tears gathered in my eyes as I watched her. I opened my mouth to get her attention but then snapped it shut again. Suddenly, I felt like a fool. Who did I think I was, traveling across the country to pop in on my sister without her okay?

A hard knot of emotion came undone in my chest, wrenching a sob from my throat. God, I'd missed her. I lifted my fingers to wipe away tears, wanting to hide my emotions before making myself known. But she must have heard or sensed me, because she reached over and powered off the old-fashioned-looking boom box sitting on her counter. Then she jerked around in a quick, defensive motion and raised the knife she held, ready to attack.

She started to lunge forward. Fast. I screamed, recognizing the fear and intent in her eyes. When they latched on to me, when she realized who I was, the knife fell from her grasp. It hit the floor with a noisy clatter. "Chloe?"

"Thank you for not killing me." I spoke in a shaky whisper but with complete seriousness, because for a second there I truly thought we were about to become one of those weird tragedy headlines. "I didn't mean to scare you. But you didn't hear me knock and the door was open. So I . . . um . . . came in."

Slicking her hands down the front of her jeans, she stared at me with round eyes, as if she couldn't believe I was really standing there. Her chin quivered. Her lips trembled. Then she started laughing in huge, gulping bursts. "Oh. Oh, God. I—I—Fuck, Chloe! I could have stabbed you!"

I too began to laugh. Hysterically. "Y-you should have seen your expression when you turned around," I sputtered. "I was sure you were going to strike first and ask questions later."

"I nearly did!" She retrieved the knife from the floor and dropped it into the sink, then placed her hands on her hips, her emotions finally under control. "Why are you here?" And that sounded like my sister: straight and to the point.

"Because I miss you."

She arched an eyebrow in disbelief. "So you hopped on an airplane without calling?"

"I did call! Repeatedly. But you haven't returned any of my messages."

Her lips pursed in confusion. Striding to the other side of the kitchen, she grabbed her cell and flipped through her directory of calls received. "I don't know whom you were calling, but it wasn't me. There aren't any phone calls from you listed here."

"That would be because I called your home phone." I rattled off the numbers I now knew by heart. "I've been trying to get a hold of you for over a week."

Her lips quirked, but a glimmer of annoyance drifted over her. "Uh-huh. Do you ever check your freaking e-mail?"

"Of course I do! And I answer your e-mails when I get them, but you didn't bother responding to even one of my messages." The hurt I'd mostly ignored sprang to life. "Why didn't you call me back?"

She sighed in exasperation. "Probably because I wrote you and told you that I'd decided it was silly to have a home phone and a cell phone, so I was dropping the home number." Her lips twitched again, but I didn't think with humor. "Like fourteen months ago."

Wow, had it really been that long since we'd talked? "Oh." The e-mail sort of rang a bell. So she hadn't been avoiding me. Relief barreled in, replacing the hurt. "I . . . guess I forgot. I always called you on the home number. They must have reissued it, because I definitely was reaching someone's voice mail."

"Maybe, but it wasn't mine."

With that question taken care of, we stood there and stared at each other, frozen in place. Sheridan turned around abruptly, as if the moment was too uncomfortable. I didn't blame her. With her back to me, she asked, "So, you said you missed me?"

"Yes. I . . . I don't know what happened to put this distance between us, but I'm sick of it. I want you back in my life, Sheri." I used her nickname from when we were kids, hoping to soften her defenses. "I want my sister back."

When she looked at me again, her eyes were shiny. She took one step forward but stopped. "Yes," she said. "That would be nice, wouldn't it? Now, do you want to stay here for dinner, or shall we go out?"

"Here. I didn't fly to Seattle to go out to dinner."

"I'll finish cooking, then. Are you staying for the weekend?" I nodded, and she tipped her head toward the hallway. "Well, I suppose there's no sense in you staying at a hotel. You might as well stay here, I guess." Her words were crisp, almost pointed. "Go get your bags. The guest room is the first door on the right."

Gee, that didn't sound too welcoming, but I'd take what I could get. "I'd like that. When I get back, I can help you make dinner."

"There's no need. I have everything under control, Chloe." She blinked, and in a slightly softer manner said, "You're probably tired from your flight. I'll call you when dinner is ready."

"Wh-what's on the menu?" I didn't really care. I wasn't even that hungry, but I wanted her to keep talking.

"Salad. Grilled salmon." She shrugged. "It's strange, but I stopped at the store on the way home and bought two fillets. As if I knew I'd need to feed two tonight."

"Maybe you did?" I crossed the room and pulled her into a hug. While she didn't resist, she held her body ramrod straight, so the embrace came off as awkward and rigid. We separated quickly. "I'm really glad to see you."

She pressed her lips together but didn't speak. I pivoted on my heel to get my bag, but also to give her a few minutes to deal with the surprise of my unannounced visit. Right before I left the kitchen, I heard her whisper, "I'm glad to see you too."

A few minutes later, I flopped down on the bed she gave me, everything inside warming as I glanced around the room. The billowy white curtains, the antique furnishings, the touches of soft color here and there—not to mention the various framed photos of me and Sheridan that sat on the nightstands—all told me that this room had been decorated with me in mind. And if she'd done that, then I'd been in her thoughts as much as she'd been in mine. We definitely had a chance.

I sat there until Sheridan called me for dinner, trying to unwind, trying to figure out how to reach my sister. When I sat down across from her, I decided to let her take the lead.

Our conversation started off stilted, nearly as awkward as our hug, but by the end of the meal, we were becoming more comfortable with each other. Thank God for that. After our meal, we brought the bottle of wine with us into the living room. With each sip, our conversation flowed smoother and easier, and before too long we were flipping through Sheridan's photo albums. Memories swarmed in, and that was what finally broke the ice between us. Suddenly, I had my sister back.

From that moment on, for the next two hours we spent equal amounts of time giggling and crying as we recalled our lives with our parents before we'd moved in with our aunt. Not that Aunt Lu was horrible, because she wasn't. She'd taken care of us in her way, and had definitely given us the best home she could. But she'd never wanted children, didn't have a natural affinity with us, and likely didn't have a clue how to meet two grieving children's emotional needs. We had every material thing we required, meals were put on the table at appropriate times and we were never left completely alone. But it stopped there.

I'm not sure if she ever told us she loved us. Hell, I'm not sure if she ever *did* love us. She'd married several years back and now lived in South Carolina. Maybe I'd call her at some point and try to find a way to bridge the gap between us. For one, I wasn't a child anymore, and also, nothing was impossible. And she was, after all, just as much my family as Sheridan.

When we'd looked at the last photo and the bottle of wine was empty, I decided to pull up my big-girl pants and ask Sheridan about the past. Clearing my throat, I twisted around on the sofa so I could see her. "I still don't understand what happened to change us, Sheri. I thought for a while it was because I moved into the dorms when I went to college and left you alone with Aunt Lu. But we were fine those first couple of years. So . . . I guess I'm just confused." I touched her hand. "If . . . if you don't mind talking about it, I'd like to know."

She narrowed her blue-green eyes. "Your memories are different than mine. We weren't fine, Chloe. I only saw you once a month or so. And you rarely called."

An immediate defensive edge hardened over me. I set it

aside because, as much as the words hurt, they were truthful. "I'm sorry. I was still reeling from Kyle, and then later I became so focused on school that I . . . I guess I forgot you might still need me. You always seemed bubbly and happy whenever we talked."

"I didn't want to worry you, but of course I needed you. You know how Aunt Lu was. She nitpicked every last thing. Way worse than when you were there." Her voice remained calm, but my sister angrily twisted a strand of hair around her finger. "By the time I graduated from high school, all I wanted was to get out of that house."

"And away from me? Is that why you came here for school? Because I'd let you down so much?" Even with her explanation, I couldn't quite grasp the reasoning for her cold-shoulder treatment.

"Yes and no." She covered her eyes with her hands as a shiver stole over her. "I don't know if I want to tell you this. I've worked to move on. Letting that part of my life go has been a struggle."

"If you don't want to, you don't have to. But I love you, Sheri." Obviously, this was about far more than my behavior back then, even if I had indeed been selfish and overly focused on myself. I tugged her hands away from her face. "Look at me, kiddo. I'm still your big sister."

Numerous emotions whisked over her as she thought about my statement. She rolled her upper lip between her teeth, trying to decide if she wanted to spill her secret. I squeezed her hand, and that one little gesture pushed her forward.

"I had a baby," she blurted. "And I gave her up for adoption. That's why I moved. I didn't want you to know I'd screwed up so badly. And since then I haven't known how to be around you, so I kept my distance."

"*What?*" I heard her words. I understood them, even. But wow.

"Yes, Chloe. Your perfect little sister isn't so perfect. Aunt Lu was driving me up a wall with all of her rules, and I was lonely. So, you know, I was a cliché. Got myself knocked up right after graduation." A strangled laugh choked out of her. "Don't look at me like that. I didn't get pregnant on purpose. But that doesn't make it any less of a cliché."

"Why didn't you tell me? I would have helped you! If you'd wanted to keep the baby, if you wanted to give her up, whatever you wanted, I would've stood by you and helped you." I shook my head, half-blind with tears. "I cannot believe you came here all by yourself and went through that. And I never knew!"

"I tried once," she admitted, her voice soft and hesitant. "We met for lunch, and I planned on telling you. But you kept saying how proud you were of me. I couldn't bear to ruin it." She lifted her shoulders in a faint shrug. "The more I thought about it, the more sense it made to just get away. So I used my portion of the money Mom and Dad left us to support myself here for the first year, and then, after I had the baby and gave her up, I went to school."

"I can't imagine." I shook my head again, trying to come to terms with this new information. "H-how did you manage all on your own? Who drove you to the hospital when you were in labor? Who was with you when you had the baby? Oh, sweetie, I'm so, so sorry you didn't feel you could tell me."

"It was a private adoption. The couple I chose were terrific. They helped me hugely, and they drove me to the hospital and stayed with me through delivery. And they held *their* baby almost as soon as she was born." She said this last part almost as if she were trying to convince herself and not me.

"Okay. Well . . . good. I'm glad you had support. I just wish it could've been me." Another thought hit. I wasn't sure if I should ask, but I did anyway. "Because the adoption was private, do the parents send you pictures and updates?" I thought that if they did, I'd like to see a picture. "She'd be how old now?"

"Twelve. But I agreed to zero contact after the final papers were signed. It's better that way. I don't see how I could've moved on while getting updates and pictures. But they know that someday, if she asks, they can give her my name. So maybe . . . well, maybe someday she'll show up." Emotion shimmered in Sheridan's eyes. "I made the right choice. For her and for me. I have never doubted that. But I never held her in my arms, I never looked into her eyes and I never kissed her. I regret that."

"Oh, sweetie." I held my arms out and Sheridan scooted closer. I squeezed her to me in a tight hug. "I am so sorry," I whispered in her ear. "I am so sorry you dealt with that alone."

"It sucked. But it was my choice." Pulling herself back, she wiped the wetness from her cheeks. "You're here now, though. And I'm so glad you are."

I nodded, but at that second something Miranda said reverberated in my head. She wanted *all* of her daughters to recognize each other. And here was another daughter, another link in our family tree, who would someday have the right to our magic.

"What are you thinking, Chloe? You have an odd expression on your face."

Plastering on a smile, I gave a partial truth. "Just wishing I could've been with you."

At that point, our conversation veered off into other areas. When midnight crawled in—two in the morning for me—we went to our separate bedrooms. The combination of exhaustion, emotions and several glasses of wine put me into a deep sleep. But I dreamed. About Ben and Mari.

About my sister. And now about a baby whose face I couldn't see.

The next morning we had a quick breakfast and Sheridan took me to Pike Place Market. I instantly fell in love with the scents—well, except for the fish market—the sights, the shops and the energy that seemed to crackle in the air. Following our trip there, we did a little more sightseeing, and I knew if I ever tired of living in Chicago that I'd be able to move to Seattle and be quite content. Okay, mostly content. Ben didn't make his home in the Emerald City. Otherwise, I'd already have been packing my bags.

Still, I enjoyed the day. I enjoyed being with my sister. We had lunch out, went shopping and returned to her place with our arms filled with purchases. Most of mine were gifts I planned on leaving for Sheridan, but I also had a few for Alice, Elizabeth, Verda and Rose.

Now, hours later, we sat on her sofa. We'd just finished watching a movie, and by unspoken agreement had steered away from any serious topics of conversation. But the hours between now and when my plane departed the next morning were dwindling fast, and there was something else I needed to go over with Sheridan.

"Hey, sis." I crossed my legs. "If magic was real and you could have one wish granted, anything you wanted, what would it be?"

"I don't make wishes." Humor glittered in her voice. "You still believe in that stuff?"

"Oh, yes. I definitely believe." I watched her carefully, trying to figure out the best way to proceed. Miranda had said that Sheridan wasn't ready for this, so spilling everything was probably not going to happen tonight. "You still don't?"

A quick, decisive shake of her head, but a tiny smile

appeared. "Nope. But you believed in Santa Claus longer than I did. Odd, when you take into consideration that I'm three years younger than you."

I grinned. Now was definitely not the time to give her the news about our heredity, but maybe there was another way. "Would you like to believe? If your common sense and"—I wrinkled my nose—"rigid rules were relaxed enough so you could, would you *want* to believe in magic? In Santa?"

She grabbed a throw pillow and tossed it at me. "My rules are not that rigid. I just happen to prefer order and logic, and I get frustrated when things don't make sense."

I sailed the pillow right back at her. "Answer my question, Sheri. Is there any part of you that wishes magic was real?"

She dropped the pillow on her lap and stared at me, curious. "I guess so. But it isn't, so your question really doesn't have an answer." She grinned. "But I suppose if I lived with the delusions you do, then it would be nice to have some type of power, something that would come in handy when things got tough." She winked. "Maybe invisibility! Or the ability to wave my hand and have money appear all around me. Or . . . or to go back in time and hold my daughter."

"I want to try something." I grasped Sheridan's hands before I lost my courage. "But only if you agree. Will you let me?"

"Um. That depends. What do you want to try?"

"To give you magic."

A laugh belted out of her. "Okay, Chloe. You go right ahead. Give me magic."

"Pretend magic is real and that there's some type of power inside all of us. One person might be able to bake wishes into cakes, and maybe someone else can draw pictures of the future, and perhaps someone else can bend the wills of others. The possibilities go on and on and on. If this were true, and if I had the ability to awaken *your* magic, even without knowing what that power would be, would you want me to?"

I had a feeling that this was what I was supposed to do. That this is what Miranda had intended. Even so, my sister called the shots here. "Still thinking?" I asked.

"I'm wondering if you've gone off the deep end." She looked at me so seriously that I knew she meant it. "But if you want an honest answer—"

"I do. Completely honest."

"Then, yes. If I lived in a world where magic was real, and leprechauns hid pots of gold beneath rainbows and fairy godmothers with sparkling wands could fix me up with my Prince Charming, then yes. By all means, I would want to experience magic."

Ha. I didn't know about leprechauns, and I'd yet to see a fairy godmother, but we did have a great-great-great-ghost-grandmother. "Close your eyes."

She did, and I followed suit.

The power came alive instantly. I opened my heart and soul, and when the magic had grown thick and heavy inside of me, around us, I brought to mind the carefully worded wish I'd been thinking about since my last visit with Miranda. As the energy continued to pulsate, ripple and surge, I silently recited,

> I wish for the magic of our ancestors to come to life in-
> side of you, Sheridan, but only when you need it. Only
> when you reach for it. Until then, your power will lie
> dormant, awaiting your command, awaiting the right
> moment. And with this wish, I expunge my power, my
> magic, from my body, from my heart and from my soul.
> No longer will this gift exist within me. No longer will I
> be able to alter the wills of others.

The power slammed through me harder than ever before. It stunned and rocked me, turned my world upside down and then back around. My breathing came out in fast, short gasps, and I was surprised I didn't keel over from a heart attack. I held on tight, as I always did, not wanting to give in, not wanting to turn my back on this wish. But God, this time, in this instance, it was nearly impossible.

I heard Sheridan giggle. Somehow, that helped me hang on. Sisterly love beat the crap out of Gypsy magic. That was nice to know.

All at once, the moment ended and my body returned to normal. I kept my eyes shut, continuing to hold Sheridan's hands, but I reached into myself, seeking the magic, trying to see if I could bring the power back to life. A shudder rippled out when I couldn't find even a trace of the magic anywhere. Relief followed, strong and furious, because this was what I'd wanted. But also a fair amount of sadness came, regret that I couldn't have had a different type of power. Something less dangerous. Something less morally ambiguous. Something a hell of a lot less addictive.

"Do I have magic now, Chloe?" Sheridan teased.

I opened my eyes. "No. But it's there, waiting for you. If the day comes where you find yourself remembering tonight and wishing for something you can't gain on your own, call me." Maybe we'd have that particular conversation before that day, but just in case, I wanted her to know to reach out to me. "Okay? Promise me."

Twinkles of mirth floated into her eyes, but she nodded. "Sure, sis. If that's what you want, then yeah. When the day comes that I wake up wishing for magic or leprechauns or fairy godmothers, I'll give you a call."

"Good. That's good." I considered giving her the scoop on our familial relationship to Alice, Elizabeth and Verda, but decided to leave it alone. Besides, I wasn't sure how to explain that connection without going into everything else. Instead I said, "I love you, Sheri. I'm so glad I came."

"Stop with the gushy stuff." She flipped the pillow my way again. "But I'm glad you're here too."

And then, knowing we might not see each other again soon, we hunkered down to talk for the remainder of the night and into the morning. I loved every sleepless minute of it.

Chapter Twenty-one

I finished ringing up Mrs. Delinsky's purchases and, after she left the store, dropped into my chair. Two weeks, one day and twelve hours had passed since my encounter with Ben. A total of 372 hours, or approximately 22,320 minutes, since I'd last seen the man I loved. Yes, I'd done the math. I'd resisted figuring out how many seconds, but only barely. Still, 372 hours without a peep.

I missed him even more than I'd thought was possible. The yearning to see and touch and talk with him, to simply spend time with him, never left me. These feelings were there, regardless of where I went or what I did. And I still hoped with every part of my being that he'd find his way back. Strangely, though, other than the aching loss of Ben, I was doing well.

Sheridan and I spoke often, and the miles between us now were just that: *physical* distance. Emotionally we were growing closer with every call, with every e-mail, and she was already planning a visit to Chicago. I couldn't wait to see her again. Maybe by then, with the help of Alice, Elizabeth and Verda, I'd be able to share everything with her—or if nothing else, the fact that we were all related. I wanted my sister to have that particular gift more than anything else.

"Hey, Chloe?" Paige interrupted my musings, stopping in front of the counter. Her voice held a hesitant quality, and she appeared unsure. Nervous, even. "I need to ask you something, and I hope you don't get mad."

"Unless you've turned into an embezzler, I don't think that's possible." I grinned, not worried in the slightest. "If you're swindling money, then I won't be able to ask if you'd like to be my partner. So yeah, that might tick me off." I'd been thinking about the idea seriously.

Her lips formed a surprised O. "What?"

"You heard me right, Paige. You know this place as well as I do, and honestly? I'd love to have someone to share the responsibility, so I can go visit my sister more. Take some trips. Become a"—I drew a circle in the air—"more well-rounded individual. And you're a business major, graduating next year, so I thought you might be interested."

"Um . . . wow. Really?" She shook her head. "I don't have money to buy in to the business, Chloe."

"We'll figure something out with your share of the profits until we're square." My grin widened. Paige deserved the offer, and I really, really wanted her to say yes. "You don't have to decide now. You'll probably want to look over the accounting and talk to an attorney. But think about it, okay?"

"Yeah, I will. And, you might rescind the offer once I tell you this."

"Doubtful. But go ahead."

"You know when you were visiting your sister? I worked that Saturday with Jen. Anyway, Kyle came in."

My interest piqued, because I hadn't heard from Kyle since I'd removed my spells. "He did? What did he want?"

Paige took a step backward. "He asked about you right off. When I said you were in Seattle, he wanted to know how you were doing. I told him you were fine."

"Oh! That's good." I wrinkled my forehead in confusion. "Why would I be upset about that?"

She took another step backward. "The shop was busy, but he hung around until we closed and we ended up going out to lunch. We talked for a long time. We've been talking a lot on the phone." Paige sighed, and then pulled in a breath. "I like him. I'd really like to get to know him better. But I—I wanted to make sure that was okay with you. Before we . . . um . . . officially started dating."

I smiled and laughed. "You thought I'd be upset because you and Kyle want to date?" Jumping up, I ran around the counter. Paige's eyes rounded and she looked ready to bolt. I laughed again. "Don't look so scared. This is great news!" I grabbed her hands and squeezed.

Paige humored me for a few seconds and then pulled away. "You're happy I want to date your ex-fiancé? That's not the reaction I expected."

Of course I was happy. For one, I'd clearly removed all magic from him, which meant I likely had from Ben, as well. For two . . . well, maybe Paige would be able to help Kyle get over Shelby. "He's a great guy, Paige. And you're a great girl. So . . . yeah, I'm good with this. He and I are still friends, you know. So why wouldn't I be pleased?"

Relief washed into her eyes, erasing her pinched look. "Wow, I was so nervous about telling you. I'm glad you're okay with it." She grinned. "And yes, I am interested in becoming your partner. I sort of hoped that might happen, but didn't expect anything until after I finished school."

"Awesome. I'll put together a profile of the business and get it to you sometime in the next week or so. And then, once you've had a chance to look everything over, we'll go from there."

Her eyes glistened. "Cool." She returned to the counter, taking the seat I'd vacated. In a light tone, she said, "There's something else I meant to mention, but forgot with all of my concerns over Kyle."

I grabbed a book that a customer had left in the wrong place and replaced it on its proper shelf. "What's that?"

"Ben called yesterday morning, before you came in."

My heart stopped beating. I waited for it start again before I opened my mouth. "Oh, yeah?" I asked, as if I couldn't care less. "And what did he want?"

"He said thanks for the gift certificate, and that his assistant loved it. I guess she's planning on taking one of our pendulum classes."

"Th-that's it? That's all he said?"

Twisting her mood ring, Paige shrugged. "Well, he also asked for the name of Elizabeth's bakery."

Every drop of air in my lungs escaped in a wheezy squeal. "Did you tell him?"

"Yeah. I recommended their peanut-butter-chocolate-chunk cookies. He laughed and said he'd have to check them out."

"D-did he ask about me?"

Paige blinked. "Nope. His call was about the gift certificate and the bakery. That was all. I'm sorry, Chloe."

"Uh-huh. Okay, then. I'm—uh—going to the back room. To do some paperwork. Lots of paperwork," I mumbled. "You . . . um . . . yeah. Paperwork."

I nearly tripped over my feet in my rush. There was no reason for Ben to call about the gift certificate, and why would he care about Elizabeth's bakery unless . . . unless he wanted to talk to Elizabeth about me? I didn't know if I should be excited or worried, pleased or scared. What I did know was that I needed to get hold of Elizabeth. Immediately.

When I called A Taste of Magic, I was told that she wasn't in. I tried her at home. No dice there, either. Frustrated beyond belief, I phoned Alice and begged her to find her sister. She said she'd try and then got off the phone in a hurry, claiming Rose needed something.

Once again, all I could do was sit and wait.

The following evening—Friday—I arrived at Alice's house thirty minutes early. I couldn't help myself. I didn't have anywhere else to be, and the mushy pile of nerves, anticipation and excitement that whipped through me left me with no other choice. Elizabeth hadn't returned any of my phone calls, which was odd and annoying, but Alice assured me that her sister would be in attendance tonight, along with Grandma Verda, so I'd be able to ask about Ben soon enough—which was the reason for my crazy emotions.

For the moment, however, Alice and I were alone in her living room. Ethan and Rose were visiting Rose's paternal grandmother, Beatrice, so the house felt way more quiet than normal. I sat in the papasan chair Alice had owned forever, and she was across from me, on her sofa.

I smiled, trying to pretend I was as cool as a cucumber. "How's Rose doing? Have there been any new magic sightings?"

Alice grinned, and the worry that had clung to her the last time we talked about her daughter's gift didn't seem as thick. "Not a one. I've decided, with Ethan's help, to take her experiences one day at a time. We'll handle them as they come along."

"That's good. You seem more at peace with it."

She laughed. "I don't know if that's true, but my life is good. I'm in love with a man who loves me, I have a beautiful daughter, a wonderful family and"—she pointed her gaze at me—"a best friend who seems to want to be around me again."

A sob caught in my throat. "You know," I said carefully, speaking from the heart, "this past year I acted like an idiot. I felt that because you were happy, I wasn't as important to you anymore, that you didn't have time for me in your life anymore. I should have just talked with you about it, but I didn't know how. So I became—"

"Lonely?"

"Yes. Defensive too. I wanted you to see what I was going through and come to me on your own. But you had a new husband and baby, and how could you see anything when I went out of my way to avoid you?" The admission slipped out along with another choked sob. "I apologize, Alice."

She launched herself at me and drew me into a tight hug. Then she shook her head. "I have my own blame. I knew something was wrong, and every day I'd promise to call you or to pack Rose in the car and go see you, so we could get to the bottom of it. But each day brought something new, and I was always so freaking tired. So, Chloe, I accept your apology if you accept mine."

"Absolutely." Not that she needed to say she was sorry.

Happy that our friendship was back on track, I decided to confess something else. "So . . . uh . . . I haven't told you what happened in Seattle yet."

Returning to the sofa, she crossed her legs and gestured for me to continue. I wasn't going to tell her about Sheridan's baby. At some point my sister might choose to tell Alice, but until then my lips were sealed. "I . . . gave my magic up."

Alice sat up straighter. "You what?"

I nodded and gave her the entire scoop. "As far as I can tell, the spell worked. I'm magic free." Though the other day, there had been this man in my store. He'd smiled. I'd turned around to grab the phone and, just like with Mari, when I turned back he was gone. I wasn't sure what that meant yet, but I was positive the will-bending portion of my ability had been dealt with. And honestly, if for some reason the rest of my gift had stayed with me, well, that seemed like a fair trade-off. Especially if I could help others.

"Anyway, I wanted you to know that you don't have to worry about what I did—using my power to make you tell me about Rose—happening again. Those days are over."

Alice scrunched her face up, confused. "I wasn't that worried about it. And Chloe, I didn't know we *could* give the magic up."

I repeated Miranda's words, then asked, "Why? I thought you liked your gift."

"Oh, I do. But maybe . . . maybe with Rose?"

"That would have to be her choice, wouldn't it?"

"Well, yeah. But I'll have to ask Miranda about this. I mean, for us, we were given the power. Rose was born with her magic. So who knows if she'll even have the choice?" Alice shook her head. "Not that any of this matters now, but I find it really interesting."

The doorbell rang before I could respond. A few minutes later, Verda and Elizabeth had taken seats in the living room. I wanted to pounce on Elizabeth for answers, but Verda had something else in mind.

"Okay, girls. I have some news to share!" She tossed me a grin, and a wicked gleam shone brightly in her eyes. I sighed but reined in my questions for Elizabeth. Verda spoke softly, but her excitement reverberated in every word. "I'm starting a business, and I hope that each of you will support me in this new chapter of my life."

A hush came over the room. Elizabeth broke the silence first. "Really? What kind of a business?"

Verda clapped her hands. "A matchmaking firm. I'm going to help the lovelorn in Chicago find their perfect matches!" She winked. "I'm quite good at it. I knew Nate was the right man for Elizabeth, and I pegged Ethan as your soul mate in the very beginning, Alice."

Well, both of those statements were true.

Alice's grin broadened. Apparently, and surprisingly, she liked the idea. "Are you going to use your fruit ranking system?"

I grinned too. Verda had an interesting method of grading men: she labeled those she considered to be top-shelf after her favorite fruit—pomegranates—while lemons were those men she ranked at the bottom. I didn't recall how the rest of the fruits played out.

"Maybe. I haven't worked out of all the particulars yet,

but I'm hoping you girls will help." Verda pulled herself up and came over to me, standing next to my chair. "And there's something else I need to tell you. Chloe knows part of it, but—"

Oh, no. "Six weeks aren't up yet!" I blurted.

She patted my shoulder. I'm sure she meant to be comforting. "That's okay, dear. Things are settled well enough now. It's time to spill the beans."

Alice froze. "What beans?"

I cringed, mentally and physically, and clasped my hands together. Tight.

"I tricked Chloe into giving me the magic back. She didn't know anything about my dream when she did it, so if you two are going to get angry, don't take it out on her."

I laughed weakly and focused on Alice. "This was before our talk. I had no idea. And I'd already promised her I wouldn't say anything for six weeks."

Alice whipped her gaze from me to Verda and then back again. I crunched myself as far into the chair cushion as I could, sort of wishing the dang thing would swallow me up. She stood and paced the room, her body tight with stress.

"Stop being so melodramatic, Alice. I know you love me and I know you're worried about me, but I'm doing what is right. And I'm not dying tomorrow." Verda pushed out a shaky sigh. "I've supported you girls from the beginning. I'd like the same from you."

Elizabeth reached out and tugged her sister's arm, forcing her to stop. "Come on, Alice. You know she's right. We should've helped her to begin with."

I held my breath as I waited for Alice's reaction. Finally, she shook her head back and forth and shrugged. She faced me and Verda but focused on me first. "I understand how wily Grandma can be, so I'm not mad at you. And I understand you had a promise to keep to her, but you shouldn't have made that promise to me, because you'd already broken it."

"No! Not really. I told you that if she came to me *from that day forward*, I'd tell her no."

"Chloe! Don't give me that garbage."

Knowing Alice was right, and wanting to move past this, I gave in. "I'm sorry. But I didn't know how else to handle the situation."

She nodded. Thank God. But then she centered her attention on Verda. "I love you, Grandma. And yes, I'll help you. But please, please don't take that dream as gospel. That's all I ask. Okay?"

Verda squeezed my shoulder. "I'm not digging my grave. So quit worrying. And I'm not sharing the dream with you all. It's mine, and it's private. But I will definitely need all of your help. Because part of what I have to do is find the woman your brother is going to marry and get things moving for them. Otherwise, they'll never find each other. And it's critical that they do."

Elizabeth piped in then. "Which brother? Joe or Scot?"

"Your stubborn-as-a-mule brother."

Oh, she meant Scot. I adored Scot, and for a while had played around with the idea of dating him—back before I knew we were family, naturally. But even then I realized it would have seemed like dating my brother. If I had one.

Verda leaned over and kissed me on the cheek, and then followed suit with Alice and Elizabeth. "I'm done talking about this. But you girls had the right to know this much. When the time is right I'll share more." She retook her seat, straightened her shoulders and gave us each a look that dared us to argue. No one did.

Before someone else made any type of a startling revelation, I took advantage of the quiet and looked at Elizabeth. "Did Ben come to A Taste of Magic to talk with you?"

Elizabeth's gaze slid to Verda's. "Yes, he did."

"Did he talk about me? Ask you questions about the magic or anything like that?"

Her mouth twitched. "No, Chloe. The bakery his firm uses went out of business. He wanted to know about our prices, and if we would do weekly deliveries for meetings with clients."

"Th-that's all? He came to you solely about business?"

"Yes. I own a bakery. He had a need for baked goods. Because of you and whatever you told him, he thought of my bakery. That's it, sweetie." She pushed a long strand of hair behind her ear. "He . . . uh . . . he looked sad, though. And if you think about it, there are tons of bakeries in Chicago. And . . . well, he's the CFO, right? Isn't it sort of odd that he would arrange something as rudimentary as buying pastries?"

Hope flared up. But Verda quashed it. "Stop filling her head with what you think, Lizzy. The man came for baked goods. That's all you know," she said in a firm, no-nonsense tone.

Elizabeth's eyes widened. "But Grandma—"

"It's time for us to leave, don't you think?" Verda stood and grabbed her granddaughter's hand. "You brought me here. You can take me home." Then Verda sort of pushed and shoved Elizabeth out of the room.

When they were gone, I blinked. One tear and then another trailed down my cheek.

"Oh, sweetie," Alice said. "It's only been a few weeks. Liz is right. There's no reason for Ben to have gone to *her* bakery. Just hold on to that for a while." My friend helped ease my strangling disappointment. "Besides, you have us."

I laughed through my tears. "This is true. You're not throttling me for giving Verda her magic back. I should be happy enough with that."

"You deserve to be happy, period. And no, I'm not going

to throttle you. I'm worried about Grandma, but I'm going to use the same thought process on her that I'm using with Rose." A soft smile touched Alice's lips. "Just take it—"

"One day at a time." I finished her statement for her, thinking I should use that philosophy myself. "You know what? I'll be fine. I managed to get my hopes up, and the fall hurt. But nothing has changed. Nothing is worse than it was this morning." And some things, such as my friendship with Alice, were better.

"Mind if I stay a while?" I asked, thinking that the comfort of my best friend would chase more of the clouds away. "Ethan and Rose aren't home yet, so we could hang out. If you don't have other plans."

Something I couldn't identify crossed her expression. "Sorry, sweetie. I do have other plans tonight." Her gaze hit the clock on the wall. "Actually, I need to . . . ah . . . start getting ready. And really, you should go home. In case Ben calls."

Yeah. Right. Go home and wait for Ben to call. I did that nearly every night. "You really have plans?" I asked.

She nodded. I didn't quite believe her, but if she wanted me to leave, I'd leave.

She walked me to the front door, gave me another hug and then nearly shoved me out. "Sorry to be in such a rush, but . . . well . . ."

"You have plans. Right. Got it."

I left then, trying to ignore the hurt. Possibly she was still fretting over Rose, and with the information about my magic, maybe she wanted to try to reach Miranda.

I nearly turned around to find out if I was right, when Elizabeth hollered my name. Her car was parked in the street, and she gestured for me to come over. Curious and concerned, I crossed the front lawn.

"Is there something wrong with your car?" I asked when I reached her.

She shook her head. "Grandma's upset. She won't talk to me, and she doesn't want to talk to Alice. She thinks you're mad at her, and won't go home until she clears the air." Elizabeth wrung her hands together in worry. "Can you"—she flipped her head toward the car—"get inside and try to cheer her up? Nate's waiting for me."

"Of course!" I didn't hesitate. I slid into the backseat of Elizabeth's car. Verda sat in the front, in the passenger seat, and her head was bent forward. I couldn't see her face, but her shoulders were shaking. God, I felt horrible—and I didn't even know why.

I patted the back of her head. "Verda? What's wrong?"

"Oh, Chloe!" she wailed. "Everything is . . . is . . ."

Alice eased in the other side of the car, joining me in the backseat. "Elizabeth got me. What's going on?"

My door slammed shut. Before I could blink, before my brain wrapped around whatever the hell was happening—again—Elizabeth crawled into the driver's seat. That's when I got it.

"Oh, come on! I do not need another intervention!" I screeched. "And if you all wanted to talk to me, we were just together. Inside Alice's house!"

Very calmly, Verda craned her neck so she could see me. "But Ethan and Rose will be home soon, and it's obvious that you're dealing with some issues regarding Ben. You need our help, Chloe!" Returning to her prior position, she whispered to Elizabeth, "We have the goodies taken care of, don't we?"

I didn't hear Elizabeth's answer.

"Why is this necessary?" I demanded of Alice. "I'm doing okay!" Mostly, anyway.

"Because we love you." She pressed her lips together. "Deal with it, Chloe."

Yeah, well, I loved them too. But this kidnapping thing was seriously getting out of control. Big time. I tried to console myself with a few facts as Elizabeth maneuvered the car out of Alice's neighborhood: I had my clothes on, I had plenty of money on me for cab fare, and . . . well, I wasn't engaged to the wrong man this time. Still, I scowled out the window. I'd once wanted a family. Now, like it or not, my family liked to kidnap me.

Chapter Twenty-two

Elizabeth drove us to the historic hotel where my prior intervention had taken place. About ten minutes into the commute, a blind and perhaps stupid hope rose inside of me. That hope increased when we didn't stop in the lobby but went directly to the room—the same room as before, by the way—and Verda dragged the key card out of her purse. I believed to the tips of my toes that Ben would be waiting inside.

When Verda unlocked the door and pushed it open, I shoved my way in first, totally expecting to see Ben lounging on the bed. He wasn't. Nor was he anywhere in the room. Just that fast, all of my anticipation evaporated. My shoulders slumped as I crossed to the four chairs that were set up: three in a half circle and one in the middle. Apparently, this really was another intervention. Yay.

Even in my distress, I noticed that the same care had been taken as the last time. Candles flickered, adding a soothing ambience to the space, soft music played and yes . . . there was a box of cupcakes in the middle of the table. So Verda had her goodies. Again, it seemed so much more like a scene set for seduction than for whatever they had in store for me.

"Okay, we're here. Who has the baby rattle?" I asked, choosing the center seat. "Let's get started."

Verda, with a pleased smile, perched in the chair directly in front of me. "No baby rattle tonight. I think we're past that. Don't you, Chloe?"

"Sure." I waved my hand at Elizabeth and Alice. "Sit down. What are you waiting for?"

Alice arched an eyebrow but did as asked. "You're handling this quite well."

"Much better than our first go-around." Elizabeth also took a seat. "A lot has changed since then, hasn't it, Chloe?"

"Yep. So . . . who wants to go first? What questions are going to be asked of me?" I crossed one leg over the other and bobbed my foot in the air. "Let's get moving." I shot Verda a grin. "Unless you'd like a cupcake first?"

The wrinkles around her eyes deepened as she laughed. "I'll have one later. But we don't have all night, so yes, let's get this show on the road."

"I'm ready," I said. "I don't have any secrets, there is nothing I'm hiding, and other than missing Ben I'm quite content with life at the moment. So . . . what's left?"

Alice spoke up. "You're still sure of your feelings for him?"

"Yes. I'm one hundred percent positive that I love and miss him."

Elizabeth leaned forward. "So if you could, you'd like to smooth things over. Is that right?"

"Yes," I repeated. "Of course I would."

"Too bad he isn't here. If he were, would you be happy to see him?" Verda reached into her handbag. "Not that he is. I'm just wondering if we should call and see if he'd come on over. Maybe if we all talked to him together, he'd have an easier time understanding our gift."

"If he were here, I'd be thrilled to see him. But no, Verda. We are not calling him and asking him to come over. And you are not to call him on your own with any of this. Okay?"

"But why not? I don't see how it would hurt anything," she pouted.

Suddenly, I had a very bad feeling. "You didn't call him already, did you?"

"No! I wouldn't do something like that without your permission, Chloe." Verda's hand remained in her purse, as if she clutched something she wasn't ready to pull out. "Why . . . I would never take it upon myself . . ."

"Give it up, Grandma. You most certainly would. It's one of the reasons we love you," Alice interjected. Focusing on me, she smiled. "But unless she's done something I don't know about, then no, Grandma hasn't called your Ben."

"Good," I said. "If and when Ben is ready to see and talk to me, he knows how. And I really want to know when"—I swallowed—"*if* that day comes, that no one pushed him into it."

"Fair enough." Elizabeth gave her grandmother a wide-eyed look. "I think, with what Chloe has said, we're ready for the next step."

Next step? "What . . . uh . . . do you mean?"

Verda's eyes sparkled. My bad feeling came back. "I did some more research on the World Wide Web and learned about a new meditation technique. It's called"—she screwed her mouth into a pucker—"the blindfold technique. What you do is sit with a blindfold on and think about whatever's troubling you. Oh! You're also supposed to have earplugs in. I nearly forgot about that."

"And why would I want to do this?" I asked as calmly as possible.

"If you can't see or hear the world around you, then you have no choice but to focus on your inner struggles. It's a great way to find peace." She did the lip-pucker thing again. "Or so I read. Will you try?"

"You're serious?"

"Of course. We love you, Chloe! This is a safe place. You can trust us." Verda batted her lashes. "Open yourself to the possibility!"

I pressed my lips together and tried not to laugh, nodding

toward her handbag. "I take it you have earplugs and a blindfold in there?"

"Yep." Verda's entire body quivered with excitement. "I came prepared."

I couldn't fathom how blocking out the world and thinking about Ben would give me any sort of peace, but I also didn't mind humoring Verda. I gave an exaggerated sigh. "Sure. I'm game. Hand them over."

She did.

Before blinding and deafening myself, I glanced at Alice. She was smirking at me, and amusement danced in her eyes. My lips twitched. "You think this is funny?"

"I think it's cute. Really, really cute."

I stuck my tongue out and then tied the blindfold around my head, covering my eyes. "How long am I to do this for?" I asked into the air.

"Not long, dear." Verda's voice reached my ears. Strangely, she sounded farther away. As if she stood across the room. "Not long at all."

"Well, pat me on my shoulder or something when the time's up." I stuck the earplugs in and gave myself a few seconds to become accustomed. My hearing wasn't completely blocked, but the sounds were greatly muted. I breathed in and out, trying to relax. I hadn't intended to think about Ben, about how much I missed him or how disappointed I was that he hadn't contacted me, but his face appeared in my mind. I saw those bluer-than-blue eyes and my heart skipped a beat. God, I loved those eyes.

The deep rumble of his voice wove into my memory next, and the husky, raspy sound of his laugh. A chiseled jaw, strong cheekbones and, oh, the masculine, muscular beauty of his body. A sigh gushed out of me. Somehow, Verda had been right. Thinking about him this way, without the distractions of the world, softened everything inside.

I let my imagination play, pictured him in my bed, in those skin-tight boxer briefs, recalled each intimate moment of that night. Heat whirled in, fast and furious. Wow. I was good at this. Scary good. Because not only could I sense Ben's presence, I could almost smell his clean, masculine scent.

The night with Mari slipped in then, and the recollection of the love, sorrow and strength in Ben's eyes as he said good-bye to his daughter took me to another place. Every part of me that had relaxed tensed up again, and the agony I'd tried so hard to set aside rolled in. Yes, my life would be fine without Ben. Yes, I could exist without his voice, without his touch, without his laughter. But I didn't want to. How could I? A man who was able to give and love and believe so fully, and let the person he loved the most in the world go because it was better for her, was one man in a million. A zillion. And I'd never, for the rest of my life, meet another man like him.

Tears filled my eyes, but the blindfold captured them so they couldn't flow down my cheeks. But they were there, and while no one else could see me crying, the release of those tears somehow, in some way, transported me to yet another place. I would always love Ben. I would never stop hearing a knock on my door or the ringing of my phone without my heart pausing, without everything inside of me hoping that he was on the other side. I would never stop wishing I'd handled things differently. But I would also, for the rest of my life, cherish every single second I'd spent with him. Those moments were precious and beautiful and had changed me.

A hand skimmed along my knee, breaking into my thoughts. Apparently, Verda had decided I'd focused on my inner struggles long enough. I swallowed before removing the earplugs. I gulped back a sob before untying the blindfold, before wiping the fabric across my eyes to soak up my tears. I closed my eyes, knowing the light in the room would seem overly bright. Also, I wanted to treasure what I'd just experienced before joining the reality of the world again.

A thumb grazed along my jaw. My breath locked in my lungs.

"Open up, Red. I need to see those beautiful green eyes of yours."

My jaw fell open, but I kept my eyes glued shut. Was I hallucinating? Oh, please, no. A choked sob escaped my throat. The thumb moved to my cheek, and fingers spread into my hair. This moment, the realization of it, almost became too much to bear.

"I don't think I can," I whispered.

"Please?" His other hand caught mine, and he squeezed. "Trust me, Red. Open those eyes."

So I did. But my heart stopped beating. My lungs refused to take in air. I lifted my chin and stared into the bluest eyes I'd ever seen—a vast, endless ocean—and in that second my heart thudded once, twice, and then began beating again as I came alive under Ben's gaze.

I blinked, half-afraid he wasn't real, that somehow my brain had conjured him up and he was nothing but an illusion brought on by my hopes and Verda's special brand of therapy. But no. Ben *was* here. And he was looking at me with that smile that melted my bones.

"You're not going to faint again, are you?" Concern etched his features, and he muttered a soft curse. "I worried this might be too much for you, but Verda insisted. I just wanted them to kidnap you and bring you to my place."

"Y-you wanted them to kidnap me?" My shock was beginning to fade. "This was your idea?"

Pulling away, he took the chair that Verda had been in. I scanned the room to see if the Gypsy brigade remained in residence. They didn't.

"Not all of it. But I remembered your tale of the first kidnapping"—a flash of humor glinted in his eyes—"and I came up with this grand scheme of romancing you."

"Romancing me?" I squeaked. "The last time we saw each other—"

"I know." He whisked a hand over his jaw. "I was kind of a jerk. It was a lot that night, Red. I don't know if you can forgive me for bolting out of there, but I couldn't come to grips with everything you told me. After saying good-bye to Rissa . . . it was just too much."

"I get that. Totally. But what changed your mind? What made you decide to"—I sucked in a breath—"romance me?"

His jaw tightened, and myriad emotions flickered through his expression. "I left that night knowing my feelings for you hadn't disappeared. But I was angry and hurt, and didn't know what to believe. So I went home and moped. Went to work and moped. Went to see Gabe and punched him again"—he blinked—"and moped."

He'd moped. About me! And his feelings . . . "I know my spell worked, Ben. I promise you that. I absolutely removed every other spell I ever cast on you."

"I believe you. I felt something that night. I don't know if I can explain it, but while my feelings remained the same, a sort of release came over me." He shook his head. "I didn't *have* to be with you. My choices were mine. But I still *wanted* to be with you. Does that make sense?"

Happiness and hope and love swarmed in. "Yes. It means that my spell gave you your will back, your freedom, but that you . . . you still care about me." I thought of something else, though. "You were very sure you couldn't be with someone who had that type of power. Wh-what do you think about that now?" I awaited his answer with bated breath.

"Your magic is a part of who you are. And you're the woman I can't get out of my thoughts." Again, he rubbed his jaw. "I guess what I'm saying is—"

I'd heard enough. Somehow, he'd found a way to accept me for the person I was, so there was no reason *not* to tell him the truth. "It's okay, Ben. I gave my power up." At his curious and startled glance, I gave him an abridged version of my recent past.

I figured he'd be relieved. Happy, even. But he frowned. "I wouldn't have asked you to do that. Ever, Red."

"I'd decided before I told you anything about my gift that I didn't want that specific power anymore. It scared me. This was my choice, and had very little to do with you. With us. It was about me, and the type of person I want to be."

He stared at me. "You did this for you and for no other reason?"

I laughed, and a solitary tear fell from my eye. "Yes. But if the side effect turns out to help us, that makes me even happier."

"Honestly, it doesn't make a difference. I'd already made up my mind when I contacted Elizabeth." He winked. "About romancing you."

Even though everything he'd said so far was good, amazing and thrilling, he hadn't tried to touch me again and he hadn't actually said what those feelings of his were. I guess, silly as it might sound, I wasn't there yet. I wasn't to the point of believing that we were going to be together. That we were going to be okay. So yes, I definitely wanted to hear about his plan to romance me.

"You said you punched Gabe?"

A rough laugh emerged. "I went to see him, because I wanted to try. For Rissa. He pointed out that I'd never punched him over Sara, but that I hadn't hesitated in doing so over you. Over 'just a kiss.'" Ben growled. "Just a kiss! His hands were all over you. My temper flashed, and I saw him touching you again, and I swung at him before the thought even processed."

A glow of pleasure whipped into me. "How'd Gabe take that?"

"He laughed his ass off. We ended up talking."

"And?"

Ben shrugged. "We have a long way to go, but we'll see. Right now, though, I'm more focused on us. I contacted Elizabeth with my idea, asked her if she could arrange another kidnapping and bring you to my house. I had this idea of a tent in the backyard, with the stars above us, a bottle of champagne . . . but then I met Verda."

I grinned, imagining. "So this was her idea."

"Yep. She said she wanted to be positive that you'd want to see me, and not just lug you off to my house without that assurance." He waggled his eyebrows. "And she meant that, but I also think she loved the idea of putting one over on you again."

That sounded like Verda. All of it. I laughed, and another tear eased down my cheek. "And you agreed."

"I wanted to surprise you." His voice caught. Longing and something else—love?—winged into his eyes. "So I agreed, and with Verda and Elizabeth's help, set the room up. And waited for you to arrive."

"You were here?"

"In the bathroom. Worrying about what your reaction would be, if you'd be willing to even talk to me, let alone what I have in mind."

"What do you have in mind?" I whispered.

He didn't answer. Instead, he strode to the box of cupcakes and grabbed the solitary one with pink icing rather than white. Returning to me, he cleared his throat. "That depends, Red. But I hope you'll hear me out."

My heart pounded. Trembles of disbelief fluttered through me. I bit my lip and nodded. "I love you. So yes, Ben, of course I'll hear you out."

He pulled a chair so close that we were knee to knee when he sat down. My eyes focused on the cupcake, wonder-

ing, hoping, but unable to actually believe the idea that
floated in my brain.

"A long time ago, when I met Sara, I believed in love at
first sight. I stopped." His voice erupted, his tenor thick and
heavy with emotion. "Then one day, I was on my way back
to the office from a meeting. I remembered my assistant's
birthday was coming up."

"Okay . . ."

"There's a flower store right across the street from the
Mystic Corner, Red. I planned on stopping there and order-
ing her flowers. As I do every year. But I saw your store, and
a compulsion came over me." His eyes gripped mine. "I *had*
to go in. I didn't know why."

"Oh," I breathed.

"I walked in. I saw you behind the counter, and my body
responded like a sex-starved teenager." He smiled at the
memory. "It shocked me. I hadn't reacted so suddenly, so
strongly, to a woman in years. Then, when I managed to
pull myself together enough to ask about pendulums—and
by the way, my assistant didn't even know what they were—I
looked into your eyes. And I fell in love. Right then, at that
instant, I was a goner."

"Wh-what? But . . . you didn't seem interested and—"

"I thought I was being stupid. I assumed my reaction was
because I hadn't had sex in a ridiculously long time, and
that my brain was confusing lust for love. So I figured your
fun and games offer would be perfect. That I'd get you out of
my system and that whatever I thought I felt for you would
disappear." He combed his free hand through his hair.
"What a deluded fool I was."

"Deluded?" The question was more of a sob than anything else. "Fool?"

"Yes, Chloe. Because I loved you the minute I saw you,
and that hasn't changed." Scooting his chair even closer,

which should've been impossible, he blew out a breath. "I love you. I know I love you. I'm done pretending that this kind of thing can't happen."

"Uh-huh?" I wheezed.

His lips quirked, and then he offered me the cupcake. "This isn't how I planned this. I was going to explain everything to you, and if that went well, kiss you. Seduce you. And then feed you this in the morning. But I can't wait."

I accepted the cupcake, every instinct I had on high alert. "You want me to eat this now?"

"No. I want you to break it in half."

Oh, God. I was right. I knew it to the core of my being. My tears fell faster and harder, and my chest filled with love for this man. My hands shook as I peeled the wrapper off of the cupcake, shivering in anticipation. Cracking it open, I saw it. And yep, I cried harder.

Tugging the ring from the chocolate center, I laughed. I shook my head, somehow still denying that every dream I'd ever had was coming true. Right now. Right at that second.

Ben pushed the chair out of the way and knelt in front of me. "Chloe, I don't know if I deserve you. You make me laugh. You've made me believe in things I never knew existed. You make me want things I stopped wanting years ago." His fingers touched my chin, and then my cheek. "I love you, Red. Will you do me the honor of making that drawing a reality? Will you marry me?"

Oh. Oh, wow. Just freaking wow.

"Yes. Absolutely. Yes, yes, and yes." A huge, booming laugh flew out of me. "Yes, I'll marry you. Now, tomorrow, a year from now. Whenever you want."

"So . . . you're saying yes?" he teased, with a grin just as wide as mine. I nodded, and he pulled the ring from my grasp and slid it onto my finger.

Awe mingled with shock coursed through me. I'd used my magic to coerce Kyle into accepting my proposal. I'd used my power to compel Ben to date me. And then I'd given up my gift, had nearly given up on finding my happy ending, when true love found me. And how incredible was that?

Ben stood and pulled me upright, the chunks of cake falling to the ground. One fast tug, and I was in his arms. I raised my chin, stroked my finger along the plane of his cheek. "Kiss me, Ben. Kiss me now."

He did.

INTERACT WITH DORCHESTER ONLINE!

Want to learn more about your favorite
books and authors?
Want to talk with other readers that like
to read the same books as you?
Want to see up-to-the-minute Dorchester
news?

VISIT DORCHESTER AT:
DorchesterPub.com
Twitter.com/DorchesterPub
Facebook.com (Search Pages)

DISCUSS DORCHESTER'S
NOVELS AT:
Dorchester Forums at DorchesterPub.com
GoodReads.com
LibraryThing.com
Myspace.com/books
Shelfari.com
WeRead.com

JOY NASH

When a girl with no family meets a guy with too much...

For Tori Morgan, family's a blessing the universe hasn't sent her way. Her parents are long gone, her chance of having a baby is slipping away, and the only thing she can call her own is a neglected old house. What she wants more than anything is a place where she belongs...and a big, noisy clan to share her life.

For Nick Santangelo, family's more like a curse. His *nonna* is a closet kleptomaniac, his mom's a menopausal time bomb and his motherless daughter is headed for serious boy trouble. The last thing Nick needs is another female making demands on his time.

But summer on the Jersey shore can be an enchanted season, when life's hurts are soothed by the ebb and flow of the tides and love can bring together the most unlikely prospects. A hard-headed contractor and a lonely reader of tarot cards and crystal prisms? All it takes is...

A Little Light Magic

ISBN 13: 978-0-505-52693-9

To order a book or to request a catalog call:
1–800–481–9191
Our books are also available at your local bookstore, or you can check out our Web site **www.dorchesterpub.com** where you can look up your favorite authors, read excerpts, glance at our discussion forum, and check out our digital content. Many of our books are now available as e-books!

"Christie Craig will crack you up!"
—*New York Times* bestselling author Kerrlyn Sparks

Christie Craig

Photojournalist Shala Winters already had her hands full bringing tourism to this backward, podunk town, but her job just got tougher. Pictures can say a thousand words, and one of Shala's is screaming bloody murder. Now she has to entrust a macho, infuriating lawman with her life—but she'll never trust him with her heart.

Trusted or not, Sky Gomez isn't about to let a killer get his hands on Shala's Nikon—or any of her more comely assets, for that matter. Her mouth might move faster than a Piney Woods roadrunner, but all he can think about is how good it must taste . . . and how she'll never escape true love.

SHUT UP
A_N_D KISS ME

ISBN 13: 978-0-505-52799-8

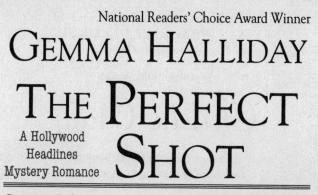

National Readers' Choice Award Winner

GEMMA HALLIDAY

THE PERFECT SHOT

A Hollywood
Headlines
Mystery Romance

Cameron Dakota is the *L.A. Informer*'s staff photographer and paparazzi to the stars. Her latest subject, Trace Brody, is an A-list actor and half of America's favorite Hollywood couple. He's about to get married in the wedding of the century, and Cam is determined to get the first shots of the bride and groom. But when Cam takes pictures of what looks like Trace being kidnapped at gunpoint, she suddenly finds herself smack in the middle of a scandal more sensational than even she could invent. On the run, under fire, and in serious danger of falling in love with one leading man, Cam must get to the bottom of this story . . . before the story gets to her.

Can't wait for all the good celebrity gossip?

Check out
www.LAInformerOnline.com
to get your fix.

"Craig's latest will DELIGHT . . . fans of
JANET EVANOVICH and HARLEY JANE KOZAK."
—*Booklist* on *Gotcha!*

Award-winning Author

Christie Craig

"Christie Craig will crack you up!"
—*New York Times* Bestselling Author Kerrelyn Sparks

Of the Divorced, Desperate and Delicious club, Kathy Callahan is
the last surviving member. Oh, her two friends haven't died or anything. They just gave up their vows of chastity. They went for hot sex
with hot cops and got happy second marriages—something Kathy
can never consider, given her past. Yet there's always her plumber,
Stan Bradley. He seems honest, hardworking, and skilled with a tool.

But Kathy's best-laid plans have hit a clog. The guy snaking her drain
isn't what he seems. He's handier with a pistol than a pipe wrench,
and she's about to see more action than Jason Statham. The next
forty-eight hours promise hot pursuit, hotter passion and a super
perky pug, and at the end of this wild escapade, Kathy and her very
own undercover lawman will be flush with happiness—assuming they
both survive.

Divorced, Desperate and Deceived

ISBN 13: 978-0-505-52798-1

To order a book or to request a catalog call:
1–800–481–9191
Our books are also available at your local bookstore, or you
can check out our Web site **www.dorchesterpub.com**
where you can look up your favorite authors, read excerpts,
glance at our discussion forum, and check out our digital
content. Many of our books are now available as e-books!

✂ ☐ **YES!**

Sign me up for the Love Spell Book Club and send my FREE BOOKS! If I choose to stay in the club, I will pay only $8.50* each month, a savings of $6.48!

NAME: _____

ADDRESS: _____

TELEPHONE: _____

EMAIL: _____

☐ I want to pay by credit card.

☐ **VISA**   ☐ **MasterCard.**   ☐ **DISCOVER**

ACCOUNT #: _____

EXPIRATION DATE: _____

SIGNATURE: _____

Mail this page along with $2.00 shipping and handling to:
Love Spell Book Club
PO Box 6640
Wayne, PA 19087
Or fax (must include credit card information) to:
610-995-9274
You can also sign up online at **www.dorchesterpub.com**.
*Plus $2.00 for shipping. Offer open to residents of the U.S. and Canada only.
Canadian residents please call 1-800-481-9191 for pricing information.
If under 18, a parent or guardian must sign. Terms, prices and conditions subject to change. Subscription subject to acceptance. Dorchester Publishing reserves the right to reject any order or cancel any subscription.